CW00688377

This is a work of fiction, and the views ex
responsibility of the author. Likewise, cer
incidents are the product of the author's ir
resemblance to actual persons, living or d⌣___, __ __
locales, is entirely coincidental.

Sunflower in the Shadows by Ambrosia R. Harris

Published by Ambrosia R. Harris

Las Vegas, NV

Cover by: Alexandre Levasseur

Line Editing by: Megan Harris

ISBN: 979-8-9861104-1-7

Printed in USA

1st Edition

Content & Trigger Warnings

Please view content warnings before reading.

More info can be found on Ambrosia's website.

DEDICATION

To the Vampire Diaries girlies who just wanted to see Bonnie get her Happily Ever-After.

WHAT PEOPLE FEAR MOST ABOUT THEIR DEMONS,
IS THAT THEY WILL COME TO ENJOY THEM.

Playlist

Toxic - 2WEI

Darkside - Neoni

Soldiers - Fjora & Neoni

Oblivion - Zayde Wolfe & Neoni

Carousel - Neoni & Aviva

Legends Never Die - Leagues of Legends & Against the Current

Outlaw - Neoni

Voices - Hidden Citizens & Vanessa Campagna

Rip - Neoni

Hypnotized - Aviva

Machine - Neoni

Wonderland - Neoni

Lilith - Halsey

Graveyard - Halsey

Boo Hoo - Neoni

Omens - Unsecret & Neoni

I'm not your Boyfriend Baby - 3OH!3

Darling - Halsey

Up - Cardi B

Up Against the Wall - NSYNC

DEMONOLOGY AND CREATURES

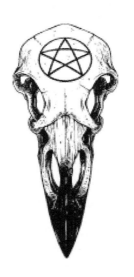

Demons

Demon Priestesses - Rulers of the Six Circles, the three priestesses are said to have created the three realms. For millennia they ruled alongside each other in harmony until a great battle grew between two. Sending one to her death and the other to a prison in the Circles.

Demon Priests - Below Priestess in terms of power. They were hand-picked by the priestesses to rule over each Circle, totaling only five. They are said to shapeshift into serpents that brought about the tale of Adam and Eve.

Nipans - These are what Demons call the mortals that have taken on Demon powers. They are rare because taking on the powers of a demon usually ends in the mortal's death. Their eyes are black with a dark golden iris. Most notable is the darkening around their eyes as their veins flood with power.

Mazarine Demons - Commonly mistaken for what mortals call angels. They aid mortals down paths of graciousness. Helpful and kind, they only mean to bring good to the mortal realm and certain circles. Their eyes are black with a deep mazarine blue iris.

Phthartica Demons - Malevolent demons the mortals are most familiar with. They love nothing more than to cause ill-will and to taunt mortals with natural disasters. Everything bad in the mortal realm can be linked to a Phthartic one way or another. They have black eyes with a deep crimson iris.

Rasasvada Demons - Demons who are neither good nor bad. They are self-serving and willing to make bargains, trades, and deals with mortals for things they want, no matter the outcome to the mortal. They have black eyes with a frost blue iris.

CREATURES

SPIRITS - Souls that have died graciously and are in existence of peace and harmony. They are kind and only dwell in Circle One.

WATCHERS - A cross between a Lyzuma and a Sori. These faceless and dark creatures usually go unseen as they creep through the shadows of both the mortal realm and Circles. If you see them in the shadows, you can escape. If you fall in their grasp, they will whisk you away to the depths of the shadow realms.

If you are unlucky enough to catch a glimpse of them in light, you will wish they that had dragged you to off, instead.

SORI - Shadow creatures that dwell in the forests of Death. They have branch-like appendages coming from the tops of their heads. It does not matter your distance from them. If a Sori sees you, you are surely dead.

LYZUMA - Creatures that resemble that of beautiful women. They lurk in the shadows and depths of swaps and blood. lakes within the Circles. They cast out sounds to draw in their prey before dragging them to their watery grave. Their sounds range depending on the person who hears them.

OMOTH - Giants that feast on flesh and act as Circle Watchers.

SISSUX - Notably the most aggressive of all the creatures. It appears as either a skeletal structure or a ghoulish smoke. Either form is adorned with six arms, metal armored chest plates, and a face wrapped in a bloodied wrapped cloth. They are the most gruesome in the dismemberment of their prey.

Pronunciation & Translation

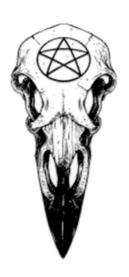

Pronunciation

Characters

Meklit *(Mic-let)*

Erius *(Eerie-us)*

Eriusazal *(Eerie-uz-ale)*

Alius *(A-lie-us)*

Alaura *(A-lore-a)*

Ennaza *(E-naaz-a)*

Dazron *(Dezz-ron)*

Jafeki *(Jaa-fee-key)*

Muffa *(Moo-fa)*

Elpos *(El-pose)*

DeMordia *(De-more-de-a)*

Tikara *(Tee-car-aa)*

Chimeriea *(She-mar-iea)*

Ozeth *(O-zeth)*

Urran *(Oo-raan)*

Drokadan *(Dro-ka-den)*

Vokuud *(Voe-kood)*

Atrox *(A-trox)*

Places

Macaria *(Ma-car-rhia)*

Kalopasia *(Kal-oor-sia)*

Malefic *(Mel-ef-ic)*

Mortala *(More-tal-a)*

Dolent *(Dole-yent)*

Note: These words have been given a
different pronunciation, but their
definition remains the same.

Translation

Mich mupfütsham rüb bup moi mate pat - I understand she
be your mate now

Ewiwpay poush zho - Ignorant little shit

Udh lab - Ink fish

Daw shakwip - Ghost fungus

Jik bush ʃup - Roast ham meat

Creamu mudh lab zil - Creamy barracuda stew

PART ONE

FOR THE WORDS OF A VOW ARE SACRED NOT

ONLY AMONG MEN AND THE ANGELS BUT AMONG

THE DEMONS AS WELL

—HOWARD SCHWARTS

CHAPTER ONE

Mira

  The thick musk of salt and sea mingled with the midsummer air, making for a beautiful Monday morning. Most people don't find joy in Mondays, being the start of the work week and all. But my friends and I kicked off the week with brunch before work to brighten the day, a ritual we have done for the last few years to spread positive energy amongst ourselves for the draining task that is work and life.

  I pushed the button at the light across from the café and waited with the few early tourists, some of which had no understanding of personal space as the heat of someone's breath blew against the nape of my neck. I took a large step forward, stepping off the curb in hopes that was a polite way of indicating for them to back the fuck up off me.

  But clearly common sense was lacking from this individual. The heat returned to my neck, burning my irritation to the surface.

I spun around with a curled lip already carved on my face. "Do you mind?"

Without waiting for an answer from the red-faced man, I turned back to find the light giving us the right of way and stormed off.

"May he always step in gum," I whispered, flicking the air behind me in his direction.

A senseless jinx, but we were just breaking out of a pandemic, and it was shit like that that caused it to spread as it had. I personally did not care to fall sick due to someone else's stupidity.

I stepped onto the sidewalk and hurried in the direction of the café, spotting Meklit already occupying a table in the balcony area. She waved happily as I caught sight of her, and I gave a wave back.

"Hey, Mickey!" I called. The smell of freshly cooked pancakes and sweet syrup hit my nose as I pulled open the entrance door.

The bright and cheery waitress, Amy, stood with her welcoming smile as she always did every Monday, our usual server and honestly, brunch wasn't as fun when we got someone else.

Her cheery smile and strawberry blonde hair always brought a sort of bright comfort that Monday mimosa called for.

"Good morning, Mina. Welcome to Martha's. Come with me and I'll get you seated with Meklit." She grabbed a menu and led me through the main dining lobby and out to the front balcony where Mickey waited.

"Hey! How was your walk?" Mickey greeted me with a teasing grin. Her dark complexion held a sard glow under the light of the sun.

"It was almost perfect," I said with a laugh as I took a seat across from her. "Some beast of a human was mouth breathing down my neck at the light."

She attempted to hide her laugh in her glass of water as she took a small sip. "Yeah, I noticed! When is your car supposed to be done again?"

"It should be finished this week." I shrugged doubtfully, seeing how they're screwing me around at every turn.

"I thought it was supposed to be done last week?"

"Yeah. That's what I thought, too," I admitted. I didn't know anything about cars, so when they told me they found something here or there that needs to be fixed, I told them to fix it. Everything was within walking distance anyway, and I still had my van to get around I just preferred not to drive it short distances.

I didn't want to ask anyone to come with me, not that that would even help. None of us were too well-versed in cars despite the fact Jasmine and I remodeled the van. We did so with a lot of help from my uncle, and I no longer had him to advise me.

I looked around the empty table with slight confusion, hoping to change the subject with our lack of drinks.

"I already ordered our first round. Amy said she'd bring them out as we all arrived. I figured she could bring mine out when one of you got here," Mickey explained.

"I always arrive first," I joked. Well, sort of. If she wasn't first, it was me. And still, I was generally the first to arrive after her in that case.

"There is nothing wrong with being punctual." She shrugged as her gaze drifted past me. "Speaking of!"

"Alright, ladies. First round. I will be back once the others arrive." Amy popped up from behind me to set our glasses down before parting with a close-lipped smile, leaving Mickey and me to our weekend catch-up.

"How was Angeles?" Mickey asked immediately. She always had a big interest in my camping trips and had joined me on a few of them, as with the rest. But recently, their other day jobs had most of their attention and weekends, leaving our only other time to catch up during the week on our small shifts at the shop.

"Peaceful, as always. You know nobody ever goes up that far."

She swirled her glass, studying the golden liquid as it spun around. "I need to get back up there. The getaway and fresh air would be nice."

"You are always more than welcome to join. It's been somewhat boring." Before I could finish, Amber's voice filled my ears as Amy ushered her to the table.

Amber and Mickey were both dressed for the summer weather but in two different styles. Where Mickey wore a pair of powder brown overall shorts with a cute light pink crop top, Amber wore a solid white top with a black maxi skirt, her dark curls piled on top of her head and wrapped in a burgundy scarf.

"Hello," she greeted in her thick accent as she took the seat beside Mickey. She flew down from London three years ago to study cooking, then COVID hit, and she found herself in need of herbs from the apothecary, and we had all been friends since. She even started working part-time at the shop.

"Hey!" Mickey and I greeted.

"Jaz is in her car. Crying," Amber added with an exasperated sigh.

"That bad?" Mickey asked. Jasmine spent the weekend with her boyfriend, who was coincidentally our coworker as well.

"I didn't hear from her all weekend. Hopefully it wasn't too bad," Mickey voiced. We all wished it was ok, but knowing Antonio and Jaz, it was anything but.

Their faces fell and eyes, focused on those entering in behind me.

"Now, now. I'm sure you guys will work it out," Amy attempted to console, but the sobbing overpowered it all.

"Worse than bad," I whispered before taking a big *sip* from my glass.

Amy sat Jasmine beside me and gave her a sympathetic pat on her shoulder. "I'll be back with the last two drinks," she informed.

"Wonderful! It's been a week," Jaz blubbered into her hands. Amy gave a faint smile before taking off again, leaving us to soothe our devastated friend.

"Jaz, it's only Monday," Meklit said innocently.

"And that's just the point, Mickey! It's already shit!" Jaz sobbed again. I wouldn't say this was common for her, especially since she focused on energies and attraction in her craft – physical attraction, I should add. It was ironic she tended to catch on to other's relationships or attractions better than her own self, but that is usually the case for those that give great advice.

"What happened?" Amber pressed kindly. Before Jaz could finish, Amy popped by with the two mimosas before darting away again. Another great thing about her: she knew when not to stick around. "Antonio and I ended things this morning. Well, he ended it," Jaz sniffled. "He didn't want Andrew down his neck about coworker relations. But it's not even corporate, it's a small family-owned business!" Tears worked their way out and she wiped them away. "I told him it was none of Andrew's business, but he was dead set on the breakup."

"Oh, Jaz. I'm sorry," I said softly to pacify her without causing a bigger breakdown. In truth, Andrew didn't care who was screwing who in the shop. He was only a fill-in manager.

"What are you waffling on about? He was a plum of a boy. Not even a man," Amber interjected.

Though her words were harsh, her tone was as kind as she could gather for the situation. She wasn't all that patient with Jasmine's choices in men. Well, none of us were. They were all quite toxic for her. And I would say if it made her happy, then I wouldn't say a thing. But she was not happy, and she never was.

"Amber!" Mickey shot as Jasmine's eyes glossed over with more tears and she finished off her mimosa. Amber's words weren't so much harsh as they were true. Antonio had a lot of growing to do mentally and honestly, he was a pain to be around when they were together. For some reason he was more bearable during the one shift I had with him.

I rubbed Jaz's back to soothe her and looked for Amy to bring another round. When I finally met her eyes through the disfiguring glass, I could faintly make out a nod as she rushed back to the kitchen.

"Maybe if you do a cord cutting," Mickey suggested in a soft voice.

"A whole banishing ritual would be better," Amber mumbled into her drink.

"Or a poppet," Jasmine said with a sigh as she placed her fingers on either side of her temple. "I have several and a few clippings of his hair."

"Be fucking for real right now," I said, struggling to hold back a laugh.

"He gave it to me willingly. There was a spell he *wanted* me to do. But I guess he forgot."

"Well, if the poppet and cord cutting don't work, we can always just have a break-up bonfire and burn all the shit that reminds you of him. Less invasive for him," Amber suggested. She was not one to interfere with another's free will whereas Mickey and Jasmine dabbled in that sort of thing.

"There you go! The spot I stay at Angeles's forest would be perfect. We can listen to the music as loud as we want and no one will bother us. Dance around the fire naked sort of shit!" I added. The first half was a serious statement, the second was all in good fun. I mean, it wouldn't be the first time I had, but that was more of a drunken rage than a ritual.

Amy stopped by and passed the second round of mimosas. "Will it be the usual today, ladies?"

We always ordered the same for brunch often enough they made a party size for us to order.

"Yes, Amy. That would be great," I informed.

She nodded as she wrote down on her pad "Grilled shrimp and arugula." With a faint smile, she left for the kitchen to drop off the order.

"I think a getaway this weekend would be helpful. If it's not your studio, it's *he-who-will-not-be-named.* Hang out with us for a bit," I said. Amber and Meklit nodded in agreement with their attention in their drinks.

"Yeah, you're right. It would be nice. I don't have any commissions this month." Jaz sniffled and wiped her tears away.

"It's settled then. We should head up Friday after work," Amber cheered.

More sniffles erupted from beside me as Jaz struggled to hold back tears.

"What am I going to do Wednesday at work?" she questioned.

"Stay upstairs with me. You know he never comes up. Just ignore him," I began. "I know it sounds cheesy, but there really are better *men* out there. It's going to hurt for a bit, but we are still young, and crying over little boys who aren't yet men is not it," I attempted to console but it came out a bit harsher than intended.

"We're almost thirty, Meems," she said with a chuckle.

"Thirty year olds who won't settle for shit stain *boys*," Amber added with a confident grin.

It was enough to pull a bigger smile out of Jaz as she pulled the glass to her lips.

"There, see? Already in a better mood," Mickey tossed in as she, too, raised her glass. Jaz and I followed suit and with an echoing clink, we changed the topic to something lighter.

Our drinks and food came out as we discussed our new weekend plans—debating the choice of alcohol and what foods to bring, how they would need to bring tents as the van wasn't built for company in mind. Luckily it wasn't any of their first trips with me and all had camping gear at the ready.

With the weekend set, the mimosa bottoms found, and our grilled shrimp gone, we paid our tab and left our tip before walking to the parking lot.

"You guys ok calling the Uber?" I asked. With a nod from each, we split ways with a goodbye.

I wouldn't say I was drunk or buzzed, but I was feeling pretty good, and the walk back in the crowd of tourists wasn't as draining as normal, making them much easier to ignore. It was the surfers on their way to the beach that provided the irritations with their whistles and ill-thought-out pickup lines.

Thankfully, it was a quick cross to my van—or home on wheels as I prefer to call it, remodeled delivery van Jaz and I picked up the summer after graduation to escape our small town. It was fun to travel in for the time and then COVID hit and we got stuck in L.A. which wasn't too bad; we found jobs, and she found an apartment while I kept the van. With the pandemic and low-paying job, I figured it would be better than living with my mother.

Not that there is anything wrong with someone my age living with their parents. The economy was trash. There was, however, something wrong with *my* mother, and I preferred living in my little van.

I slid open the door to the angry yowling of my cat, Prometheus, a little black fur ball with big green eyes that showed up outside the van just before lockdown a few years back. I wasn't much of a cat person, but he had been my partner in crime ever since.

He zoomed over my feet in a crisscross pattern, making it near impossible for me to get in.

"Would you excuse me!" I shot to him. The sudden noise sent him flying onto my bed, flicking his whiskers in irritation.

"Yeah, I know. It's coming," I droned as I pulled out one of his canned meals. "I have to get ready for work. Hopefully you can manage on this can for the evening." I plopped the mush into his bowl on the mat before turning to start my shower and prepare for my night readings.

The apothecary I worked at also had a connecting spiritual shop. I didn't do particularly well with herbs, so I spent most of my time with the occult merchandise. I was mostly hired to run divination readings—tarot decks, bone tossing, pendulums —all of that was work I took pride in and was one of the best readers in L.A. I tried to stay humbled, but when A-list celebrities came for readings, that was a bit of an accomplishment for not only me but the shop as well.

After I had finished my shower and twisted out my hair, I found a comfortable spot on my bed to begin my meditations.

I took a deep breath, focusing on the thoughts that passed by, silencing out the world around me until my body and head felt light. The temperature dropped slightly, lifting the hairs along my arm and creating goosebumps along my skin. It was never an extremely comforting feeling, but this time it seemed a bit gloomier than normal, colder and not willing to present itself as it swirled around me. I stayed quiet, allowing the spirit to study me as they often did.

My van was my sanctuary, protected with sigils and amulets—hung satchels of protective herbs, a salt lined threshold, along with weekly smoke cleanses. I felt safe, and any spirit that passed through, no matter how cold, was not malevolent enough to be blocked.

After several long moments of the icy chill against my skin, the space around me warmed, signaling the spirit's quick departure. Most were only curious, some stuck around, and even fewer actually made contact in a way for me to understand—obscure tarot readings and odd pendulum responses that did not seem to fit the questions.

My eyes opened slowly to adjust to the bright light that spilled in from the windows. I focused on the furry creature in front of me, his tail flicking from one side to the next. His pupils were thin slits as he glared at me, a usual stance he took during my indoor meditations.

"Will you be a good boy while I'm gone? I don't want to come back to those filthy little hairballs on my pillow again or you'll be sleeping with the seagulls tonight," I warned as I slid from the bed.

The green in his eyes nearly vanished while his pupils rounded, as if recognizing it was only me. He released a soft purr as he jumped down and sauntered to the front to take his place in the passenger's seat.

The sun sat low in the sky, gradually making its way towards the moving waves. My heart sank as I jerked my head to the small digital clock over my single burner.

4:45 PM

"Fuck!" I spat, racing to grab my deck and bones to shove into my bag. There was no time to think about what time I had lost. It was a twenty minute walk to work. If I had my car this wouldn't be an issue, but the stupid piece of shit had always been unreliable. Now it was just unreliable and costly.

The bike it is.

I raced out to the back of the van where my bike sat, locking the van door with a click of a button, and headed off. I tugged the beach cruiser over the curb in a rush, ignoring the whistles and hoots from the passing surfers who usually hung around the lot. They were easy to ignore as I jumped on and kicked off in a hurry, tucking my skirt under the thigh harnesses I decided on wearing.

I crossed at the light, riding past the tourists with ease as I headed to the next corner. The Green Coven was hard to miss with the dark green paint and old-fashioned look in the center of a very modern looking L.A. When I hit the corner, I turned down a narrow alley that led to the back of the shop where the bike rack was kept.

Without bothering to lock it up, I ran to the front and pulled open the door. The heavy scent of herbs and spice filled my nose instantly as I entered the cozy-styled shop. Dimly lit planted light fixtures hung from the rafter beams of the open apothecary lobby. Potted herbs lined the three windowsills with more potted plants scattered around and tucked into any corner and slot available. Poster-sized monographs of various herbs hung along the walls, and herb-filled jars lined the countertop. Along the back wall sat a large, antique styled apothecary cabinet with a dozen tiny drawers.

I turned the corner in a rush, nearly running into Jordan, one of my other coworkers.

"Slow down there, what's the rush?" He laughed, pulling a white stick from his mouth. Jordan was also a part-time worker, as he did graphic design and was the one who designed the herb posters around and all the shop's advertisements. Mondays were his one and only shift. Being a graphic designer and all, his days are usually spent hunched over his iPad, sketching out his designs. He was also still in school and was an intern for a big company.

Which sucked because the shop only paid about ten bucks an hour and was basically part-time if you didn't work from open to close all five days. Not much for a college student in L.A., if you asked me, but who was I to comment on his job choices?

"I have clients today," I panted, my eyes falling to Andrew as he entered from his back office. He held a tray lined with honey-pops as he greeted me.

"Hey Mina, you ok?" he asked with an overly enthused smile. Rather than stopping to stock the pops, he met me at the counter.

"Yeah, I'm fine," I assured with breathy words.

"I'm not going to fire you if you are a few minutes late, Mina," he reminded. Truthfully, I didn't think there was much I could do that would make Andrew even consider firing me. I was the only one free to work the shift I do, which was every weekday and more than him. Besides, I was the only one who provides readings, and that was the biggest customer draw.

"I know, but I have clients today," I reminded him.

"Oh, just one. Ms. Lee called and said she would be unable to make today's reading," Jordan interjected.

"She's working late." A usual case for Brenda as her work

seemed to be very demanding, from what I could gather. Jordan nodded and continued leaning.

"Oh, well. I guess I could have walked."

Andrew pulled one of the honey-pops from the tray and handed it to me. "My mom and Lily want your review specifically," he informed.

I took the pop and looked it over for a moment. "What flavor is it this time?" I inquired. Mrs. Williams and her daughter crafted all the blends and candies the apothecary carried and I was their favored taste tester. Not a problem with me. It gave me a reason to snack on sweets.

"Calendula and chamomile."

I tilted my head and looked past Andrew to Jordan. "Is that what you have?"

He nodded, not removing the stick from his mouth to muffle the words, "It's good."

Pointless. Jordan couldn't tell the difference between the flavors of lavender and mugwort. I popped the sucker into my mouth, enjoying the sweet blended honey and herbs.

"Much better than the last ones. The lavender ones weren't it," I muffled.

"That's what I said!" Jordan pipped from his spot.

"Well, these ones will do well." I smiled to Andrew and nabbed another pop before heading upstairs to my reading space. I hardly spent my shifts in the first floor apothecary as I have a horrible habit of scorching the tea.

The second floor was the spiritual shop where I spent the majority of my time. Being that I was no green witch, Andrew placed me up on the second floor with all the occult like shit, saying that my style generally matched the aesthetic he was aiming for: a gothic cottage core vibe to match the downstairs theme while also giving off a "witchy" vibe.

Because I conducted my readings, I had my own personal "office" space which was very much a second room for me. I kept an altar, and most all of my books and crystals there since there wasn't much room for them in my van.

I walked in, flipping the switch for the dim light. Skulls, bones, and statues lined the shelves along with a multitude of mini jars of powders and herbs. Pillar and taper candles sat wherever I could safely place them without catching shit on fire.

It took about five minutes to light each candle and start the incense, giving the room a spicy, bitter smell. The space filled with smoke, slowly escaping through the thin slit under the door, a very simple way to cleanse and provide the sort of ambiance my clients felt most relaxed in.

Once the mood was set, I began setting up the reading space. I didn't have any tables or chairs, aside from a simple pullout for some elderly clients who were unable to sit on the floor. Today wasn't necessarily a day for the chair. It all depended on Mrs. Halbert and how she was feeling for the day.

Mildred Halbert was one of my widowed clients, and she came in every third Monday of the month. During our first reading together she had informed me it was a significant day, as her and her late husband would spend it as date night. Understandably, she held that date near and chose to visit me the moment he had passed back in early 2020.

She also bought a ton of the sleep tea blend from the apothecary to help her sleep through the night. We took the liberty of pre-pouching it for her so she didn't have to worry about measuring it and possibly messing up the dosage. From what she said, her nights have never been better.

I set to work arranging the throw pillows around my reading mat and placed all the tools I usually used for her readings in the center of it all. When everything was to my liking, I sat in my spot and took the time before the meeting to center myself.

Readings were draining themselves and my readings with Mrs. Halbert usually ran over an hour. She had mentioned it would be a special night during her last reading.

I sat on the floor with a few of the pillows tucked behind me and flipped to my playlist of song bowls on my phone. With a deep breath, I closed my eyes and began my meditation.

Thoughts passed my mind's eye in disconnecting ways, showing me memories and wishes and random things that made no sense. After a few more deep breaths, my mind settled on faint images, —shapes, and colors, flashing sparks of pure nonsense.

Then, a shadowy figure stood before me in a dark room. The only light flickered directly above me and the enormous shape. Glowing, white eyes crept open to peer down at me. They were hard to read, but I sensed a certain curiousness about them.

The shadow creature leaned down, tilting its head to the side as if to examine me. In doing so, it gave me the opportunity to examine it back.

Its massive body faded into the darkness that surrounded us, so there wasn't much to be seen there, but its head was long like a horse—maybe a goat. The ears and whatever growths that came from the top of its head faded as its body did.

Suddenly, the creature was at my back, circling me as it studied me. I moved with it, not wanting to have my eyes off this strange thing but just as curious in it as it was in me. It wasn't strange for odd entities to visit me this way; it was just rare.

"Hello…" I greeted.

Its head tilted again as three knocks rang through. The lights flashed, returning to the dimly lit room I began in.

"Good evening. Sorry I'm late," Mildred greeted from the doorway.

"Late?" I repeated as I grabbed my phone, realizing the song bowls had ended at some point. An hour-long track. I hopped up to greet her properly, stumbling slightly from the cramping in my legs and back.

Mildred stood in a bright red dress with a beautiful black fur covering her shoulders. Pearl earrings with a matching necklace and ring added a nice little pop. Some would call it all costume jewelry, but if they knew Mis. Halbert, they would know nothing about her was fake. She was dripping with high class and money.

"I lost track of time, dear," she informed me, stepping to the pile of pillows positioned across from me.

"It would seem I had as well," I admitted. "Would you like the chair for this evening's reading?"

"No, no. I can sit perfectly fine. Thank you." Her box dyed red curls caught the light of the candle behind her as she took her seat, creating a sort of raging flame look on top of her head.

"You said today was a special Monday?" I reminded. If I hadn't known already, it would have been an easy guess.

"It is our anniversary," she informed with a soft smile.

"Awe, how lovely," I cooed, holding my hands out to her, pendulum in my right palm. "Well, happy anniversary to you." I closed my eyes and took a deep breath, ready to channel Mr. Halbert into our space. She took my hands and, after several deep breaths, I pulled from her grasp and held the pendulum over the mat between us. A cool chill wrapped around the room as a spirit found its place.

"Hello, Richard. How are you?" I greeted, holding the pendulum over the mat and allowing it to sway with the energy. It swung quickly to the letter H before moving to the letter I, his usual greeting.

Using pendulums wasn't the best way to hold full conversations, leaving his responses to a minimum of one word. Some days were more emotionally paining than others. There was an intimacy about divination readings between myself and my clients. Very personal and life-changing events were often shared as if I weren't there, a line in the conversation rather than an actual person. But that was ok I didn't find insult in it. If they felt comfortable enough with me, that only meant they were gaining something from the readings.

They spoke for over an hour before Mrs. Halbert grew weepy-eyed and tired, rightfully so. I helped her to her feet, and she thanked me sweetly before leaving with her back hunched from the position she had sat in. I watched as she slowly made her way to the steps, and once she was out of view, I began my cleaning ritual, snuffing out the candles and cleaning with a rosemary bundle.

"That was a long one, huh?" Andrew's voice came from the doorway. I turned to find him with his usual smirk that he held on Mondays after my readings. He jerked his head toward the office across the hall and headed off before waiting for a reply.

There was one thing I forgot to mention about my boss, Andrew. We hooked up. Quite a bit, actually. It wasn't something either of us intended. That's usually how it starts, right? Fucking my manager in the upstairs office of his ill mother's business wasn't something I like to go around bragging about.

I would love to say it was some big romantic story, but really, we were just closing late one night, and one thing led to another. Now it was a bit more often than either of us expected, and I was not looking for anything too serious. But Andrew was not shy about wanting to move this past the office setting—dates and family introductions. Though I already knew his mom and sister due to work, he had a much different introduction in mind.

He didn't have bad dick. Quite the opposite, actually. And it was not as if he looked like a troll. He was decently attractive with blond hair and green eyes and his personality wasn't horrible. I just didn't plan on sharing my space with anyone anytime soon. Besides, why fuck up what we had now? It was consistent dick without the worry or hassle.

I jumped up and followed behind him without a word, staying quiet to avoid suspicion from the downstairs peanut gallery. Andrew never seemed to care all that much, but again, it wasn't something I wanted to brag about. It was more than juvenile. But so was sneaking around his mother's apartment since he lived with her to help out, and the van didn't provide much in the way of space. So the office it had been.

I stepped through and the door shut with a soft click. His hands slipped around my arm and tugged me until my back pressed against the smoothness of the door. He held my face as his lips took mine in a swift movement, kissing me roughly. When he pulled back, his face was already flushed. "I thought she'd never leave."

"You've been waiting, have you?" I teased.
His hands left my cheeks and slid down to my legs where his fingers tangled in my fishnets. "You know how I am with your lace and nets." The snapping sound of strings tearing echoed in the quiet space. Our lips collided as he struggled to remove his belt and push his pants down. He pulled away once more to dig through one of his pockets for a condom. I wasn't sure when he found it or put it on, being too focused on his neck and removing his shirt.

I only knew he had accomplished putting it on when he shoved my thong to the side and thrust into me without warning. I cupped my hand over my mouth to muffle the moan that begged to break free. He let out a relieved sigh as if he truly had been waiting all day. After a moment of adjustment, he began grinding into me, slowly at first to not cause noise from the door or from either of us.

The heated room grew hotter, and every silent moan seemed to echo louder as we went.

Andrew held me up with one hand while his other worked at figuring out which direction to pull my top. Each failed attempt inspired deep thrusts as he grew frustrated at the constricting shirt. With an agitated grunt, he gave up on the shirt and buried his face in my neck.

The silence in the room soon filled with the breathless moans, squeaking wood, and the slap of sticky skin.

"God damn!" he grunted out, pausing his movements in attempt to hold his finish. Like a gentleman, he made sure I finished first. He took my mouth again, his movements slow and deep. The building friction and fire began in my low belly and spread down my thighs. I rolled my hips against him, aiding in the sensation, blinded by the building tension, a delicate and thin line that could be just as easily shattered. He sucked in through his teeth as he began pounding into me.

"*Fff-fuck.*" The one word that snapped that thin line, pulling me from my body for a moment. I gripped his shoulders, his shirt, and whatever else my hands met as I rode the waves through. Andrew's hands slipped over my mouth again as he pumped into me, chasing his own finish as his hips bucked wildly.

A quick fuck in the office wasn't the most romantic of places, but I never said there was anything romantic about what we did. He was to me what I was to him, a quick and easy lay, and with the way the world was going, that was really all I had that gave me a sense of control.

"What are you doing after work?" he asked. I wasn't surprised, but I hadn't expected it either. I thought after our last conversation he would understand.

"Drew," I whispered, "we talked about this."

He pulled free with a deep groan. Pure disappointment pinched his brows as he backed away from me. I stepped down to adjust myself, fixing my skirt to hide the ripped fishnets.

"You head out first. I have to grab some paperwork anyway." He buttoned his pants and walked around the desk. He didn't have to be so upset about it, but as long as it ended the conversation. I was sexually satisfied and happy, so I didn't see any problems.

What we had was perfect how it was.

I headed out of the office and back to my room to collect my things and leave for the night. Since I only had to worry about readings, and the little after affair, I didn't have to stick around Mondays to help lock up.

"Oh, Mina! I forgot to mention. We have a shipment drop-off coming in tomorrow at two. Just a heads up," Andrew called from the office.

I paused at the door of my room, turning back to see Andrew popping his head out from the open door. "Ok, is there anything special I need to do?"

"Just stock everything. It isn't much, just a few more things for up here."

Anything to do with upstairs was usually left to me, and since Andrew only worked on Mondays, it was up to me to sign and stock inventory.

"Will do, boss man." I stepped into the room and for a split second, in the far corner near my collection of animal skulls, was the faint outline of a figure. Just a second for my eyes to adjust and it was gone.

I sucked in a breath, fighting the shiver brought on by the cool chill that ran over my skin. Again, a common occurrence I had learned to ignore, though my body still senses something off and reacted appropriately. Despite my constant, subtle run-ins with the spirits that visited this plane, my body continued to react with a flight or fight response.

I spun the ring on my finger with my thumb three times, my special charm of protection, as well as a habit to ensure it was still there. It was a quick cross over the floor to the back shelf where I kept my bag. After snuffing out the candles, I headed out through the lobby.

"Bye, Andrew. Later, Jorden," I called, heading out the door and around to the back to grab my bike. But when I turned the corner, my heart sank to my stomach as I stared at an empty rack, my last means of quick transportation gone.

"Fucking wonderful," I huffed, stomping from the alleyway. I couldn't say I was surprised. I didn't bother locking it up. It was a broken-down piece of shit that needed replacing anyways, so it wasn't all bad.

The smell of freshly fried funnel cakes grew stronger as I crossed the street, a much-needed treat after the evening I had. Pair it with some wine and the bike wouldn't even be a concern anymore.

I tracked down the funnel cake stand and slipped right in line. Was it the healthiest of dinners? No. but I am a twenty-eight-year-old woman, and I want a funnel cake, damn it.

The sweet scent taunted me the whole wait, burning my stomach with a hunger I wasn't aware of until presented with the sweet treat. When it was finally my turn, I stepped up to the cart with a large grin. "Hello," I greeted. The small menu on the table had very few options, but I didn't what anything special. The same thing as always.

"Just a powdered cake please," I ordered. The boy couldn't have been any older than sixteen running a funnel cake stand. But then again, usually it was an older gentleman named Burt, so maybe it was a family business.

"$1.99," he said with a sigh, pulling the tongs and wax paper out. He wrapped up the delicious snack and handed it to me as I handed him a five.

"You can keep the change," I offered with a smile.

"Wow, thanks," he said dryly before tossing it into the drawer.

I shrugged it off. I wasn't going to let him ruin the evening anymore than it was. Me and my funnel cake would enjoy the waves over on the bench that faced out into the water.

Before I could take my seat, my ass buzzed with the ringing of my phone. I put the cake in my mouth and pulled my phone out with a grumble.

Parasite #3

I tried to shrug off the message, but the heat filled my chest and face as I took a bite of the cake a bit too aggressively. First my bike, now my younger sister texting me when I thought I had made it excruciatingly clear I did not want them contacting me.

I took a deep breath in through my nose, forcing my shoulders down to relax as I counted to five. I had much more to be thankful for. I did not need these small things interfering with the peace and happiness I had constructed over the last few years.

When the heat washed away from my cheeks and my breathing was less harsh, I sat back to look over the ocean as planned, allowing the wave of peace to flood over me.

I had the cake, the amazing sex, and the tranquil feeling of the calm waves of the ocean to melt my senses back into bliss.

A simple job, low debt, a free life, and the freedom to eat what I want, when I want. What more could I ask for?

CHAPTER TWO

Mira

A box truck with the words "Books and Crystals" painted on the side, sat parked in the lot as a man unloaded several boxes onto a trolley. The delivery Andrew had advised me about, only a full three hours earlier than expected. I barely got everything set up and open, and now I had to worry about stock on top of it.

Wonderful.

The door opened with a ring of the small jingling bell as the man pulled the trolley of boxes through.

"Hello," I greeted kindly, using my best customer service voice and smile.

He turned to look at me. Even with his dark sunglasses I could tell he gave me a quick size up. He moved his head up and down, so it wasn't like he was trying to hide it. He didn't smile or offer a hello in return, just pulled out a clipboard and looked over it for a moment.

His blue button-up was stained in sweat and what I hoped to be coffee. The undershirt that poked through was clearly once white but now held an uneven dinginess to it like it hadn't been washed in months. The appearance alone would have led me to believe the man underneath it all was an unkept beast. But the attire did not match the face. The man was well trimmed with a clean-cut beard, hair combed and slicked back as if he was some late 90s time traveler.

"Delivery for—Andrew Williams," he grunted. This was not the usual delivery driver. Couldn't be a trainee in that used jumpsuit. Must have been a fill in.

"That's my manager. He is not in, so I will sign for it," I informed, dropping the smile. I waved to the lobby where the deliveries were usually left. The boxes were never heavy enough for me not to be able to carry upstairs alone.

"And you are?" he grunted.

"Mina." I wasn't about to give off my last name to him.

He pulled out what looked to be a list of sorts and gave it a quick scan. Once he found what he was looking for, he gave a stiff nod and began unloading the boxes without having me sign for anything.

He left just as quickly and without saying a word as he stormed back out to load the trolley onto the truck. Getting deliveries was always eventful but usually because of what Andrew ordered. He never knew what to order when he was set to do it by himself, always needing me or one of the other girls to help with the list. But this exchange was weird as fuck.

I got to work taking the boxes up to the second floor. Of the four boxes delivered, only one of them was a bit difficult to lift. I had to plop it on every other step as I brought it to the top floor. Most likely it contained the book orders since we were running a bit low on stock after the summer sale.

I grabbed some box cutters from the counter and opened the first case. Sage, lavender, and rosemary came out in a puff, flooding the floor with the fresh fragrances, a box full of herb bundles and loose powder incense. I slid it over to the cabinet that held such items and moved on to the next one.

Crystals wrapped in tissue and bubble wrapping filled two more boxes that I placed alongside the display tables. The final box was fine where it was. I left it for last at the top of the steps.

The incense and bundles were quickest to unpack. The crystals, however, would take much longer since I would have to unwrap them, find a spot for them, and place them without knocking the rest down—extremely time consuming. It would be much easier for me to wait until Amber arrived.

Instead, I headed over for the box of books and cut it open. I was greeted by spells to modern witchcraft books along with several copies of the Wicca and pagan books we carried. Four copies of *Daily Witchcraft* were first to be placed. It was a copy we were sure to keep in stock, and I'd read it a few dozen times during slow hours. A decent read but very much "love and light," with a heavy emphasis on *light*.

The bell at the door announced a customer's entrance, breaking me from stock duty for the moment.

"Welcome to the Green Coven. I'll be right with you!" I called, setting the last of the *Daily Witchcraft* on the shelf.

"Meems, it's me!" Amber called, already making her way up the steps.

"Hey," I greeted when she reached the top. Her eyes fell on the shipment boxes. "You're early."

"Yeah—I'm regretting it now," she joked with a laugh.

"It hasn't been too bad," I promised, moving back to the box of books. Next to go up, *Sabbets and the Wheel of the Year*.

"I'll start the teas," she said, looking over the box of crystals. I didn't mind if she manned the apothecary while I finished stock so long as I didn't have to work with the teas and herbs.

"Do you have any readings today?" she asked before heading down.

"Nope. Once I'm done with this, I'll be down."

"Ok, have fun," she teased as she disappeared down the steps, leaving me to my work amongst the books and crystals.

I chipped away at the box by title until I pulled the last copy of *Magic in Colors* free and slid it onto the lower shelf. A sudden loud thump in the box caused me to jerk up, knocking my head on the shelf above.

"Ow!" I hissed, rubbing the new sting. I looked into the box to see what it was that had made such a noise. It had to be a heavy book, which would account for the extra weight.

At the bottom of the delivery sat an enormous leather book with tattered binding. Clearly not newly printed, or even of this century, if I had to guess.

I pulled it out to look for a name, but the covers were blank of any legible words. There was some faint etching that may have been a title but from what I could make out. It wasn't anything in English. Even stranger, there was no significant text written on the first page. Flipping through the thick parchment offered little aside from odd sigils and sketches.

"What the fuck?" I whispered. One of the pages was covered with black charcoal smeared all over on both sides. It had not faded onto the other pages but left the residue all over my hand. I rubbed it between my fingers, an odd slippery feeling rather than dusty.

"Ew, gross!" I groaned, wiping my fingers along the old cover. It wasn't a copy we ever carried, nor had I seen it before. Andrew could have ordered it for display, or it could have been an accident entirely, but I got up and placed it on the back counter. A problem for later, and not even mine.

I headed to the downstairs lobby where Amber worked over several herb-filled bowls. Almost all her blends ended up on our house menu and we tended to hear a lot of good things about them. My favorite was her divination tea. Not only was it delicious without honey, but I also felt it helped in my readings.

"You done already?" she called.

"I'll do the crystals later." I shrugged with a laugh. "What are you blending for this one?"

"Stress relief, with skullcap instead of lavender," she said, as if I would understand the difference aside from taste. Amber took a large scoop of the flaky herb and tossed it into the bowl. "Have you spoken to Jaz at all?" she added.

Just as the words left her lips, my phone began buzzing with an incoming message.

"I bet that's her now." I laughed as I pulled my phone out. Sure enough, the name on the screen read *Jaz*.

I called out today.
I'm exhausted.

-Jaz

All that late night hexing
will do that.

23

it was a cord cutting.
I'll tell you how it went
when I get up.

-Jaz

I set my phone on the counter. "She's staying home."

"That so? Will she be staying home tomorrow as well?" Amber scooped another cup of herbs into the bowl and began mixing.

"She didn't say, but seeing as how that is their shift together, probably not. Honestly, I wouldn't want to be around that," I said. It was the last thing I wanted to be around, them fighting like a high school couple. I couldn't deal with it. I had a few clients anyway, and it would all around be better that one of them stayed home.

"Shit. I forgot to grab the pouches," she hissed.

"Probably up in storage."

With a groan, she set the wooden spoon down and headed upstairs to the storage room. While she did that, I made my way over to the computer to check if I had any last-minute readings. There were none.

"They aren't on the shelf!" she called.

"Try behind the counter!" It was the only other place I could think they would be if they ended up in a shipment I had up there. I would have definitely left them behind the counter to bring down at a later time then instantly forgotten them.

"Ah ha!" she cheered.

After a few moments, she came back to the counter with the disposable tea pouches in hand. "Hey, what's that dusty old book up there?"

Perfect example, because I had already forgotten that ugly, old thing.

"It came in today's book shipment. I have no clue what it's about. I think it was a mistake or decoration."

The bell chimed with a customer's entrance, cutting our conversation short and officially starting the workday.

"Welcome in," we greeted. The short haired woman smiled and waved as she headed to the stairs. I waited until she was at the top before I followed behind to not seem as if I were hovering. It was a courtesy I enjoyed when I shopped.

While she looked over the books, I headed to the counter, available but not in the way.

She grabbed a few copies, then slowly examined each table of crystals. When she had collected her share of stones, she sauntered over to the checkout.

"Hi," she squeaked, spilling her finds over the counter, an annoying habit of most customers. It didn't make anything harder or easier; it was simply rude.

I bagged everything and rung her up for $89.90 with a smile. She took her bag and was on her way to inspect the apothecary. Her lively chatter carried up to the second floor as she admired and questioned Amber about her accent. I turned to head down as well, noticing the book had been left open from when Amber was looking it over. Oddly enough, she flipped to the charcoal covered pages as well.

I closed it on my way out, getting the odd, nasty substance back on my hand. Even stranger was the fact that it didn't appear to rub off on any of the other pages, at least not all slippery as it did on my skin.

"Hey, did that book leave a black goo on you, too?" I asked Amber as I came down.

"I didn't look at it that long," she said as she scooped the new blend into a pouch. When she finished with the one, she slid me a paper towel she had near her.

The rest of the shift went smoothly with a few dozen customers for both floors. We decided who would do clean up and who would drop the drawers.

"I did the drop last week," Amber scoffed. "It was Jaz's turn."

"Well, she earned herself two weeks," I groaned, snatching the envelope from the counter. The second floors drop was quick and simple, making an even $700 for the afternoon.

"I'll put these large crystals up for you," Amber said as I headed down the steps.

"Thanks."

The apothecary's drop was not as much but far timelier because people often paid for the cheaper teas with quarters. By the time I had finished the drop, Amber had finished cleaning both floors.

"I would have grabbed your bag, but you had all your cards and books out. I wasn't sure what you take with you." she said.

"It's fine." I made my way up the steps for the last time. The energy in the room felt a bit heavier than usual, lifting goosebumps along my skin. Fear wasn't something I encountered often in there. It was my protected space, but fear chilled my bones in that short moment.

I rushed around to collect my things, trying to ignore the static that tingled my skin. On my way out, I caught sight of the dingy brown leather of the old book sitting open on my altar. I was known to collect creepy things, but Amber should have known me better than that. Even if I did like how it looked, I could not get past the weird residue it left.

On my way out, I snatched it up and carried it to the back counter where I originally left it. Checking the order will be first on my list tomorrow to see what the thing was called.

Amber waited by the front door, ready to lock up and head out. "Did you bike it today?"

In all the oddness of the day, I completely spaced on that junkie old thing. "Oh, someone stole it yesterday during my shift." I shrugged.

"'*Oh, someone stole it.*' So unbothered." We stepped out and I locked up since I had the spare keys.

"It had a fucked-up gear. Besides, I need to get my car from the shop."

"It's still in there?" she shot.

"They keep finding things wrong with it, and I don't know if they are being honest or trying to hustle me."

We turned from the shop and headed to her car parked far in the back of the lot so no one would hit it.

"Why don't you ask one of the guys to go with you? I think Andrew mentioned he rebuilt his sister's whole engine."

Andrew would be the last person I'd ask. I didn't want him to get the wrong idea from it. On the other hand, asking the other guys we work with would just cause Drew to ask why I didn't ask him first.

"I don't want to bother him. He has his mom to worry about," I reminded.

"Mhm," she hummed suspiciously. The girls knew Andrew had a thing for me because he wasn't too secretive about that. But they didn't know we were already hooking up, and I kept telling them he wasn't my type and the whole boss card. They weren't buying it.

"Well, you really need to get it out of the shop. I know your van isn't that far from here, but you know how the nights are, and I worry about you walking," she said as she dug in her purse for keys. When she found them, she unlocked her car as we approached it.

"I will. I just don't want to be overcharged for bullshit."

"Are they not charging you for holding it there?"

"Only after a month."

"Climb in." She opened her car and climbed in with a look of confusion. "How long has it been already?"

I ran around to the passenger side and hopped in. "Twenty-four days." Truthfully, I had no idea what to do. I didn't care all that much for cars. I just drove them and put gas in, the occasional oil change. But the engine and all of that? I hadn't a clue.

When she was finished hounding me about my car, I told her about the delivery man and how he was fucking weird. We laughed about some drunk tourists crossing at the light and chatted about other nonsense things as she pulled into the lot of the beach, parking in the empty spot behind my van.

"Thanks for the ride. I'll text you tomorrow."

"No problem. See ya!" she called as I slid from the car and waited to pull off until I opened the door. I gave her a final wave and stepped in as she honked in return and drove off.

After such a long day, I wanted nothing more than to shower and relax with the book I've been reading on my Kindle. It was just getting to the part where the main character finally fucks the dragon and honestly, I'd been interested in reading how that played out.

I stood over the old book and examined the charcoal covered page a bit closer than before. Under the glow of the light, the indentation of written text was faintly visible.

"*Bübså nuj.*" The language that came from me was not one I knew nor one I had ever heard of. I wasn't even sure if I pronounced it right. Further down the page was what appeared to be a list in the same odd language.

"Mina Karim?" a deep voice called. I looked up, unsure why my last name was needed, or what random customer would even know it. But the creature before me was neither a man nor a customer. A dark shadow stood across from me with eyes as white as snow. It reached out to me, and I stepped back, holding my arms up to block it.

I shrunk back as best I could, digging my back into the counter. My clammy hands slipped from the edge as I attempted to pull myself onto the granite top.

The shadow creature dropped its hand to the book and pointed to something on the page. Pounding its finger with urgency against it caused a deafening thump that rattled my head. Keeping a comfortable distance between us, I peered over the page where it was pointing. Before I could make out the letters, a sudden pounce on my chest stirred me awake.

I jerked up from my bed to a yowling cat, demanding his morning meal. Dim, gray light peeked in from the slit of the curtain.

"Prometheus!" I groaned as I reached for my phone.

5:33 A.M.

"Damn it, cat. Can you let me sleep in for once?"

He sat impatiently beside me, flicking his whiskers and tail in annoyance.

"Fine. I'm up." I slid from the bed and began the morning routine of feeding the cat prince. After he was settled eating his meal, I grabbed my yoga mat and headed outside to the foggy beach morning. The surfers were zipping up their water suits and heading out. The few that often saw me this early waved with a smile. The true regulars were respectful.

I didn't care for the wakeup call, but I did love early mornings at the beach. Something about the fog and salty smell was relaxing. After I had the mat set out and the music playing on my phone, I began my stretching. They say yoga is about breathing and relaxing your mind, but I spent most of the positions worried if they are proper or focusing on not toppling over.

Once my joints were nice and flexible, I sat for my morning meditation. I had a dream to interpret, and that was the subject to reflect on.

The memory of the text on the book was faint, so I wouldn't be able to gather much from that. My focus would have to center around something clearer. I wasn't sure of the surroundings now that I thought on them. Thinking back, it wasn't a concern at the time, but it seemed as though I was in a dark room with one light or a very bright room. Either way, the surrounding area clearly wasn't important.

That left the shadow figure and its very insistent need for me to read a particular part of that page as it pointed to the bottom, a section I would look over once I got into work as well as check the order Andrew put out. I was sure if I could find the name, I could search up what it's about.

Warmth spread over my face as the sun finally made its appearance through the fog. I slowly cranked my eyes open to the blinding light. The blur cleared, presenting my fuzzy black cat, sprawled out in the sand to sunbathe.

"Such a king," I teased. With a swish of his tail, he rolled to his belly. I gathered everything and headed into the van. With the short time I had left of the morning, I ate and got ready for my shift. Wednesdays I had a few readings to conduct: weekly readings for two of them, biweekly for the last, making this particular Wednesday a busy one.

My phone buzzed on my bed with a message. The notification read *"Jaz: I'm not coming in today"* across the top banner. It wasn't surprising she'd call out today, too. It was the shift we worked with Antonio, and she would have been stuck alone with him while I conducted my readings now that I realized the day.

I knew things for them were turning sour when one of my readings was interrupted by their fighting. I wouldn't say they were yelling, but it was loud enough to travel.

I don't blame you.
Will we see you tomorrow for dinner?

I wouldn't miss that!
-Jaz

I shoved my phone and other needed items into my bag and headed off to work. My shift wasn't until noon, but the extra time would give me an uninterrupted moment to look over the book. I didn't know what I expect to find in it with how messy the page was but I was invested now.

The clear, bright sky provided no shade from the heated summer sun, but the cool ocean breeze brought with it the salty sea scent and calming mist, making for a lovely day to walk before I was trapped in the freezing, overpowering air in the shop. I would adjust it, but Andrew kept the thermostat locked.

With all the extra time, I walked slowly to take in the warmth and natural energy while I could, enjoying the day before trapping myself behind the glass wall of the shop. Unfortunately, no matter how slow I moved, or tried to move, I still found myself looking over the forest green paint that began to peel from the shop's sidewalk sign.

I unlocked the door and stepped into the mix of different aromas. The dark lobby felt colder than usual, so I headed up to my room where I kept a small space heater. There would be no focusing for me in the freezing cold, so it came in handy during many readings. I placed all my things down on the small table, grabbed the heater, and turned to head out to the counter to plug it in.

After getting the space a bit warmer, I flipped on the computer and waited as the struggling fan kicked on with a loud whooshing sound. It always took it a minute to load up and, for whatever reason, the cold made it run much slower. While it did its thing, I went to grab the book from the back counter where I had left it. I began looking over the front and back cover, the spine, and anything else before flipping to the page in question.

Once the computer finally loaded, it automatically pulled up the stock list Excel page. I clicked the order list tab and returned to the book, knowing that it would take another few minutes to load that next screen.

I looked over the pages under the light, searching for the indentations I saw in the dream. Unfortunately, that was all it had been, a simple dream because the page I looked over now was textured only from thick parchment and layers of dust.

The odd words now faded from my memory. I was back to square one.

The screen flashed as it finally switched over to the order list. I scanned it from top to bottom and again three times over, finding only the titles I knew, along with the amount ordered, and the old book was not included.

Hm, an accidental shipment. I immediately snapped a picture and sent it to Andrew with a short text. It wasn't the first time we got an accidental order, and we usually ended up selling it at whatever price Andrew set for it.

> *Hey, this used book came in the shipment yesterday. What price do you want me to set it at?*

While I waited for Andrew's response, I headed downstairs to set everything up and get ready to open shop starting with the house teas that needed to brew, which Amber had already measured out and prepped for me.

While I set out the pouches along the counter, Andrew finally responded.

It's ruined. Toss it
or keep it. Nobody
is going to buy that thing.
                                    -Andrew

I hadn't thought about keeping it, but throwing it away didn't seem right. It made it this long and even if I couldn't read it, it would add to the creepiness of my room.

I headed up to set the book in one of the altar cabinets, adding a purification incense to give it a quick cleansing while I prepared everything downstairs.

It didn't take long before all the displays were set and the tea brewing. With nothing left to do, I waited until Antonio arrived before I headed upstairs to prepare for my readings. I still had two hours until the first one, but I didn't have much to say to Antonio. He was never my favorite person to work with, but now, what was there to even talk about? Aside from work, which was a given.

We shared a polite hello before I made a swift retreat to the second floor to finish putting away the crystals I had left out, as Amber only stocked the small tumblers. The tables were already well cluttered with all sizes of stones in all forms and colors. I wasn't all that sure why Andrew thought we needed more, or why he thought we needed so many large towers. But I started the task by shifting stones around to make the needed space. Which wasn't much, so I did what I could and took what couldn't fit to Andrew's office.

On my way back I stopped at the apothecary computer to check my client schedule. It was much faster than the one upstairs, and it was the only one with the program for the scheduler. Nothing new for today, just the three as planned. But tomorrow held a newly filled slot for one named Tim B, an alias for a celebrity that often came in.

Jaz, Mickey, and I always loved the heads-up because we never knew if the paparazzi would figure it out and swarm the shop. And not only did we want to look our best, but Andrew had made it clear he wanted the shop in the best-looking shape for such publicity. I texted them the news and returned to the second floor.

Readings were uneventful with common questions and answers. There were no customers up top and only a handful downstairs. Not that I was complaining. Fewer customers made for a simple clean up and, in a blink, I was heading out the front doors into a pouring thunderstorm. I enjoyed the rain enough to not care about walking through it, but this was a downpour.

Well, I wasn't asking Antonio for a ride, and I definitely wasn't waiting for an Uber to pay over $25 for a two-minute trip.

"See ya, Antonio," I called as I locked up the doors.

"Later," he said with a twist of confusion as he pulled out his keys. I spun around and headed off, not waiting for the invitation I would have to reject. I didn't think I would accept a ride from him even if they hadn't broken up or dated. As I had said, he wasn't my favorite person.

I pressed the button at the light and waited with two other people who decided to brave the storm. They were so engrossed in their own conversation that they had to practically scream over the rushing wind. When the light finally flashed for us to cross, I rushed to the other side to escape the icy bites of wind that burned my skin. Each drop felt like blades cutting me, which was odd for a summertime storm. Usually the water was just as hot, but this was near freezing.

I nearly ran the rest of the way to my van, crossing onto the lot with my eyes locked on my blurry home. The wind shifted, tossing the water droplets more frantically in all directions to distort my view further. Through the darkness and rain, I could see someone near the front door of my van, looking into the windows at my cat as he swatted angrily at the glass.

"Hey!" I called out as I picked up speed, not too sure what I would do once I got there. I was a solid five foot five and had no fighting experience aside from the handy kick to the groin and keys to the eye sockets. Other than that, I could quite easily be overpowered. I slowed down, realizing the true danger as the person froze to look over at me. I couldn't make out any distinctive features in the dark, but it wouldn't have mattered. They took off down the beach toward the pier before I could say another word.

Traveling in a van alone as a woman was dangerous in itself, and boondocking on a beach had its challenges, break-ins being one. It wouldn't be the first time, and I had installed new security, but there was always risk hanging above that someone will still break in. Thankfully, it had been a few years and since I hadn't been here so long, most of the locals knew me well enough to keep a good eye on things.

I stepped up to the door with caution, my keys tucked between my fingers. The loud yowling broke through the door as Prometheus cried for his food, igniting my own anxiety of someone still lurking around. I worked frantically to unlock the door, missing the keyhole a few times before I finally shoved it in and slid open the door. I squeezed in through the small gap I allowed myself before slamming it closed once more.

With my back against the cool metal, I let out an exasperated sigh while Prometheus continued to scream at me, completely unaware of the dangers I had just faced to get in.

"I hear you!" I shot as I attempted to clear the short distance to the cabinet while he circled my feet.

"Can I get there, please? Gods!" I tossed my bag on the bed and got to work for the *king* of the van. The stench of salmon and chicken attacked my nose as I plopped the mess into his bowl and set it down. Now to feed myself.

Order in, or figure something out with the few ingredients I have?

I opened the small fridge to find three bottles of water, some condiments, and salad dressings. Other than that, I was sure I had some instant oatmeal in the cupboard.

Order out it is. I pulled out my phone and swiped to the Any Where Delivery app. They had some of the best salads I'd ever had, but I was feeling more like burgers than salad. I punched in the order, the card info, and hit submit. Before I could even close out from the app, I received a notification that my order was in the works. It came with an estimated delivery time of thirty minutes.

To pass that, I sat in the driver's seat to watch the raging ocean waves and keep an eye out for the stranger. With all doors locked, I found comfort in the storms that crashed against the sands. It was one of two locations I found complete serenity in.

Lightning flashed again, followed soon by the loud roaring of thunder.

On calmer nights, looking to the ocean was like gazing into an endless star-filled sky. Normally, the light tide reflected what was above, mirroring the constellations. But this night, the raging storm thrashed and tossed the waves about as if sea gods themselves were in a fierce battle over who would claim the sandy beaches I watched from. It made it easier to discern from the sea and sky for a beautiful show of nature, a balance of calm and chaos that likened the balance I felt between earth and sea.

CHAPTER THREE

Mira

    I didn't usually practice lucid dreaming, mostly because I was never aware I was in a dream despite how obvious it was. But there was something about this dream that allowed me to acknowledge that it was in fact a dream.

    I looked at the clock on the nightstand beside my bed, which was the first indication I was dreaming. The numbers read 31:05 EA, which made no sense. The sound of my brothers and sisters running downstairs ignited the resentment that rested deep in my chest. I groaned as I rolled to the opposite side of the bed, hitting something hard.

    My fingers twisted in the coarse hair of whatever stuffed animal I had beside me. Another wave of joyful screams came from downstairs.

"Ugh!" I grunted angrily. My eyes flew open, meeting a mess of black and gray hair that spilled over my pillow. I jerked up straight, my eyes still on the mass beside me. Before I could make another move or escape the bed, a single eye opened between the thick, matted strands. The rectangular pupil gazed at me, and I could feel it looking my soul over like a meal.

The creature lifted, rising until its head met my ceiling. Long fur covered it from head to toe, spilling over my bed. I fell back onto the floor with my eyes locked on the odd creature—no face, no arms, no distinguishing features to indicate what was creating a dent in my ceiling.

The resentment that had filled my chest was instantly replaced with a grating ball of fear as the thing took a frightening step towards me. My stomach dropped, pulling my lungs with it as air escaped them. I struggled to draw in labored breaths as I sat frozen, watching it near me. No bending knees, no fault in the dismount. It practically glided over the wood floor.

I followed its body up to where I assumed its head was located. Between the thick strands of matted hair, two odd-shaped eyes glared down at me. Fear anchored me in place, keeping my focus locked on the mound of horrific fur.

The scream grew deep in my chest, balling up enough energy to project the howl. Icy chills spread over my skin, raising goosebumps along the way, and my throat closed, muting the sounds I struggled to release.

The creature tilted its head to one side as it continued to stare.

"Mina! Mina!" My siblings' cheerful screams burst through the door with a loud BANG as it hit the hard wall.

The sudden sound flung me from the comfort of my bed and tossed me to the hard floor. My head hit the cabinet while my feet became twisted in the comforter, and the alarming movement tossed Prometheus into the air with a hiss.

"Ow!" I groaned. Smoggy gray light peeked in through the curtains, signaling the early morning. I removed my bonnet, irritated that the enchantment had run its course once again, a monthly charging to keep nightmares away that I would soon have to redo. Returning to my childhood was included in that list.

I ran my hand over the growing bump that began to welt from the collision, wincing at the stinging pain the contact brought.

"Great," I groaned, wobbling to my feet. The van spun around me for a moment and when it settled, I grabbed a bottle of cold water to hold against the bump. Once I felt well enough, I gathered myself and began my morning. With the celebrity client and girls' dinner after work, I planned on a cute lacy black skirt, a crop top with lacy sleeves, and a bra harness under it. My makeup, however, was not as dedicated to one color.

I wasn't here to say *"I am not like other girls."* I most certainly was and I loved makeup. With that being said, the craft of glamour magic was also incredibly soothing and empowering.

With eyes and face complete, I moved on to my hair. The thick halo of blonde curls sat wildly around my head. I parted out two small chunks in the front center for two small braids. With those sectioned off, I pulled all my curls into a pineapple at the very crown of my head. I freed a few random pieces for a slightly messy look and then laid my edges. The two small braid pieces were quick and easily tucked behind my ears.

A look, for sure.

With my bag packed and the cat fed, I headed out early to grab breakfast before heading to work. The beach and the foggy mornings were calming, but after last night, I preferred an indoor session, giving me peace to meditate comfortably without fear of someone running up on me.

Prometheus meowed as I closed and locked the van, his cute way of saying goodbye. He'd most likely spend the day in the window watching the seagulls and surfers. Aside from that, I really didn't know what else he would do.

I headed to the small burrito shop on the way to grab their most famous breakfast burrito. The mouthwatering scent of sausage, egg, and cilantro had me racing to the shop for the privacy to enjoy it.

The apothecary smelled of incense and herbs, but the food in my hand was stronger. I locked the doors so no one walked in thinking we were open and pulled up a seat in the lobby.

After my delicious breakfast, I headed upstairs to prep my room. Feeling a bit of weight was normal considering I communed with spirits, so the energy had always been a little thick. But this day it was overly weighing with a frigid air circulating much colder than usual. Nearing the protection of my room didn't make anything better, as the odd feeling continued to crawl along my skin.

Once over the threshold of my protected room, the clenching grip the energy had around me released. I took in a deep breath and dropped my bag beside the door as I looked over the book on the opposite altar. The energy felt more concentrated near the mysterious book.

I'd have to cleanse that before opening. Now that I thought about it, it would probably be wise to add an extra cleansing during the week, just in case. Clearly, that book brought with it more than simple curiosities. It would have to be cleansed and bound today.

With a heavy sigh, I got to work setting up the cushions and pillows along the floor. I removed my cards, pendulum, and mat from the bag to set up as well. Once the room was as I liked it, I moved downstairs to begin setting everything out.

Since Amber had premeasured and bagged everything for me, opening throughout the week has been much easier. Setting up was simple. It kept me and my mind busy, but once everything was ready and the doors unlocked, I was left waiting. Thankfully, Andrew wasn't a strict boss and allowed us to pass the time on our phones when it was slow.

Guess who comes
in tonight!

There hadn't been a paparazzi moment yet. The few celebrities that came were very good about their aliases and keeping a low profile when they visited. By law, we couldn't give out that information, so we just hoped someone slipped up.

Merrill or Rory?
-Amber

Rory.

Rory recently starred in a new paranormal movie and had been acting since he was a kid, though his appointments were always scheduled under a Tim A. His ballcap and sunglasses disguise wasn't doing much, at least not for us. I'm honestly surprised nobody else has figured it out yet.

The tea kettles began to whistle out the steam, announcing their arrival at the proper temperature. I turned down the heat on the stovetops and tossed in each tea pack to steep. Once everything was set, I made my way upstairs to grab my charger. The energy in the room hadn't died down in my absence. Instead, it felt as if it grew more unstable. Bumps lifted along my skin, raising the hairs across my arm with a sudden chill. An echoing click sent my heart to my throat, making it hard to swallow. A loud thump followed that I could feel rattle through my feet.

The air fell still and quiet, muting out the sound of the low chatter on the first floor. Even the A/C seemed to go silent, replaced by the loud thump of each quickened heartbeat.

I turned toward the source, finding my altar cabinet slowly creeping open and the book lying flat on the shelf, barely peeking out to push the door further. My hand instinctively connected with the keyring in my purse to ensure it wasn't a prank, though I didn't know who would know to prank me with this book in such a way.

A frigid breeze brushed over my arms and legs, causing rippling tremors in my bones. I took in a deep breath and marched across the room.

On second thought, I don't need this book, nor does the shop. I snatched it up and headed out to the floor trashcan. I might have used a bit too much force as I heaved it in, but oh well and good riddance. I didn't like the feeling of creepy crawlers moving over my skin. It was the type of dark energy that set my nerves on edge.

As a necromancer, you'd think I would feel at home with the dark and paranormal, and usually I did, but heavy energy like that was too much.

I lit a rosemary bundle and set it in my small cauldron to smoke cleanse the room while I waited for everyone downstairs. I could more easily distract myself with my phone there without all the suffocating discomfort.

It didn't take much for me to get lost on a stream of videos, passing an hour with ease and no customers. I decided to do a walk around the lobby to stretch my legs and give the cameras something to look at since I was shoved off behind the counter where it couldn't see much else than my hands.

The door chimed and their roaring laughter announced their arrival at the shop.

"You two are ridiculous!" I joked with a laugh. They came dressed to impress with Amber in her soft, flowing white dress, and Mickey in an adorable skintight black dress, makeup ready for the night for both the client they would barely see and the dinner after work.

"Is this all for the hopeful paparazzi or later at the restaurant?" I quizzed.

"Dinner, of course," Amber said, snickering.

We walked to the back counter and spent the next few hours planning more for the following day's camping trip, setting on some few minor details before time clicked closer to my client's arrival.

"I'm going to head up now. You two behave," I joked, making my way up the stairs. The weighing energy from earlier felt a bit heavier and the feeling of being watched nagged at me as I crossed the floor.

I left the door open as I readied the space for a second time, cleansing and prepping the mat for the reading. With everything going on and the extra weighing feeling that seemed to be making its home, I decided to take the rosemary bundle out to the floor to ensure the entire space felt as clear as possible.

If the energy was bothersome to me, it would only be frightening to my clients, and fear didn't make for a great reading experience. Most often it called to and invited in more malevolent spirits. After the weight lifted, I made my way back to the room to center my mind in my usual spot on the floor.

"Knock, knock," Rory's voice rattled over the calming silence, breaking my hour-long blissful peace and reflection.

"Good evening, *Tim*," I greeted without turning to him. "Please come in."

Rory didn't often speak with those who have passed on. Mostly he just wanted insight into his career and family life. His wife wasn't much of a believer, but Rory credited it for his whole career—not anything he conducted with me, but the previous practitioner he went to. He had been seeing me since they started filming here three months ago.

"Thanks again, Mina." He pushed a bill into the small jar I kept on a shelf beside the door. It wasn't meant to be a tip jar and tips were not required, but they did come in handy. Besides, whenever I did attempt to tell them that it wasn't necessary, they'd find a way somehow.

"Have a good night, Tim," I said, gathering the crystals and cards spread out on the floor. His footsteps drifted off behind me until they ended with the chime of his exit.

"There," I huffed as I tossed the last pillow. Feeling proud of my half-ass work, I grabbed my bag and headed down to meet with the girls.

"Jaz said she will meet us there!" Amber informed me as I hit the bottom step.

We met at the lobby door and headed out to lock up. Steak and Whiskey was a simple tavern near the pier with some amazing lamb shanks and great bourbon. Like with our Monday brunch, our Thursday dinner was equally needed to decompress the stress-filled week.

"She said she was pulling up and would get us a booth," Amber informed us. We crossed the lot and headed toward the tavern a block away.

"Hey, Meems. Does Rory have bodyguards?" Meklit asked.

When I thought about it, I had never really seen Rory enter the shop. He always came right upstairs where I already was. I didn't often greet my clients in the lobby since I prepared for the reading beforehand. But I never knew him to come with anyone, especially since it had never been brought up.

"I'm not sure. Why? Did he have some today?"

"I didn't see anyone, but we didn't have any customers your entire reading time. I thought maybe he had them outside, shooing off customers."

"Hm," I hummed. "He's never mentioned anything to me. I figured the disguise was well enough."

We shrugged it off as a coincidence and turned onto the path for the restaurant. Their large open windows in front gave clear visual to Jaz in the booth already enjoying the house bread.

She waved to us through the window as we stepped up to the door, greeting us with a wide smile as we walked in, a complete turnaround from earlier in the week.

"Hey!" she cheered as we all slid into the leather seats. The night looked to be a busy one with every booth and table full. The bar was packed from people in the stools to people standing around the counter to order.

"There is a wedding rehearsal going on. I was able to steal us a booth, and some of the groomsmen sent over the bread!" Jasmine said joyously. She had to yell a bit over the volume of the crowd, but we all nodded in response.

The waiter came over after a few moments. His hair stuck out in every direction as he frantically raced through the house menu. We came often enough and already knew our order and didn't need time or menus.

"We can put our order in now, if that makes it easier for you," Mickey offered sweetly.

"Oh, yes, please, Ms. Meklit." The waiter, Tyler, sighed with relief. We gave him our orders for food and drinks, and he was off again, dodging hands and squeezing through the patrons to get to the back.

We discussed more plans for the weekend now that we had Jasmine to see what she planned to bring and if we needed anything extra. By the time our drinks came, the celebration from the other groups had carried on to roaring, drunken laughter that resulted in pushing and three broken beer mugs.

The three individuals were escorted out by the bigger bartender that doubled as the restaurant's unofficial bouncer. He tossed them out the front into a passing crowd of people. I'm not sure why—there didn't seem to be an immediate danger—but my heart suddenly picked up as if I had run a marathon.

I searched the crowd for something unknown until the feeling subsided and my breathing fell even again.

Damn anxiety. I turned back to the table with my bourbon freshly refilled. I took a long sip to ease the rest of my nerves as I tried to settle into the cold leather booth.

"Damn, Mina!" Jaz gasped. "Slow down."

Along with traveling in the van and being my best friend since elementary school, she had seen my struggles with my family. She had also been there for my many ups and downs, especially my relationship with alcohol. I wouldn't consider myself an alcoholic. It wasn't affecting my life negatively, and I didn't wake up thinking about drinking. But when I did drink, I tended to go for the harder stuff. Really, I just wanted to have a good time quicker than four drinks deep.

"You have to walk home," Jaz reminded, pushing the glass from my lips.

"I'll drink water when the food arrives," I assured, taking another long sip.

"You don't want to be hungover for the drive tomorrow. You know how you'll be dragging all day. You have to drive," Amber reminded.

"Yeah, yeah." I waved them off with a chuckle and we carried on with the previous conversations.

Our dinner arrived a bit cold but honestly, with what they had going on, it wasn't a surprise. The noise wasn't dying down and we all wanted to hurry and leave. We rushed through our meal, pushed Tyler a tip of eighty, and left. The feeling of the bourbon had dwindled to a steady headache and heavy eyes.

"Night, see you all tomorrow. Text the group when you get home!" I yawned and we parted ways, agreeing to make that notification of safety once we made it home.

I crossed the street with a small group of tourists that broke off to nothing and headed into the lot of the beach I park at. There wasn't much illumination in the area after dark, mostly the pier lights and the moon. I had a few dim solar bulbs out around the van, but other than that, it was all shadows.

Prometheus sat in the windshield, his attention out to the slow washing tides. I stumbled to the door and unlocked it, having a bit of trouble with the keys, but once I got it, I was good to go. The door slid open, and I climbed in, tripping over my cat as he zoomed down from his perch to greet me.

Despite being drunk, I ensured every door was locked and shut the front windows in case anyone saw my stumbling ass enter the van alone. With the little energy I had, I sent a sloppy text to the chat, undressed, and washed my face. I managed to pull my bonnet sloppily over my curls before falling back on the pillow for the night.

Chapter Four

Mira

I spent the morning at the grocery store, stocking up on food, drinks, and ice, as well as some extra firewood despite the bundle I had tucked away at my site. There was always the slight chance someone actually found the spot and used it, but that was rare, if ever an occurrence. I packed all the ice and perishables into the cooler and loaded the mini fridge with water and soda.

The lot across the shop had a few cars scattered around, so I parked directly in front of the main window and headed to start my shift. According to the prior day's investigation, there were no clients to be had today.

After setting up the apothecary lobby and starting the teas, I headed up to my room. The looming energy still weighed heavily over my shoulders as I crossed through the door. My attention immediately fell on the wide-open cabinet where the book sat with its cover facing out. My heart felt as if it were ready to leap from my chest as the sight seared into my brain.

"What in the poltergeist fuck is this?" I whispered, forcing myself to continue into the icy room.

The now bone-chilling air swept over my skin, making my throat dry as I struggled to swallow. I looked around the room to see if maybe the girls were playing a trick on me. But they had no idea I even kept the book, let alone the fact I had thrown it away.

I reluctantly stepped forward, my eyes glued to the book as if it were tugging me in. The sound of steady breathing and a racing heart were all that filled my ears as I reached out for it. A loud chime from the entrance door rang through the shop. The sudden sound jerked me up and I whacked my hand against the hard wood of the altar.

"Ah!" I cried out as I fell back hard on my ass, hitting my head against the bookshelves. "Ow, fuck!"

I rubbed the sore spot on my head and jumped to my feet. "Welcome in! I'll be right down." I turned to rush out.

Another chill shook my body, pushing me through what felt like a thick film as I exited the room. I sucked in a breath and raced across the lobby to the stairs. "How can I help you?" But when I looked over, the lobby was already empty. There was no way I was returning to my room until Jasmine or Meklit showed up. I needed someone else to witness it before I drove myself insane.

I waited for them in the apothecary lobby. The dark energy of the book fluttered about upstairs while I pretended to ignore the nagging feeling.

What time are you guys getting here?

I wasn't too proud to admit I was a bit scared. As I mentioned, the shop gets odd paranormal happenings here and there. But I had never been around to witness much else than the shadow figures running past the corner of my vision.

Omw now. Is it busy?

No. I'll tell you when you get here.

I set the phone down on the counter, keeping my head down to avoid even the slightest glimpse of whatever was going on upstairs. It wasn't exactly quiet anymore. The sound of soft shuffling and scraping came in spurts.

Meklit's car pulled into the lot next to my van. She hopped out of the blue Mini Cooper and jogged up to the door. Her attire definitely read after work camping trip.

"What happened?" she called, busting through the front door as if the news was that drastic. But her arrival did bring silence to the second floor instantly. I sucked in a steady breath, ready for the odd looks and questions.

"Remember that dusty book that came in with the shipment Tuesday?" I begin. She nodded slowly with a concerned twist to her lips. There was no need to sugarcoat it. "I need to show you something." I led her up to my reading room, stopping at the closed door to explain what she was about to walk into.

"So, I tossed it out yesterday, but when I got in this morning, it was back."

Her blank stare was answer enough. It sounded just as bizarre as I thought it would but it felt so much better to say aloud.

"I am sure it is just an old book, Meems. You spend too much time in here by yourself. All those skulls and demonology books are getting to you," she said with a nervous giggle.

"You think so? Because I'm not usually scared to hang out in this room."

Mickey stepped back with a lifted brow, her eyes on the door. "This isn't some prank, is it?" she asked skeptically.

I shook my head and gave a dry laugh as I opened the door. "I wish." We walked in. Too scared to look in its direction, I pointed to it. "See."

Meklit looked around, confusion forming on her face before concerned eyes fell back on me.

"See what? Your messy altar?" She shrugged.

I turned to look at the cabinet, finding the door shut once again. The weighing energy still pushed down on my shoulders, but I needed to know for sure. I walked over and reached out for the door, holding my breath as I pulled it open to reveal the tattered old book now lying flat with its spine toward us.

"What the fuck?" I whispered to myself.

Meklit leaned over to get a better look at it before I shut and locked the cabinet. "Well, that is an ugly, old thing," she said with a scrunched nose. Her eyes flickered back to me with concern. "Are you going to be ok to drive?"

Perhaps she was right and it all was just in my head. So much incense smoke couldn't be good for me.

That's it, because that's the only explanation for all this.

"Yeah. I think you are right, all those demonology books," I said blankly, my eyes still on the cabinet door.

"If you are bothered, just stay downstairs with me," she offered with a smile. I agreed and we stepped out, being sure to shut and lock the door behind us. My bag was downstairs anyway, and I didn't want to come back up. The deep cleanse would be a problem for another day. Tonight was to be enjoyed.

Our phones buzzed wildly on the counter as we descended the stairs. I raced over, finding the notifications were all from Jaz and Amber in the group chat. It was just them letting us know they had met up at the dispensary and Jaz would be coming with Amber to make the cleanup quicker.

"How much do you think they got this time?" Mickey asked with a grin.

"Enough for the week if Jaz has anything to do with it," I joked as I sent a response.

We helped three customers in the apothecary before we saw Amber's red convertible pull up on the opposite side of the van.

"Are you going to tell them about the haunted book?" Mickey teased.

I shot her a pointed look and shook my head, my curls bouncing around my face as I did. Taunts from her were well enough. I didn't need all of them piling on me about it.

Another twenty minutes or so passed before Amber and Jaz walked in with high spirits and bright smiles. They, too, were dressed and ready for the trip, while I was in my usual attire.

"We left everything in the car. I figured we could move it once we leave," Jasmine said as she headed to the back to join us.

"Hopefully it's slow enough and we can leave early," Amber

said with a sigh.

We spent the next few hours talking about the burning we would conduct while camping. We had few enough customers that Jasmine decided to text Andrew in hopes he would allow us to close shop early. He gave us thirty minutes. If no one came in that time, we were free to close.

"I'm going to get everything switched over to the van. Meems, can I see your keys?" Amber asked with an open hand.

I dropped the set in her palm and got to work cleaning the downstairs with Mickey while Jaz took to sweeping the upstairs for me.

After the thirty-minute checkpoint and zero customers, we texted Andrew that we were heading out. I grabbed both mine and Jasmine's heavy-ass bags before heading out to lock up.

"Do we have everything?" Mickey asked. She was always the one to make sure we were well prepared, wise and mature despite being the youngest of us. Amber gave a quick look through her car and with a final nod we jumped into the van and took our places.

"Pro-pro!" Jaz greeted Prometheus as he ran to her, his second favorite person besides me. He would make his rounds, but Jasmine was always his first stop for attention.

Amber and Mickey took their spots on the bed while Jasmine and I took the front two seats. The van wasn't constructed with more than one other passenger in mind, so the bed was the next feasible spot. Not necessarily the safest, but I ensured everyone was seated and ready before pulling out of the lot.

Traffic was light when I turned onto Pier Avenue and made my way for the freeway. Different songs ran for a second or two before Jasmine skipped them in search of the right travel song. Once she found it, she turned the volume up. We all had the same taste in music, even on her wild shuffle. Taking us from late 90s to early 2000s and current, she had it all.

Our conversations ranged through different topics during songs we didn't care for, turning it down for one only to turn it up for another we enjoyed. The actual topics never resumed as we drove the hour up to Angeles. It wasn't until we hit the lightless dirt road that we turned the volume to zero. Even though we crossed into the park, we still had a bit of a journey up and around until we were at my spot, and for some reason I felt I could focus better with less noise, as if that helped me see any better.

"Damn, Meems! You make this trip every weekend?" Amber

asked from the back.

"Yeah. I enjoy the peace and quiet. It is refreshing after a week of the usual noise from the city," I responded as I pulled into the final turn and slowed to a stop.

"We're here," I announced as I jumped from the seat.

Jaz and the girls got up to begin rummaging through their bags for their gear.

"I'll start the fire," I offered. It was already dark enough, and they would need the light to set up their tents. We all agreed that it wouldn't be fair for one of them to get the bed and the other two the floor, and my bed isn't built to fit four people. Luckily they all had tents from previous camping trips.

I tugged the bundle of wood out and tossed it by the pit as I made my way for the bushes I had shoved the last bundle of wood under. I reached my hand under the brush, finding the logs just as I expected.

Back at the pit, Jaz was pulling out the drinks from the cooler, and Amber was grinding down weed to roll.

"You guys can't set up your tents in the dark but can do all this?" I laughed as I stacked the wood and shoved some kindling into the center. It took me a few tries to get the lighter going, but once the spark hit the dry wood, it lit up within seconds, consuming the logs in an inferno to illuminate the small space around us.

"Ah, better!" Jaz called from the side of the van where she was mixing drinks. Amber moved closer to the flames as she began rolling a few joints for the night. With the fire set, I headed back to the van to turn up some music.

The flames kicked up smoke and embers into the sky while we sat back drinking our variations of alcohol—Jack and Coke for Meklit and Jasmin, wine for Amber, and the Bumbu Rum I kept stashed away for myself. None of them cared too much for rum, which meant more for me.

"What else do you usually do out here, Meems?" Amber quizzed.

I shrugged. "Get drunk, smoke weed, and stargaze. A full moon ritual or two. Did you have something else in mind other than the burning?"

"No, that sounds good to me," she said as she licked the paper she was rolling.

"Does anyone need more to drink? My bottle is done," Jaz quizzed. We all raised a hand with a wave of *"me"* to follow.

"Oh, grab the bag and more papers!" Amber tossed.

"Yeah, yeah," Jaz slurred back as she disappeared into the van.

I took another sip of my rum, leaning my head back to gaze at the stars above. I was never great at constellations and their names, but the two I knew well and could spot with confidence were the Big and Little Dipper. Not that that was anything to brag about. Most people could point them out given the right description.

I took a moment to locate them, giving myself a mental high five once they had been spotted. I dropped my head to Amber who was grinding up more weed to roll another joint.

"Hey, Meems!" Jaz called from the van.

"Yeah?" I called, letting my head roll back.

"What's this?" Her voice held a low amount of disgust to whatever she was referring to.

Mickey, who sat across from me and had clear view of Jaz, let out a sharp gasp, her eyes widening at the object.

I turned around to see what the fuss was all about, my heart dropping to the pit of my stomach as my eyes landed on what she held up.

The haunted book.

I turned back to Meklit with an "I told you" sort of gaze as I called back to Jasmine, "Where did you find that?"

"Your bag. It's fucking heavy!"

"Very funny, Mina!" Micky scoffed.

Amber's brows lifted as she tuned in to our conversation.

"When would I have had the time?" I countered.

Jaz had made her way over with it, flipping through the pages curiously as I had.

"Is that that odd book that was mixed in with our order?" Amber quizzed.

"Yes, and Mina thinks she is being funny by acting like it's haunted," Mickey slurred.

"I am not acting. Try looking it up," I offered, taking another sip of my rum, welcoming the numbing heat that spread over my cheeks.

"Where's the title?" Amber asked as she pulled out her phone to begin her search.

Jasmine looked over the covers and flipped through the pages, her face falling more concerned as she looked back at me.

"There isn't one," I smiled triumphantly, as if a nameless book validated any sort of haunting at all. "The only thing of interest is the blank page that's covered front to back in nothing but charcoal."

"The charcoal page isn't blank," Jasmine informed quickly.

I shot my gaze up at her and the book as she flipped it around to show us. Across the once blackened page was an odd language written in white ink. I jumped up and snatched the book from her to look over the page. I had looked over it a few too many times before to not have seen the writing.

"Excuse you!" Jaz snapped. They crowded around as we all looked over the words on the page.

"Is that Latin?" Amber asked as she studied the words.

"Mina, you studied Latin, right?" Mickey asked.

"Only a semester, but this doesn't look like Latin," I warned as we looked over the page more closely.

"I'm sure it's the same thing," Jaz slurred innocently. It most certainly was not the same, though the words did look a tad familiar as I skimmed over the lines, finding one in particular I knew very well. I pointed it out to them.

"That says ritual," I said with confidence. I looked over the rest of the passage, very simple when I combined it with the few words I taught myself from the demonology books I had.

"It's a manifestation ritual!" I cheered. But my excitement was only met with skeptical looks.

"In that ugly ass book?" Jaz asked.

I turned the book to face them, pointing to each word and explaining the meaning. "Basic—entry-level," I slurred with pride.

"Ok, we will take your word for it," Mickey said slowly, taking her seat back on the log. Amber and Jaz broke off as well, returning to the van to collect what Jaz had originally intended.

I continued to look over the etching in the page, slightly amazed the words were there and mostly in awe that I finally found out something about the silly book. There had to be a reason it showed up at the shop, why it kept appearing everywhere I go. It wanted me to read it, and what more magical way to display that other than presenting the words under the full moon's light?

"Let's do it!" I suggested, pausing everyone in their tracks as they turned to gawk at me with arched brows.

"Oh hell no, Mina!" Amber laughed from the van.

"Yeah, girl, be fuckin' for real. You spent all week obsessing over this book and claiming it to be haunted. Now you want to do a working from it?" Mickey added.

"Uh—yeah, maybe it needed to be read under the stars or something. Look, it even has the diagram. All we need are a few candles and to draw a circle," I slurred happily again.

"You are wild. How drunk are you?" Mickey laughed.

"Yeah, the weed isn't even that great. What's up with you?" Amber admitted.

"I mean, I'm down. I have some things I want to manifest this full moon anyway," Jaz finally added as she returned with more bottles.

Amber looked up to the moon with pressed lips. "I suppose it wouldn't hurt."

"I got candles inside." I jumped over the log, enthused with the plan and headed into the van to collect the black and white pillar candles I had. Now, if you knew anything about anything in witchcraft, you would know there are a number of protections that must be placed, a clear mind and body, and knowledge of what you are doing. Speaking Latin, or in this case, the given language fluently may also help. Being drunk and half-assing any of those was a clear recipe for disaster.

But alcohol and weed does a number on your judgment and, despite knowing all of this, we continued on with making the most horrific-looking summoning circle in the sand around the pit. Mickey eventually joined in by looking over the diagram in the book for anything we had missed.

"Oh, you decided to join?" I teased Mickey.

"What else are witches to do late at night in the middle of the forest?" she teased back.

I lit the candles over the fire and set them on what looked to be a north and south location, and we all took a spot around the circle. Mickey handed me the book, I assumed because it was my idea. Not that I was upset over it. It was my book, after all.

I looked over the text with a deep breath, sounding the words out in my head a few times before projecting the chant out for the rest to hear. *"Audi, Eriusazazl. Exaudi causam meam!"* I began, repeating the phrasing a few times until the girls joined in.

"Audi, Eriusazazl. Exaudi causam meam!" we chanted. I flipped the page to continue the passage but it ended after two more chants. I paused and looked around, unsure what to do or say next.

"Do we just say our manifestation aloud?" Amber asked suddenly.

We looked around at each other for a moment before falling into a fit of laughter. I am not sure what we all expected from the chant or the circle.

"It would have been cool if the fire kicked up or something. Like real magic," Mickey giggled with enchantment.

"Real magic?" Amber laughed from her side of the circle.

"Yeah, like levitation and broom riding. Potions and spells. Magic," Mickey explained.

I couldn't really disagree. A way to physically see and audibly hear my clients' loved ones would be amazing.

It could also be the added liquor and weed was making me more agreeable, but I couldn't see a con in Mickey's suggestion. We didn't have anything to lose, and it was giving us something to do. Besides, it was the most I got from the book. I might as well take advantage.

"Like *Hocus Pocus*?" Amber laughed.

"Laugh all you want, but wouldn't you want your teas to go beyond medicinal use? Rather than it taking time, it's instant," Mickey explained to Amber. She turned to Jaz and continued, "And you, you talk about looking at people's auras all the time. Wishing you could see it sooner."

"She has a point," I tossed in over the fire.

Amber and Jasmine shared a look of defeat. The examples given and the added liquor was more than enough to convince them.

"So, we agree?" Mickey confirmed.

"Yeah," Amber and Jaz sighed in unison. I nodded and looked to the page for anything more. To my drunken surprise, words began forming over the black charcoal. I read out the words as they appeared, *"We give you our soul for four desires."* I looked up at them with a lifted brow. The fire flickered aggressively, casting shadows over the page that shifted the words again. *"Gratias tibi."*

As the words left my lips, the fire flared up and out, shoving us back with its heated rage. A booming clap rang through the forest as if an explosion erupted from the pit. The force of it all pushed us back, causing me to stumble over the log. I struggled to grab at anything to break the fall, but my head connected with something hard. Everything flashed white before fading to black and the words *"Audi, Eriusazazl"* echoed until it to, faded into the dark silence.

CHAPTER FIVE

Mira

The throbbing in my head woke me, or maybe I was just coming to from being knocked out. I sat up, holding my hand to the lump on my head. "Ow."

I waited until the spinning slowed and the throbbing was bearable before wobbling to my feet. I'd had worse stumbles on nights out, so this wasn't anything new. But it was unexpected.

I scanned the camp, finding the book opened beside me with the charcoal page blank once again. I snapped my attention to the girls who all lay scattered around the fire in much more comfortable positions than me, not thrown back from any fiery explosion. Even the circle appeared to be snuffed out of the dirt.

My empty rum bottle leaning against the log explained everything. With a soft laugh, I scooped up the book and climbed to my feet. "What a wild dream," I said to myself.

A sudden snap rang through the silence, jerking me up straight as I searched the direction of the noise. I locked eyes with two that reflected the fire as they gazed back at me. Too small to be any sort of mountain lion known to the area, but too big to be a dog. Unless of course, someone lost their Great Dane.

I whistled off to it in case it was a dog, but it didn't react beyond a simple blink.

"Hey!" I called next. My sight adjusted to the shadows, and I could make out more of the creature. I squinted at it to be sure what I was seeing was what I thought it was.

Is that a fucking goat? I know goats had been seen around but usually with their farmers and in small groups. Never this high up, this late, or alone. It also wasn't a breed I recognized. Lucky for the little lost critter, I adored goats. How fantastic for us both!

I slowly stumbled my way over so as not to frighten it away. But it didn't flinch at my clumsy approach. It just stood there watching me. The closer I got, the more I realized it hadn't a reason to be frightened of me in the slightest. It was large, almost towering over me to the point I had to look up to it as I got closer.

A magnificent black goat with large swirling horns just as dark.

"You are a glorious guy, aren't you?" I slurred, drunkenly reaching my hand out to pet it. The goat remained still, only blinking its odd eyes at me.

My palm pressed against its warm snoot. I waited for it to jerk away but after a while, it seemed to lean into it. I rubbed its nose before bringing my other hand up to scratch beneath its furry chin.

"Oh my! You are a friendly goat!" I giggled as I continued to love on the wild animal. I remembered the bag of baby carrots I had shoved in the back of the mini fridge last week, a pleasant snack for a good boy.

"Would you like a treat? Up here all by yourself, you must be hungry," I cooed, withdrawing my hands from the thick fur. It shook its body and tilted its head to the side as it looked down at me.

"Well, come on!" I turned from the goat and headed back to the van, not too sure if it was following or not.

I opened the door and stepped in, Prometheus running onto the bed with a frightened hiss.

"Sorry, buddy. There is a friend outside. You should see!" I slurred to the poor cat as I rummaged through the fridge until I found the bag of carrots. "There you are."

I pulled them free and left the van, struggling to open the bag, "Ok, Mr. Goat, they are small so please try not to eat my fingers…" My words were cut short as I looked up, dropping the bag as I stared at the goat standing carelessly in the center of the firepit. Air froze in my lungs, weighing them down to my stomach as I tried to make sense of the sight before me.

Flames wrapped around the goat, dancing and licking at his horns as he stood unbothered by the heat. Even his fur remained unsinged from the blaze.

He reared up onto his hind legs, the flames rising as he did, twisting around him until it engulfed him completely in a loud, crackling inferno. Smoke spread out over the girls, blanketing them and the forest around me in darkness while thrashing winds picked up as if the choking smog wasn't enough.

I looked back to the raging firepit where the goat was, but it was not a goat that stood there. I wouldn't so much call it a human either. The horns remained the same while the thing they were attached to changed entirely. It had skin that looked like the universe personified into a seemingly humanoid shape. Stars and colorful moving nebulas swirled under his skin. Aside from the claw and thrashing tail, the creature was the shape of a man. A very naked man.

My eyes trailed down to his hips, just above the flames and in perfect view was a very… *unique* looking dick – if I must say. Probably a bit weird to notice that out of everything, but when it was just out and about in my face like that, what was I supposed to do?

"Mina Karim?" his deep voice thundered, rattling my body to the core and oddly warmed me in places I did not expect it to. The sound of voice had a magnetic pull on me, moving me until I was standing before the thrashing flames. The creature tilted his head again as he waited for a response.

I gave a slow nod. The smoke and wind still circled us, picking up speed once I answered. His snake-like tail whipped around me in almost a curious way, as if to inspect me. It twisted and tugged at my wrist, pulling me closer to the creature.

"I have come for the souls offered," his voice thundered again.

"Souls?" I echoed. I didn't believe we offered any such thing.

"Souls," he repeated slowly as he leaned over me. I thought over the ritual I had assumed was a dream. Maybe this was all a dream, too. A very vivid and intense dream.

"You wanted magic. I have come to provide that request. I only need the souls promised," he urged with a bit more annoyance as if I was the one who was bothering his drunken dream. I looked over to where the girls were lying, but I was still unable to view them through the smoke that twisted around us.

The wind picked up, pulling embers of the fire around.

"Are you a demon or something?" I quizzed.

His lips twitched at a smile, but he continued to glare down at me. He took my right hand in his as he spoke again.

"My sweet. You asked for powers, and I am here to provide them. All I require are the four souls promised," he repeated in an entrancing tone, pulling me closer. I gasped as he glared at me with inhuman eyes, black with a glowing iris that flickered until the illuminance died down, leaving behind frost blue eyes that chilled my soul. But as frightening as they were, I couldn't pull myself to look away.

"Do we have a deal?" he purred, pulling me closer until the heat of his odd skin pressed against my chest. A dizzyingly sweet and enticing scent of vanilla spilled over me, dazing my mind and nearly melting me at my feet.

"I can give you whatever you want. All I need is your soul," he whispered.

I would have loved to blame the alcohol for my weakness, but really, I was just a sucker for a deep voice.

"Deal." The word slipped from my lips with a low exhale that escaped.

His hand tightened around mine as he pulled back to look over me with a wicked smile. "Wonderful," he purred, flicking his wrist to initiate the shake and seal the deal. The wind kicked up into a vicious cyclone, thrashing and pulling with such force my feet left the ground. The forceful wind whipped my loose curls about wildly, stinging my face as strands snapped against my cheeks. Between my hair and the smoke, I could see Jaz, Amber, and Mickey twisting around like rag dolls in the air. Blue, glowing substances circled each of them for a moment before breaking free into the creature that held me captive.

An electric charge pulsated through my body, coming to rest in my chest like a thick ball. I could feel it crawling through me until it seeped from the tips of my fingers in a glowing blue plasma. It spun over his arm and dissolved into him, which looked to bring him great delight as a menacing smile spread his lips to display shining fangs. He closed his eyes with a deep, pleasurable inhale, savoring whatever it was he clearly enjoyed about my soul in particular.

"Mina Karim," he called, "your soul is the sweetest I have tasted in centuries."

The pain in my hand ignited, spreading up my arm with fury as it scolded and tore at my skin. I pulled back with no luck of his release.

"Great, now let me go!" I ordered frantically.

I struggled to pull my hand free of the…whatever it was, but he held me in a firm grip. The pain continued ripping and tearing its way up my arm in what looked to be deep cracks. I yanked back again, only intensifying the pain. The clear splits that worked their way up my arm began to emit a golden glow that charred the edges of my wounded skin.

An agonized scream broke through my lungs as I tore back at my arm, crying and begging for him to release me, but it was as if his hand was locked in place.

"What did you do?" he bellowed, pulling back against me as he attempted to break free as well. The wind continued to howl and rage around us. Horrid screams echoed through the darkness, growing louder the longer we struggled to break free.

We pushed against each other, desperately trying to release from the pain carving into my arm. I cried out, yanking back once more with success. Our hands released as the wind came to a sudden stop and the smoke cleared just as instantly.

The sudden drop pulled air from my lungs as I gasped out, not realizing how far up we had gone. My eyes remained on him, slowing time as he watched me without care before vanishing.

I sucked in a breath, only to hit the ground and have it knocked out of me once again. I coughed, gasping for air as I climbed to my feet. Dust continued to swirl around and blind me as I tried to find the girls around the fire. I reached out, noticing an odd yellow glow pouring out of gaping cracks in my skin, a wound that devoured my hand and wrist all the way up to my elbow with a searing pain that buckled my knees. Each bone from my fingers to my shoulder felt as if it were breaking one by one, snapping and cracking into place.

I cried out with silent screams as I grappled with the unknown pain on a cold stone floor. The hard chill shocked me up for a moment, long enough to take in what was around me, and it wasn't that of the calming forest, just a dark and cold chamber that echoed off my gasps and weakened cries of silent screams.

Pain returned to center its rage on my right hand, feeling as if my skin were being pulled from my bones. Pressure began to build in my head, bringing with it a deafening ringing in my ears. I covered either side of my head as the ringing continued to grow and the pressure continued to build.

Another shrill scream ripped through me, weakening my legs to nothing. I fell flat on the ground of familiar dirt. Tears pooled into small mud drops in the dirt as the heat of the fire warmed my now chilled skin. A wave of tranquility washed over me, riding my sore muscles to bring a calming sensation over me. My body grew limp as the pressure subsided and the ringing faded. I watched the dancing flames in the pit as darkness crept around it, stealing it into the night.

The scorching pain in my right arm jerked me awake. It rested over the stones beside the blazing fire, red and raw from the heat. I peeled it from the rock with a hiss and struggled to my feet with a heavy and groggy mind. I looked around the fire at our snuffed-out circle and the girls laying peacefully in their sleeping bags. Other than our own footprints and mess, there was nothing. No goat tracks, no dropped carrots. Come to think of it, I didn't even keep bags of mini carrots in the fridge.

I shook out my curls, ridding myself of the memory of the dream. "Wild as fuck alcohol dreams," I muttered to myself. The book was lying beside the fire, closed and undisturbed. I grabbed it and headed into the van. My arm began to throb from the burn, and at first, I tried to ignore it as I tossed the book onto the bed and searched for the first aid kit. But the longer it took for me to locate what I was looking for in the kit, the more unbearable the pain became.

From an annoying ache to a throbbing sting, I shot up, tossing the kit to my bed and spilling myself over the sink. I turned the knob to cool and dunked my hand under the water. But that did absolutely nothing as the pain continued to build until I was screaming in tears. I fell back onto the bed, gripping my hand to my chest, moving in and out of consciousness as the pain flared up and died down repeatedly.

A deep growl shook my van, sending Prometheus into a hissing fit as he raced around like a wild animal.

"Prometheus! Stop it!" I groaned out. A loud, thunderous crack rang through the sky, shaking my van and sending my cat into another hissing and spitting fit.

"What did you do to me?" a voice growled from the darkness. His glowing eyes appeared first, lurking in the front of the van.

My body slumped over from alcohol, exhaustion, and the many blows to the head. I landed on my side, the coolness of the mattress relaxing my pained arm.

"Mr. Goat?" I mumbled mindlessly but received no answer. I slurred out a few more disoriented words before the pain became far too unbearable.

Erius

Mortals performing rituals in the forest was not unusual. They typically did unsafe things in unsafe places. But this group of female mortals had been the most unsafe in their trials. The smell of alcohol of all kinds hung heavy around the air, indicating this was already not well thought out. They only set up their circle with two candles, and the fire in the center was vastly unneeded. They left half-empty bottles of alcohol near the flames as they conducted their highly unprotected summons, which was simply just unsafe.

When the chanting had faded and the fire died down, they looked about themselves with confusion. After a brief discussion of what to trade, the fire kicked out and sent them toppling back. I only needed to wait for one to wake —I only needed the one. And she clutched the book as if it were her final lifeline.

A sweet, mouthwatering scent twisted around my nose, coaxing me forward. I was sure they were much too out of it to notice me poking around, but I needed to see which of them smelled so delicious – their soul needed to be saved for last.

I stepped around the debris and bottles, following the ever-growing fragrance—spiced honey with a hint of something I could not place. Fire tore through my throat, leaving behind a dry ache as I neared them. I followed it to the leader of the group, the one who read the scripture and set forth the deal.

How interesting.

An unlucky turn of events for her all around, but I suppose it was better me than *Elpos* or *Ennaza*. A scent so sweet must be enjoyed, and they would surely rip through her with little remorse or care for savoring such a creature.

I crouched down to get a better look over my target. Her curls lay scattered about, covering her face and the book like a blanket, blocking me from viewing the deliciously scented treat. I mindlessly reached out and brushed her hair back from her face. The movement sent her scent lofting into the air, stilling me in place as I stared down at her, a sweet floral that set my mouth on fire. A soul begging to be devoured.

I leaned down further, inhaling her once more. I imagined her soul would taste just as delicious, and now, it was all mine.

She crinkled her nose as a soft sigh fell from her lips.

It is time. I stood up and headed to the tree line of the forest, cloaking my appearance to that of something she'd find most appealing and safe.

Tucking into the shadows, I waited for the mortal woman, watching as she sat up in the dirt. A look of confusion, along with sand, clung to her face as she looked about the fire. She climbed to an unsteady stand as she looked over herself and the scene around her. Drunken confusion flushed her face, making my task even simpler. Intoxicated mortals were most easy to manipulate. It was gaining their attention that most of my kind found difficult, but it had been my specialty for centuries.

I shifted my weight, pressing down on a loose twig until its snap echoed through the clearing. She instantly scanned the darkness, freezing when her wide eyes found mine through the dancing flames. She took a moment to study me, trying to make out what had come for her. Most would be shaking with fear by now, but she held no scent of it as she gazed into the unknown.

"Hey?" she called out unwaveringly. An instant curiosity lit her face and she stumbled her way to me with a bright smile, unafraid of what was before her. She stopped at an oddly close distance, captivated by the vision I gave her of my appearance. Her full lips curved upward as she looked over me as I did her.

She was quite small, even for an average human. Her brown skin held a bronze flushed glow from the alcohol she undoubtedly consumed. Her disheveled curls fell back from her face as she tilted her head back, her smile widening, an antithetical reaction to that of most mortals.

"You are a glorious guy, aren't you?" She looked around me before meeting my gaze again.

I leaned down to be level with her as I spoke, but before I knew it, her palm was resting on my forehead, patting me as if I were some household pet. If she did not smell so delicious, I would have stopped her, but the warmth of her hand against me spread the scent more aggressively, and I wanted to savor it before it was gone.

"Oh my! You are a friendly goat," she slurred out. While one hand ruffled my hair, the other moved under my chin. I froze, focusing on maintaining the disguise and not the absurd warmth that flooded me uncontrollably.

My chest ached to rip her soul clean from her body, to claim the meal before it had a chance to grow rancid with fear. The thought of souring it with such emotions kept me locked in place. My claws dug deep into the earth beneath us to anchor me down for the moment.

Finally, after the agonizing seconds passed, her hands fell from my hair. "Would you like a treat? Up here all by yourself, you must be hungry."

Yes, very much so.

"Well, come on!" She swung around and headed off to her camp, a playful giggle leaving her lips. I followed close behind, the pleasantries over. I was summoned with the promise of four souls and that was what I was here to collect, but it was hers I would enjoy the most.

She stepped into the tiny house on wheels, speaking softly to something out of view. Her distractions in searching for the snack provided enough time for me to step into the dying fire to feed life to the flames once more.

"Ok, Mr. Goat, they are small so please try not to eat my fingers..." She breathed as she looked up from the bag of carrots that soon slipped from her hands.

The fire around me raged, spitting embers into the air as I kicked back. I dropped the guise to present myself as I truly am. My tail whipped out from behind me, slithering around her with interest. Her eyes widened and her mouth fell open, but no scream broke through. Despite my true form presenting itself, her gaze fell to my waist and her head tilted before her eyes returned to my face. Blood flushed her cheeks and sweetened her scent to an overwhelmingly irresistible degree.

"Mina Karim?" I inquired in an ominous tone ready to get my hands on the tantalizing soul. A bouquet of the most delicious scent twisted about her clothes, most distinctively not fear, a reaction that needed further inspection as I pulled her closer, the sweet scent fanning out around us. I looked over her once more, noting the number of stones and sigils that covered her. A mortal witch with nothing but charms to protect her. Normally they did nothing, but this one had placed some sort of true essence to it.

"I have come for the souls offered," I pushed out, fighting the distracting scent.

"Souls?" she echoed back with slight confusion.

"Souls," I repeated. "You wanted magic. I have come to provide that request. I only need the souls promised."

Confusion befell her face, pinching her brows at the center as she turned to look over the three others laying drunk in the dirt. When she turned back to me, I had expected concern and fear to flood her eyes, tears even, but they were only filled with wonder and excitement.

"Are you a demon or something?"

Or something? I was not sure what else would trade souls. It was the one assumption the mortals had correct about my kind. That and reason to fear us, but this one didn't seem to run on such an emotion.

"My sweet," I began with a softer tone, "you asked for powers, and I am here to provide them. All I require are the four souls promised." I drew her closer to me, locking eyes with her to gain the proper connection. "Do we have a deal?"

I draped over her like a cloak waiting for a verbal response to pull from her lips, but all she put off was the mouthwatering scent. My throat ran dry and my stomach burned, begging for the soul already in arm's reach.

"I can give you what you want. All I need is your soul." I smiled. My mouth watered with anticipation for the meal to come. I held my hand out to her to seal the trade. Without waiting a moment to think or consider her options, she looked up to me with set eyes.

"Deal," she whispered, slipping her hand into mine.

"Wonderful." I gave her hand a firm shake, projecting myself around her to set everything in place. Wind ripped around us, tearing smoke and flames into the air as we lifted from the ground in a display I had not managed before. But then again, I had never taken four souls at one time, and this one seemed to hold a powerful essence. No matter, once I had her soul and could leave, there would be only one thing to worry about.

I pulled the souls from the other three women first, wanting to enjoy the best for last and knowing theirs would be delicious but not satisfying. Turning to my prized meal, I pulled everything from her; soul, humanity, essence, and all. I could not help myself; it was the most delectable thing I have ever consumed. I closed my eyes, savoring the flavor as it flooded my body.

"Mina Karim," I hummed blissfully, "your soul is the sweetest I have tasted in centuries."

As the words left my lips, a raging pain spread up my arm, clawing and pulling me as our hands gripped each other.

"Great, now let me go!" she snapped, yanking me toward her in her tight grip. Normally mortals were much weaker after soul draining and a bit too dazed to speak coherently. I shot my attention back to her and our locked hands. Crackling fire split our skin with an intense glow that seared me down to the bone. She cried out as she continued to struggle, a sense of fear finally etching her face as she pulled at me.

The splitting burn intensified with each attempt to break free, but the mortal and I were tightly bound by whatever magics they had placed with their ill-created circle.

"What did you do?" I growled out, pulling back with as much success as her at breaking loose. Wind and howls of shadows circled us, echoing the fear back to her as wind thrashed her hair about her face.

How did this disoriented little creature manage such a capture? If I had to take her arm, I would. Mortals could live full prosperous lives with one, both weren't entirely needed.

I motioned to grab her shoulder with my free hand when she pulled back one last time, breaking us of the hold. Without my power holding her up and the immediate stop of the twirling wind, the mortal fell back the few dozen feet we had climbed. With a quick inspection of my now-seared arm, and four newly consumed souls, I flashed back to Ion's Inn where my entrance back into The Circles and possession of unregistered souls will go undetected.

I arrived at the bar while Ion cleaned up some glasses from the night. He didn't turn upon my appearance as he continued to work. I took a seat and began to inspect the damage done to my arm.

"Welcome back, Azal. What was it this time?" he joked, turning to me with a large smile that fell instantly. "*Thie*! What happened there?"

Whatever power the mortal had, it cracked open my skin and left a permanent scar across my hand and wrist, discoloring the night sky within me with stationary constellations. Agitation rumbled deep in my chest the longer I inspected the mark. The memory of the pain began searing into me once again. The odd dots and cracks began to glow gold, brightening with the throbbing that began accompanying it. My head filled with the same burning affliction as before. I balled my hands to fists on the bar top, fighting the agony that ground into me while Ion watched in confusion.

As the pain grew in my arm, a blinding ache flooded my mind to swell my brain. The golden glow brightened, pulsating with the growing torment.

"What are you doing?" Ion finally asked with furrowed brows.

"I am not doing anything—*she* did this!" I growled out before my body ripped from the stool and was thrown back into the mortal world.

I landed hard in a tight space, my legs and tail folded up to my chest and my horns dug into some soft material I couldn't see. The pain in my hand subsided as I regained control of where I was. The space smelled of nothing but the sweet tasting mortal, warm and fragrant. A bed with a mound of pillows and blankets sat before me with an odd hollow door to my left and a tiny shower to my right. The narrow walking space wasn't ideal and didn't aid in trying to maneuver to a stand, a useless notion when I simply needed to return to the Inn so I could go home.

I pulled forth my shadows, calling them to take me back once again. With a swirling gust, I arrived on the stool in front of Ion.

He stumbled back from the counter upon my sudden arrival. "What was that?" he asked with raised brows. He hadn't left his position. In fact, he looked to have been inspecting the space as if the stool was the cause.

"I am not too sure. There was something strange about the mortal. I am positive whatever this is is her doing. I just do not know how." I gestured to my scarred hand.

"Did you think to ask her?" He didn't have much of a dislike for the creatures; in fact, he was most interested in mortals. A bit too much if you asked me. But that was why his Inn was between realms.

Before I could gather an answer, the pain seeped in again, slowly at first until it was nearly unbearable. It came back with a vengeance as it scolded my skin, tearing me piece by piece to toss me back into the mortal world.

I landed in the small space as I had before, rocking whatever it was from side to side. This time, a tiny head popped up from the pile of pillows on the bed. Its ears flicked up straight as its eyes turned to thin black slits on bright green orbs.

"A cat!" I growled out, scrambling to my feet. The beast hopped down with a fierce hiss, pinning me to the front cushion where my horns had dug into earlier. I bared my fangs with an equally monstrous roar that didn't seem to faze it, fearless as with its master. It hissed again, swatting its paw at me but missing. My tail whipped out, knocking the ball of fur into the hollow door. Unbothered, he returned with an out-of-this-realm yowl.

"I do not have time for this," I growled, calling up my vapor to carry me back to the Inn for the last time. The cab filled with black smoke, but I did not feel the light breeze of my flight. The air did not shift to the musk of mead and oak. Instead, it remained sweet and tantalizing. When the shadows cleared, I remained on the hard floor, staring at the same bed as before. The cat returned to me with its swatting and noise, this time rousing whoever lay in the bed.

"Prometheus! Stop it!" she groaned out with a wavering voice. Pain coated her words as she rolled over, her hand clutched to her chest with the same odd swirls. Heat flooded me as I shot up, the cab illuminating with red from the forming colors that raced over my skin. I ignored the beast that swatted at my legs as I marched over to the insolent witch. "What did you do to me?"

She did not move much aside from looking up through slit lids, her lips pressed together as she tried to make sense of what stood before her.

"Mr. Goat?" she mumbled, allowing her head to fall back onto the pillows around her. "No refunds on the souls."

Chapter Six

Mira

My van shook with a mechanical grinding squeak from the thrashing wind, scaring Prometheus into a snarling, hissing fit as he zoomed around the van.

"Would you quit it already?" I groaned as I cranked my eyes open. Blinding light poured in through the back windows of the van, adding pain to my already throbbing head. I struggled to sit up, holding my head in my hands to cover my eyes from the brightness. "Ugh! What a wild as fuck nightmare." I rubbed my eyes and reached for the half-drunk water bottle shoved in the blankets. I drank it down as if my life depended on it, not realizing how dry my mouth was until the water touched my lips. When I was done with it, I tossed the bottle into the small can and reached for the fridge to grab another when a pair of oddly clawed toes caught my attention from the corner of my eye.

I froze, my attention still on the fridge handle but my peripheral locked on the figure I could hardly make out. We remained unmoved in that position for a long moment while I tried to figure out what to do. Scream? Run? Grab my bat? All of which didn't seem too logical in the grand scheme of things. Yeah, my van is small and can make for a quick escape, but from the looks of those feet, I wasn't dealing with an average intruder.

The creature suddenly stood, rocketing Prometheus onto the bed as he continued to spit and hiss at the thing. I fell back on my ass, my back hitting the wall of the van as I locked eyes with the demon from my nightmare. The sun shone through the windows and blinds so I could see him more clearly, though he was exactly how I remembered—a bit dirtier, with his black hair coated in a thick layer of dried mud that draped over his eyes and face. He stepped forward, his legs hitting the bed in two steps.

Prometheus sprang into action again, hopping into my lap and swatting at the nearing demon. He didn't seem too bothered by my cat's attempts as he leaned over my bed. His face was a blank sheet of the sky, but if I had to guess an expression, he was definitely pissed off about something.

He continued to lean over until he was nose to nose with me. His nostrils flared as he huffed heated air my way. I remained still, with my back against the wall and my cat thrashing wildly in my arms to attack the demon.

"What do you want?" I shot after a long moment of staring.

"What have you done to me?" he growled out. I didn't know what he meant by "what I've done to him." But he was the demon, not me. I didn't even know what language was in that book.

My gaze fell past him to the seat he had been in, the book wide open on the floor with the charcoal-covered page present. Before I could look back to him, I was being jerked up from my bed, my arm burning from his touch as he pulled up my oddly scarred wrist. My skin crawled from the contact, filling me with a boiling rage as my free hand cut through the air. The van filled with a loud crack as my palm connected with his cheek. Not that it bothered him. He didn't even move aside from yanking me up until I was on my feet. His chest rumbled with a deep animalistic growl as he held me still.

"Don't touch me!" I pushed through clenched teeth.

His hand gripped mine as he ripped it up for me to see, placing them alongside each other. The night sky stared back at me, chambered in a beastly arm with odd consolations I'd never seen.

"What are you showing me?" I snapped at him. Another rumbling bellowed through his chest as the night sky washed away from him. His horns retreated into his scalp, leaving behind his thick, muddy hair. His tail slipped from my leg, releasing a numbing pressure that shot down my thigh and into my foot. I stumbled to the side, thrown off balance by the sudden lack of feeling. He yanked me back up to hold me in place, shaking me a bit until I looked up to his hidden eyes.

Instead of a naked demon with wild skin stood a naked man with skin as pale as a vampire appeared. The slight pink undertone told me he had some sort of pulsating blood heating his body. Mud and dirt clung to him all over, falling from his hair as I tried to struggle away from him. His grip held firm as he tried to present our arms again. This time, I could see what he was trying to show me. The odd scar that covered my hand up to my elbow mirrored one on his right arm, near identical in the odd swirls and bumps, matching in the same black ink color. More like an unwelcome tattoo than a scar.

As I examined the twin markings, the sliding van door flew open, spilling light and noise into the small space.

"Mina!" the girls gasped. A mix of confusion and concern laced their cries as they looked to us with wide eyes.

"Let her go!" Jaz shot after a few silent moments of processing the sight. They rushed in, trying to grapple me free and push him from the van. Even Prometheus got back to his attack. But the demon only looked to grow more irritated with a tightening grip.

"Who the bloody hell are you?" Amber pressed as she pulled her phone out. In a blink, it was in the demon's hand. Crushing metal filled the van as he crunched the phone in on itself with ease. His grip grew tighter around my arm, and I swore I heard crunching and creaking of bone.

"Ow!" I cried out.

"I do not have time for this," he grumbled as he stepped free of the van, tugging me with him. The aggression only seemed to set the girls off more as they chased us out, hurling insults at the demon. He dragged me out to the firepit and tossed me into the dirt before him.

"What the fuck is your problem?" Jaz cried out as she and the others raced to my side.

"You," he barked, pointing to me. "Run." He loomed over us with a dark, weighing energy that matched the stupid book that brought him.

"Run?" I climbed to my feet and dusted the dirt off me, confused at the request and lack of explanation. "Why am I running?"

"Just run," he said stiffly. I could feel the girls readying themselves to conduct another well-deserved verbal attack. But if it meant getting away from the demon, I really wasn't going to argue. I wasn't even sure why he'd stay around anyways. The matching tattoo scars weren't that interesting, and watching me run couldn't be worth all this.

Before anyone could speak, he leaned down over us. "It will amuse me." I was sure there was an accent of some sort, but his voice was deep and gravely, so it was too hard to tell.

"Gross!" Amber spat out. "He's a pervert!"

"Or a killer!" Mickey tossed in with a shaky voice.

The demon stiffened, melting away his human disguise to present the monster he was. The girls stumbled back, grabbing at my arms to follow as they decided they no longer needed answers to their questions.

"Now run," he growled again. This time, the girls tugged me along as we ran into the woods with no sense of direction. It wasn't until we were a few yards from camp that I stopped to look back at the demon. He stood at the edge of where we entered, watching us as we made our way.

"Come on, Meems!" Mickey urged.

"I'm not running, you guys. I'm not leaving my van. I don't care if he's a demon. He's the one from last night, don't you all remember?" I turned to continue on our path, but I was walking that shit and knew another way around for us to sneak back into the van.

"Remember what?" Jaz questioned first.

"The ritual," Amber said blankly, her attention off in the distance as she searched the forest around us.

Ravens crowed loudly as we passed, swooping down from the branches before disappearing into the depths of the forest. Beams of light poured down through the thick leaves, giving a clear view of the passage before us. It would have been a beautiful day if it wasn't overpowered by the scent of pine and musk or topped with a looming dark energy from the night that still waited for us back at the camp.

"Are you telling me we summoned a demon?" Jaz clarified.

I didn't feel it the right time to tell them I had made a deal with him because I did not want to hear the lecture that would undoubtedly come. Making any deal with a demon seems pretty ill-advised to begin with. and I did it while drunk.

"Yeah, and now he thinks I did something to bring this about." I lifted my arm to them to present the new scar. We stopped again so they could examine it and me more intently.

"Does it hurt?" Mickey asked, tracing her fingers over the swirls.

"Not anymore. Last night it felt like I was holding it under acid."

We began walking again, their questions coming one after the other, aside from Amber being sort of out of it. But who could blame her? None of us expected this to work. Now we were walking through the woods with a demon making home at our camp.

"You don't seem too worked up over all this," Amber pointed out. I hadn't realized it, but I guess waking up to a naked creature should have been a bit more frightening for me, but all I felt was annoyance.

"I think I'm just in shock," I offered, knowing that was a bullshit excuse but it wasn't like I was the only one a bit numb to what was going on.

"What about you guys? You see me being manhandled by some dirty naked man and you don't run to call the cops or anything?"

"Honestly, Meems, what are the cops going to do in this moment? If he was some crazy killer, we would have been dead by the time the cops got up here," Jaz explained.

Which was sadly true. It would take anyone on average thirty minutes to get here from the entrance. Luckily, the demon didn't seem to be a killer of any sort, not that I wouldn't put it past him.

We neared a clear trail and crossed right over it to continue through the thickest part of the woods to keep out of sight and make it difficult for the demon to spot us. We didn't even make it all the way across when the scar began to tingle and itch. I ignored it at first as we continued to step into the bushes once again. For several yards, the itchiness grew to a scolding burn that brought with it the yellow glow from the night.

"What's happening?" Mickey inquired.

I shrugged and pushed through three more steps before the pain began to carve down to my bone. My arm pulled back and away from me as if to be tied to a rope, suspended in the air, and exceeding the slack allowed.

"What in the Hell is that?" Jas asked, looking over my glowing arm.

I thought over the morning, the words and questions the demon did provide, most of which involved what I had done to him. But it all began to make sense—why he was still here, why we had matching scars. I didn't know what it was or what it meant, but clearly, he was unable to leave.

"I think we should go back to camp," I said blankly, my eyes still on my arm.

"Why would we—"

"Does this look like something a doctor can help with?" I protested.

The girls fell silent as they looked at each other while I looked back to my arm. The brighter the glow, the more painful the throbbing became, and despite not wanting to return, I knew the only one with answers to provide would be the demon waiting at the camp.

We reluctantly headed back to the van where the demon had returned to his human disguise. This time he was decent enough to cover up with a collared button-up and pressed dress pants. Where he got such clothes, I was unsure, but he was a demon, so he probably just summoned them from Hell for all I knew.

I couldn't assume demons had rules when it came to taking souls, and I was sure manipulating drunk women into offering them was top of their list. How would I even know if we got what we wanted in return? Other than having the pain in my arm and the demon attached to me, I didn't feel any different. For all I knew, this could have been some twisted trick to capture me and force me to do gods knows what. I would not be the vessel for the next Lucifer, fuck that.

Once we cleared the last of the trees, I marched up to him with a pointed finger, shoving it into his chest.

"This is your fault! You tricked me!" I hissed.

He looked over me with an unmoved expression, at least what I could see.

"A deal is a deal. Four souls for four magical gifts," he said in a thick English accent.

We all looked to him in shock at his words. I would have never assumed a demon to use the Queen's English of all dialects, but then again, I wasn't too sure what voice I would expect from a demon.

"Wait!" Jaz shot before anyone could continue, "What do you mean *four* souls?"

Chapter Seven

Mira

We sat around the firepit with the demon hovering behind me.

"Let me get this straight," Jasmine began. "You sold our souls, too?" Her words were laced with understandable irritation.

"I thought I was dreaming. How often do any of our rituals work out like this? Never!" I reminded. Had I felt it was anything other than some drunken hallucination, well, I didn't really know what I'd do. But trading our souls would not be on the top of the list.

"How are we so sure it even worked?" Mickey began before dropping her voice to a whisper. "He seems just as pissed about all of it. Look at him!"

We all turned to inspect him together. I hadn't even told them that he kept saying this was somehow all my fault as if I was the one who tricked him into taking my soul.

"What did you give us?" Amber jabbed.

He inhaled deeply, pressing his lips in a line as he glared down at us.

"Suddenly he can't speak," Jaz complained, tossing her hands up in irritation.

"I remember Mickey suggesting powers," I spoke up.

"Oh yes, the *Hocus Pocus*." Amber sighed, her attention still not entirely with us.

Jaz looked at me for a moment before considering the trade with a shrug, while Mickey began flicking her fingers, watching as if sparks were to fly off.

Amber's head snapped up in his direction, her eyes locked on him. "And what does that have to do with *him* still being here?"

He folded his arms over his chest but didn't respond to her comment.

"Apparently, I did something. But he just keeps asking what I did and not saying what it is."

"*Jí ewiwpay poush zho*," he snarled from behind me in an odd, rough language that hardly sounded human.

"Whatever that means." I shrugged.

Amber narrowed her eyes at him. "It sounds like an insult."

Despite his hair covering his eyes, I knew a death glare when I saw it, and the way he set his jaw oozed hatred.

"I think he is still here because of this." I held up my arm to them. "It looks like we can't go very far from one another."

They inspected my arm as they had in the forest before attempting to look over the demon's, but he kept his arms strapped firmly over his chest.

"How do we know he really took our souls and gave us anything in return?" Amber questioned, garnering a displeased scoff from him.

"I guess we have to wait and see," I began. "Do you feel any different?"

"Not at all."

"No."

"Nothing." They each shot off in a collective wave.

I looked at the demon through a narrowed gaze. "Well, if we don't feel anything in a few days, at least he's stuck here to fix it."

His lips pulled down as he leaned over me, mud and dirt raining down from his hair. "I will be departing before the day's end. I am simply waiting for you to part with your guards," the demon said darkly.

"You're not taking her anywhere without us!" Jaz snapped.

The demon turned from us without a word and headed into the van. No argument or anything.

"I don't think it would do us well to argue. The sooner we can get back and get this removed, the sooner he can go back to wherever he came from." I made the deal, after all, might as well deal with it without any hassle.

"You cannot be serious. Do you really think we will leave you alone with him?" Amber added. As much as I appreciated them for their concern, I wanted him gone just as desperately, and if it meant dropping them off to see what can be done, then that was what was going to happen.

"Come on, lets pack up and head home." I sighed, climbing to my feet to start breaking things down and cleaning the site. They didn't say much after that, knowing we would just be going in a circle.

I gathered the last two half-empty bottles and headed in to set them away. Prometheus sat on my bed, still hissing and screaming at the demon who sat in the passenger seat of the van.

"Do you know how to fix this?" I asked him.

He kept his focus on the world outside the windshield. "We do not need to speak."

I gave him an incredulous sneer at the nonsense and left the van to help the girls break down their tents.

We loaded everything into the van, cleaned up any trash, and made sure the fire was completely out. The entire time, the demon did nothing more than watch us from the window. He clearly wasn't much of a talker but, with how rude he was, it was probably best he kept quiet until he had something more useful to share.

"Ok, that's everything," I called as I stepped into the van. I sat in my seat on the driver's side and buckled in. The heated gaze from the demon at my side reminded me he was there. I looked over him and then back to the girls who had all found spots on the bed, far away from the demon and far away from me.

"No one is going to sit with me?" I quizzed, ignoring the demon already in place as I did not want to be beside him for the next hour.

"None of us want to be next to him either. Besides, it looks like he prefers you just slightly more than us," Amber informed.

"Prometheus can sit with you," Mickey offered. My sweet guardian cat jumped into my lap and immediately turned to face the demon with a spitting hiss. I patted his head approvingly before starting the van.

"Good boy," I whispered to him as I pulled off.

We headed down the path as fast as the van would allow, knowing the sooner we could get in town, the sooner he could figure out how to undo this. He had his attention on the book as it sat opened on his lap, searching for a way to fix this all, I hoped. When he wasn't looking at the book, he turned his whole shaggy head toward me. I assumed he was glaring but it didn't have the same effect when I couldn't see shit but his nose and permanent scowl.

We didn't learn much more from him during the long drive back to town, and it was mostly silent aside from Prometheus's random bouts of hissing anytime the demon moved. By the time we got off the freeway, it was closing in on noon and we had one final stop before I could see what this demon had set for us.

I pulled into the lot of the shop as promised and helped the girls unload their things into the cars, thankful to be out in the fresh air and out of the dark and gloomy energy that surrounded our new *friend.*

"Are you sure you want to be alone with him?" Jasmine asked as she hugged me. "We can follow behind in the car if you want."

Regardless of if I felt safe or not, I didn't know what this demon has planned, and I didn't want them getting hurt from it if it was bad.

"I think, if he was going to hurt me, he would have done it. But I will keep you posted," I assured her as I climbed back into the van. I waved a final goodbye and closed the door, now alone with the demon and unsure what his next plans were.

I went back to my seat, picking Prometheus up as I sat and resting him back in my lap. He was the best protection I'd have for now since the demon didn't seem to like him much either.

"Head to the Four Seasons," he ordered stiffly.

"The Four Seasons? Hotel?" Of all places to go, I didn't think demons enjoyed luxury hotel stays. "Do you have a room there?" I couldn't imagine a demon would have any interest in human things, especially one that didn't seem to like them all that much.

His expression of displeasure never changed as he waited for me to pull off. I forced a stiff smile and headed to Burton Way. A thirty-minute drive if I was lucky—but I was in my van and it's Cali traffic, so what would be a short thirty-minute drive soon turned into an incredibly silent hour. I could feel the anger of the demon heating up with each passing minute he felt was too long, but he never made a sound.

When we finally arrived, I turned right into the parking garage.

"Park on the top," he ordered. Again, I did as told without further questioning, taking the van all the way to the top floor and parking it in the far back, which probably wasn't the brightest move if he was planning on killing me. I certainly opened the opportunity for it. But something told me killing me wouldn't do well for him, or else he would have already done it and been done with this stupid link.

I reached the top floor and threw the gear into park. Before I could even unbuckle, the demon jumped from his seat to hover over me. The moment my buckle was unclipped, he gripped my arm and pulled me up to my feet.

"Hey!" I barked as I stumbled forward, catching myself on the passenger seat before crashing into him. He ignored the swats and hisses from Prometheus as he tugged me from the van. I managed to shut the door before he proceeded to roughly tug me across the lot to the elevator lobby.

"Ow, you don't have to be so aggressive!" I snapped, but he continued, stopping only when we got to the elevator doors. He pressed the button while still maintaining a firm grip that began to numb my arm.

"It's not like I can run away," I grumbled.

He looked down at me but said nothing, as expected. The elevator doors opened with a ding and he tossed me in, finally releasing me. I stumbled forward and hit the wall. He pressed the button labeled L and turned back to grab me. I shrunk back, pressing myself into the corner to escape him, but his hand snaked around my upper arm once again.

"Follow me and do not say a word," he ordered.

I narrowed my eyes, ready to test the waters. "I don't think I have any other choice but to follow you."

His face hardened as the elevator came to a steady stop. After a few long moments, the doors slid open to an empty hall and before I could take a step, I was tugged into the clean-smelling lobby, one that was an odd mix of newly bloomed flowers and bleach cleaner.

We rounded a large white table that held a cluster of pink flowers reaching high up toward the enormous chandelier. Directly before us sat the check-in counter with a single woman manning it. Several large vases scattered the top with more colorful flowers blooming from each.

People chatted and moved about without notice of us as the demon continued to tug me faster than I could walk, only stopping once we reached the reception desk where a blonde woman stood with a welcoming smile as she greeted us, not seeming to notice anything out of place despite the bone crushing grip this *"man"* had on me. I was sure my arm was purple by now.

"Welcome, do you have a reservation?" she asked.

The demon leaned over the counter and spoke that odd language to her. Whatever he said seemed to pull all the emotion from the woman as her face fell vacant and gaze drifted off to something unseen. She nodded softly before walking to the phone that hung on the back wall. As she dialed, I was tugged away again and led to a nearby bench where he shoved me down to sit.

"Sit here and do not move," he ordered rudely before storming away.

"Please is a thing here," I grumbled to myself as I attempted to get comfortable.

There was nothing else to do and nowhere to go, and as much as I hated to admit it, this was my fault. Not too sure how, but summoning a demon while drunk was on us. I made the deal, and I shook his hand. This is the exact outcome one would expect from summoning anything while under the influence.

He walked up to the receptionist and spoke a few more words. As if under some trance, she walked around the counter and ushered him to the back and through a door.

The sudden emptiness of the lobby became very apparent. I could have sworn it was filled with noise a moment ago, with people walking and moving around. But now, it was silent and empty. Odd for a tourist hotel in a busy city, especially in the middle of the day.

The thing about stillness in an open space is it left room to notice the little movements fluttering past you. The ones you'd miss if you were too focused on the day to day. The shadows that drift past the corner of your eye become more active in stillness and quiet.

Shifting shadows caught my attention from the courtyard beside me. Birds flew and chirped behind the glass, but it was not the animals that caught my attention. I stood and crossed the short distance to the window for a better look at what sat hidden in the shadows.

Despite the sunlight that shown through, darkness covered the floor beneath the trees, twisting and jerking to life until it sat directly under the sun like a puddle of darkness against the white marble tile. It vibrated against the flat ground like the bellowing of a gator beneath the surface of the water. The glass rattled and the ground rumbled, matching the dancing movements of the shadow puddle.

Twisting up toward the sky, it began to morph into something new before my eyes.

"Mortal." A hand gripped my arm and spun me around. "Did I not tell you to wait over there?"

I blinked at the demon for a moment and turned back to the court. The dark shadow had gone and was replaced with a few people touring the path and plants. The lobby filled with the sound of chatter, as it was now filled with people all over talking amongst themselves, oblivious to what just occurred.

"Is this her?" a man with thick locs asked. He held a bright smile on his lips that tugged at a long scar that trailed from his brow to the corner of his mouth.

The demon grabbed my right arm to present to him alongside his own. The man looked over it quizzically with pinched brows. "This is keeping you from returning?"

"It not only pulls me back to this realm, but it brings me directly to her."

The man looked from the demon to me and back, a small grin spreading his lips. "And the distance?"

"Not far enough," the demon scoffed, gripping my arm again as if I were going to run away.

"I am right here!" I snapped, attempting to pull away and when that didn't work, I tried prying his fingers off with even less luck.

The man's eyes popped open as he looked at me, his grin growing wider. "Oh! She speaks," he said curiously.

"Yes, I speak. I can hear as well. Now, what is going on? Who are you?" I asked him before turning to the demon, still working to pull him off. "Who are *you*?"

"You haven't introduced yourself?" The man chuckled.

"For what purpose? I will be free of her soon enough." His words were hopeful, but the man's face fell slightly.

"Come. Bring the mortal." He turned and headed back through the lobby. The demon grabbed hold of me once more and tugged me along. He led us back to the elevators and pushed the button to go up.

The doors opened and we stepped in. Well, I was pulled in. the man kept his eyes on me, only shifting them to the demon when the doors closed. Without looking, he pressed a dark red button at the bottom of the keypad.

"Release the mortal," the man ordered.

Instead, the demon's grip only tightened around me.

"Ow!" I gasped, my attempts at breaking free grew more frantic as I tugged and tore at his hand, shoving against his arm and pulling at my own, but nothing caused even the slightest shift in his stance.

"Why?" He growled the words to the man, who didn't seem bothered at all by it.

"You aren't going to like what I'm about to say. And I would prefer not to have a mess on my hands. Release her," he explained. But the grip continued to tighten.

"What do you mean?" he asked, ignoring my struggles to break free. The man reached for me, but the demon yanked me back with a deep chested rumble that froze us all.

"Dazron is here. I do not think a scene is what you wish to cause, my friend," the man said again as he slowly reached out for me. His words seemed to register as the demon's grip loosened around my arm. The man took my scarred arm and held it next to the demon's again.

"You have been tethered, and by the looks of the markings, it's a pretty solid one," he informed in English, but then instantly switched to the other language and said, *"Pa bù tåk ůtå. Tou můzhmou bìs màd."*

Whatever the man said only seemed to upset the demon even more as his head snapped toward at me. The man held his hand up. "It is not the mortal's doing."

"How do we break it?" the demon grunted.

The man looked over my arm more thoroughly.

"There is only one with the power that may be able to help."

"May be?" he echoed.

"Alaura is gifted, but she is young. I cannot expect much, but I can ask. It's just…"

"What?"

"Alaura has been missing in the Underground for some time now. I can send one of my serpents to search for her. She is familiar with them, but I am unsure how long it will take. Right now, she is the closest help you have."

"What am I supposed to do until then?" the demon pressed, his grip returning to cut the circulation from my arm. I sucked in air through my teeth at the pain as I tried to wiggle free again.

The man looked over me once more. "I am not too sure. But you will want to get her off grounds before Dazron catches wind of this." He turned to me with a grin. "Now, now, little bird, he will not harm you."

"Don't call me that!" I snapped, attempting to shake the hand from my arm.

He pulled back with a lifted brow. "An audacious little thing."

I groaned at the statement and tugged at my arm some more.

"She is going to give you trouble in more ways than one," the man said with a chuckle. But the demon looked down at me with a scowl.

"Let me know when Dazron leaves," he ordered.

The elevator doors suddenly opened, and our new *friend* backed out. The demon pressed the button to take us back up to the garage floor, his grip never loosening around me. Not that I could run anywhere. From what I gathered of the conversation, this demon and I were stuck together for who knew how long, so manhandling me was completely unnecessary.

The elevator rang as we hit the top floor and once the doors were open, he was pulling me out.

"You know, I can walk," I spat.

"You walk slow," he grunted back, still towing me through the lot.

"You have long legs. I don't."

He stopped and spun to face me, leaning down until he was eye level with me. "Yes, you are quite small, aren't you? A bite-size snack when all is said and done," he huffed.

"Are you going to eat me—"

He tossed me over his shoulder before I could finish and sped across the lot.

"Ah, put me down!" I cried out, kicking and swatting at him. "You put me down right now!"

"Enough," he growled, shoving me off his shoulder. I landed off balance on my feet, throwing my hands back at whatever was near to regain control. My palm caught the side of my van before I fell flat on my ass.

"Get in and take us to wherever it is you call home," he ordered.

"You can say please here and there," I muttered, scrambling to my feet to unlock the door. We took our seats in silence, all except my cat, who proceeded as if we hadn't left. It had been consistent enough that the demon ignored it and us by facing the window. Not sure how he could see anything through all the hair and mud, but hopefully he wasn't expecting anything as fancy as the Four Seasons. He was going to be greatly disappointed when he found out he was sitting in my home.

I pulled out and headed to the beach without argument.

Something told me I should save that energy because this felt like it may be an extended stay.

I eventually pulled the van into my usual spot on the beach and pushed the gear into park.

"We're here!" I said.

He looked around the beach and the lot from the windows, confusion twisting his face. I got up and moved Prometheus to the bed so I could start setting everything out for the week. I stepped outside to connect the tanks and reconnect the water hose to the spigot. When I got back in, the demon was looming around the door.

"So, this is the main living space. Shower, kitchen, bed." I pointed to everything respectively. "The bathroom is over there—it's public. Please don't eat anyone." I pointed to the small building just within our distance of under twenty yards. "And... that's about it."

No response.

"Ok, well, I'm going to take a shower." I turned to gather my things, not hearing any sort of movement on his end. I spun back to find him looking around at the walls mindlessly.

"Did you hear me? Get out!" I urged, shoving him from the van and slamming the door behind him. I wanted a moment of peace before I sat and struggled with him about what we are to do next. Which I guessed should be a talk on rules and personal space.

Prometheus took a spot by the door, his tail flicking from side to side. It is said that cats were guards to the Underworld in some beliefs. I wouldn't say it was a stretch, but clearly my cat had something against this demon.

"Good boy," I praised, turning the water on high. The heat was instantly relaxing as I stepped into it. I drenched my hair and quickly washed out the dirt as I thought about how to go about this whole thing.

I supposed I couldn't be a dick the entire time. It wasn't in me to be mean for extended periods. It was too draining and I preferred to spend my adult life happy, not busy worrying about someone who couldn't give two shits less about happiness. We didn't have to end this being besties, but I could be cordial, even if *he* couldn't.

By the time I finished my thinking and body washing, the water had run cold. I cut it off and stepped out to dry before my usual routine.

Prometheus held tight to his spot in front of the door, unmoved and unbothered. I figured I'd allow the demon back in before I got started on my hair since that would take a while and wasn't a task that called for privacy. With a deep breath, I slid open the door for him. He stood with his back to me, turning slightly at the sound.

"You can come in." I moved back to the bed to gather my hair supplies to place away. He didn't speak or acknowledge I had even welcomed him back in. I wouldn't have even known he stepped in if it hadn't been for the door sliding shut. Prometheus jumped onto the bed, his eyes on our new guest the entire time with a clear malice in his paper-thin slit pupils.

By the time I had finished my hair, my stomach was screaming for food. Not surprising since I missed breakfast, and it was well past my usual lunch.

"Do you eat food?" I asked him, figuring he would remain mute.

He didn't turn from examining the hanging raven skulls on my wall, "This body can survive on mortal food."

It wasn't much, but it was progress. If he was going to be here, I needed to ensure I was not a part of his diet—especially after that snack statement.

"I will take that as a yes." I grabbed my bag and turned to leave, colliding with the demon. There wasn't much room, and we were going to have to figure out some rules. He leaned over me as he tried to find space in the small area. The heat of his body was suffocating, crowding me in the corner of the cabinet and the bed. I shuffled around him, careful not to touch his overly heated body. Not that he made it easy, standing there like a tree.

It was a little after one, which meant most lunch menus were open for the pier restaurants. I wasn't too sure what he ate, but I guessed I would figure it out. Hopefully he wasn't serious earlier in the parking lot about eating me.

"Come with me, I guess." I squeezed by him to grab my bag from the front and headed out. It took him a moment before he stepped out wearing a black hoodie that covered his head. I thought about asking if he wanted to shower first, but figured if he wanted to, he would have, and clearly he wanted to be seen as a dirty mountain man. So long as he stayed a few feet behind me as he had been, that could be a problem for him.

We walked across the lot and tucked into a small crowd waiting to cross the street. Their loud conversation carried over the tides and the seagull's cries. Everything was far too loud and too bright now that my hangover had a chance to catch up with me. I needed a dark and quiet place to eat.

I knew a small seafood tavern a block from the shop and headed there. It was always slow and dimly lit. More of a romantic setting. But it was the one place I could count on when I had bad hangovers. I figured I wouldn't need his approval; he was following and had nowhere else to go.

By the time we arrived at the tavern, my stomach was growling up a storm. Luckily it was self-seating and no wait. I found a booth and slid right into the spot, my new demon friend taking the seat across from me. The dim light cast shadows over him to further hide his hair and features. The light that did catch his face gave me little to work with, but I could see the goat from the night before when he had let me pet him and wanted carrots.

"They serve mini carrots here if you want some," I offered to break the tension, but he remained quiet.

The waiter came around with the two menus and a bright smile. He seemed a bit jumpy as he set them down and pulled out his order pad.

"Hello, welcome. Can I get you started on drinks?" he asked nervously.

"Yeah, I'll just have water," I said.

He looked to the demon, who just nodded as if that were answer enough, but the man scribbled something down and ran off.

"You don't say much, do you?" I pressed, but he gave me nothing. I continued, "If we are going to be stuck together, you could respond."

"When you begin to say something of interest, I will respond," he suddenly answered.

I lifted a brow at the insinuation that I was boring.

"I'm always interesting, so you'll start speaking soon," I said confidently. "Besides, you can't answer questions?" I added, but before he could respond, the waiter came by with two glasses of water.

"Are you ready to order?"

"Not just yet," I say back. With a nod, he was off again, and I pulled my attention back to my new companion, waiting for an answer.

His lips pressed to a flat line under his unkempt hair, but he remained silent.

"Let's start with your name," I pushed. Unsurprisingly, he gave no answer and took a long sip of his water.

Clearly, he was not intending this to be a social stay, so I didn't bother asking anything after that. The waiter was due to make his reappearance soon, and I needed to get my order together.

I searched the menu for a burger and fries. They carried a fish burger, but from word of the waiters before, it had a small amount of salmon ground into the beef. Nothing special. I closed the menu and pushed it to the side for when the waiter returned. The demon sat there, his attention glued on me the entire time.

He didn't bother turning away when I glared back, as most people tended to do. But then again, he wasn't like most people.

"Boo!" I shot. Still no movement from him. I leaned back, defeated, and pulled out my phone to text the girls and let them know I was alive. Opening the group chat, I had about fifteen missed messages between Jaz and Mickey since Amber's phone was trashed. The messages ranged from asking if I was ok to wondering if they needed to stop by.

I'm alive!

OMG I was already in my car
-Jaz

What happened?
-Mickey

The text buzzed back-to-back before I could type out an answer.

To start, he is not gone.
We are "tethered" and have to wait
for some girl who MIGHT be able
to help.
And there's apparently, some underground
demon shit at the Four Seasons.

I hit send and waited for their response. It was a lot to unpack at once, and the waiter was making his way back for our order.

"Are you ready?" He addressed me first, a clear avoidance of speaking with a demon even if he wasn't aware of it.

"Yes, the fish burger, please," I told him.
He nodded and scribbled it down before hesitantly turning toward the rude demon. "And you, sir?"

I hid a snicker with a sip of my drink. He didn't respond in words. As he did with the water, he simply nodded, and somehow the waiter seemed to know. He jotted something down on the pad and disappeared again.

My phone went off on the table with messages from the group.

"Does that incessant buzzing ever stop?"

It was my turn to not answer as I pulled open the messages, one after the other of shocked emojis. I told them I'd give them more information later and shoved my phone back into the bag. The new scar that took up my right arm caught my attention. It wasn't painful, unless of course the demon was too far, but other than that, it was as if nothing were there.

"What do you think went wrong?" I asked, mostly as a thought to myself as I continued to look over the markings.

"*You* cannot perform a simple summoning ritual properly," he said stiffly.

I dropped my arm to glare at him. "Isn't this your job? Soul taking? Perhaps you should have double-checked the fine print."

CHAPTER EIGHT

Erius

I sat in the only spot with a decent amount of space to accommodate this body. My time spent as a mortal was usually done in my flat where I had ample amounts of space. This was a can of a home, hardly suitable for anyone, even for her size. I kept my focus on the raging sea as it washed up the beach, watching as it closed in on the small distance between where the van sat and open water.

How the mortal managed in such a confined space was beyond me. Perhaps she had a death wish and wanted the tides to sweep her away in this flimsy submarine.

"Do you sleep?" Her voice came from beside me, steady but gentle with only a slight hint of irritation. The taste of fear was vacant from her, unlike her three guards who still held a subtle hint of it. She shifted to the side, stirring her scent around us as she waited for an answer. Despite my clear attempts to avoid her, she was relentless in trying to communicate.

Though I supposed it would not hurt to keep a mutual line of communication. This form could handle that much.

"This body requires the same as yours in order to function," I said with my eyes still on the water. A mess of blankets and pillows fell into my lap, sending her scent into a cloud around us. What I had once found sweet now taunted me as a reminder of my own selfishness.

"What is this?" I barked, shoving the torment from my lap.

"Stuff for you to make a bed." She gestured to the less than a meter wide space on the floor between us. I looked to the mattress, an area coated in her fragrance, and then to the small space on the floor. I'd rather struggle to control this form than be subject to sleeping on the ground like some mongrel pup.

"There is a bed right there," I pointed out.

Her eyes widened as she stared at me in disbelief. "Yes. My bed. I'm not going to share with you." She plopped down on the soft mattress and folded her arms.

"You expect me to sleep on the floor as if I am a common pet?" I stood from the seat, grabbed the cushions and blankets she had given me, and made my way to her.

"Uh, yeah. Your hair is filthy, and I don't want it getting on my sheets. Besides, you don't even like me. Why would I share my bed with you?"

I dropped the blanket and pillows on the bed and made space for myself on the mattress, ignoring her failing attempts at blocking me and the concentrated scent that attacked my senses. "I do not need to like you to sleep."

"You won't fit, so," she argued next. But I situated the space well enough. I pulled one leg up and rested it at an angle with a hidden grin.

I fit just fine.

"UGH!" she growled defeatedly as she glared over my new space. "Please take your shoe off my bed," she ordered, forcing kindness into her tone.

I rested my hands behind my head and leaned back against the wall, enjoying the flush of blood that pooled across her cheeks. The scent around us shifted, changing to a mix of oak and smoke with soft notes of the familiar sweetness.

She can feel anger.

If she hadn't had the sense to fear me before, without her humanity, she wouldn't ever find it. But if I could have her anger for entertainment, that would work just as well.

"No decorum," she grumbled under her breath as she tried to make do with the little space I left her. While she struggled to find comfort, her stomach rumbled—the only sign I knew of that indicated their hunger needs.

"Again, Mortal?"

She looked up to me with furrowed brows before looking down to her own stomach as it rumbled loudly for a second time. Her head snapped back to me, the blood resurfacing in her cheeks again.

"Um, yes, *Mr. Goat*. Sometimes if I'm feeling extra wild, I do it three times a day, maybe more," she said as she pulled her phone out and began tapping against the screen.

"Have you only been feeding that body once a day?" she suddenly asked with a pinched expression. Mortal cuisine was hard enough to get down, but this form had always functioned fine on the amount. Perhaps she was ill and required more nutrition from it.

When I didn't respond, she returned to her phone with extreme focus. Once she had finished, she got up to move over the bed, struggling to maneuver around my leg as she crawled the short distance to the opposite wall. Her attention fell back to my foot, flushing her skin a deep bronze.

"Get your shoe off my bed!" she snapped, shoving my leg off. The contact shocked me up until we were nose to nose. The smoky oak fragrance ignited once more, stronger and more potent as it twisted around me.

Rage. That much has remained.

"Do not touch me," I pushed out in a near growl, but none of it bothered her. She kept her eyes locked with mine and didn't even flinch at the movement. Her nostrils flared as she inhaled deeply.

"Get. Your. Shoe. Off. My. Bed," she repeated, articulating each word as she pushed them through her teeth. Her essence flared out, pushing against me as her hands lit up with a green flame. She didn't appear to notice as her gaze remained on me, but I allowed myself to look down at the sight. Interest flooded me. Most trades I conducted didn't end with such a latching. I had never witnessed my gifts in action or seen the outcome of my own power within another. Perhaps this wouldn't be such a waste if I could witness how she developed them.

I brought my gaze back to hers. "Fine." I leaned back to remove my shoes and set them beside the bed as she ordered.

"Thank you," she offered as she returned to the wall to pull down a white sheet. When she was finished with that, she came back to adjust a small yellow box above our heads. She reached up in a contorted position to access the device and flipped a switch. I remained still, with my attention on the sheet before me, holding my breath and ignoring the nagging pull to look over at her.

The space filled with a low humming sound as the sheet lit up to a blank white screen. She returned to her spot in the small space and began flipping through her phone, tapping it a few more times until a black screen with a red **N** at the center pulled up. With a few more clicks she was navigating through several dozen options of their modern cinema.

The highlighted selector moved through two categories before landing on horror. Without reading any titles, she skimmed through the options before landing on one with an elevator door as the cover. The title *Devil* sat in the upper lefthand corner with a small description. With a few more taps, the screen flashed as the movie began to play.

I gave in to the pull and turned to find her already glaring at me.

"I'm sure you'll be able to relate to this one," she said sarcastically before returning her focus to the screen. The colors and lights flashed over her face as I continued to watch her, weighing the options I had left myself. Killing her would cause me more troubles, and the very thought triggered a searing pain over the healed wounds on my back. Less than wise, just as it was to take her soul for myself. Avoiding her would have been easier if she lived in a mortal house and not whatever this was she called home. Befriending the creature did not seem wise – I simply had to endure her.

It wasn't long into whatever movie she had put on before three knocks rattled the door. The bed shook as she lifted up to her knees, her eyes searching for mine under the thick strands of hair. I made no motion to move, as she had not asked, but it was clear she expected it. Before she had a chance to touch me, I pulled my leg up for her to climb over without issue. She did so without making any contact and answered the door.

With some words shared and an exchange of money, the cab soon filled with the bland scent of cooked meat.

She climbed her way back into her spot and placed the bag between us. "I ordered you the same as me. A cheeseburger. You're not a vegetarian or anything, are you? Are you ok with gluten?"

I looked at her blankly, unsure what any of that meant, and I was only slightly familiar with the dish she mentioned. She pulled out a white box and handed it to me before opening her own.

A mess of bread, lettuce, and meat sat slathered and stacked with a gooey yellow substance dripped out of it. I examined the mess, unsure how anyone could eat such a questionable dish, but the mortal didn't seem to have a problem. She took a small bite, chewing it slowly as she looked over me, ready to pelt me with more questions. I followed the action before she could think to ask, chewing the mixed mush quickly before swallowing it. I ignored the taste, not registering it as good or bad to get it down.

She stared at me with a raised brow and twisted grimace. "It's ok to enjoy the food," she commented before biting into hers again, chewing it slowly. Remaining in this realm was not my plan, and sitting here with a mortal *"enjoying"* food was far from my idea of entertainment.

After we ate, she shoved me out onto the beach so she could change again. Not that I was interested in seeing anything she had, nor was it anything I hadn't seen, but mortals were oddly modest. The clean air was also refreshing and clear of her scent. I took in as much as I could, desperate to clear my system of the grinding annoyance. The washing waves over the sand did little to soothe the tension and anger that gripped me.

The door slid open for my return, and the mortal headed back to her bed without a word. I entered to find her creating a barrier down the center of the mattress made of thick quilts and other pillows she had hidden somewhere. I waited for her to finish and cover herself before I climbed in. With the little bit of space and the concentrated attack on my senses, I tried to relax with no success.

Every twist and turn she fought shook the entire space. Her cat remained fixated on me from the front, his slit eyes never rounding, a protector that had not backed away from his post. Even more frustrating was the fact all of this was no more her fault than it was mine.

Eventually, the mortal's breathing fell steady, and I was able to calm my own mind and welcome sleep.

I was woken to the bed shifting as the mortal sat up. She looked around until her attention fell on the door with a blank stare.

"Yeah. I'm coming," she grumbled in a muffled voice. Her hands pressed against my chest as her leg swung over me. In my half-asleep state, I reached for her, but she was gone, already at the door and sliding it open. The ominous clicking of a creature that mortals had no sense of, soon filled the van. She leaned her head out as the clicking grew louder. "Hello?" she called.

I shot up, reaching across the small distance to yank her back and slam the door shut, locking it instantly.

I had not known Watchers to venture this realm, but I did not usually spend my stays out on the mortal streets, keeping tucked to my flat at the Seasons where they are forbidden to roam. This may add a layer of difficulty if they wandered the area too frequently.

I turned back to the disoriented mortal. She shook her head, confusion painting her face as she tried to make sense of what happened. She looked up to me with squinted eyes before she seemed to realize what she was looking at.

"Where were you?" she asked in a groggy voice. Perhaps she is one that gets caught in the dream state a bit too heavily.

"In the bed. You climbed right over me," I informed her.

She looked at the bed and then at me, her eyes dropping before shooting back up to my face.

"Why are you naked?" she quizzed.

I looked down to find her words true, though I couldn't place how it happened. I would assume the rush to shut the door sent my body into defense and burned the fabric free, but such things would be pointless to explain to a mortal. With a snap, I called forth some shadows to cover myself for the time.

"Keep the doors locked at night," I ordered her.

"Why?" she pressed quickly. Her maddening questions were never ending. With any bit of needed info I gave she requested more. I walked back to the bed and climbed in while she gathered herself off the floor.

"My world is not so frightening," she groaned as she, too, returned to the bed. This time she was far more careful as she climbed over me, avoiding any contact.

"Your world is no longer your world," I countered.

She tucked herself under the covers and turned toward the wall as I fought to find comfort once again.

A comfort that lasted what felt to be a few moments before the cramped cage began shaking with the mortal moving about. She stomped around the cab, opening the windows and doors, complaining about some smell that displeased her. I attempted to stretch out in the little space I had available.

"Good! You're up," she spat. "Do you shower? You smell like dirt, and now my bed has all these mud clumps in it!"

I looked to her tiny shower and back to her. Her eyes were locked on the shower as she considered something that twisted her face into a hard grimace.

"On second thought, I can't risk you clogging that drain. The sink just pours into a bucket that can be emptied," she said.

I looked at the even smaller kitchen sink. This woman lived in squalor and traded her soul for magical powers rather than money or a fancy home as most mortals did.

"Oh." She suddenly groaned. "You're kind of big for that, too."

I looked around at the obvious issue, the cramped cab, "Perhaps it is you and this tiny bucket that are too small."

Her mouth snapped shut as she pointed to the mini bowl. "Just lean your head into the sink. I'll do it."

"Is hair your profession?"

"No, but my hands can fit in the sink with your big head without getting water everywhere. So, if you don't want to sleep on the floor, you'll let me wash your funky hair!"

Be it my luck I get trapped with a mortal who lost her sense of fear and respect. "I will not have some mortal in my hair."

"And I will not have some demon fucking up my bed and my peace," she countered with a firm stance. I blinked at her, ready to push back further when she snapped her fingers and pointed back to the sink.

"I can take you to a salon and have some random person do it instead. Because you are not sleeping in my bed with that mess, nor will you clog up my drains with the mud and gunk you've accumulated in there."

I looked over her blankly, considering the new bed arrangement and the endless cramped pain it would cost me.

Her hands would be far more pleasant than any other mortals. A thought I should not entertain, but this body warmed under it. I moved to the miniature sink while she gathered whatever she needed. After dropping everything on the counter, she pulled out a stool and set it behind me.

"You can sit on that," she informed. I crouched down, my knees folding up to my chest. She looked me over before studying the sink to figure out how it all would work.

"Ok, just put your head under the water." She turned the faucet until the water was flowing freely at low pressure. We looked at each other for a moment before I did as requested, dropping my head into the small space and letting the water run through my hair. Muddied, brown muck rinsed down the drain as my hair became saturated.

"Ew! Have you ever washed this?" she asked as her fingers began picking through the mud chunks and splashing water over my head. When it began to run semi-clear, her hands found their way into my hair with a soft scent of chamomile and honey. I scrunched my nose at the new fragrance. Everything in here smelled of a mortal woman.

Now it clung to me.

Her hands continued to scrub suds into my hair as she grumbled to herself about the mud. I waited patiently, arched over in the uncomfortable position as she began rinsing the soap free. Before I could lift my head, her hands tangled into my strands once more with another overly fragrant cream.

"Have you ever thought about combing this out?" She huffed. Grooming was a top priority in most cases, but I had spent the better part of Friday trekking through forests and hidden puddles of muck.

After the cream, she began pulling a comb through my hair, simply extending the torment. She pushed my head up, wrapping a towel at my neck before running her fingers through like a comb, sweeping my hair from my face as she did.

Her hands froze as her eyes locked with a clear view of mine for the first time, a reminder of what she was sharing space with. She pulled free with a gasp and a slight tremble of her lips.

"Done," she blurted before gathering the supplies she had pulled out and setting away just as quickly—an attempt to avoid me, which was splendid. It gave me peace while I attempted to search through that bloody book some more. I did not get far before she woke up on Saturday and now, I had nothing but time.

I found the book resting on the floor of the front seat where I had left it. If there was anything to reverse it all, it should have shown up on the pages by now, but each piece of parchment remained blank. I flipped to the summoning page, coated in oak charcoal yet still blank. It should not have been difficult to follow, the words were simple, basic Demric that any mortal could pronounce. Unless her impaired state caused her to butcher the scripture. It would not be uncommon to mispronounce something, I supposed. But to this degree? There must have been more.

I continued to flip through the book when the door slid open and shut again. The concentrated scent of the mortal cleared slightly to signal her departure from the van. I took the risk of making eye contact with her cat and looked back to the empty bed. At least she took that thing with her to give me peace. Guards of the Circles, whether they knew it or not, were never pleased with my kind's presence.

A jarring buzzing rattled the space as her phone went off, vibrating itself off the counter and onto the floor where it did not cease. I had tried to ignore it, but the buzzing persisted to the point of annoyance. I got up and crossed the short distance to snatch up her phone. As I tossed it onto the bed, I noticed the message displayed in the bar.

SOMETHING HAPPENED TODAY!
-Amber

CHAPTER NINE

Amber

Steam drifted into the air, carrying the minty citrus of eucalyptus with it. I stirred the bundle over the surface of the water to release more of the fragrant oils, a calming bath after an overly exciting Friday and out-of-this-world Saturday. I relaxed back, leaning my head against the cool wall as I tried to silence the noise from outside.

Chatter rose from people already making their way to the beach. Normally I didn't mind people passing by my garden. I even set out a community basket for them to take as they please. But lately, the early-morning tourists had been rude. Some had even stepped into the garden to pick off the trees and I'd had to put up more fences around the yard.

I did not want to remove the basket, but if people couldn't learn to respect property, it may have to be done.

The talking and laughter grew as I tried to soak, causing too much of a distraction for me to sink into any sort of meditation. With a low groan, I stood from the water and grabbed my towel. There was a clear view of the garden path from the bathroom. White flowing curtains helped to shade the room and provided decent coverage from any gazers below while providing me perfect clarity.

I looked around, not seeing anyone within the garden, and figured they were carrying on alongside the fence. Nothing was planted there that could be ruined by anything, so I let them be as I got ready for work. I needed fresh herbs to take in anyway. Hopefully they left by then.

After dressing, I grabbed my coat and toque from the hook to tuck into my tote bag. When all was ready, I headed to the garden to collect the few herbs my boss, Ashton, had requested. With the harvesting basket in hand, I began my trail around the herb bed, clipping and plucking the parsley and cilantro for the evening.

The lot from earlier had not left and continued their conversation despite my presence. One would think people would quiet their discussions when someone unknown entered, but that was not the case for this group, carrying on at a volume I could clearly hear, and what they had decided to be the topic of their discussion was the soil I used. They shouldn't even be close enough to examine it, let alone critique it.

My ears heated, spreading wildly down my neck and over my shoulders as the irritation grew. I wanted to remain quiet, but I wasn't about to sit here and have my work dragged like rubbish.

"I'm sorry? What would you know about soil?" I asked as I stepped around the corner to surprise them, but I was met with only a wheelbarrow full of my soil mix. The conversation fell from its obnoxious volume to a low whisper.

"Hello?" I called out, but no reply was granted. I scanned the area that couldn't harbor an appropriate hiding spot for even a small dog, let alone a person. The whispers continued as I looked near the cluttered fence, still seeing nobody.

It's all in your head. Probably a reaction from the demon. I took several deep breaths to center myself before returning to collect the remaining herbs. After I locked up, I headed out to the car. Prime Steak House was a thirty-minute drive if the freeway was clear, forty-five on the main streets, and I started work in forty minutes.

Freeway it is.

I turned the volume up and rolled the windows down to drown out the faint whispers that continued to drift into my head, a perfect distraction until the freeway where a sea of red brake lights flashed from the traffic. With a quick glance at the dash, I figured it would be close, but I could make it. I squeezed into a clear space and flowed with traffic at a steady but not overly daunting pace until I reached my exit.

After speeding through the two short blocks, I pulled into an already crowded lot with a line poking out of the front door. I sighed and searched for a spot, finding one free space at the far back right after a customer pulled out. I pushed the gas, going a little faster than I should have in a parking lot, but I managed to get the space just as someone turned into the lot from the second entrance.

I threw the gear in park before fully removing my foot from the gas, causing the gear to make a harsh grinding noise—not the first time I had done it, but that one sounded rough.

I grabbed the basket of herbs and made a dash through the back employee entrance to clock in.

"You're late!" the line cook, Danny, greeted.
I tossed my coat on and pulled back my hair for my toque. "By a few minutes. Technically, I was in the parking lot on time," I corrected, placing the bundles down to fill a bowl of water.

"Sure. Did you bring the herbs? We just ran out of parsley." He scooped up the herb in question and tossed it into the metal container.

I pulled the bundles out of the basket and submerged them in the water. "Of course."

After a moment of soaking, I ran each bundle under cool, running water one by one, placing proper intent into them as I handled and prepared them. It was a ritual I did for not only food I created at work, but all food. And what better time to test the demon's gifts?

"Danny! We have a return. They said they wanted it well done with no onions," one of the waitresses called as she barreled in with a half-eaten steak.

Danny looked over the plate with pinched brows.

"That shit is as gray as ash. As for the onions, do you see any onions?" he argued.

Tiffany looked over the plate with a heavy sigh. "No, but the customer insists—"

"What customer is this?" I interjected. There were a few regulars we had. One in particular was well-known for this behavior.

"Walters," she said in an exasperated tone. "Mrs. Walters." The kitchen filled with collective groans as everyone released their displeasure. No matter, parsley was great for purification and healing, something Mrs. Walters was in desperate need of.

"I'll cook it," I offered.

Danny moved from the burner, grateful not to have to deal with it. However, I did send him off to gather everything. We even double-checked that no onions were included in the produce gathering. He helped chop everything except the herbs as I worked at chopping the parsley and garlic. I whispered my intent as I dropped them each into the pan to sauté. Though I wanted her to heal with her soul, I also wanted her to humble herself. From here on, she would eat anything placed before her and enjoy it, whether it be what she asked for or not. Lying for a free meal was no longer tolerated, and without Ashton present, I was technically next in charge.

"Here," I called out as I placed the onion free, overly cooked slab of steak on the plate to send out. Before Tiffany could take it, I sprinkled fresh parsley over it for an extra kick. We walked over to the order window to watch as the plate was placed in front of Mrs. Walters. She looked over it a moment before a forced smile lit her face. She looked to have thanked Tiffany kindly before sawing into the dry brick. It was a wonder how people could enjoy such a deplorable cut of meat, ruined by overcooking. But there she was, chewing away with a growing smile.

"She shouldn't be sending that back." Or anything else, for that matter. Hopefully nothing too drastic or magical happened other than her not returning it for a second time.

My shoulders slumped with slight disappointment. How was I supposed to know anything? It wasn't like I had the manual living with me to give instruction, not that I thought Mina was having much luck with that either, but at least she had something.

I walked to the back to finish my work with the herbs and check the sprouts we had growing for the salads. I was growing them at home but figured it would save space for me and make access easier. We cleared out the smallest walk-in fridge to use and filled it with three, four shelved racks, a small operation that saved Ashton thousands in the end.

I stepped into the chilly air, snatching the clipboard from the wall as I made my way over to the first shelf. Ordered by date planted and type, I began with checking the water of the most recently spread seeds to the oldest. After the water, I grabbed the few finished bunches and got to work with separation. Harvesting the trays and packaging everything was also simple.

As I cut out a square of the broccoli sprouts, faint whispering began to tug at my ears. At first, I shrugged it off as noise from outside, but the longer I tried to focus on my task, the clearer the whispering became. I figured I'd drown it out with music and pulled out my new phone to pull up a playlist. Once I settled on a song, I turned the volume to high and continued with the sprouts.

I pulled the last tray toward me to finish, dropping my attention to an odd center sprout that was slightly bigger than the rest. As I reached out to pluck it free, my fingers grazed the elliptic-shaped leaf and it fluttered out in response with a soft squeak.

I drew back, watching it with wide eyes as more leaves pulled back into what appeared to be a tiny hat. Small black, twig-like arms lifted toward me as large, black, bug-like eyes locked with mine. I held my breath as we stared at each other in disbelief—mostly on my end.

It squeaked again as it reached for me, lifting its roots from the container soil to crawl onto the other sprouts. I released a shuddering breath, unsure what to say as it looked up to me. The tiny leaf head tilted to the side curiously and continued to reach high.

This must have been the magic I had been waiting for because nothing else would explain it. Not that there was much that could explain summoning a demon and trading our souls, which I still didn't grasp the full meaning of. If I hadn't a soul, shouldn't I feel numb or hopeless? Morally corrupt even?

I felt perfectly content, aside from a bit of shock from this new little creature that sat before me. The leaf hat fluttered out again. This time the colors shifted from a light green to a deep orange.

"Hello?" I greeted softly to it. The leaves around its head stopped and returned to their normal shade of light green. I offered a soft smile, and it mimicked the movement.

"Do you have a name?" I asked, but it just looked up at me wordlessly. I guessed I couldn't expect it to know much, since it just became sentient. It most certainly couldn't stay here and would be hard to explain. I couldn't even wrap my head around it myself.

Without thinking, I grabbed one of the empty sprout containers and began poking a few holes over the top. I layered the bottom with a few folded sheets of damp paper towel and set it beside the creature. Once that was fitting enough, I held my hand out to the creature. It climbed in with ease. The little twig fingers and fluttering leaves tickled my palm as I moved it over to its new temporary home.

When I was sure the creature was secure, I finished cutting the sprouts and placing them into the packing containers. By the time I was finished, the creature had made itself at home in the damp paper towel, resting in the corner without care.

After placing the sprouts in place on the Outgoing rack, I text the group the update.

You guys!

I have news!

SOMETHING HAPPENED TODAY!

I couldn't wait for a response as I grabbed my new little friend and rushed out to the kitchen to help with the lunch rush due to start. I tucked him gently into my purse and assured it was out of risk of getting bumped before returning to the kitchen line.

By the end of the night, I headed back to the fridge to collect my phone and bag, seeing a mess of messages from the girls asking what I was talking about. It was far too much to explain over text so I told them I would call them when I could and headed out to the kitchen one last time. Everyone was breaking down and cleaning for the night, ready to leave just as I was. I kept the container in my bag as I helped with the washing and mopping, and within an hour I was on my way to my car.

I pulled out the box with caution and gently creaked it open to check on the leaf pile. It still rested in the corner with steady breaths that lifted its leaves in a quick rhythm. It was clearly new to the world, like a baby. I wasn't sure how it came about, if I somehow made it or if it's just a reaction to the gifts. But clearly, I was in charge of it now, and I didn't even know what to feed it.

The creature sat up in the container with its eyes on me as we sat in silence. Communication wasn't going to work until we establish it had an understanding of anything. I had gathered a few things from the garden shed that would possibly be considered plant food, but I also brought a few raspberries and blackberries that were the perfect size. I placed each in a small pile before the creature to allow it to decide for itself because that seemed the best course of action to learn from it.

Its leaves twitched about as it moved toward the blackberry pile. After it ran its tiny hands over some of the bunches, it pressed into them, spilling the purple juice over the paper towels. It pulled the pulp out and brought it to its mouth before looking up at me. After a moment, a small smile curved up its tiny lips and it took a bite of the fruit.

I waited until it ate its fill of the blackberry and moved onto the raspberries. To my surprise, the bundle of leaves ignored the actual plant food. I would probably want to avoid leafy greens, but I should test other things as well. Hopefully, none of this harmed it.

"You need a name," I informed the creature. Its hat of leaves twitched and fluttered in response. "Hm," I hummed as I thought of a few.

"Sprout?" I admit, it wasn't original, but it was the first thing to pop in my mind.

The leaves on its head twitched and fluttered as they turned to that deep orange color again, a reaction I assumed meant no. For now.

"Ok, not Sprout. What about... Twitch?" The moment that name left my lips, I instantly didn't like it, nor did the small creature.

"No. I don't like that either," I rushed out. Thinking of a name for a plant was harder than I imagined it ever would be. I looked around, trying to find an idea. My eyes landed on my keychain and all the anxiety trinkets I loaded onto it, one of which was a mini olive-green spinner.

"How about Fidget?" I suggested.

The creature's lips pulled up into a more noticeable smile, calming the leaves movement as they returned to the light green color.

"I'll take that as a yes." I giggled.

Chapter Ten

Mira

When the sun finally peeked through the curtains, I was more than ready to get out of bed. Unfortunately, as he had been all night, the goat man was in the way. He stole my blanket to use as an extra pillow and left me cold while he lay overly comfortable and relaxed. His loud and irritating snore was about to end.

"I have work today," I announced, but his snoring continued without interruption. I waited a moment longer before making another attempt. "Mr. Goat," I sang. His snore pattern was only slightly disrupted as he inhaled deeply.

That's it, away with the politeness.

"Hey, get up. I have work!" I barked out as I shoved at his arm until the snoring came to an abrupt stop. His eyes cranked open to glare at me as a low growl rumbled through his chest, vibrating the bed from the tenor.

I glared back. "Yeah, ok." I guess this was my new morning routine: sleepless nights and a demon who looked at me as if I was the problem. If he had slept on the floor, there wouldn't be an issue of him having to move.

He somehow managed to stretch out, pushing his knee further into my space. On second thought, he would still take up the little walking space.

He shifted again with a yawn that displayed eight pointy teeth. Eight fangs for who knows what. With what he had said about me being a bite-size snack, I would imagine they were for ripping and tearing like any other carnivorous animal.

He snapped his mouth shut and gave me a look with vexation. His chest rattled again with a feral growl. I looked up to his darkening eyes, realizing I had leaned into him as I was enthralled with his fangs. I leaned back, searching the cab for a distraction from the questions that began to burn on my tongue.

When he stretched again, it created an opening for me to escape. I slipped off the bed before he had a chance to block me some other way.

Another con about van life was having to leave to use the restroom. But in this case, the space was more than needed if it got me out of this stuffy, demon crowded van.

I grabbed my bathroom bag and headed out. I enjoyed the heat of the morning sun and the early fresh smell of the sea before midday hit and it was fish central.

After doing my business and washing my hands, I took a moment to look myself over in the dingy mirror. I pulled my bonnet off to fluff my hair out to the best of my ability. The reflection was more of a blur of colors, so I couldn't really make out much other than the shape.

I took a deep breath, preparing myself for the return to the van. I wasn't sure what he could do while I was at work, but I couldn't have him hanging around while I was trying to perform readings, and I had a client today.

I stepped out from the bathroom, making a sharp turn to the van, and crashed into the demon. He wasn't paying attention to me despite the collision, his focus on the closing door.

His hand clamped down on my arm, and soon I was being towed

off to the van. I struggled for control of my own self and the ability to walk without being leashed or pawed at. But the tightening grip didn't ease off until we were back inside.

"What is your problem?" I spat. "You get all pissy when I shove your foot off my bed, but you can be grabbing and pulling me every which way?"

He watched me with an unmoved expression as he stepped closer, blocking me in with his arms as I pressed against the counter. His frosted eyes bore into mine as his body took up space around me, clearly trying to intimidate.

"Things you were once blind to will not lurk so quietly anymore." He grabbed my scarred arm with his. "This links you to me in more ways than you realize. Do try to listen and do as I say."

The invasion and order lit my skin as I shoved him off me. "I'm not listening to you—you stole my soul!"

"You traded it."

"You tricked me!" I snapped back.

He looked me over from half-hooded eyes, unbothered by my protest, but he didn't deny it or respond. Must have reached his limit on communication for the day. As well as his limit on clothes; he wore the same as yesterday which meant we had to go shopping if I was to be seen out in public with him.

I scanned his attire from top to bottom as I stepped away from him with a disgusted grimace twisting my lips. Come to think of it, I hadn't even seen him shower.

"Do you have other clothes?" I began.

He looked over himself and then back to me.

"Are you able to go buy yourself some clothes, and something to sleep in? Because the nakedness isn't going to fly."

He gave another slow blink with no verbal response.

"I will take your silence as a yes. Now, I need to get ready." I turned to gather my clothes, again not hearing any movement on his part. With a quick glance over my shoulder, I found him focusing on the hung skulls around the van, as if that would detour me from kicking him out.

"You cannot be in here while I change. I don't understand why I need to explain that." I opened the door and gestured for him to get out, which he did without a fuss.

With him gone, I dressed in a plain black top and waist-high shorts of the same color before allowing him back in.

He watched me intently as I did my hair and makeup. Oddly enough, it was the only time throughout the entire morning he didn't look annoyed or irritated.

When I was done, I fed the cat and sent a text to the group about not being able to make our Monday brunch. If he was going to live with me, he needed more than clothes.

"I assume you shower?" Knowing I wasn't going to get an answer, I continued, "Well, you will while here. Sharing a bed is one thing but I draw the line at toiletries. Come on."

We left the van and headed for the bus stop across the lot. The clear day meant the streets would be crowded, which in turn meant the buses would also be packed. I led him across the street to the stop. Luckily it was clear of anyone, but there were still a good ten minutes before the next bus was to arrive. I sat at the bench while Mr. Goat scrutinized the display with a displeased twist turning his lips.

"Have you no car, Mortal?" he asked. I guessed names were not a thing where he comes from.

"I have a name, and my car is in the shop," I answered stiffly as I looked up to him.

His brows furrowed with confusion over clear mortal blue eyes, making him appear like an actual mortal than some creature trying to be one. I sucked in a breath, trying to not be obvious about the slight pause. His brows deepened as he waited for a response to a term that was clearly not one he was familiar with.

"My car is being worked on. I don't know much about cars, and they keep telling me things are wrong with it, so it's in the shop being worked on."

I wouldn't say his silence bothered me; it felt surprisingly normal. When you spend a year talking to a cat, you tend to get used to no verbal response.

The bus pulled to a steady stop with the odd whooping sound. I paid for the both of us and we took a seat near the middle. He sat closest to the window, and I figured he'd enjoy space between us so I left the middle seat open. It was a bit of a bus ride to the mall and back, so I got as comfortable as I could and pulled out my Kindle.

The mall was about six stops away, making it easy to keep track of while I read. He found comfort looking out the window and I in my book, making the ride more bearable since neither of us felt the need to entertain.

It wasn't until stop four that a large group of chatty people stepped onto the bus. I didn't pay attention as they entered, but a weighing energy filled the space that caused my skin to tingle. My stomach twisted to knots, drowning me in that annoying feeling that gripped the lower pit of your stomach and inflamed it with a nagging tug I couldn't name. It clawed at me as I scanned those who entered, but nothing seemed out of the ordinary for those gathering in.

I returned my focus to my Kindle, ignoring the new riders as they shuffled into their seats to wait. The volume climbed slightly but was nothing too distracting from the smutty scene that the book was getting into.

"Hey," a voice called from beside me. I generally ignored interactions with men on the bus. They never had anything kind or intelligent to say. For whatever reason, some men found the bus to be a romantic spot to try and hit on women.

Newsflash, it's not.

"I see you like to read," the voice said again, but I continued to ignore him. If he was talking to me, and he can see that I am reading, then I don't understand why he thought that would be a prime time to conversate.

"What are you reading there?" He tried again.

I could see him leaning forward out of the corner of my eye, waving his hand to gain my attention. He was very much talking to me. I pulled my device closer, acting as if I never heard him.

"Oh, you're an uppity cunt?" he instantly spat.

Normally, I would ignore this as well, but this time, I looked up to him. The man had greasy red hair that came down over his ears. His lips curled up into a sinister smile that displayed tobacco-stained teeth.

"And you're an insecure waste of space." As soon as the words left my mouth, I knew I fucked up. I turned back to shove my reader into my bag and prepare for whatever verbal abuse was about to come my way.

"What the fuck did you just say, bitch?" He jumped to his feet and leaned over me in my seat, the heavy stench of cigarettes and Rumple Minze poured off him.

"Why don't you take a seat?" the demon suddenly said.

"And what are you going to do about it, *mate*?" The man barked, horribly mimicking his accent. Before I knew it, I was being lifted from my seat as Mr. Goat moved between us. He towered over the small man. I'm not sure what the man saw in his face, or if he heard the deep rumble of the demon's chest, but whatever it was, it caused him to cower back in his seat without another word. My new friend sat down in my previous spot and kept his attention forward.

His random act of chivalry wasn't unwanted. I just didn't expect for him to step in at all, let alone as *"gentlemanly"* as he did. My body flushed with heat as I tried to ignore it and get comfortable in my spot.

The bar cannot possibly be that low. Get it together, he still took my soul. I repeated the soul part to myself the rest of the ride.

When we finally made it to our stop, I stood from my seat and waited for him to do the same. Coincidently, the man got off at the same stop, keeping a few feet distance between us. It could have been his stop, or it could have been him wanting to be a creep, who knows? But Mr. Goat was sure to keep closer than usual until we entered the mall.

"Does that happen often?" he suddenly asked with a slight hint of irritation as if the exchange was an inconvenience to him and him alone.

"Well, I am a woman. So, yeah. I usually don't respond at all because men tend to get aggressive."

"He was aggressive before you spoke," he pointed out. I gave him a quick up-down, surprised it seemed to bother him. "It would appear I have that effect on your gender. Mortal or demon. Thanks for your help, though." I cut right, heading for the bedding store with the demon close on my heels.

"I do not particularly want to be attached to a mortal, least of all a dead one." He spoke in a low rumbling growl that surprisingly went unnoticed by the small family ahead of us. I shook my head as if to shake out the oddities in his casually stated words.

"What does that mean?" I didn't understand why he must give such half-assed answers, but this one felt more like a threat than a warning.

"You are fragile and weak," he said as if it were a fact I should be well aware of.

"Ok, thank you," I pushed sarcastically, not seeing where he was going with all of this.

We were greeted kindly by the man standing at the counter. His large grin fell slightly as he looked over us. I guess it was something I would have to deal with during his stay since it seemed to be a common reaction. I gave the man a wave and headed straight for the pillows with Mr. Goat following close behind.

"Pick a pillow," I ordered as I walked around to the covers. I needed a new satin case anyway, so it all worked out. He was at my side after a moment, a large memory foam pillow in hand. I found a cover in the same size and tossed it to him. With how high his body temperature seemed to run, I didn't think he would be acquiring a blanket.

After we paid, I led him to the next shop to get clothes and whatever else he needed while I sat in the shoe department to wait with the previous purchases. The smell of leather and heavy cologne was more suffocating than it was enjoyable.

I informed the group chat of what was going on and what happened on the bus. I left out the part about how wildly attractive it was, mostly because I could be reading into it. It was Monday, and I was pretty sure I'd trained my body to expect something on this day. Even replaying the events to detail them out to the group had my body in a traitorous heated fit.

"Mortal," the demon said from behind me. I looked back to find him holding his bundle of clothes—no bag or receipt. He looked around the small department of shoes, eyeing each table display.

"Are you done, or did you want shoes, too?" I shoved my phone back in my bag and stood, shaking off the feeling from moments before.

"I do not need shoes," he said with a slight note of disgust.

"Ok…Did you pay for that?" I looked over the tags on the shirts and pants, coming to a quick conclusion with or without a response.

He looked down at me with his same unbothered expression before turning without a word as he headed toward an exit we did not enter through.

"Wait! Check out is that way and the bus is on the opposite side of the mall," I huffed as I power walked to keep pace with him.

"I am not sitting in that mortal-infested canister again," he said, reaching into his pocket.

"Did you want to walk instead?"

He pulled out a ring with two keys attached.

"Where did you get those?" He didn't have keys to speak of when we left, and I highly doubted he bought a car in the mall in no less than twenty minutes, which left one explanation. "Did you steal them?"

Nothing but a heavy sigh in response.

I followed him out to the parking garage and up to the third floor. He seemed to know exactly where he was going, which would be hard to know if he did steal it. Then again, he was a demon—his ways of acquiring things were probably not on moral grounds.

With a click, he sent out an echoing chime that came from a black GT at the opposite end. He marched over while I scurried behind him, nearly running until we arrived at the questionable car.

"This doesn't look newly bought," I protested, but I was ignored again as he opened the door and let himself in. I looked over it, knowing there was no way he just came by this. It was definitely stolen.

"What happened to the owner?" I questioned, only to be answered with the loud rev of the engine.

The window slid down as the demon leaned over the center console. "I do not plan to ride in that tube again. Now, you can either join me or be dragged along. Your choice." My reflection rolled up with the window to stare back at me with a hung mouth. He had said earlier he didn't want to drag around a dead mortal. Tugging me behind a car would most certainly solidify that for him.

The car began to reverse, and I flung forward, gripping the handle with a hard tug. I fell back on my ass as the door flew open and the car screeched to an abrupt stop, followed by deep laughter that rumbled through the parking garage. I gaped up at him, shocked to not only see a wide, face-splitting grin but hear the most musical laughter. I would have assumed it to be more haunting or chilling. However, his was warm and welcoming.

Granted, it was at my expense. But it was something, a decent sign he didn't completely have a stick up his ass.

I climbed to my feet and dusted off my shorts before sliding into the passenger seat. The new car smell was still seeping from the leather. An empty water bottle lay in the center of the back seat, and a pack of gum sat in the cup holder at the front.

"Mr. Goat?"

He threw the car into reverse and backed out with ease.

"Did you steal this car?"

"Yes," he said without remorse as he pulled out. The tires screeched over the asphalt as he sped off to the exit. He didn't even look both ways as he turned onto the main road and headed toward the freeway entrance without instruction. Cars and buildings passed by in a blur as he weaved between traffic to race home.

I looked over at him, calm and relaxed as he hardly used any of the mirrors to make his lane changes. A quick peek at the speedometer had me nearly choking. He was going well over 110 with ease, practically flying undirected and I was sitting there just as calm. No clammy hands, no hyperventilation, no phantom break pressing. I was completely at peace having no control of a car a demon was speeding in.

I sucked in a deep breath, trying to feel the nervousness I usually felt in these situations, but it felt as though I was digging into an empty hole and suddenly, the feeling of despair that used to plague me felt more like a memory I couldn't grasp.

"How are you doing that?" I finally asked, turning my attention back to the probable cause.

"Doing what?"

"Keeping me calm?" I blurted.

He huffed, taking his eyes off the road to look at me. "I am not doing anything to keep you calm. You simply lack your humanity without a soul."

I stared at him blankly for a few seconds, trying to make sense of his riddles. "What does that mean?"

His hands tightened on the wheel as he made the merge for the exit. "It means you will notice some of your emotions slip away over some time."

His words repeated in my head for a moment, but it was as if they were not processing properly. I couldn't bring myself to worry or care about the loss of emotions, because what does that really mean?

"Which ones?" I pressed again.

His shoulders fell with an exaggerated sigh. "Looks like fear was one to dissipate first." He turned to look over me. "Not surprising," he added.

"Then, I will be losing more? Like what?"

He pinched the bridge of his nose with irritation. "I am not your manual, Mortal. You will simply have to wait and see for yourself."

I figured that was his sign to indicate he was through with answering and talking all together, so I sat back and combed over what emotions I had felt over the last few days. The morning I met him I didn't feel afraid, so it must have started then. But since then, I had felt irritation and annoyance. I had felt content and frustrated, but I hadn't felt sad or scared in what felt like forever already.

After several more proper turns, it was safe to say that for a demon who didn't seem to care for humans all that much, he clearly knew more about us than he cared to show. The mounting questions were too much to contain any longer. He would just have to answer or deal with me asking nonstop until he does.

"Mr. Goat?"

"Eriusazal..." he corrected stiffly.

I looked at him blankly for a minute "Is that your name?" It sounded familiar, but I couldn't place where I would have even heard it from, and it seemed like a mouthful. He nodded once.

"I will just call you Erius. Are there cars in Hell?" I asked. He hid a quick grimace at the new nickname before shaking his head. "No. there are no cars where I come from."

"Where you come from? Is that not Hell?" I perked up in my seat, finally getting some interesting answers. Honestly, Hell would have been the first thing I asked him had we started out on a more pleasant greeting.

"Hell is a place you mortals created. Demons, creatures, and all things your lot find dark and frightening, come from the Six Circles," he informed me nonchalantly, as if he didn't just drop the biggest religious discovery known to humankind.

"The Six Circles?" I repeated, mystified by all the new information I had always wanted to know.

"It is where the lost souls of your realm roam, but they are not the only ones," he explained. Surprised with his sudden willingness to answer, I pressed for more while he turned onto the lot at the beach and pulled the car into an open space by the van.

"So, it's like the Underworld?" I asked, hoping he didn't decide to check out at any moment.

"The Underworld?" The name seemed to confuse him.

"Yeah, the afterlife. Where souls go when they die, to be judged for their life sins or whatever," I explained.

"There are no judgments cast out in the Circles by anyone other than the soul itself."

Ok, vague but something. If Hell wasn't real, nor was Heaven but if the Underworld or something like it isn't real—then what the fuck were these Circles like?

"If there are no cars in these Circles, how do you know how to drive?" I pressed.

He looked me up and down, another thing I'd noticed he did right before ignoring my question.

As predicted, he left the car without responding. While he grabbed his bags, I went to unlock the van. I placed everything down on the bed before walking out to give him the same respect I demanded when I'm changing.

Prometheus followed me out for some fresh air. A small walk along the beach would probably do us both some good, and he could prowl for his mollusks. We kept close to the van, walking in a half circle around it while we waited. On our last turn, the door slid open to present

Erius.

He stepped out in a gray button-up and black slacks, the same style as before only now he added a black Rolex to the outfit. He ran his hands through his hair as I walked up to him, lifting his shirt a bit to display the sharp V line at his waist.

Heat flushed my face, but I didn't bother to look away. When he noticed I was staring, he dropped his arms to adjust his shirt.

"Your rent has to be paid some way," I joked, but he didn't find it so funny as his eyes bore into me like daggers.

"Come on, then." I sighed. "Not on joking terms yet, I guess."

CHAPTER ELEVEN

Mira

"I get off at seven, so you can meet me here. There is an all-natural store that is within our distance," I informed Erius as we stepped up to the shop.

"What is there for me to get there?" he asked gruffly. How he understood some human concepts but not the bare minimum was beyond me.

"You need to brush your teeth and wash your mortal body and hair." I scrunched my nose as I looked him over, "I can tell by the way you drive that this isn't your first go as a human, try and act like it. I don't have time to teach you basic skills."

A blank stare was all I got in return.

"Ok, well, I'll see you when I'm off then." I turned and headed into the brightly lit apothecary without waiting for a response I knew I wouldn't get.

"Hey, Mina!" Andrew greeted happily, a wide grin split his face. He tapped his thumb against the countertop with each step as I approached, his eyes locked on me the whole way.

"Hey, Drew. Where's Jordan?"

His smile grew wider. "He called out today."

Heat flushed over my skin with anticipation. It was as if I had deprived myself for months. There was one client I had to get through, and it wasn't normally a challenge. But today I felt a bit more in need of the relief.

His eyes flash to my right wrist, creating an instant pinch between his brows. "What happened to your arm?"

"Oh, a painting accident for a project in the van," I lied, pulling my arm up to inspect.

"It looks like a nasty burn," he countered.

I shrugged, heading up the stairs. "Would I lie about a burn, Drew?"

"I guess not," he said as he returned to the papers on the counter.

I smiled and headed up to ready the room. The energy on the second floor felt heavier, a noticeable difference that only grew the closer I got to the door. A mix of warm and cold tingles flushed my skin, covering my arms and shoulders before falling all the way down my stomach and through the souls of my feet. I crossed the threshold, the weight only growing heavier. It sent the prickly feeling over my body into an erratic wave.

Not much different than the feeling the book gave while it was here, except the exhausting weight of fear didn't cling to me as it had. My breath remained steady despite the creeping feeling that slunk over me. I felt more on edge and anxious that my space was not as clear as it appeared.

I tried to shrug off the odd feeling and took a seat in my pile of pillows. Perhaps clearing my mind and a moment of reflection would help me sort out what emotions I could discern from. With crossed legs and a pillow under each knee for comfort, I closed my eyes. A new weighing aura instantly fell around me, clearing my skin of the crawling chill. It wasn't painful or frightening; it felt more like peace and comfort, relaxing my body into place.

My heart fell in line to a steady beat as I drifted into a trance. Cool air drifted around me with a light pressure sending the feeling of solitude away until the smell of cigarette smoke and peppermint filled the air, giving me reason to open my eyes.

Across from me sat an older woman, I would say mid-sixties. A green and yellow scarf wrapped her hair up into a puff of white curls at the top of her head. Her full lips turned up into a smile as she looked over me. She was not a client I had read for before, and I didn't even look at who was supposed to come in.

"Hello, are you here for a reading?" I asked politely.

Her eyes rounded as she straightened up, her lips pulling even wider. "My dear," she began, "you can see me?"

"Yes? Why wouldn't I?" I asked slowly.

"Usually you do not," she began. "Oh, how wonderful. You can tell my sweet Melody more for me." Her voice was shaky but hopeful.

I tilted my head as I continued to examine her for a moment more. She didn't look to be a ghost, at least, not how I always thought they would look. She wasn't transparent or pale, nor was her skin rotting away. She didn't float or hover as she sat connected to the floor like any other client. Vibrant, lively eyes looked over me with an elated glimmer, not cloudy or white like a corpse.

I studied the familiar features of a younger client I saw frequently, recalling the photos she had once shown me of her late mother.

"Vivian?" I choked out. Melody had explained that her mother passed last year. Ever since the funeral, she'd come to see me for readings and connections.

"What?" Melody sniffled from the doorway. She was often in tears long before arriving, even more so upon leaving. But she never left unsatisfied with the answers.

"Oh, nothing, please have a seat so we may start," I offered. My eyes fell to Vivian as she settled in the back.

Melody took a seat where her mother had just been moments earlier. They both had their hair done up in a matching style I assume Vivian had taught Melody. With them side by side like this, I could really see the similarities, especially in their eyes.

"What would you like to share today?" I asked, holding out my hands for her to take.

Melody had started college recently and her mother had passed before she left for university. Despite offering to stay for her dad, he begged her to go and finish her education. Most of her readings consisted of her telling her mother about classes and how she was coping with it all while without her.

After a few steady breaths, we opened our eyes and I pulled out the pendulum, "Go ahead," I instructed.

"I got the internship, Mom!" Melody gushed.

I looked up to Vivian who was still in the corner. Her smile grew, and she pulled her hands to cover her mouth. When she pulled them down, her lips mouthed what looked like "I'm proud of you."

"She says she is so very proud of you, Melody." My eyes were still on Vivian as hers were on mine. I ignored the pendulum as it swung from letter to letter, but I was sure Melody couldn't tell the difference.

"Tell her I love her, and I hear her every night." The woman's whispered words echoed through my head. When it cleared, I looked to Melody, unsure of the meaning.

"She says she loves you, and she hears you every night." Melody's eyes rounded to disks. "W-what?" she stammered.

Vivian was at my side, placing her hand on my shoulder without warning. An icy chill rained over my body that was soon replaced with a static charge that lit the scar over my arm.

"Melody, I am not disappointed in you. You had been backed into doing what must be done. I cannot fault you for that." The voice that came was not my own. I hadn't even meant to speak, but when I finished, Melody jumped to her feet.

"What the fuck, Mina? Is this a joke?" she cried.

"No. It's not a joke," I assured, but my tone and lack of reaction didn't help my case.

She stormed from the room in a rush, not wanting to hear any explanation. It wasn't like she would understand the one I had anyway.

I turned my attention back to Vivian, who stood just as shocked as me.

"Well…maybe next time, you can give me a warning." I offered.

"I did not know you could do any of this," the ghostly woman said.

"Me either. Perhaps try and convince her to come back somehow. Leave signs for her. I've told her you would." In past visits I had suggested Melody look to her and her mother's favorite activity in bird watching for signs of her mother. Thus far she said she has had some signs but nothing she could decipher alone.

"Yes, I remember." Vivian grinned.

"Have you always been here? I mean, during my readings with Melody?"

"Yes. Every visit. You do not seem too frightened, dear," she pointed out.

Oh, that is because I traded my soul for this ability. The demon said I would lose a bit of my humanity. Apparently, fear was first to go. I wanted to tell her, but it didn't seem appropriate for the moment. I shrugged my shoulders with a slanted smile, no lie to give in its place.

"Well, I am overjoyed to better connect with my Melody," Vivian gushed before placing her hand on my shoulder. She gave a soft smile before fading into mist, causing the flame on the candles to flicker.

Erius gifted me something after all, a neat little trick that would come in handy during future readings. Maybe they would appear as my emotions slipped away. A true trade, a piece of my humanity for a gift.

I should ask Erius how many emotions will slip. All of them? Some? Most? Was it only fear I lost? Because I could feel annoyed and angry. I had felt content – I wouldn't say I'd had a moment to feel happy so I couldn't completely disregard it.

With my mind reeling with questions, I began my nightly cleanup. When I was finished, I headed downstairs to help Andrew since Jordan was gone. He gathered a few documents from the shelf under the back counter and handed them to me with a slick grin. "Can you take this to my office for me?"

He slid the papers over to me with a wink and went back to pulling things from the counter, his way of getting me to the back and out of line of the cameras while he locked up.

I took the envelope with a smile and walked to his office in the back. I placed the sheets on his desk and by the time I turned to the door, he was shutting it behind him.

When he faced me, there was a split second where the heat between us fanned out. He looked over me, as if to take me in for the first time. His eyes trailed down to my hand, softening them in a way I hadn't seen. Within seconds he was across the floor and holding my scarred arm. "Are you sure this is nothing?"

"Like I said, it's just from a project. It should fade in a few days," I lied, pulling my hand from his grasp. I didn't come here for tender moments, and he should know this.

"Does it hurt?" he pressed again.

"No, I don't feel a thing." I offered a reassuring smile, hoping he would move on from it before my mood dwindled away.

I moved his hands to my waist where he struggled with the row of buttons on my shorts. His mouth connected to my skin wherever he could reach without throwing him off from what he was trying desperately to get to. He spun me around so my back was to him and tugged the shorts down around my thighs. His lips never left my skin, following a trail over my shoulder and neck. The clatter of his buckle fell to the floor, followed by the sound of his zipper echoing in the small space.

My body flushed with anticipation, waiting for what I had been desperately craving for a week. I impatiently rolled my hips against him while he worked on the condom. He let out a breathy chuckle, trailing his nose over the curve of my neck.

"Impatient today," he hummed. The soft snap stilled the room, signaling the success. My breath hiked as I arched my back, pressing my ass against his dick.

"It's been a long week," I purred.

He gripped my waist and thrust into me until he was buried deep, pausing with a low groan. I could feel myself throb around him, slick with need. I coaxed him by pulling nearly off, stopping at the tip before slowly rolling back. His body stilled as I began slowly twerking on his dick.

Fingers dug into my hips as he matched my pace, pounding into me mercilessly. I cried out, gripping the edge of the desk for better support. Fire quickly began to heat my stomach, filling my mind with a building pressure. His breathing came out hard and labored as his hands wandered over my body.

"Deeper," I pleaded, causing his movements to become more frantic. The desk scraped against the floor with each thrust until it was banging into the wall. A few frames fell off, missing us as they clattered to the floor, but Andrew didn't pause.

He held me in place with one hand while the other slipped around my chest, teasing my nipple through the shirt until it found purchase around my neck. He pulled me to him so my back was against his chest and his lips were near my ear. His heavy panting grew ragged as his hips jerked against me, signaling a finish I had to beat.

Thankfully, I was close. My skin flushed and muscles coiled, ready to reach my peak. The building pressure felt as if my head would pop, and just as it all was about to boil over, the thrusting slowed to a damn near stop as Andrew came. The once throbbing bliss died just as instantly, and the mood was shattered.

"Wow," he panted, "I don't know about you, but that was…. That was something." He pulled out with a heavy sigh. It would have been something for me, had I finished, but some nights it was like that, especially with someone usually working in the lobby. I was just hoping since nobody but us were here, I would have had a more enjoyable outcome. After the week I'd suffered, it was all I was hoping for to take the edge off.

Just pointless.

I quickly pulled up my shorts and adjusted my top before turning to him. I didn't feel like bothering with hiding the disappointment—not that he noticed. He finished buttoning up his pants with a stupid, satisfied smile.

"Bring the nettle and yarrow jars when you come out." He gestured to the two large jars of herb on the back desk as he picked up two gallons of oil and headed out to the front.

I may have been less annoyed by it if I knew I had the freedom and privacy to go home and handle it myself, but I didn't even have a room to sneak off to.

I fluffed my hair before gathering the two jars in my arms to give a bit of time on the cameras.

The entrance bell rang with a late-coming customer, followed briskly by Andrew's greeting.

"Welcome to the Green Coven," he said cheerfully.

I don't know why he wouldn't have locked the door. Thankfully they didn't come in three minutes ago. That would have made for an awkward greeting and sell. It was also irresponsible. Anyone could walk through those doors, and we weren't exactly being quiet.

I headed out with the two jars and a new feeling of dissatisfaction over the entire situation. If it wouldn't make me look like some sex crazed nympho, I'd bitch that demon out about this, too. What more can he take from me?

"I am here for Mina." Erius's voice gave me pause at the hall entrance, instantly killing my pleasant mood. His gaze shifted from Andrew to me with a fixed expression.

"Oh, do you have a reading?" Andrew asked.

Erius's gaze drifted back. "Yes," he said slowly, clearly not even understanding what he was asked.

Andrew motioned toward the computer to check the schedule I knew he wouldn't see. Besides, it was way too late for me to have any clients.

SUNFLOWER IN THE SHADOWS

"He's a late walk-in," I interjected as I placed the jars on the counter and turned my attention to the demon, "Come with me and we will just reschedule for another day. We are closing in a few." I marched past my new van-mate and headed upstairs to my room. I didn't stop to see if he was behind me because I figured he was, but when I turned around, he was barely reaching the top step.

"What are you doing here? I told you I'd meet you at the light," I said to him when he reached the room.
"I grew bored," he said stiffly, walking in. He took notice of the altar of skulls and made his way over to it. "What are readings?" he questioned as he looked from the altar to the wall of more skulls.

"Tarot, pendulum, and bone readings," I informed him. I wanted to tell him about Vivian, but I knew he wouldn't give two shits less of a care about it. I pulled my phone out and began typing into the chat.

You guys!
I see dead people lol

Ok, that was a cheesy movie reference, but I still giggled about it.

Ew, that sounds scary
as hell!
-Jaz

Right! Meems, that
does NOT sound fun.
-Mickey

They look just like us

How do you know
they are dead then?
-Amber

It was during a reading,
and she sort of appeared.

I turned back to Erius, who was still enthralled with the walls, looking over my decks of tarot and oracle, the bowl of lavender bundles, the various skulls I collected, and other such things I stocked. Things said to ward off negative energies and entities, yet there he stood in all his dark gloom and attitude.

He picked up a bundle of blue sage and examined it. When he lost interest in that, he made his way around until he was in front of me.

"Did you enjoy your tour?" I quizzed. He looked me over with a slight scrunch of his nose and a look of disgust.

"What?" I snapped.

He made an odd snort of amusement and a half smile as he turned back to the wall. "Did you kill those animals you are displaying there?" he asked, pointing to the altar of fox and raven skulls.

"No, I find them in the forest when I camp. Why?"

He continued to examine more of the shelf for a moment longer. I figured he wouldn't answer and moved to cross the room, but he blocked me.

"You requested necromancy strengths, correct?"

I didn't specify what powers I wanted; we all just sort of agreed to ask for magic. Clearly, he gifted it out how he pleased.

"Um, sure," I confirmed.

He grabbed the raven skull and leaned down to be eye level with me. A crawling feeling crept over my skin as he flipped the skull around in his hand.

"Can you please be gentle with that?" I requested softly, reaching for the bone as he pulled it back out of reach. My hand fell through the empty air, and I stumbled forward, crashing into him with a shriek. Before I could push off, his hand covered my face as he shoved me away.

"Ah!" I fell back, landing on the soft pile of pillows. I glared up at him as he stood there with his arms crossed over his chest, looking as displeased as ever.

"What did you do that for?" I snapped.

He kept his same unmoved expression as he offered a slow shrug. "I do not care to be touched."

"You caused this! Amongst other things." I shuffled around, struggling to climb to my feet.

"It is best you keep your distance." He shrugged half-heartedly and returned to looking over the skulls.

"Oh, because you'll make a meal out of me. Was my soul not satisfying enough?" I groaned.

I struggled to work myself up from the cushions, nearly colliding into his chest again. His darkening eyes set on the door. His lips pulled down briefly before twitching at a brief smile.

"I imagine you would taste just as sweet," he purred, widening his eyes as he spoke. It stirred the same heated feeling between my thighs that I silently cursed at. A heavy knock broke the silence and his grin widened.

With my eyes on him, I stepped over and placed my hand on the door, the smile only growing—an actual smile, displaying all his fangs and white teeth.

"Ok?" I said slowly, turning back to the door. I cracked it open enough to poke my head out and found Andrew in the doorway with drooping brows and a look that reminded me of a lost pup.

"Is everything ok?" I asked him.

"Ugh, yeah. I just heard something –"

"Yup that was me," I shot quickly. "I fell."

His brows furrowed "You—fell?"

"Yea, I'm a klutz. Was there something you needed?"

His gaze fell on the man behind me, a look of unease falling over him.

"No, just making sure *you* were alright," he said.

"Yup, all good. Just going over the schedule for the week. I can close up if you need. You don't have to wait for me." I began to shut the door when Andrew caught it with his foot.

"Yes, I know, but I was wondering, what your plans were after this?"

His odd interruption and questions grew meaning before my eyes.

Erius made a noise in his throat, his presence a lot closer than before. A discomforting heat lit up around us, engulfing me in the aura of him.

"Andrew, I don't think now is the appropriate time for that question—"

Before I could finish, Erius pushed against the door, shutting it in Andrew's face.

"That was rude," I cracked.

"As is cutting in on our rescheduling of this… reading," Erius pointed. He had just shoved my face away from him, and now he cared about interrupted time.

"You didn't even know what a reading was two seconds ago!" I hissed.

"You're going to get me fired." I pressed my ear against the wood, listening as the footsteps disappeared down the stairs.

"Listen, you can't be doing stuff like that. I don't need you getting me fired because you're rude!" I huffed as I gathered my things. He didn't say anything aside from offering an indifferent shrug.

"I don't know why you couldn't have waited by the pier," I grumbled as I pushed past him to leave. I heard the door shut behind me as he followed me out.

Andrew wasn't at the counter when we hit the bottom step. The back-office light was on, with the sound of shuffling papers drifting out.

"Bye, Drew!" I called, rushing out the door. The humid summer air felt sticky and hot, which did nothing to help how wired I felt from the evening.

"Do you drink? Alcohol?" I asked. He looked down at me with a slight nod. Good, there was at least one thing we had in common. "Come on."

We headed across the street as I navigated us to the bar Agave Azul. It was a tourist spot but had the best botanical highball, and I loved snacking on their appetizers.

To my delight, there wasn't much of a crowd, giving us a decent pick of bar seats. I wasn't surprised when Erius sat beside me. He didn't really have anywhere else to go, and clearly being on his own didn't last long. Maybe if I could get him to loosen up with a few drinks he would be more open to talking.

The tender dropped two menus in front of us and shuffled off to the back as if we were a bother. I already knew what I was going to order so I didn't need it, but Erius looked over it with a face of dissatisfaction.

"What's wrong?" I pretended to read his menu before looking him in the eyes. "Oh no! They don't carry souls here. Pity. Pick something else."

I leaned back in my stool as the tender circled around with a more pleased expression as she made a beeline to Erius. I mean, I know he's conventionally attractive, but fuck, am I now invisible?

"How can I help you, sir?" she asked in a breathy voice.
Erius crinkled his nose. A slight hint of disgust twisted at his lips, and he did not even try to hide it. He really didn't like mortals. He glanced at the menu once more. "Jameson whiskey," he said stiffly.

The woman turned to me, her smile falling. "And you?"
Ok, rudeness.

"A botanical highball and an order of the calamari, please," I ordered kindly. I didn't like spit in my food, and though she did deserve a bitchy response, I kept it to myself.

"Coming right up." She left us once again and I turned to the demon at my side.

"You know that's the whole bottle, right?" I advised, and he responded with a nod.

"It's pretty exhausting when you are so talkative one moment and then mute the next. This," I held up my scarred arm "Clearly won't be fixed in a few days, so you can be cordial—or at the very least, use your words."

"What do you propose we speak on?" he asked gruffly.

"Well, you never answered me about being human before. We can start with that," I said.

His eyes flickered from me to the bartender lugging his very large bottle of whiskey and a glass with round ice in it to him.

"The highball will be right up," she said as she began mixing it before us, making me wait even longer for the answer. When she was finally done, she set it in front of me and headed to the back room.

"So?" I pressed. He looked me over for a long moment.

"Pick a different question," he ordered.

"What?" I whined.

He poured himself a glass and took a deep drink before turning back to me. "A different question."

"Is it personal business or something?" I guessed.

"You can say that," he muttered into his glass. I was ready to snap back when the woman came around with a huge plate of calamari. Clearly a serving size for two, I pushed the tray between us and took a ring to nibble on.

"What are these?" he asked suddenly.

"Calamari? You've never tried it?"

He shook his head, eyeing the piece in my hand.

"It's fried squid," I hummed as I enjoyed another bite. He hesitantly picked up a ring to examine.

"You dip it." I laughed, doing as said while dunking the ring into the marinara sauce they provided.

Erius followed along, popping the piece in his mouth, giving me a clear view of his fangs again.

"You have fangs?" I blurted. With a little alcohol in me, I didn't feel the need to hold back on the questions as they came.

He paused his chewing to shoot me a darkening glare before swallowing. "*Fangs* are what your lot calls them. To me, they are just my teeth," he said.

"Is that a rude question to ask?"

"Yes, it is." He took another dunked ring and popped it into his mouth.

We didn't talk about much after that, not because I ran out of questions but because I got caught up in the calamari and my drink. He poured some of the whiskey into my glass a few times at my request, and it wasn't long after the second pour that I was probably ready to be cut off.

A man and his friend that had taken over the stools beside me began to get louder with every drink they ordered. I turned to face Erius and put them at my back, but the one behind kept bumping and tapping me as he moved around.

"My bad," he grunted without turning around. I ignored it and turned back to the empty plate of calamari with a frown. When I looked up to Erius, he was enjoying the last piece. At least he was eating more, I supposed. Maybe that was why he had such a shit attitude.

The man bumped me again. This time he did not acknowledge me. And though it was more of a tap, he had one more bump before I lost my shit.

"Oh," I shot, trying to distract myself, "I didn't tell you earlier, because you know, you don't really seem like you care about much. But since you shared with me, I'll share with you. I saw a dead person today."

The bartender happened to walk by at that moment and gave us an odd look but shrugged it off as simply drunk talk, I was sure.

My bar stool slid closer to him with a scraping sound. "Now that, Mortal, is what I consider *interesting*." He poured the last of the whiskey into both of our glasses. "I am curious to see what you will do with my gifts."

He tapped his glass to mine and shot the drink back. I followed along only for the man to elbow me again. I flew from the stool, smacking into Erius's chest and spilling the whiskey all over us. He shot up from his seat, pulling me into the warm vanillic scent of his chest. Blinded by his arm and dizzy from the alcohol, my body jerked with his.

"Take a walk," he growled to the man as he shoved him. Shattering glass silenced the bar with a following echo of rage filled words. His arm tightened around me with a low, rumbling growl.

Erius took a step as the men continued to hurl insults and slurs our way. I don't know what happened next; I was much too preoccupied with his dazing smell. I just know the two men cut their words short as another deep growl rattled into my ear.

I leaned into him as everything seemed to settle down. This time he wasn't as quick to push me onto my ass. He did pull away from me like he was peeling a leech off, but it wasn't his usual aggressive way.

The warmth returned between my thighs in a traitorous way. Erius tilted his head, ready to say something when the bartender raced in from the back. She looked over the slightly battered man and his friend, then panned over to Erius and me.

"You four need to leave," she spat angrily. "I don't give a fuck what happened, just go."

I was ready to leave anyway. We had already finished eating and the bottle was empty. Erius tossed an oddly folded bill onto the bar and grabbed my wrist. With a light grip, he walked me out to the front and pulled me around to face him.

"Now, tell me of this spirit you have seen."

Chapter Twelve

Jasmine

The faint mildewy smell of new canvas filled the studio along with the stale acrylic paint. Natural light illuminated the open space, shining in at the perfect angle. With the clear sky, we'd have about two hours of good lighting to work with. I stepped up to the model and adjusted the fruit and flowers for the perspective painting we would be working on today.

"Ok, class, happy Monday. I hope you all had a lovely weekend. Please get your brushes from the back. Today, we are painting a perspective piece," I announced, pulling a thick band off my wrist to pineapple my locs. Despite the rec keeping their A/C on full blast, the art room always seemed to get poor circulation during the summer months, making for a stuffy sauna of a painting space.

I took my place at my desk as the "students" collected their materials. My class ranged in age from elementary to high school children who signed up for summer workshops, and my studio offered the classes out to the recreational center for nine months of the year. So, in other words, I was an art teacher.

The children took their spots at their aisles and got to work sketching the objects at the center of the studio. It was fun to watch them because other than seeing the creative process spread out amongst age groups and skills, I could really gather a story from them, mostly the high school grade students who had more drama in their day to day lives.

Two of my students were very clearly a couple. They signed up together and showed up in the same car, so it is safe to say they were dating. However, on my off days I enjoyed painting nature scenes, and it would seem I was not the only one. I caught Francine with Travon at the canyon last week, and Travon was not her boyfriend. Franklin was. Yet here she sat, cuddling up to Franklin while Travon stewed in jealousy on the other side.

Messy. But oh so delicious.

It made it better that they had not seen me themselves. I did not like when children begged me not to say anything. I didn't ever plan to in these situations; I didn't enjoy being involved in their meaningless drama aside from a spectator. But I did wonder how today's events would have played out had they seen me.

Since it didn't appear like anything was going to pop off, I began plans for the next project. Being the middle of summer, they were already well-established with several different mediums. This week we did paint, and I was thinking next week we'd work with clay.

"Ms. Deboys?" Francine said from beside my desk. I didn't know how many times I had to tell these kids.

"Just Jasmine, please." I looked up at the girl, taken aback for a moment. Faint fumes of several colors seemed to seep from her skin into the air where it floated around her. I blinked and rubbed my eyes in case it was me having the issue, but when my vision cleared, the colors had brightened. Distinctive red, green, and violet shades twisted around her body.

"Are you ok?" she asked.

My gaze fell to the other students finding the same substance, in a variety of shades, slowly seeping out from each child. They didn't notice it, or at least they didn't appear to. It wasn't a bothersome smog, and it didn't have a smell.

"Uh, yeah. Excuse me for a moment," I said, excusing myself to the restroom to see if I, too, fell victim this mysterious fog. On my way I passed two other volunteers with the same cloudy hue. One had a mix of colors while the other only had a deep forest green. They waved with a smile as we passed, oblivious to what was around them. I waved back, hoping my face didn't give away my growing concern.

When they turned the corner, I pushed through the door to the bathroom and marched to the mirror, finding I had a lovely pink cloud lofting around me. Faint, painless, and odorless—which didn't get me any closer to finding out what it was.

Flipping the faucet on, I cupped my hands under the running water to splash over my face. I kept my attention down as I dabbed my eyes with a paper towel, catching notice of the pink cloud swirling around my hands. My heart dropped to the pit of my stomach as I looked back to the mirror with no change. A fluttering breath escaped my lips as I stared into the mirror at myself, watching as the color continued to twist and turn around me, covering me in its beauty and wonder.

The magic that demon gave us...Finally!

I stifled an elated squeal and cleaned up the water mess before heading back to class. By the time I entered the studio, the students had moved from sketching to painting. No troubles or outbursts, and with them focused on their work, it gave me time to research what was going on. Not that I would know where to start.

On my way to my desk, I passed both Travon and Franklin gathering more paints and having a surprisingly pleasant conversation. But it wasn't the strangeness of their dynamic; it was the colors that lofted around them. Travon held a deep red hue while Franklin had a soft violet shade, colors that most certainly matched their personalities. Not too sure why Francine would want a literal red flag when she has a soft violet beside her. I looked to the girl in question, the two colors swirling around her own.

I sat down with my eyes darting between the three of them with a forming realization.

I can see auras. I sucked in a breath as I looked around the room at the rest of the colors. None as mixed and intertwined as theirs. Despite it being messy drama, it was quite lovely to see. The mix of colors in relation to the personal connections, not the actual cheating.

Time seemed to tick by as I watched the students' auras shift in colors throughout the hours. I still wasn't sure how it all worked but moods and shared energy looked to be a big factor.

When class ended, they cleaned up their paints and brushes and took their canvases home, leaving me with little left to straighten up—which was a good day for me and considering the developments, I needed the extra quiet time to think. It would be wise to know more before I presented it all to the girls. Amber didn't really explain in depth what she could do, and I was sure she was still trying to figure it out herself. I'd rather learn without everyone asking me about it throughout the day.

It would be easier to bring up when I had a better understanding of it myself. Seeing auras wasn't that big of a deal; some people had trained themselves to do it and honestly, it wasn't like it was a hard task for a novice practitioner. I needed to understand what it meant and the color significance. Whether or not I can do anything with it other than see it and what all that could mean.

If the demon wasn't such an ass, I'd see if Mina could ask him, but I knew she was dealing with her own battles on top of him invading her life. At least I would see her tomorrow. I could bug her about it all then.

After wiping down the sink, I reorganized the paint tubes and brushes in the cabinets. The only thing left out was the reference model for tomorrow's class.

With everything done and away, I grabbed my bag and began the short walk back home, with one quick stop on the way. Between my apartment and the rec sat a small crystal shop that carried a far more extensive library than The Green Coven, most of which I knew to be on auras and aura reading. For some reason, Andrew kept neglecting my request to get a few copies at the shop, leaving me with no other choice but to go elsewhere.

I walked through the near empty lobby, noting each color and person that passed as I left the building and hit the sidewalk. The journey to the shop was just as magical with each person I saw. They all held their own shade or mix of shades that gave a small hint to their life. I may not yet know or understand the colors, but having a peek into personal connections made me feel like I knew things I shouldn't.

And I loved knowing things I shouldn't.

The heavy scent of sage and lavender incense wafted a block away from my destination while intense tremors shook the ground at my feet, growing stronger the closer I came until it was a full thumping in my chest as I stood at the front entrance. It was a new sensation I could only assume was a part of my mystery gifts. I hadn't felt anything like it before, and the demon would be the only explanation. It wasn't anything painful, just a tad annoying.

Florescent signs with sigils and pentagrams flashed from the windows caught my eye as I looked over the new display. Tapestries of moon phases and herbs hung along the glass to shade the inside from the bright lights of the street.

I stepped into the low-lit occult shop, ignoring the humming that buzzed against my skin as I took a moment to admire the maximalist setup. Though it was much smaller than the spiritual floor at The Green Coven, it had far more options packed and cluttered in any space things could fit. The center table was chock full of bones and jars of deceased creatures submerged in formaldehyde or whatever liquid was keeping them from decomposing. I had only been in a few times, and the last time I did not see the dead animals and skulls, so those must have been new. The walls were covered in mirrors of all sizes and frames, posters with occult sigils and art, along with taxidermy animal heads decorated like cute characters.

I would have to remember to tell Mina about it. With everything going on she would love the dead animals and bones. Shit, I might as well just bring everyone and make it a girls' trip. We all could use it after the last one.

"Welcome in," the cashier called from the front. I waved with a soft smile but kept looking around. The vibrating energy fluctuated against my skin while I skimmed through the tables. When I was done admiring the collections, I headed to the back where the bookshelves sat, a whole wall lined with rows of books from modern-day witchcraft to wiccan practice, they had a wide variety to choose from. They even had a section of leather-bound journals to collect.

I focused on scanning the titles until I found three on auras and grabbed them all. On my way to the checkout, I passed a nearly hidden table full of rose quartz and amethyst. They sat behind a coffin lined with shelves of crystals. Different waves of vibrations hit my skin, sending a heavy weighing energy through me that almost knocked me back.

Another mysterious gift, it seemed, something to study more closely along with these colorful auras. I moved my hand over the rose quartz and then the amethyst, feeling the different pulsations they gave off before returning my attention to the rose again.

I walked around to the front of the coffin and held my hand over each cluster of stones, admiring the different vibration patterns that radiated from them. Most of the crystals on the shelves were heavy and wild in what they gave off, and I didn't feel like that would do well in my apartment. Besides, most of what I had were clear and rose quartz.

Their calming vibrations brought me back to the table full of the powder pink rocks. A large sphere sat at the center with different sized raw stones around it. From there it was a mix of polished stones in many sizes and shapes.

Picking up a palm stone and a small raw quartz, I welcomed the soothing tremors into my hands, crystals with a much calmer vibration that soothed my nerves from everything else around me. With everything in hand, I made my way to the counter to check out.

"Did you find everything alright?" the man asked as he typed in all the items by hand.

"Yes." I smiled, pulling out my card to finish the transaction. He wrapped and bagged the stones and set the books in their own separate paper bag before sliding them all to me with the receipt. I wished him a good day and headed out with better insight on my gifts. Now all that was left was figuring out what it all truly meant.

The three books sat open and scattered across my kitchen table. Each had a color chart for auras, but all the information conflicted with one another and didn't provide shit other than what little I already knew, which meant my research would need to be hands on, and that seemed tedious.

I leaned back in my chair and looked over the new crystals I brought home. The steady buzzing of the rest of my collection thumped through the hall and rubbed against me. I hadn't thought to take a look at my other stones when I had gotten in, too focused on finding the answer in the books to study the crystals around me. They all gave off the same steady rhythm as the new ones I just brought home. But I wanted to feel the differences in each one despite them being the same type. I could feel various rhythmic movements, as if the base of several different songs were playing through one subwoofer.

I opened the door to the deep thump reverberating through my feet and into my bones, nothing too fast paced, and if I had to say, it sounded like the beat from the movie *Jumanji,* only less intimidating and anxiety inducing. Upon my dresser that doubled as my altar sat a glass geometric terrarium with an opening on one panel and Himalayan salt covering the bottom to cleanse and charge my crystals.

I crossed the floor with the slightly off rhythm stones in hand to place them in with the rest. A cleanse and charge should allow them to match up with the current beat of the whole room. With a quick blessing, I lit a rosemary and lavender bundle and set it on the salt stone plate to burn while I straightened up my altar. Once everything felt balanced, I grabbed some clothes from the top drawer.

"I shall see you tomorrow," I whispered to my crystals before retreating to the shower for my well-needed spa night.

Chapter Thirteen

Mira

I locked the van and began to make my way across the lot to the bus stop when the chimes of Erius's stolen car rang. The jarring sound made my skin crawl as it echoed in my ears. I ground my teeth and turned to see him leaning against the trunk, rolling his sleeves up without a care. He combed his hands through his hair, displaying his human eyes. Despite them looking a clear crystal blue, there was still something wildly inhuman about his presence that they didn't really hide. If I didn't know he was a demon, I would still guess there was something unnaturally off about him.

"You don't think that may have been reported by now?" I

pointed.

A devilish grin flashed his lips as he turned to head for the driver's side of the car without response. The car kicked on with a mechanical growl, reminding me of the other option I had available—by force.

I marched over, yanking the door open to throw myself in. "For someone who doesn't want to drag around a dead mortal, you sure enjoy hinting at the fact you'd love nothing more than my death."

He looked over me with an unmoved expression, probably fantasizing about it.

"Don't try and envision it too hard there," I groaned as I buckled in.

The corner of his lips kicked up before he turned to pull out. Despite the A/C being on full blast, the cab was overly heated with static energy. A nagging sensation clawed at my arm, digging down to my bone until it felt as if they were vibrating. I tucked it into my side and tried to focus on the passing cars. I didn't want to ask Erius about it. If it wasn't silence he responded with, it was riddles that didn't answer my question without me having to ask for more.

Other than the attacking discomfort, taking a car was preferable over the bus since Erius wanted to take me to the cemetery for some reason. I haven't yet taken the bus that far, but I was sure it would take too long, and I had work at noon.

"Do you know how to get there?" I asked, pulling out my phone to get the navigation. As I typed in the cemetery name, a text notification dropped down.

> Hey, I have a new recipe
> to make and I was wondering
> if you'd help out.
> -Andrew

My stomach tightened at the true meaning behind the text. It wasn't his first time asking me to help out so I wasn't new to what he's really asking for—date or at least his way of easing into one. Even if I was up for it, now would not be the best of times to be out dating. Not with this dark cloud around me.

I tapped the notification bar to see what else had come in. Ever since Amber's announcement of her gifts, I didn't want to miss when Jaz and Mickey found theirs. Several bars filled the screen, mostly of social media notifications. I scrolled down to the last one, freezing at the name. My muscles locked, clenching my jaw as I looked over the message.

Missed Call: Parasite #2
Voice message from: Parasite #2 — 3 min 06 sec

That's three minutes and six seconds too long. I slid the bar to the left and hit delete before I allowed any questions to ruin my day. I hadn't spoken to my siblings in years, and I didn't plan to any time soon. I thought they would get the hint by now.

I flipped back to the maps app to find directions when Erius pulled to a stop in a near vacant parking lot. Only one other person was parked far off by the cemetery office.

"How did you know…" The slam of the car door cut me off as he left and headed toward the entrance without me.

Always so rude.

I got out, taking my time as I followed along behind him, not stopping until he reached the hidden entrance gate, cluttered with overgrown vines and bushes. An enormous willow tree hung over the gate to drape its long branches over the sign in an intimidating fashion. Pink rose bushes poked through the black steel fence that surrounded the stones, hinting that it was managed, just not in this general area.

By the time I caught up to him, he was examining the closed off gate. With a brief inspection, it was obvious this area was closed off to hold more plots and instead of removing the gate for a full fence, they just let the plants take over.

"I don't think we can get in this way."

He moved his hands over the blockade, creating the same vapor as before. With a low echoing groan, fog began to seep out from the fence line, crawling to our feet and spreading up the foliage and iron. It twisted about the vines and leaves, engulfing them until they were no more. It did the same with the iron gate, dissolving it to nothing before our eyes. Once everything was displaced, it left an opening into the cemetery, spilling a mossy, sour wet wood scent out over us and filling my nostrils with an irritating itch.

"Why are we here?" I groaned, rubbing at my nose.

"You said you saw a spirit. With that and what happened the other night…"

"What happened the other night?" I interjected.

He glared at me for a long moment before turning to enter the opening as he spoke. "The other night you projected your essence. I want to see what more you are capable of."

Projected my essence? What the fuck was he talking about? I followed behind, entering the cemetery through the new gate. It felt as if I crossed through a bubble or sticky film that coated me, causing my skin to become increasingly sensitive to the rough clothes I wore.

"What does that mean?"

He looked to my hands as he spoke. "When you removed my shoe from the bed. Your hands produced power."

I pulled my hands up to inspect them, as if that would give me any answers or replicate it. "Ok? Can you explain what that is or means?"

"No, you will find out for yourself." He grabbed my hand and tugged me onto a patch of grass with a few headstones lined together. A pressing weight fell on me as he pulled me closer to the first grave.

Once he released me, my skin ignited with a prickling sensation. "Why am I so itchy all of a sudden?" I groaned as the irritations intensified.

"It will fade. Call to this one," he ordered.

"Call to this one? Who is *this one*? How would I call to them?" I probed.

Erius's eyes darkened and his nostrils flared. A low rumbling growl emerged from deep in his chest. I don't know what kind of display it was, but it did nothing. I continued to look at him, waiting for a response. I made an expression that I hope read "proceed" when he didn't say anything.

"Push out your intended energy. Which is calling upon..." he looked over the headstone, "a Charles Rhodes." Still, a very vague explanation, but that was probably as much as I'd get from him.

I turned to the final resting place of Charles Rhodes and closed my eyes. I took a moment to clear my mind and center myself to focus on the person I had never met or seen. I took in another deep breath, balling it in my chest as I focused on the name. With my hands hovering over his grave, I called out to him as instructed.

"Hey! Charles, you there?" I asked casually.

The demon yanked me back with an irritated growl. "Is this a game to you, Mortal?"

"If you would explain things in a way I could understand—"

"I cannot explain to you how to sense and feel the energy around you. Now, what do you intend to do?" he interjected.

I looked back to the gravestone, taking a moment to feel the heavy, chilling weight of the spirits that surrounded us.

"To see a soul," I said slowly.

"And how would *you* feel you would call to them?" he asked again, this time his voice was smoother, like it had been the night of the deal. I let his words rest on my ears for a moment.

It wasn't that he wasn't trying to help me; he was, in his weird way. But they were my powers, so all of this was a personal practice. He wouldn't be able to give the answers.

I closed my eyes again, envisioning my focus as energy moving through my arms, concentrating on that feeling as it pushed to my palms where the warmth of it began zapping across the tips of my fingers. With another deep breath I held my hand over the grave and sent the energy down into the earth. Before the heat left me, I caught hold of it, gripping it like a rope. I pulled up on the taut connection, ensuring I had reached something before drawing it out.

Chilling air poured down on me with a slight breeze that lifted the hair on my arms. My eyes cranked open to find a stout man with white, glowing eyes. His body wasn't solid, nor was it completely translucent. The headstone was still visible through his ghostly body, but it was obscured and distorted.

"Hello?" I greeted kindly.

The man's eyes rounded as he looked from me to Erius with a wide gape.

"Can he not hear me?" I asked Erius.

"He can hear just fine," he said before turning back to the ghost, "Speak, ghoul." The thunderous demand sent the man shriveling back.

"You don't have to be mean!" I hissed to the demon before returning softer eyes to the man. Erius chuckled with a wave of his hand and stepped back out of my way.

"Sorry about him," I offered with another step forward.

"You can see me?" the ghost stuttered out, his vacant eyes darting from me to Erius.

"I don't think I would be speaking to the wind." I laughed.

The ghostly body began to shudder and cower back towards his grave. "Are you here to take me to Hell?"

Erius leaned around me to look over the headstone once more. "It says you passed in 1993. It is a tad late for your journey."

I wanted to ask what he meant, but Charles began sputtering

incoherently as he looked over the stone for himself.

"1993," he finally muttered, "What year is it?"

I looked to Erius, ready to ask but he swiftly answered before I had the chance, "Time is not the same for them."

"Oh," I turned back to the man. "It's 2022."

His eyes widened even more as he looked about the cemetery. "If you are not here to take me, why is a demon with you?" the man whispered to me, his eyes on Erius.

I looked to the demon in question, seeing the human form he'd been in for the last four days. His lips pulled up into a devilish, fang baring grin as he looked over the ghostly man.

"He's a human," I lied, but the heat of Erius's body consumed me more now than earlier. A large mass hovered over me, and I didn't even consider it was him.

"Spirits will see me as I am, no matter the cover," Erius explained.

"It has deceived you!" The man gasped.

I held in a laugh. In a way, he wasn't wrong nor was he entirely correct. "Only slightly."

Erius leaned down so that his lips were at my ear. The sudden contact froze me still. He did not care to touch me unless it was to tug me around. The heat of his breath brushed over my skin as he spoke, lifting the hairs on the back of my neck. "Now, try and control him."

"What?" I whipped my head around to face him, surprised by the close proximity he suddenly allowed. The vanilla scent of his breath dazed me instantly, but he didn't move away. Instead, he grabbed hold of my wrists and guided my hands up.

"Envision what you want to do and do it. Control him," he ordered. It was difficult to envision anything other than the demon touching me. His sudden closeness was far from what I was used to over the last four days.

He moved to the other side of my head to direct me some more. "You will feel it when you are connected," he whispered. I could only imagine how frightening it looked to the ghost as his eyes widened further.

I definitely felt something but it wasn't the ghost in front of me. My body heated up, flushing my skin until it was sensitive to the touch. I pulled away from him and his new infatuation. His arms fell to his side, but his hardened expression never changed.

We glared at each other for a moment more before he cocked his chin toward the spirit.

The man looked at us in disbelief. He trembled wildly as he took another step back. "A witch!" he cried out as he pointed an accusatory finger my way.

"But I'm a good witch," I said in an attempt at soothing the situation, but the ghost was having none of that.

"Witch! Demon!" he cried before chanting a prayer under his breath.

"That will not help you." Erius chuckled darkly.

"Just calm down," I urged, taking a step toward the man with my hands out. The second his eyes locked with mine, he froze stiff and silent. A tingly warmth rippled over me, clinging to me like a tight dress.

"Hm, good job, Mortal," Erius praised, walking around the ghost as he inspected it. "Lift your arm."

I'm not sure what I did or how to do it again, but I did as requested, lifting my left arm high in the air. The ghost did the same, mirroring me down to each steady breath. I lifted my right leg next, watching the ghost do the same. An overcharged excitement shot through me. I dropped my arm and leg, noticing a greenish hue floating around my fist.

The concentrated essence Erius mentioned. The green flame flickered around my hand and fingers. I examined the odd mist that radiated from my palms like fire. It wasn't cold or hot, and it didn't cause any pain. It was as if there was nothing there entirely. I looked back to the spirit, still following my every movement, even the mist that came from my hands, though his was more of a white smoke.

"Interesting," Erius hummed. The ghost and I looked at him with curious expressions. He lifted his scarred arm, shifting it to the black-clawed hand with the twisting black mist and rested it on the man's ghostly shoulder. Mist and smoke wrapped around the spirit as Erius pushed him down into the grave once more.

The grinding rocks and soil churned together as Charles disappeared into the earth, cutting the connection I had made. The itchy feeling returned with full vengeance as it engulfed my arm in the irritating tingling.

"Was that it?" I asked, scratching the shit out of my right arm. Erius looked at my infliction and nodded before turning back to the headstone. "Yes, it was most insightful," he said. The corners of his lips twitched from a frown to a flat line as he thought about whatever it was that occupied his mind. I, on the other hand, had things to share.

I pulled out my phone and immediately began filling in the girls on what had happened. Once the message was sent, I looked back to Erius who looked just as ready to leave as I was. Granted, it was fun to learn a new power, but it was draining, and I still had a full shift to trudge through at work.

We headed out to the car. This time he was polite enough to wait until I was in before starting it up with a loud, unnecessary noise. The clock read 11:45 and we were a good thirty minutes away.

"Will you be able to make it to the shop by noon?" I quizzed.

He threw it into gear and revved the engine once more but didn't respond. I'd have to take that as a yes. Thankfully I opened and didn't have to really worry about being a few minutes late. Not that I had to before, I just didn't like it.

He sped out of the lot and onto the road, taking the freeway with ease as he weaved between cars. The stolen GT fit perfectly between the tiniest spaces that even I thought were far too small for the car's size, yet somehow he managed to glide through smoothly and get us to the shop lot at 11:59. Thank gods I couldn't feel fear, because that would have been a highly stressful ride.

I exited the car and searched through my bag for the shop key. Erius's door slammed shut with his exit, which reminded me. With all the discoveries from the morning, I forgot to figure something out for him to do while I worked. I knew I hadn't any clients to read for and I'd be with Amber and Jasmine, so I wouldn't have to explain much if he came in.

I climbed out, ready to ask him, but he was already halfway across the lot. It's like he can read my mind or something. Gods I hope not. I trotted along behind him, taking three steps for his obnoxiously large one. By the time I caught up, he was already waiting by the door.

"Do you do everything fast as fuck?" I panted.

His gaze raked over me, a small smirk curved his lips. "Depends."

I narrowed my eyes on him. Something about the way he answered was weird. Probably because he may have been teasing, but I had yet to see him crack a joke. Maybe with the loss of emotions, I lost a sense of being able to read others as well.

The doors unlocked with an echoing click and a chime followed as we stepped in. The overpowering aroma of herbs and spices filled my nose and clung to my tongue.

Someone must have forgotten to seal the herbs again. The last time Amber came into a jar left open, everyone had to endure the hour-long lecture from her. I loved her, but I didn't want to deal with that today. I walked to the back to see what was left out. But upon further inspection, I found nothing out of place or uncovered. Everything was perfectly sealed down tight.

I shrugged and got to work pulling everything out. While I got all the tea mixes ready, Erius took to inspecting the lobby as if he were going to give me an in-depth analysis of it. He followed me upstairs, doing the same while I pulled out all the displays, entertaining himself by looking over all the books we carried.

After ensuring the shop was ready, I took my post at the upstairs counter.

"You can hang out in the room. I have more books in there," I offered as I waited for the computer to kick on.

He didn't respond as he stepped into the room, but he wasn't in there long before returning.

I tried to ignore him, focusing on work by skimming through the upcoming order and adding what was needed. He moved around the counter to where I was, heating my skin with his presence. I wasn't sure what had gotten into him, but he needed to back the fuck up off me for a second.

"You cannot be back here," I muttered, turning to face him. He held up one of the raven skulls in one hand and a fox skull in the other.

"Why do you keep touching my stuff?" I asked blankly. He set them on the counter beside me and waited. As I waited for an answer, the same itchy feeling from the morning spread over me.

"It's rude," I add.

Black mist seeped from his fingers, covering the raven skull. Before anything more could happen, I figured it best to let him know of the security system in place.

"There are cameras up here," I informed him.

The black vapor dissipated instantly as his hand dropped. He picked up the skulls and headed back to the room without a word or second glance.

I followed behind him to ensure he placed the skulls back, but also, I was a bit interested in what he was about to do.

He set the two skulls on the center of the back altar and leaned against it with his arms folded over his chest. "Call to them," he instructed.

I looked from him to the skulls. First he wanted me to call to a spirit, now he wanted me to call to skulls. I wanted to see him *call* to something.

"And how do I do that?" I poked.

He pinched the bridge of his nose with an exasperated sigh as he often did when irritated by my questioning. "I cannot explain everything to you, Mortal."

"You do it then. Go on," I ordered back.

A low, rumbling growl came from him as he gave me a heated glare.

"Yeah, yeah. Roar to you, too. Now, *please*, show me," I ordered.

His nostrils flared with an irritated huff, but he held his hand over the raven skull to demonstrate. Black mist swirled from his fingertips and covered the skull in seconds.

The vapor spilled off the edge of the altar and left a ghostly raven in its place. Its head twitched from side to side as it looked between us. With a loud, echoing cry, it took to the air and flew around the room three times before landing back on the altar.

"That's pretty cool, Mr. Goat," I shot.

His lips fell at the name as he turned back to the altar. "Call to the fox," he ordered bluntly, no further explanation provided.

"Hey, I know this sounds wild, but there is this word we use here. It's called '*please.*' We use it when we want something," I explained as if explaining to a child. He didn't respond with words, but his expression was more than enough.

I turned to the fox skull and held my hand over it with closed eyes. In the cemetery he told me to envision what I wanted. I was sure this would require the same.

Flashes of a silver fox crossed my mind, a gentle and majestic creature with fur as smooth as silk. I thought of the cute creature bounding through tall blades of grass as a feeling of connection heated my palm. I opened my eyes, watching as a green mist poured out of my hands onto the skull. It wasn't a majestic dance as Erius's vapor was—more of a spilling mess as it fell over the bone and altar top.

An icy prickle spread over my hand and drained out with the vapor. It cleared out just as Erius's had, leaving behind a ghoulish fox with green smoke circling its feet. It tilted its head at me and twitched its tail before bounding into my arms. Warm fur snuggled my skin as if the fox were living.

"Oh, I can feel him!" I gasped as it continued to snuggle into me.

I looked up at Erius. A slight look of disbelief crossed his face as he looked over the creation.

"Death is the source of your power. You'll want to keep a bit of it with you. The more of it you can draw from, the more you can use it to your benefit."

"Will any bones work?" I inquired.

He looked around the room and my grand collection. "You can draw from bones and any type of dead matter. However, to reanimate them like this, you will need the skull." He tilted his head down to the fox I had *"reanimated."*

I ran my hands through the fur with a smile. "What else can I do?"

Erius leaned down to be at eye level with me. I wasn't sure why he felt this was the best way to speak with me, but it felt patronizing. "I am growing exponentially interested in that as well."

"You mean you don't know?" I said with a raised brow.

"I gave you the power you asked for. That is all I know." He reached out to the fox, receiving a snarl and snap instantly. It would seem even my animal spirits disliked him. I giggled and set my new friend on the altar, pulling back the energy I had sent out to it.

Smoke swirled around my hand and up my arm until the fox was nothing more than a skull. With the number of bones I kept in the shop and all the ones in my van, I had a near endless supply of energy to draw from all around me. If that was the case, it would be best to figure out how to incorporate them in my everyday attire.

"Well, what else can you show me?" I pressed, confused by his sudden lack of knowledge. He literally just showed me how and had been guiding my powers all day. Now he didn't know shit.

"It is basic death magic. As for the extent of what more you can do, that is to be determined."

"*These* are basic?" I snorted.

"Yes. The rest will appear just as your emotions will fade. Consider it a trade." He looked about the skulls again with a half grin.

"Show me something else and I'll try and do it," I demanded.

He scoffed, his eyes still on the shelf. "In due time, Mortal."

"What was the point of you showing me now?" Before he could respond, the entrance bell rang as customers stepped in.

"I was growing bored of you not doing anything with the gift you summoned me for. It was beginning to feel as though I was attached to you for nothing." He turned to look at the door with a hard scowl.

"The ones who speak for you have arrived."

Before I could answer, they were stomping up the stairs and across the lobby floor like a great stampede. I spun around to open the door before they decided to transfer that energy to their fists and pound the wood down.

I flung it open, pausing them halfway through the lobby. "Why are y'all stomping up the steps like that?"

Jasmine lifted her brow at me and then to the one behind me. Amber caught sight of him as well, their expressions twisting to the same hate from Saturday.

"See you're still here," Amber spat at him.

A soft breeze blew a loose curl forward as the heat of his body pushed against my back. The heavy scent of vanilla filled the air, stunning my senses as usual. But clearly, it hadn't the same effect on them as they stepped back with wide eyes.

"Are you afraid of him?" I chuckled.

He spoke into my ear just as he had in the cemetery, dazing me further with the warming smell. "Their humanity will run differently than yours." He switched to the opposite side just as he had earlier with Charles. "Fear is a stronger emotion for them both. You did not run on it as they did."

Their eyes widened once again as if they were looking at a monster. I turned to find the demon looking as mortal as he did a moment ago, unfrightening as ever.

"What are you doing to them?" I snapped. He looked down to me with a growing grin.

"I lifted the veil of my cover from their eyes. They see me as I am," he said with a vindictive smile.

I turned back to Jaz and Amber and their even wider eyes. "Are you saying you are really some big monster right now and I'm just seeing a human?"

"No," he said flatly before turning back into the room to look over the books I had on the shelf. I glared at him through slit lids, always so vague.

"Stay in here. Try not to destroy my skulls," I ordered to him as I stepped out, shutting the door behind me. "Sorry about that."

"Mina, what are you doing in that small room with him?" Jaz flustered.

"He isn't as big as whatever it is you saw, and he was showing me what I can do." I shrugged.

"And how's that going for you? Easy, I suppose," Jaz snarked.

"No, why would it be easy?"

They shared an awkward glance before turning back to me. "We don't have a live-in demon to show us the way."

"As if he makes it any easier. You all seemed to be having a more eventful practice. All I had was seeing dead people up until today." I laughed.

The door behind me creaked open and the hovering fright the girls held on their faces returned.

Jaz's eyes remained wide as she pulled me closer to her. "You have been stuck in your van with *that* for three days?" she whispered.

I turned to look at Erius and his basic human form I'd been seeing. When I looked back to Jaz and Amber, they looked awestruck.

"Erius hasn't been that bad. A little annoying and in the way, but he hasn't been completely rude," I informed them.

"Erius? Is that his name?" Amber shot.

"That or Mr. Goat."

The girls gave an awkward giggle as their eyes fell on the demon once more.

"Why must you three speak of me as if I am not present?" he grumbled as he came up beside me.

"Oh, wow. Listen to how he speaks. So proper," Jaz gasped. I wasn't sure why I hadn't thought about how he spoke before. Despite being rude and rough, he didn't yell or swear or even really say vulgar things at all which, for a demon, I would have thought would have been their M.O.

I looked back at him. He had in fact been a decent person as far as vulgarity went.

"Mr. Goat, do you cuss?" I teased.

To my surprise, the corner of his lip twitched up a bit. "Do not test me, Mortal. My patience for *you* is thin," he warned, doing that odd eye thing again. It didn't seem as aggressive or threatening as his usual warnings went.

Jaz shifted her gaze between us, her brows furrowing with each second before she snapped her eyes closed.

"Are you alright?" Amber asked.

Jaz lightly shook her head and peeled her eyes open. "Yeah, I'm fine, just dizzy."

"Let's get you downstairs for some tea. Were you in the studio all night again?" Amber consoled as she guided her toward the stairs.

Jaz nodded weakly as they made their way down.

Jasmine was known to get attached to whatever painting she was working on, sometimes spending days in her studio until Amber, Meklit, or I went knocking to pull her out. Her few days at the shop were a nice break from the paint fumes, but she may need to consider a few more days out of the studio because clearly, the paints were beginning to affect her.

I did not want to spend my free shift locked away in the room with Erius, and he didn't particularly enjoy their company. As long as he didn't mess with anything, I turned to tell him not to harm my skulls if he chose to stay in the room, but his attention was hard on the window, staring into the orange and purple sky over the sea.

"I'm going downstairs with them. Try not to bust anything," I said, making my way to the steps.

"It is going to rain," he muttered.

"Whoopie," I say dryly as I descend the stairs.

Amber and Jaz were standing around the tea jars by the time I reached the lobby, a kettle already prepped and heating on the burner behind them.

"So, have you noticed anything else?" I asked as I joined them.

"Like what?" Amber shrugged.

"Your emotions?" I pried. They shared a look between themselves before looking back to me.

"What do you mean?" Amber asked slowly.

"Without our souls, we don't have a sense of humanity. At least that is what Erius explained to me. In his words, our emotions will slowly slip away from us. Have you not noticed anything?"

"Well," Jaz began, "I wouldn't say I am lacking anything. That's why I couldn't get to bed last night. I had so much inspiration to put out. It felt as if it was an endless supply of motivation. I didn't work on one piece; I completed seven of them before I noticed the sun rising."

Amber and I gawked at her and her words. No wonder she wasn't feeling well now.

"That would explain why you are dizzy. What about you, Amber?" I turned to her, waiting for her response as she thought back over the last few days in her life.

"Less anxious, I suppose."

"Ok, but having less emotions wasn't what we traded our souls for, Meems," Jaz popped next. "All I can do is feel crystals and see auras—and I'm still not even sure about how much of that I can understand."

"The full extent of your gifts will present themselves in time," Erius said from the bottom of the steps.

Amber clicked her cheeks as she looked over him. "And we are to take your word for it?" she challenged.

"If you do not try, how are they to develop?" he asked as he made his way over. They took a step back into the counter as he came up and stopped at my side. Why he suddenly wanted to be so near was questionable, and it clearly tripped them out.

"Stop doing that," I said to Erius as I turned to him.

An amused, slick grin rested on his lips as he broke his gaze with them to slowly turn toward me.

"They speak to me less this way."

CHAPTER FOURTEEN

Mira

I wouldn't say the afternoon was as relaxing as it usually was. Sure, it was slow where customers were concerned, but the tension between the girls and Erius never subsided. Mostly because he seemed to get a kick out of taunting them with whatever version they saw of him. Keeping a pesteringly close distance between us as he followed me around the shop.

"Meems, will you be able to come out Thursday?" Jaz asked me as we headed for the door after closing.

"Yeah. Why wouldn't I?" As soon as the words left my mouth, I knew what she meant. Her eyes shot up to Erius who stood to my left.

"He's a demon, not my dad. I'm sure he can find something to do nearby."

We stepped out to a building storm. Thick and heavy thundering clouds swiftly blanketed the sky above us with crackling lightning that sizzled across it. The flashing lights were soon followed by the heavy crack of booming thunder that only seemed to send down more vengeful icy drops to pelt our skin.

"I'll see you Thursday, you guys. I'm out of here," Amber called as she ran off to find shelter in her car.

Jaz pulled me in for a tight hug. "Will you be ok?" she whispered.

I pulled away with a laugh as the cold rain began to slowly saturate my hair.

"I've been fine this long. I'll see you tomorrow," I assured her, turning away from her to head back to the van. Erius followed behind, finally at more than an arm's distance from me.

I should have listened to him earlier when he said it was going to rain, not that it would have prepared me for the storm we were struggling through now.

"How did you know?" I asked him as we crossed the street. He looked at me blankly but didn't answer so I pointed up to the sky, "The rain. How'd you know?"

His sopping wet hair clung to his face and dripped over his eyes, but he didn't seem to care as he looked up. "I could smell it."

"You can smell it before it starts?" I pressed, more interested in what he could do.

"It had already started about sixteen kilometers – uh – ten miles out when I caught it." He gave a disinterested shrug and dropped his attention back to me. His brows pinched at the center and the color of his eyes flickered, illuminating from the darkness that surrounded them, most likely through with answering, but I was only getting started. We crossed the lot toward the van while more questions bubbled up.

Ten miles out. "You can smell things that far?"

"Further."

As interesting as it sounded, it also seemed unpleasant considering we were by the ocean. Most days it was a nice fresh sea breeze, but during the summer times, on exceptionally hot days, it smelled like gutted fish. I couldn't imagine that being pleasant.

By the time we got to the van, sticky rain dripped down into my socks and boots. My hair was heavy with water and my clothes were soaking down to my bra. The chilling wind and rain bit at my skin with an icy vengeance.

Prometheus could be heard carrying on with his anxious meowing behind the door. I hurried to find the keys and struggled with sticking it in the lock with shaking hands. Once the door was finally open, Erius and I stumbled in, dragging muddied sand over the floor.

I kicked my boots off and tossed them under the van to dry. When I turned, Erius was surprisingly doing the same.

Other than dinner, I really wanted to wash out the rainwater from my hair and off my body, but asking Erius to wait outside wouldn't be fair.

"I'm going to shower. I don't expect you to wait out in the rain. Can I trust you won't do some weird demon shit?"

He looked me over with a raised brow and, without responding, headed to the front of the van to sit in the passenger seat. While he watched the battling waves, I took to gathering clean clothes and a towel.

Normally, I would wait for the water to heat up, but undressing and waiting would have to be done at the same time. I stepped in, took the soaked clothes off, and maneuvered them into the string hamper in the side cabinet. I tossed one last look through the small crack in the curtain to ensure Erius was looking away and turned the faucet to the hottest it could go. Not that it would be hot coming out.

The ice drops stabbed at my skin, shoving me until I was pressed against the equally chilling wall.

"Ah!" I cried out as the water hit my feet, burning them with the cold. The chilling drops gradually heated, allowing me to peel from the wall and rinse off properly. Once the sticky feeling had washed away, I grabbed my co-wash and began on my hair.

After scrubbing my body and rinsing everything a final time, I cut the water and peeked out to ensure Erius was still where I left him. He sat facing the windshield out into the storming ocean. I moved to the other side and slid my hand out of the shower to the empty hook that usually held a towel. I poked my head out to search the hook then the floor, finding both empty. Instead, the towel sat neatly folded on my bed along with my clean set of clothes and a pile Erius must have set aside for himself.

Fuck.

I looked back to him, his head still facing away from me stuck on the world outside. With my eyes darting between the bed and the demon, I slowly opened the shower curtain and took a silent step out. I checked back with the front, Erius completely unaware. I closed the distance to my bed and quickly snatched the towel to fling around myself. I gave one last look back, seeing the back of his head, and released the burning breath I had been holding the entire time.

I leaned over, grabbing my clothes to return to the shower. Turning around, I nearly crashed into Erius, now suddenly up my ass again. He stood a breath away, leaning over me to accommodate for his height. How he managed to move around so quickly was beyond me, but his sudden appearances at my back were becoming increasingly annoying.

"Why do you keep doing that?" I asked blankly. His jaw flexed as he leaned closer to me, his gaze holding mine. I sucked in a breath and leaned back, the bed providing little help as his chest pushed against mine. A shudder shook me despite the fight I made to contain it, a response that didn't go unnoticed by him as his gaze slipped down to my hands gripping the towel at my chest.

My body flushed and heart sunk to the pit of my stomach, an idiotic betrayal of my own body yet again. I swallowed against the hard rock in my throat, ready to push him away, but my hands clung to the towel covering me.

His lips turned down as he pulled away. The rough cloth of whatever he grabbed brushed against my arm as he brought it between us, thankfully giving me a reason to look away. In his hand, he held the other towel for himself. With a few more grueling seconds ticking past, he turned away and took the small step to enter the shower, releasing me from whatever trance he held me in to finally breathe.

I couldn't say I didn't like the way I felt when he looked at me, but I didn't need to be lusting over a demon that would be gone soon.

I figured he'd need more privacy than the shower would allow, so I quickly threw on my panties and shorts under the towel and tossed on the tank. I kept my entire body facing the back of the van as I gathered my mirror and hair supplies. It took a bit of moving around before I found a decent angle that kept my back to him without also giving me a clear view of the shower through the mirror.

With the passenger seat in view behind me, I began the process of braiding my hair for the night. I parted it down the middle and had completed one side before the shower cut off and the curtains scraped across the metal bar. I tried to focus on my reflection as I combed through my curls, but he drifted into view.

With his back toward me as I did him, the towel wrapped around his waist gave a clear view of two large scars slashed across both of his shoulder blades. Not a clean looking wound, one that looked to have been tortuous to endure. Identical in size and placement but uneven sawing and tearing clearly occurred.

He ran his hands through his wet hair, flexing his back as he did. I hadn't taken the time to really look at him, though, he hadn't had his naked back to me. I pulled my attention back to my still unfinished braid, taking my time to twist the strands and keep my eyes trained on my hair. That did not stop my peripheral vision from seeing him moving around behind me.

Sweet Gaia, please help me.

A black mist suddenly appeared, wrapping around the towel at his waist and transforming it into a pair of what looked to be sweatpants of the same color. I spun around with my eyes on the pants as he turned to face me, filling my line of sight with more than I needed.

This is not what I mean, Ms. Mother Earth!

I did not think demons would be attractive. None of anything I have seen has depicted them as such, but perhaps Joseph and Guillaume Geefs's depiction of Lucifer wasn't so far off.

My gaze shot up over his oddly toned body up to his hardened gaze as heat flushed my cheeks.

"Did you just turn my towel into sweatpants?" I asked, and he gave one stiff nod.

"You can keep them," I said. My stomach rumbled, reminding me of the delivery I never ordered. With a quick search, I spotted my phone and snatched it up to look for something that would still be open.

"Do you have any food requests?" I asked him, knowing that he would probably eat what I ordered for myself.

"Whatever you are having," he grumbled.

Predictable. I pulled up the Anywhere Delivery app and typed in my usual order, marked it for two, and hit send. After a few seconds, a notification pulled up on the screen, alerting me the meal would be to us within the next thirty minutes. I tossed the phone down and returned to braiding my hair. It was a nightly task he watched every time, so I didn't know why I thought this instance would be any different. But he stayed behind me with a hard expression as he studied my hair which would have been easy to ignore if he wasn't directly behind me with his dick print right over my shoulder.

The heat of his eyes burned into the back of my head as I finished the final braid. I dropped my hands and glared back at him through the mirror with the same dark expression as his.

"Boo," I snipped, but he just continued to stare me down. I gathered everything in my arms and turned to him. "You have this whole van to sit in, and you choose to be up my ass."

He glanced back to the front, which wasn't far. With a shrug, he stepped back to the chair and sat with his body turned enough that he still faced me while I put everything up. These were the odd, scrutinizing looks I didn't care for from him.

After setting the supplies away, I pulled down the sheet for the projector and got to work setting that up. His focus never left me the entire time.

"If you take a picture, it will last longer," I grumbled, leaning back to flip through the streaming apps. Before it could even load up, he came to stand beside the bed to glare down at me, or better yet, my hair.

"You have an odd infatuation with my hair."

"You have an odd infatuation with my body," he countered.

My face flushed with heat again as I turned back to my phone. "No, I don't."

He sat on the side of the bed and leaned against the back wall, his gaze still on me, a small smirk curving his lips. "I give you the power to raise the dead from their graves and you use it to grow out your hair?"

"I didn't use it to grow out my hair. It's called shrinkage," I explained, but it was clear by his expression he hadn't a clue what I was talking about.

I released a heavy sigh. "My hair is curly, as you may have noticed. The weight of the water stretches it. When it dries, it curls back up and makes it look shorter. My hair is quite long."

He didn't respond, not that I was expecting him to have much to say in return. I did, however, expect him to stop examining my hair so closely, but that continued until a heavy pounding shook the van. I jumped off the bed, being sure to keep my body from touching his as I did and crossed the short distance to the door.

I slid it open to greet the delivery woman who held a white paper bag in hand. She looked up to us with widening eyes and a slack jaw while her gaze danced between me and the demon.

"Hello," I said impatiently. If he *was* my man, she was rude to just stare like that and I'm hungry.

"Oh yeah, sorry. Uh, $28.50," she sputtered.

The weight of my right braid lifted from my shoulder as he examined it. I waved his hand away and reached for the tip on the counter. He didn't drop it immediately, so I waved him off again as I traded the money for the food.

"Thank you," I said as kindly as possible, but I slammed the door in her face harder than I intended. With my hair still captive in his hand, I moved to the counter to set the food down. Once my hands were free, I spun on my heels, whipping my hair from his grasp. He did his little eye thing and gave me his devilish half-smile as he dropped his arm. With one small step he was crowding me between my counter and bed with a twisted grin. My heart sped up, banging against my chest which only grew his smile more. This close, I could see he had a small dimple on his cheek deepening the longer I was stuck on it.

"What do you want?" I barked.

An ominous rumbling surrounded us, and I was pretty sure it was a laugh, just not a mortal one.

He leaned into me, shuffling through the bag to grab his food at an agonizingly slow pace, locking me between his chest and the counter where the faint smell of spiced vanilla drifted down from him. I tried to fight the full body tremble, but I bit back the soft whimper at the familiar ache between my thighs. His smile widened as he pulled back his takeout box and moved around me to his spot back on my bed, taking the heat and smell with him.

He sat there with a triumphant smirk on his stupid lips. He was doing some freaky demon shit to me. There was no way he was oblivious to what he was causing. *He knows what the fuck he's doing and he's doing it on purpose.*

"What is this? Did you get bored of being quiet and moved on to… Whatever *this* is you are doing?" I snapped.

"You can say that." He chuckled softly.

I stared at him in disbelief, just another personality of his to keep up with, though him being friendlier wouldn't be entirely bad. We shared a bed anyway.

Ugh, listen to yourself. You can't fuck a demon, Mina.

But who really made that rule? I could just ask, there really wasn't anything to lose by him saying no. Especially if I knew full and well he would say no. But what if he didn't? What if ten minutes from now I could be getting my guts rearranged? It would just be casual; I could do casual sex.

Casual sex with the demon who took my soul. Because that sounds justifiable.

"Are you going to eat, Mortal?" he asked, pulling me from my conundrum.

"Huh? Oh, yeah."

Stupid, sounding just like the delivery girl.

I grabbed my box and climbed my way over to my side of the bed. Setting the food down beside me, I pulled open whatever streaming service I had left my phone on. I flipped through a few categories, unsure if he'd ever even watched movies. He didn't seem to care about what I was putting on before, but I felt perhaps it would be kind if I included him.

"Do you like movies? Are they a thing in these Six Circles of yours?" I asked.

He took a bite of the burger as if I hadn't asked him anything. I waited for him to finish chewing before deciding if I'd need to be more direct.

"I'm a demon, Mortal, not an alien," he said with furrowed brows.

"I don't know anything about your world," I argued.

He pinched the bridge of his nose between his thumb and forefinger, clearly annoyed with the questioning while he ate. "Yes. I know what movies are."

"What would you like to watch?"

"I do not believe you would know of any of the movies I prefer."

"The film industry a bit different where you're from?" I teased.

"The movies I enjoy are much older than you, Mortal," he said. He hadn't mentioned his age before now, and I was a bit curious as to how old the demon I shared my van with truly was. Ok, I was super curious about it. I didn't really want to be lusting after a thousand-year-old demon, now that I thought about it. I didn't want to be fantasizing about a demon at all. But I was, so maybe his age would put me off.

"Mr. Goat, are you trying to say you are old as fuck?"

His lips kicked up as he turned to me. "I have watched this planet grow for eons."

I blinked at him, taken aback. Eons? Multiple? He wasn't just old as fuck. He was ancient as fuck.

"Oh!" I blurted. "Why do you look like you are maybe pushing thirty?"

"This is the mortal body I have always gotten. I do not know its physical age."

"So, you've been here before? What do you mean you have always gotten this body? You didn't choose it?" I poked, pulling my food out from its box.

"It is a mortal form. I have as much control over how it appears as you do with yours." He took a bite of his burger and chewed slowly, probably hoping I wouldn't ask anything more. But joke's on him.

"If you don't care for us so much, why do you come here?"

"It is not by desire, Mortal."

"So, you're forced? Why?" I pressed again, but he simply gave me the blank stare.

"You seem to have things ready for you when you come here. Do you have an ID, a wallet perhaps?" I pushed. If I wasn't going to learn about his previous times here, I guess I could try and find out his age.

He stopped chewing as he thought for a moment before a black vapor swirled between us. When it evaporated away, it left behind a black leather fold. As he went to wipe his hands on a napkin, I snatched the wallet and opened it to find the ID.

The date read July 27th, 1989, and it was currently July 19th.

"This says you're about to be thirty-three. Happy early birthday," I teased. "Or do you not really age, are you just frozen like this?"

"Just this." He leaned into me and took the ID to examine further with a lifted brow.

"It's better than being seventeen indefinitely," I whispered, very clearly aware of his proximity more than he was. He had been much too friendly and it was really affecting the whole "he's a demon who took my soul" argument. I pressed my hand to his bare chest and gave him a slight push. His skin was blazing hot, more so than I think it ever had been.

His body froze at the contact and his nostrils flared as he looked over me with his freaky demon eyes. The disproving disposition was a heavy reminder of what he was and why he was here. I pulled my hand, ignoring the sudden ache to place it back, and returned to my phone to keep busy.

Erius

The ocean was the only decent thing these mortals had going for them. It would be better if it took up more of the planet. Perhaps they could adapt to water living if they would just try.

I kept my eyes on the washing waves and not the silly mortal behind me. Not the fact that she was nude and only a few feet from me. I figured she would be easy to ignore, but this form was not reacting how I thought it would. It usually didn't find desire on its own until I went out and sought it myself. Now I could hardly even control it around her and that blasted scent.

Her long list of questions and curiosities mixed with my own didn't aid in trying to avoid her, either. We would be separated soon, after all, and she could go along her way with the gifts I have provided, free to practice and master them how she saw fit. Though it would be nice to see how far my gifts would expand with her.

Weight lifted from my shoulders at the consideration, warmer and more welcoming than the hollowing feeling that dug into me at the thought of never knowing. She was just a mortal I had been tethered to by her doing. I should not care to leave her here in the hands of that inadequate male.

The water to the shower turned off and my eyes immediately flashed up to the rearview mirror angled perfectly to face the shower. Her hand smoothed across the wall in search of something forgotten. She had left the towels on the bed before entering the tiny wash closet, clearly forgetting the placement now. I dropped my eyes to the water as her head poked out from the curtain. Her every movement begged for my attention as the sound clung to my ears. I forced myself forward, ignoring the urge to entertain any idea of her.

My past regard already forgotten amongst my form's reaction.

The metal rings of the curtain silently scraped against the pole as she pushed it back. One foot touched the floor, followed by a long pause, and then the other step fell silently. My eyes shot up to the mirror, catching sight of the delicate curve of her back. Water cascaded down her hips and thighs, soaking the floor as it dripped from her saturated hair. Before the final thread of sanity dwindled to nothing, she quickly covered herself.

What would I truly be risking? It was not like she would fight me if I eased into it. She leaned over the bed for something, I was not sure of. It was hard to focus on anything other than what the towel didn't cover, giving me view of her dripping cunt.

Heat raced to my groin, shooting me up and across the van instantly. My hands ached to grip down on her soft skin, to pull her to me and hold her there until we were both sure of what we wanted. Her sweet scent bloomed around me, fogging my focus. My muscles flexed, ready to grab hold of her when she suddenly turned with a gasp and wide-held eyes.

"Why do you keep doing that?" she pushed.

With her, I was beginning to feel unsure why I did anything. But her words pulled me back to reality, and most certainly the tightness I felt in my slacks.

I leaned over her, keeping hold of her gaze so she did not drop hers any lower. I clutched the second towel, pulling it between us to block the erection.

A wave of her arousal lofted about, stirring my dick again. She moved around me to the front of the van. I didn't wait to see what she was doing. I had other things on my mind.

I shut the curtain, released the clothes around me, and threw the water on in hopes the chilling liquid would put an end to the madness. But the water was warm, and all that plagued my mind was thoughts of how warm my mortal would be. I gripped my dick in one hand and braced myself against the wall with the other.

I began stroking hard and fast, envisioning her lips, her cunt, I wouldn't care what she allowed. The very image of her bent over the bed burned against my mind. If only she hadn't turned so soon, I would have ripped that flimsy towel from her. Just running my hand along her supple skin would be satisfying. The sound of her breathless moans, whispering my name. Just the thought sent chills down my spine.

I worked the building fire in the pit of my stomach, thinking of all the ways I'd fuck my mortal in whatever form she begged. Her perfectly soft lips around my cock were mind-numbing to even fantasize.

The building pressure had me seeing stars, but I continued to push myself until the euphoric release struck my body. I rocked back, pressing against the wall as best I could manage without making too much noise.

"Fuck," I breathed. My dick throbbed as the waves pulsated through me. The release was immaculate, but I couldn't continue like this for an unknown period of time. It was torturous in a different way than I had originally suspected being tethered to her would be.

This mortal shit sucks.

Once my body finally relaxed and I had control of it again, I washed with the soap she provided me, rinsed, and grabbed the towel. My mind felt clearer than before, but I would rather not look her in the face yet. I kept my back to her, changing her towel into a pair of pants that seemed most popular last time I visited the realm. When I had left, they appeared to be a big deal, and I wasn't sure if they still would be. But the van filled with her scent full of lust, and I figured that was answer enough.

I turned instinctively, locking eyes with hers. Blood pooled across her cheeks, flushing a golden bronze over her face.

"Did you just turn my towel into sweatpants?" she asked. Her voice may have appeared even and calm, but her body continued to betray her.

I nodded, keeping my mouth shut and the taste of her from my tongue. This limited space was enough to drive one mad, and it tormented me daily.

"You can keep them." She sighed before looking around herself and spotting the phone on the counter. She grabbed it, an appropriate distraction for us both.

"Any food requests?" she pressed, never willing to maintain any sort of silence.

"Whatever you are having," I pushed out, and she began tapping away the order once again.

When she was finished, she tossed it to the side and went back to work on her hair. Every morning she shortened it, but by night she grew it out, a complete misuse of the powers I had granted. She could do much more.

I watched her ritualistic process every time and still did not understand why she did this. What benefit did a mortal have in adjusting the length of their hair? I did not see the purpose.

My phone vibrated in my pocket, another perfect distraction for the moment. I pulled it out, expecting a response to a message I had sent before we left the apothecary.

He's still here.
But I have convinced him
that you are searching
and once you return, I will
notify him. I am
waiting on his departure.
-Alius

I ground my teeth as I glared at the words. I was trapped in this tin can, despite it being the safest place for the mortal until Dazron left and I could figure out what to do with her until the tether was broken.

My phone sounded off again, pulling me from my train of thought and filling me with more irritation.

Ennaza: What is taking you
so long? Are you having trouble ....

I opened the message and explained that my searches had led me down a more meticulous path, but otherwise facing no issues. She'd more than likely take that to Dazron and grant me more time in figuring out what to do with my new mortal.

This little endeavor had become more bothersome with each passing day. It was clear Dazron was anxious for whatever hit he planned, but this collection seemed to be most prized to him. Perhaps being kinder to the mortal would not hurt. She may be able to help me figure it out before too late.

I centered my attention back on the mortal who had returned to styling her hair. Her normally soft and gentle features were pointed with a small pinch between her brows as she focused intently on her task. Hopefully her lack of humanity wouldn't interfere.

"Boo!" she suddenly snipped, searing a pointed glare into me from the reflection.

CHAPTER FIFTEEN

Mira

Rough hands slid over my ass, pulling me into a comforting warmth. I rolled against it, feeling a firm grip dig into my skin. Reality clicked into place, shocking me back to my bed and whom I was forced to share it with.

"Hey!" I shouted as I jumped up, shuffling around the covers to flip the light on. The unbothered demon remained still in the bed.

"What are you doing?" I belted.

He stared at me for a moment as if to not understand the question. "It is you who sought comfort from me," he said blankly.

I glared at him as if that made it any more reasonable to grab on my ass.

"What does that mean? Why do you talk like that?" I snapped.

He widened his eyes briefly with a slick grin as he had that first night, and that stupid flutter lit my stomach the same way. "Talk like what?"

"Cryptically," I pointed out, snatching the thick quilt to place back between us. "You aren't allowed to touch me, or you can sleep on the floor."

His body shook the bed as he laughed. "I would not dream of touching you, Mortal. I was simply moving you away from me."

I flopped down on the bed and tugged the blanket over my shoulder. "Perfect." Snuggling back into the warmth, I tried to find comfort and sleep again. But the white flash of my phone screen burned against the back of my eyelids.

A low groan rumbled through me as I opened my eyes to my flashing phone. A few alerts and missed messages pulled up at the top bar, but all I noticed was the time displaying 8:21. Demon roommate or not, I still had a life to live and things to do before work, and today was unfortunately one I'd had to repeat for the last month.

Erius stretched a leg out on the floor, bending the other in a way that provided a slight gap. This gave me space to slip around him and off the bed as he usually did every morning.

His frost blue eyes stayed glued to me as always while I gathered myself and the little information I'd been keeping during each call about my car. I didn't like that they always had something new to fix with it, but I didn't know much about cars either.

I dialed the number and waited for the ringtone. Today it rang only two times before someone answered hopefully that was a good sign.

"Rusty's Mechanics. This is Billy speaking. How can I help you?" the man said politely. I had yet to speak with Billy, which meant a full rundown of the situation... Again.

"Hello, Billy. My name's Mina Karim and I have a 1999 Hyundai Sonata in with you guys. It's being worked on and I am checking to see if it's done. It's been there close to a month now."

"The 1999 Sonata? Uh—give me one moment to check on the status of that," he said, but it didn't sound too positive.

"Thank you."

He clicked the line over to hold and hung me with some slow tune elevator music to wait.

"Your car has been getting looked at for a month?" Erius suddenly asked.

I turned, finding him towering over me once again with a dark

163

gaze burning into my phone.

"Yes. Like I mentioned, it's being worked on." I pressed my palm flat against his chest to push him back off me a foot or two.

"But you know nothing about cars," he confirmed with a downturn of his brows. It could have been out of concern or out of pity. His expressions were hard to read, especially after spending the better half of the last few days avoiding answering questions or talking in general. And his roller-coaster personality wasn't helping me.

"Correct," I informed him slowly.

"Hello, ma'am?" Billy greeted.

I return my attention to the man on the other end. "Yes."

"It looks like a blown fuse was found for the blinkers. They were looking to work on it today but our guy who handles that is out. It should take—"

Erius took the phone and ended the call.

"Hey!" I shouted as I tried to snatch my phone back, but he pulled it out of reach, holding it behind him as he leaned down to be eye level with me.

"Where is this place?" he asked. The frost blue of his eyes brightened before shifting to the mortal blues. His vanilla spice breath twisted over me, sending a heated ache to the pit of my stomach.

"It's this new auto shop on 24th Street," I sputtered out, overwhelmed by his entire being weighing down on me.

His brows pulled together as he thought of the location given. "Get ready, and we will be on our way then," he ordered calmly as he pulled away from me, placing my phone back in my hand.

"On our way to where?"

His lips twisted up into a devilish grin. "To retrieve your car."

My body flushed again, filling my stomach with the stupid butterflies I hadn't gotten since I was a child. Of the few men I've connected with over the years, not one caused that fluttering feeling. It was the reason I'd moved on from them and one of the reasons I hadn't moved forward with Andrew. Settling was never an option, but I just thought maybe it was them—no, just me—I was the problem. I was apparently only attracted to men who were not human and took my soul.

Seemed about right.

There was nothing wrong with him helping me get it back. I was sure he knew more than I did when it came to cars, and if I was not going to argue with the mechanics, I wasn't going to argue with him. Besides, it would be fun to see how a demon gets a car back.

I wasn't sure what he had planned but I figured if I needed to run, I would want to do so freely. I tossed on my gym shorts and a tee-shirt, threw my hair up into a high bun and everything else before stepping out to let Erius do the same. Once he was finally ready, we made our way out to *his* car.

"What all have they informed you is wrong with it?" he asked as we climbed in. I thought over the list I constructed over the month. I had called once a week and each time it was something new that kept my car there for another long stay.

He threw the car in reverse and peeled out with an obnoxious screech while he waited. Speeding out onto the clear road headed to 24th Street.

"I had taken it in to have the brake line tightened. Then they said the transmission was weak or bad. After that, they said fixing the last issue caused the A/C to stop working and from that we are here—with a blown fuse."

"You did not suspect anything?" He lifted a brow in disbelief.

"Why would I? It's their job to know." I shrugged.

An amused chuckle rumbled through him as his scarred hand hovered over my lap. Soon the black vapors twisted from his fingers, raining down into a foggy cloud. When the cool mist faded away, it left behind my fox and raven skull. "I have a feeling you will be needing those. Keep them close."

The raven skull was easy to slip a chain through and hang around my neck. However, the fox skull was a bit tricky. I didn't want to crush it by accident in my purse, but walking into any business with a skull would be seen as morbidly creepy. Which I was, but that wasn't everybody's business.

There was only one other option, and it would be decent practice since he anticipated I'd need them. With a deep breath, I pushed my intent and focus into the skull as I had the first time. Life poured into it with a greenish mist that twisted into the small fox from before.

It curled up into a ball on my lap, comfortable and content with where it was.

"Best to keep it in the shadows until needed," he advised as he pulled into the lot on 24th and Valley Drive.

I waited until he was fully parked before sending the fox out to the nearest shadows to wait. He bounded happily towards a thick bush that sat under a full tree. Once my sweet little fox was tucked into the darkest part of the bush's shadows, I made my way to leave. However,

Erius pulled me back in, his brows pulled down and his lips pressed flat as he looked out of my opened door. His body ignited with a deep inhale and his hand tightened around my wrist.

"Do not hold back your rage," he said softly, pulling his eyes back to me to curse me with his wicked eye tricks yet again. I looked at him, confused by what would cause me to become rageful. It's just a cheap, junk car.

"You want me to use your gift for revenge?" I probed.

His lips kicked up into a wide smile. "Precisely."

I looked over him skeptically, but he held my gaze with a confident grin, filling the small space with a choking static that zapped over my skin. With his smile still wide, I watched as his fangs shrunk down but were still unnaturally sharp.

I nodded slowly and he released me to head out of the car. With a few more mind clearing breaths, I stepped out and met the demon at the trunk. Erius inspected me briefly before turning to head for the cluttered entrance.

The shop itself still looked as though they were just moving in with tires and junk parts laying all around the garage area. The sign was still written on a temporary board that sat outside the front door which did seem odd a month ago when they had first got here, but now it dug at my stomach annoyingly. I couldn't place why, aside from the fact they were dicking me around with my car.

The heavy smell of oil and gas stung my nose as we cleared the door. But it was not just my sense of smell that felt under attack as ear-splitting drills sounded off, blaring against my ear drums. I covered them to drown out the noise while we waited. Thankfully, it was only a few seconds before a man stepped up to the counter. His familiar greasy hair and crusty complexion brought an instant tightness to my chest. I clenched my jaw, grounding my teeth to what felt like nothing as I looked at the man from the bus the other day.

Erius stepped up behind me, causing the man, who I assumed was Billy given the name tag, to cower back like he did on the bus. I looked up to the demon and his twisted expression as he eyed Billy.

"You knew," I accused in a whisper.

His smile grew, silently answering my question. There wasn't time to wonder about how he knew it was the same man, or how he knew I'd be upset by it. I had a car to retrieve.

I pulled my attention back to the one at the counter. I hadn't spoken with him before—at least not in this setting. Which could only mean he was new, and what a poor day for him to be new.

"Oh—eh—Welcome in!" His voice broke as he stuttered out his words. He kept his eyes on Erius despite the fact it was me he was rude to.

"Save it, *Billy*. I'm here for the Sonata—where is it?" I snapped instantly.

His face fell as he began frantically clicking through files on the desktop before him, uttering about parts and wires and things I didn't care to understand. It was beginning to look like they didn't have my car. From the window I could see three cars being worked on, none of which were mine and there wasn't a very crowded holding space.

The temperature around us dropped to the point I could see my breath as we stood there waiting. The TV they had on fell silent and even the noise from the back faded away to nothing. All that could be heard was the low chattering of Billy's teeth as he looked at Erius with wide eyes.

"Send off your fox and raven," Erius whispered in my ear.

I turned to find the corners of the lobby fading into shadows, but no demon to be seen. Phantom hands slid over my arms and neck, twisting in my curls as it crawled over me. I tried to ignore it and focus on pushing the energy out like before. The essence engulfed my hands in the green, glowing flame that illuminated the room.

The shadows continued to crawl toward Billy as he gaped at me. I didn't waste time asking what Erius was doing to him. It was clear he was taunting the man with different forms of himself that I couldn't see.

With a snap, my fox crawled out from the shadows that flooded the floor. The raven flew from my chest and around the lobby with an echoing call. Billy's attention turned to me, wide-eyed and filled with fear I could not feel for myself.

"I just want my car." My voice echoed ominously through the silent air, sending the weak man into a whimpering fit.

The room around us faded entirely, turning the once brightly lit lobby into an endless pit of dark despair. Fear flooded the floor as it drained from the man begging for his life. His sobs and whimpers didn't echo through the darkness like Erius's deep chuckle, a sound that only sent the man into more hysterics.

I looked over him with indifference and a slow shrug. "I guess I'll have to look for myself."

Without instruction, my fox ran off through the door Billy had entered from. As he dashed away, the darkness around me faded, shifting to shelves full of tires and tools scattered about the floor. I watched as the sight bounced around, running over and under three other men blinded by fear as they cowered on the floor from something unseen. Without pausing to check, the vision shifted to the cars, the ones above that were being worked on—gutted from the bottom for all they had. The sight moved around to the back where three more waited on brick stacks, none of which were mine.

When the vision melted away, I slipped back into the lobby where Erius continued taunting Billy with whatever sights he was unleashing upon him.

"It's not here," I hissed, regaining focus on the whimpering man in the corner.

Erius filled the dark space with a rumbling growl that rattled the lobby and shook the ground at my feet. His hands gripped Billy's hair as he pulled his head up to face him, receiving a pleading yelp in the process.

"No need for that. I do not offer mercy. Now, where is her vehicle?" Erius snapped with a sharp jerk of the man's head.

Billy cried out as he looked up to me, blubbering his words out incoherently while tears and snot spilled over his face.

"I'm sorry," he finally sputtered out through the waterworks.
I couldn't hide the grimace as I looked down at him, more disgusted than sympathetic. "Just tell me where my car is," I snapped.

He shrunk back, or at least attempted to. Erius snapped him back up so that he was facing me.

"You sold my car off for parts, didn't you? That's what this shitty place is? A chop shop?" I berated, allowing the anger and annoyance to control me this one time.

"Accidents often happen in mechanic shops. Another catastrophe for the news." I waved my hand, admiring the green mist that began to ignite at my palms. Erius's deep rumbling chuckle shook the room in a haunting echo that had little effect on me in the way of fear. But Billy and the men in the back cried out, screaming for help and to make it all stop.

I pushed the flames out, not too sure how they worked apart from my skulls and intent, and my intent in this was to shut this shit down. It wouldn't have been long before they were caught anyway, and a small fire wouldn't hurt the surrounding legal businesses.

The moment the thought settled in my mind, the flames twisting at my hands faded from green to yellow with a slight heat. It engulfed the counter and computer in a magnificent inferno that soon spread across the floor to the back. Screams filled the air along with fallen tools and shattered glass. The lobby quickly flooded with the dancing flames as I held my sights on Billy.

The fire swept around him, licking at his shoes and legs but never consuming him as it did the others. Over the fire I could see Erius beside the man, whispering into his ear. I'm not sure what he said or what he was doing, but Billy's gaze fell vacant and his expression grew blank. When Erius pulled away and returned to my side, Billy's body fell limp on the only patch of the floor that wasn't on fire.

The demon grabbed hold of me, tugging me out as he waved his free hand about the air to clear the flames. "That is enough. We must go."

As much as I would have enjoyed staying to watch it all crumble, Erius knew more about whatever it was we just did: committed murder—arson—revenge?

He didn't release me until we were at the car where he pressed me against the passenger door.

"Interesting. You will have to think of something more creative than fire next time," he mused.

"Next time?" I was unaware he planned to make this a frequent thing. I only wanted my car and since they didn't have it, I figured helping others would be the next best thing. I didn't think I had enough anger to make this a consistent hobby.

"How else do you plan to extend this power?" He trailed a finger gingerly down my scarred arm, stopping at my wrist. My face lit up and I hoped with all his extra senses that he couldn't hear the wild beating my heart was laying against my chest. I shifted to ignore the sensation building between my thighs. Not the best time or place to be fantasizing about getting dicked down by a demon, yet that was what began to flood my mind.

His lips kicked up at the corner as he leaned around me. I waited, holding my breath while I watched him. The car beeped and the demon politely opened my door.

"Get in so we can go," he demanded with an authoritative tenor.

Before I could think to control myself, the words were spilling out of my mouth. "Yes, sir." My face flushed with heat, and I spun around to enter the car before he could say anything.

We drove to the shop in silence because I was too focused on ignoring the heat that began to flood my body. I wasn't sure if it was from Erius himself or just from me being so charged after possibly killing people. I know I should have probably felt something. Someone with a soul would. But I felt content in my decision—not even empty or hollow. It was something that needed to be done and I did it. It would be easier to navigate what emotions and feelings I did still hold if I knew exactly what ones would fade.

"Do you know what emotions will stay?" I pushed out.

Erius looked over me, not a hint of concern over the morning, "There are a few that commonly stay for most mortals. Anger, pride...lust—to name a few."

Surprisingly, his short answer explained a shit ton.

He pulled into the lot of the shop and parked alongside Andrew's truck. It wasn't uncommon for Drew to work any other day aside from Monday. It was just extremely rare, and he usually didn't have much to do. There was no way I could have Erius following me around with Andrew also on my ass. I still enjoyed my Monday nights, and the demon had ruined enough for me.

"My boss is here, so it would be best you didn't come in," I warned as I opened the door to leave without waiting for a response I knew I wouldn't get. His energy slipped from me as I crossed the threshold of the shop, replacing it with a more weighing energy that held a discomfort to it as it scratched against my skin.

I was greeted with the strong fragrance of mint and sage, one of my least favorite combinations because it irritated my nose, and this day it seemed to be exceptionally sensitive to it.

"Mina! There you are," Andrew greeted with a bright smile.

"Hey, Drew. You working with us today?" I made my way to the back counter to check for clients before heading up. With him here, I wouldn't have to man the apothecary.

"Yes and no. I came to check a few things, but I did have a question for you," he began.

A creeping sensation crawled over my skin at his words. I hid the shudder as I waited for yet another attempt.

"What are you doing after you get off today?" he asked with a hopeful smile.

My shoulders slumped, tired of this same old conversation, and after this morning, I just didn't feel I had the time for it. I had more things to worry about.

"I am busy with a few things actually."

"With that new client of yours?" He shot.

"Which one?" I tried to play it off, but I could tell by his face he knew that I knew who he was referring to.

"The one that was in here yesterday with you for your entire shift," he pointed out.

Fuck the cameras.

"Did you not think I checked the cameras? Come on, Meems, you know me better than that."

"He wanted to learn about how to conduct readings. I offered to help him and said he could shadow me for a few days. No big deal," I lied.

Drew lifted a brow in understandable disbelief. "*That* guy wants to learn how to conduct readings?" He chortled.

I nodded with a hopeful smile. "Yeah, why is that funny?"

"Have you seen him?"

I mean, how could I not? I had seen entirely too much of him in two different forms. That didn't mean he couldn't learn to read tarot if he didn't already know. I didn't really think a demon would need cards to speak with spirits, though.

"What about him?"

Andrew cleared his throat as he tried to find the right words. "He just doesn't look like the type to be interested in all this occult stuff. You know?"

"No," I said slowly, narrowing my eyes at him. "That seems judgmental, Andrew. We shouldn't judge our clients."

"I'm being serious, Meems. Just be careful, please." He smoothed his palm gently over the scar on my arm with growing concern. I fought the sudden urge to shrink back from the odd crawling feeling it gave me.

It was a bit too late for being careful, and I no longer felt it was only the demon I needed to be concerned with.

 Chapter Sixteen

Meklit

My grandmother's book sat open, and the instructions on how to craft a poppet stared up at me as I contemplated the other avenues to deal with this situation.

"We have tried all the proper, mature, normal ways – this is my last hope. Mina's demon better have given me something," I say out loud as I leaned over the list of materials, all of which I had coincidentally already picked up last week.

I headed to my altar to gather what was listed. Everything was neatly tucked away in the cabinets and shelves, so it took me a minute to collect everything. Once all the items were gathered, I placed the small bundle of twigs and straw in my cauldron along with a strip of red fabric, broken chunks of charcoal lying around, and the wad of twine I had sloppily twisted into a ball. It was not the most aesthetically pleasing collection for the ritual, but magic was not about looks. And my grandmother's magic and tools were far from organized or pleasing to look at. Half of it was hard to even read and faded. Wooden tools that had been chipped or charred along their journey in her path, all passed down to me since she knew I was more interested in her practice and religion than my sisters.

With everything in hand, I returned to the book and set to work on the poppet. I looked over the first *"order."*

"Something personal or a picture. Hm." I didn't have any personal things from my neighbor, and the only photo I had was a blurry screenshot from my doorbell camera.

That will have to do. I pulled out my phone and selected the shots in question. With a few more taps on the screen, my wireless printer kicked on.

While those printed, I bunched up the straw and twigs to shape a small doll, then wrapped the red fabric around the torso and placed the charcoal bits for eyes. It was not the best-looking thing, but it was made of twigs and scrap fabric. It only needed to represent the person; it didn't need to be an exact match.

With the doll complete, I lit another puck of charcoal and set it in the cauldron, adding a sprinkle of black hexing powder for an extra kick, a recipe right out of my grandmother's book, as most of my spells and workings. She was and is the only connection I have to the voodoo practice. Without her, I dabbled only in what is in her book, aside from that I practiced mostly hoodoo.

But my neighbor and his sexist, bigoted attitude called for some of her darkest magic. What better way to test the demon's power and get back at my neighbor for all his shitty behavior? Now that I apparently didn't have a soul and had true magic, though I did like to attribute his most recent lost job to my last full moon hex. He apparently got another one a few days later. I want him to get evicted no matter how that came to be.

"Let's see you steal packages now, *Billy*," I muttered to myself as I sprinkled more powder over the charcoal.

Billy was the pathetic dick in question. He moved in a few months back and ever since then, three out of four packages had been stolen from my doorstep. It was what caused me to get the camera installed to begin with. And you'd think the idiot would notice—but no. I had lost thousands of dollars in prized fabric, and I didn't even know what he was doing with it aside from tossing it. Unless he had an idea of the price and knew anyone with taste and knowledge. Highly doubt it.

Smoke began to rise from the small iron cauldron as the powder lit up, sending the potent sting of chili, ague weed, and patchouli into the air. I moved the poppet through the smoke, repeating the incantation as written in the book which was hard because it was in Kanuri and most of Gran's books were written in it. Thankfully she taught me how to read a good number of the spells and rituals, but after her passing, I had to teach myself.

After chanting and coating the doll in the smoke, I set it at the center of my altar along with the printout of him in the act of stealing a bolt of powder blue shantung fabric I needed for an upcoming show—expensive as fuck and reordering it had cut me back a month's time.

I hope he fucking suffers.

I allowed the candle to burn out on a fire-safe plate while I bleached my roots and showered before work. Thankfully, the client had been super understanding about the fabric being stolen. After I showed them the picture and police report, that is. Not that the report to them or my landlord did shit. Like I said, I had tried every proper and mature avenue available, but Billy apparently knew people on the force and I wasn't too sure what relations he had to the landlord.

They would be the next ones to get poppets.

I headed out, tossing a glance at Billy's door, but I was pretty sure he left for work already.

Good. Hopefully his misfortune starts there.

The buzzing of sewing machines sounded through the entrance of the studio. We only had two of them to work with and now that we were crunched on time, we had been struggling to get the undergarment done. That way, when the fabric arrived, we would only have to worry about the outer portion. This was a risk because we hadn't seen the shantung fabric in person and if the shade was even slightly off from what we had made, we were fucked.

I looked over the two shades being worked on at each machine. "What's this one for?" I inquired.

"In case the color match was off," Milly, my eldest sister,

informed me.

"Mom thought it would be wise. So we've been in here since four this morning. Thanks for joining us, Mickey!" Molly, the youngest, tossed in.

"Well, excuse me. I have another job and my own boutique to worry about. Where is Mom?" I tossed my back onto my desk as I headed to my mom's office, knowing that was where she'd be.

"Where else?" Milly called after me.

I pushed open the door without knocking and shut it just as soon as I entered. "Hey, Mom! Did you bring it?" I asked immediately.

She looked up from under her thick halo of a fro with a smile. "Yes. It took some digging, but I found it in a trunk along with all her other...things. I had your father help me bring it all up. I figured you'd get better use out of all of it than your sisters or anyone else in the family. It is heavy, though, so your father will help you get it home when you get off. I already told him."

Ever since my dad's retirement, she had him wrapped around her finger with every little thing, including helping us girls with anything to everything.

She pointed to the wall under the window where an enormous, worn leather trunk sat. The edges were rubbed thin to nothing and the brackets at the corner were clearly once painted black, but that had since worn down to the gold then silver coloring of the metal. The straps across the top had buckles missing, and the ones that were supposed to be on the bottom half were torn off at the center stitching. It drowned the room in the smell of Gran as it sat there under the sunshine. A welcoming and familiar comfort embraced me as I walked over to it, feeling her presence the closer I got. It was pure and clear, with a small scent of tangerine.

I slid my hand over the top before flinging it open to see what treasures she held dear to her practice. Aside from old, tattered books and dusty jars of unknown substances were black candles, carved and anointed. In the center sat two skulls of the same size. One was clearly a small dog of sorts, but the other looked more like an oversized, dried-up locus head. Beside them was the only book with the cover facing up and the title written in Kanuri.

"What's this mean?" I held the book up to my mom. She knew a little more than I did when it came to the language since Gran spoke it more than she spoke English in my mom's youth.

"It's a book about shrunken heads," she said with a disgusted sneer as she eyed the book, not interested in the dark magic Gran was.

"This is perfect!" I whispered as I looked over it all. I turned to the trunk with a smile. Tomorrow was a full morning free to test that demon's powers more closely than a simple poppet and hex.

The rest of the day passed in a fog, and before I knew it, I was pulling into the lot of my complex with my dad following behind. I raced upstairs to unlock the door for him and stepped in to turn on the lights, ensuring the front room was decent to avoid a lecture. I may be twenty-six but I would always be sixteen to him. On my way out and down the steps, I nearly ran into Billy on his way up.

Looking funky as ever with his grease-filled hair and dingy face, his jumper was torn at his knees and stained in what I hope wasn't shit. I was used to seeing him covered in grease, and I'd never seen it look like that—or smell like that.

I pinched my nose as I passed by him, ready for his rude greeting, but he was silent with a blank stare as he headed to his door.

That's definitely shit.

"Billy, are you ok?" I blurted absently. My eyes began to water from the foul smell creeping through my hand blockade. He didn't turn or pause or even acknowledge I had spoken to him. He just continued walking to his door until he needed to unlock it, at which point he pulled out his keys like a robot on autopilot. He didn't even really appear to notice how he looked or smelled, as if he had spent the day swimming in the sewer.

"What in the shit is that smell?" my father choked as he lugged one end of the trunk up a step, "That's your neighbor? I see why you wanted all this stuff!" He held back a gag as I helped him pull it into the front room.

"I can unload it from here. Thank you so much," I said with a smile.

"Are you sure you are safe with that one next to you?" he asked protectively.

We all decided not to tell Dad about the fabric thief, Mom included. It was she who advised me to take legal actions and if my father found out it was him, he'd kill him. Plain and simple. I couldn't have that while I was building a case against him.

"I'm fine. Did you see him? He wouldn't stand a chance," I teased.

My father wrapped his arms around me in a deep hug. "I don't trust it. I'll install a better security system for you this weekend." He placed a kiss on top of my head before heading out with a final wave. I watched as he pulled away before heading in, stealing a glance into the open window where Billy lived. His lights were off, so I assumed he was sleeping or hopefully showering.

I locked up and headed to the trunk to start pulling out the things I wanted on my altar to honor Gran, starting with the book on shrunken heads along with the two heads it came with. I hadn't seen a locus head so big, but I'd also never been to Nigeria and wouldn't know if it was average. I set them on the coffee table and flipped open the book to any random page. Each and every one of them had writing scribbled along the side with English words.

"How to enlarge head" was scribbled on three pages where several had something along the lines of shrinking them. I looked back to the heads on the table, the locus one in particular. A shudder shook my body while I looked over my grandmother's work.

"Did *you* enlarge this?"

CHAPTER SEVENTEEN

Erius

"I need you to stay here. I can't have my manager seeing you on the camera so much," the mortal advised. I did not know why she thought hiding me from her mate would pacify anything for him. His essence flooded with envy at the very sound of her name on my tongue.

"Ok. Well, I'll see you when I'm off," she said with a sigh after a while of my silence. I waited until she entered the building before I circled around to the back alley as I had the day before. I simply wouldn't gather a thing about the gift's progressions from a pier bench.

I slunk back into the shadows, hidden from mortal eyes as I moved from one section of darkness to the other. The alleyway was well-shaded and the door leading into the back of the shop was left ajar. Clanking glass echoed through the narrow hall as I crept in. The shadows managed to carry me to the opening of the lobby where the mortal was busy handling enormous jars of dried herbs. She scooped out piles and dumped them into a muslin sack before setting that aside to hurry onto some other tasks without another mortal in sight.

Alone with no blond male to hover and question her over my presence.

I followed her to the second floor, remaining in the shadows while she set things out by hand. It had been a tediously slow progress waiting for her to do anything on her own, to stretch the limits of her power and see what she could do. Yet she chose to continue to do her mortal work rather than conjure the number of skulls she had waiting to conduct her meaningless tasks around this insufferable asylum.

Eventually, she moved into her room of skulls and endless things to draw power from. The only light came from a strange glowing pink rock and several candles, enough illuminance to guide her as she tossed cushions about the floor and enough shadows to keep me well hidden during her reading.

The mortal lowered herself to the floor as she moved the cushions around to her liking. When she finally plopped down in the pile, she crossed her legs and closed her eyes. I waited until her heart slowed and her breathing grew steady before peeling my back from the wall for a closer look.

Hmm. Mortals partake in the breathing trance as well. Interesting.

I supposed a great deal of focus would be needed for whatever it was she did for the others. She should have had the power to present the spirit to her clients if she would simply try rather than continue with these mortal antics.

Her shoulders rose and fell in sync with her steady breathing, trapping me in a trance this form could not seem to escape from. I eyed the delicate curve of her collarbone down to the low dip in her shirt. My claws ached to press into the softness of her skin, to feel the tender flesh give at the pressure and draw the beautiful crimson blood. I didn't usually partake in blood consumption, but with a scent so strong and a soul so sweet, I could not begin to imagine the taste of the rest of her.

She sat there, perfectly still for more than an hour, allowing me to silently torment myself as I basked in her scent and fought the plaguing need to reach for her. I was almost at ends and about to give in when the entrance door opened with a chime to break the hold.

"Mina? You here?" the one named Amber called up, disturbing the mortal's concentration. Her eyes fluttered open as she took a sharp breath, looking around herself with slight disorientation.

"Meems?" the voice called again.

"Yeah, up here!" she called back as she stood from her cushion pile. With a quick dust off of her fluttering skirt, she headed out of the room. Without need to follow, I remained in the room and waited for the client and reading I had been anxious to see. I would prefer not to listen in on the mortal women's conversations, but alas, it was not as if I could tune out the volume.

I tried to busy myself and mind with the objects and books around the room. The bowl of rosemary bundles sat untouched from my last visit, so I assumed she hadn't attempted to use one.

"Hey, Amber!" she greeted. Her voice drifted down the stairs as she met with the one who shared the same accent as my mortal form. The dialect was a bit different, though.

"Is your new friend here?" she asked, thick detest lacing her voice.

"No. I have a client, so I sent him off for the evening."

"I thought you two couldn't leave each other's side," she countered again.

There was a slight pause before my mortal spoke. "Basically. I'm sure he's near."

"What does he even do?"

"I don't know. Demon things. He's not much into sharing anything unless he wants to."

I tried to drown them out and continue waiting in peace, but not even the honking of the cars or chatter of pedestrians silenced the women's conversation.

"What if he is slithering around in the shadows of the shop, just watching you?"

I waited for my mortal to respond as her silence very clearly indicated she was considering it.

"He doesn't give a shit about me enough to spy." She laughed. I would not say I was spying. I was merely ensuring she made use of my powers—which she was not.

"You're right, he probably gets enough of you at the van." Their conversation trailed off to things less interesting, allowing me to return to looking over her collection of books, quite poor for as much space as she had. She did say she had more on that tiny white device, but I was unsure how she'd fit any sort of reading material into that, let alone a vast number of books.

It wasn't long before the other woman showed up and their conversation found its way to more interesting matters. The one my mortal called Jaz had acquired a sight for essences of a particular sort that she had yet to locate. The other, referred to as Amber, seemed to have a connection to foliage, simple things with no hint of darkness to be seen. With my power in them, they should be using the gifts for much more.

The one could use her skill to pull vines from the earth, deathly tendrils to snag anyone she saw fit. The other could use the gift of sight to manipulate those around her. And my mortal could torment that blond pest in his nightmares. Yet there they sat, discussing simple fluff that held no malice.

"I'm heading up," my mortal finally said as her footsteps climbed the stairs. I pressed myself into the deepest corner of the shadows and waited for the show to begin.

She walked in and immediately adjusted the pillows on the floor. When they were to her liking, she lit some smelly sticks and waved the smoke about the room. I was not sure what she thought the floral scent was protecting her from, but it mixed poorly with the sweetness of her own.

As I settled back in the corner and she readied her space for her client, a slow shift in temperature moved across the room, draining the warmth to replace it with the frigid cold and maddening silence. The cause of such a shift appeared before her as two ghostly puddles reached across the floor for her. She appeared to notice it as she watched the shadows rumbling up to form two individual spirits of a peaceful essence. No taste of fright nor amusement drifted from her, but she studied the newcomers intently.

"Hello," she greeted in a soft voice.

The two souls bowed their heads but did not speak. Most in this state did not have that capability something she would hopefully soon learn.

"Are you here for the reading?" she inquired next. Again, the souls bowed their heads and settled into their spots in what looked to be a seating position and she quickly followed along, taking her spot across from the spirits that have yet to find their way to the Circles. She looked over them for a moment before a smile broke her lips, a gentleness not meant for the power it was holding and it would either change on its own in time, or—with a slight push—be molded into a fine power that could match my own. It was my gift, after all. Perhaps if I stayed and guided her, that gentleness would grow some jagged edges to it.

Creatures as kind as her were easy prey for predators such as myself, and no mortal with my gifts would be seen as simple prey.

"You must be here for Gian," she guessed. They nodded slowly, reassuring her power further. The bell rang again, announcing someone's entrance to the shop.

"She is up waiting for you, love," Amber called to them. Soon, slow footsteps made their way up to present a short woman with jet-black, pin-straight hair. The spirits straightened in their place as the woman gave a light knock to the door before stepping in.

"Hey Mina," she greeted brightly.

"Hey, Gian. How are you?"

"I'm good. Well, as good as one could be I guess." She shrugged and took her spot across from the mortal.

"Ready?" Mina asked with her hands held out for the girl. When their hands connected, they did a few deep breaths before my mortal pulled out a small mesh pouch with odd trinkets inside. The souls gathered closer to them, watching as she tossed the objects over a dark mat with odd etching across it—sigils of her creation, I would assume. They were not any I was familiar with. Nor were the odd collection of bones and teeth she had spilled over the floor.

I shifted to the darkness that overlooked my mortal's shoulder, keeping myself out of view as I took a closer look. With the souls not of the Circles just yet, they wouldn't sense me, but Mina, with all her miraculously growing gifts, might.

The spirits moved forward, guiding each piece to lay in a meticulous pattern. My mortal looked over the collection and their placing with great intent before looking to the spirits at the woman's side. With a few silent breaths, she explained the meaning and gathered the objects for the next question. This proceeded in that fashion for up to ten meaningless questions from the woman, all of which Mina repeated the answers whispered to her with great care until the meeting found its end.

"I think I have some research to do then." The girl sniffled as she climbed to her feet. Mina and the spirits joined her, exiting the room together.

The chime sounded to alert her exit and I crept out, keeping to the darkest parts of the wall as I made my own retreat. As I swiftly made my way towards the back door, I noticed the rest of the group had joined as the four of the women crowded around the counter.

"Meems, will your demon be joining us?" the kindest of the four asked. They did have plans for a dinner of sorts tonight. If it meant space from that tiny can, I could bear spending the evening with them.

I slipped out as quickly as I could and headed around to the front where a small bench sat. It usually took them a bit of time to clean after they locked the front doors, but their conversations were very much mortal women's conversations that I did not care to flood my mind with. I got comfortable for the wait, watching the various shades of mortal essences that drifted by. Many of the faces were dark, eyeless succubuses that found themselves a mortal to latch onto. Harmless for a time, none of them seemed too malevolent towards their host, but they were also unpredictable creatures. So long as they did not notice me, they could continue their hunts while I continued my mindless wait.

As predicted, the women were stepping out after thirty minutes of waiting, quickly taking notice of me.

"Oh look, Meems. There goes your best friend!" the tall one, Jasmine, poked.

My mortal shot her friend a look of annoyance as she made her way over to me. "We are going out to eat. You are more than welcome to join if you want. Or you can find something to do around the area, but we are driving," she informed politely.

I looked off to her friends who waited for her a few feet away, they would be overjoyed if I didn't intrude. Perhaps it would irritate my mortal all the same, and an irritated mortal was an entertaining one.

I stood without a word and followed behind her as she walked back to her group. Disbelief struck two of the three's faces as they looked back at me with wide eyes before turning on her once more.

"He sits with you."

We arrived at a place they called Catch, which apparently served seafood. My mortal did say they had more of the fried squid, and that was enjoyable at the last restaurant. She also mentioned they had a selection of whiskey and a bar.

"Will you be sitting with us?" Mina suddenly asked me.

I pulled my gaze from the window to look over the several expressions directed my way. It was clear two of the four did not care for me to join. Not that I cared to join them or be tormented by their constant chatter. With a shake of rejection, we exited the cramped car and made our way to the entrance.

I followed behind them into a rustic-styled dining area with a decorative tree at the center. The heavy scent of cooked fish clung to every inch of the building, not that any of the mortals seemed to notice.

All but mine, that is. She looked around with a slight pinch to her brows and scrunch of her nose. Her breathing slowed to short inhales as we walked to a small podium.

"Four, please," Amber told the waiter.

My mortal looked back at me with a faint smile before heading off with her group. I, on the other hand, located a spot at the bar and planted myself far away from the few other mortals that sat along the stools. Mina and her friends took to a booth where I could see them. She and the one called Mickey sat facing me while the two that seemed most distasteful toward me sat with their backs in my direction.

"What can I get for you?" a dark-haired man asked me. I was not familiar with their selection, but most bars and inns were all the same, keeping similar lines of drinks in stock.

"Whiskey," I tossed off.

He nodded, turned to grab the selected bottle, and slid a glass my way before pouring it halfway. As I brought the glass to my lips, my phone buzzed with the following dinging alarm. I took a quick sip before checking the notification.

How's it going?

-Alius

I hit the dial button and brought the blasted thing to my ear. He took to mortal technology a bit quicker than I, but I do not have the patience to send messages back and forth. It was no different than sending a serpent in most cases, waiting just as long if not longer for a reply—yet text messaging is supposedly instantaneous.

The tone rang through twice before his deep chuckle greeted me.

"Do not patronize me," I grunted. "Have you any news on Dazron?"

"No." He snickered happily.

"Then what do you want?" I snapped.

"Exactly what the message says. How's it going? How's little bird? Still alive, I hope."

I took another deep sip, my gaze falling on the mortal while I waited for Alius to finish his laughing.

"Yes, she still breathes. Besides, even if ending her life solved the situation, you know I cannot do that. My sentencing is more than enough, and *this* is worse."

"Come now, being stuck with her cannot be that horrible—"

Alius' words were cut due to a rowdy group of men that took the seats a few stools away from me, quieting down to a whisper only after they ordered their rounds.

"What's that noise?" Alius asked.

"These mortals have me out in a restaurant while they dine and drink," I grumbled.

"And where are you?"

"The bar," I pushed.

"Azal! She is a pretty little thing. It wouldn't kill you to be kind to her," he scolded.

"I do not need your lectures on impressions. Besides, I am being kind. She is still breathing, as I have said before."

The group beside me began discussing the looks that likened the description of my mortal and her friends. They glanced back toward the table, their essences dripping with malevolent desire.

"Just order them a round," one said.

"Do you think the bartender is going to let you pour it? How do you expect to get that in their drinks?" Another shot. The first looked to the tray before him with a grim smile.

"He always leaves them there like that."

Clearly, this wasn't their first go at whatever it was they were about to do. Nothing good, by the taste of it, and the one that looked to be the head of the group was much more pungent than the rest. The sickening scent grew stronger as the ringleader waved over the bartender. He proudly ordered four rounds of some bubbly named drink.

"For those beautiful women over there," he told the tender. With a stiff nod, the dark-haired man gathered the glasses and began pouring the drinks, doing exactly as the leader had said by leaving the freshly poured drinks unattended. Either the bar tender was in on these dealings, or he was daftly ignorant and poor at his job.

"I have to go," I finally informed Alius before hanging up and returning to my own drink. I listened intently to the group as they dumped a thin powder into each drink and gave them a quick swirl. By the time the man returned with a round tray, the drinks had settled with a glistening finish.

I looked over to the group in question, unsuspecting and unaware as they laughed and joked in their own world. I moved my attention back to the tender as he pulled the tray up onto his shoulder. My body was in motion before I had time to think, sliding free off my stool as he headed for their table. I cut around two tables, trying to avoid an inhuman speed as I raced to reach the booth before him.

He crossed my path with perfect timing, crashing into me. The tray flew back and clattered to the floor, sending bits of broken glass and ice across the smooth tile. The man fell back onto an unsuspecting family in the booth beside my mortal and her friends.

"Sorry, sir!" he said frantically, shuffling around the floor to collect the broken glasses and tray. I turned from him to the mortals as they stared up at me with looks of irritation. Ignoring their glares, I walked over to Mina and leaned over her so that only she and her friends could hear.

"What are you doing?" she hissed angrily as she leaned away from me.

"You see those men at the bar?" I said, holding my attention on her.

Her eyes darted to the location in question. "Yes."

"They had plans to drug you. By the sounds of it, they do so frequently to unsuspecting women. So, I will be joining you." I slid into the spot next to her, shoving her over a bit so that I had clear view of the men at the bar.

"What do you mean?" she snapped. I broke my gaze from the men to look down at the creature I now had to protect if I did not want to be blamed for her death. Amongst other things, her demise was the last thing I needed attached to me.

"That was no accident," I pointed out.

"Yea, I gathered that. How do you know that's what they were doing?"

"I heard them, then I watched them."

She blinked at me, a bit dumbfounded as if I was in the wrong. "Why did you let them get that far?" she asked with furrowed brows.

"I wanted to see how far it would go, but then I thought it would be the perfect opportunity for you to use those gifts of yours." I looked to the rest of the group with a slick grin. "All of you have the power to punish them for such disrespect. I urge you to use them."

They looked at me with wide eyes for only a moment before each one of their faces twisted with ideas.

My mortal's scowl turned to a wicked grin as she looked to her friends and back to me. "You said they do this often?"

"That is how it sounded," I informed.

Her eyes darkened the same way they had when we went to get her car. The inhuman tint of black clouded the whites of her eyes as a faint golden glow took to the deep brown. The sweetness of her scent flooded with the scent of rum and anise. It clung to the back of my throat in a pleasing way that was as enjoyable as the taste of her anger.

She turned to her friends and the soft brush of her curls swept across my nose, sending another wave of the potent fragrance my way. I pulled away from her, not realizing I had leaned over her to the point of crowding, but she didn't seem to notice the invasion.

"You guys up for some fun?" she asked them.

"What do you mean by fun, Meems?" the tall one whined.

Mina looked back to me with a growing smile, the smell of the spiced rum twisting around her as it grew in intensity.

"Just a little alteration on their sight." Mina shrugged, turning back to her friends. They shared a look around before returning their gaze to me.

"Is he going to make them see something?" Amber asked as if I were not there.

"I can," I responded stiffly. All except for my mortal turned to look at me with distrusting glares.

"Like what?"

"Whatever she requests." I pointed to my mortal and waited for her answer. Without hesitation she leaned into me, cupping her hand to whisper into my ear, sending the sweet and spiced mix over me.

"Whatever you did to Billy," she slurred and pulled away to add, "but wait until we are up there."

"What about everyone else?" Meklit asked innocently.

"I will ensured they have no clue as to what is taking place," I informed her with a nod.

Surprisingly, the other three nodded in agreement after another brief glance around the table

"Wait for the signal," Mina slurred. They began gathering their things and heading up to the bar where the men waited with wide eyes. It wasn't until they sat beside them that I realized I hadn't been given any signal to look for. But that wasn't the only issue that plagued me.

Tension coiled in my muscles as I watched the leader of the group scan his gaze over Mina. It wasn't a feeling I had intended to consume me, but the clawing feeling dug into me the longer I watched. I ground my teeth impatiently as I waited for the mysterious signal while they chatted calmly with the men.

The leader leaned into my mortal, wrapping his arm over her shoulder. Normally, I found I had better control of myself, having never felt territorial over one of them before. But the contact brought my blood to a boil, and the pain of holding back the shift seared my skin. My mortal hands began to melt from my talons the longer I waited. The need to pull her from him carved into me as deep as my own claws.

The longer my mortal entertained the man, the darker his essence grew. It twisted his face the same way it did most mortals with a blackening soul, misshaping them into eyeless ghouls with overly stretched faces. Not that the mortals would see it, if they could, it would be easier for them to avoid the ones that meant them harm, such as this one.

He draped over her shoulder and pulled her into his chest without regard for the clear disgust that carved her face. I gripped the table, ready to launch myself between them when her eyes locked with mine. She gave a slight shake that held me in place. My hand bit down, digging into the wood until it crumbled into splinters with a low, echoing crunch.

After several agonizing minutes of the men pawing over the women and many attempts to buy them more drinks, Mina looked over with a mischievous turn to her lips.

That must be it. I can only assume it is.

I did as requested, casting shadows toward the men while avoiding the other patrons who dined, oblivious to what was to come. At least in a sense they would be.

As my shadows reached the group of men, I could taste the fear that washed over them like the frigid chill that filled the floor. That I could not help; every mortal nearby would feel the steep drop in temperature. But as for the enclosing shadows making their way around the men, those went unnoticed by everyone other than those they were intended for.

Mina, however, did notice them as she backed away from the invading arm and tucked into her friends, pushing them back away from the group with a darkening grin.

Each man began to convulse as they watched the darkness spread over their vision. Screams and shrill cries began to fill the bar as the men began acting erratically. They jumped from their stools, shrieking about the bartender being of the living dead. Two of the men began vomiting in between incoherent ramblings about maggots falling from the liquor bottles. The man that held my mortal got the worst of it all. For him I not only gave him horrible visions, but I cleared his veil and allowed him to see me as I truly was.

He looked upon me with wide eyes and colorless cheeks, motionless as those around him began swinging their arms and carrying on at anyone who came near to calm the situation.

The women rushed back to the table to flee the new commotion that drew in everyone's attention. The bartender frantically dialed the phone before shouting to whoever picked up on the opposite end.

Mina tucked herself into my side as she slid in to give enough room for her friend as they watched on with prideful grins. When they were able to compose themselves a bit better, they turned to watch as several security men came out to subdue the flailing men.

"What did you make them see?" my mortal whispered, poking my side.

"For three it was their deepest fear, but for that one, I allowed him to see me." I shrugged and took a sip of my scotch.

"Well, thanks. That is actually pretty decent of you, demon," Jasmine offered.

It took several minutes for the guards to shuffle the men from the restaurant and when they were gone, the people began clapping and cheering as if some great monster had been subdued.

Unfortunately for them, I was still with them.

Once all had settled down and the dining area returned to calm chatter, the tender came over with fresh drinks of what had been knocked over, including another whiskey for me.

I remained with them through the meal and left with my mortal while the others ordered what they called an Uber to come get them. I could manage getting us to her home through the shadows much quicker than some vehicle stuck on the freeway. However, I did not account for towing a drunken mortal through them. Not that she was frightened; I would have preferred that. No—she was simply too interested in everything and asked a dozen and one questions until we were finally standing at the door of her van.

"Can you get your keys, or do you need me to get them?" I asked.

"I can get them," she slurred as she began digging through her bag.

"Go on then," I urged, knowing she was failing miserably at it.

After a few more grueling moments, I reached over and removed her hands to search, finding the keys in the side pocket of the bag. I pulled them free and unlocked the door while she leaned absentmindedly against the side, oblivious to the cool air that escaped her van, leaving me no choice but to carry her to the bed. I plopped her down to search for water. With how small she was, it didn't take her much to become inebriated beyond belief.

"Thank you," she grumbled as she fell back into the covers with her legs dangling off the side of the bed. I grabbed her to move her further up with very minimal help on her part. When I was sure she was on her side, I examined the tight top she decided on, along with the lacy skirt. I was not sure how comfortable it was, but it did not look too much so. However, I doubted she would be too pleased with me removing them.

Her hand slid gingerly up my arm before falling limp onto the bed again. The taunting bloom of her need twisted around us, pulling my attention up to her face just inches from mine.

"We can have sex if you want," she suddenly offered.

I paused, my hand on her waist as I stared at her. Fearlessness was one thing, but what mortal offered their entire body to a demon?

"What?"

"Sex, Erius. We can do that if you want to—together," she slurred shamelessly.

My mortal form sent heat to my groin as I looked down at her. This body clearly didn't oppose the idea, but I did not think she would be appreciative of it in the morning. Drunk mortals did not make the best decisions clearly or else I would not be stuck here.

"I am not having sex with you, Mortal." I pushed off and returned to searching for water, anything to keep my mind away from her.

"Suit yourself," she sighed peacefully.

CHAPTER EIGHTEEN

Mira

I shifted with a groan, rudely awoken by the pounding in my head and a stiff dryness in my throat. I blindly reached out in search of water, only to come in contact with the warm body I forgot about.

"It is early for you." His deep voice came from beside me, close enough that I shot up. I struggled to focus on Erius's faint outline in the darkness.

"What are you doing up?" I questioned between a yawn.

"I do not require as much sleep as you." He gave a low chuckle that shook the van and sent heat over my skin. I pushed the feeling aside. I wasn't going to allow the deep sound of his voice to distract me this time.

"What does that mean?"

"That I am up long before you," he said much too calmly. There wasn't much around to keep him entertained and he clearly kept the projector off. I highly doubted he would read anything I owned; he hardly understood how my Kindle worked.

"What do you do that whole time?" I probed and waited for an answer I assumed I wouldn't get, and for once, that made me nervous.

"Do you watch me sleep?" I guessed, partly joking.

"You are not that interesting." He snorted.

"So," I said slowly, "what do you do?"

Again, he was quiet, his glowing eyes on me.

"Your silence doesn't make me confident that you don't watch me sleep."

He cocked a brow and flashed his fangs in a slanted grin. Before I could think to ask anything else, heated hands bit down on my arms, tugging me over his lap so that I straddled him. I may have been drunk, but I wasn't that drunk, and he just told me no. Why say no if he was just going to wake me up with it later?

I pushed against his chest to break free, but he had me locked in, and all I could feel was his dick pressed against me.

"Um," was all I could manage. A hand slid up my back before gripping a chunk of my hair and with a firm tug, he opened my neck to him and whatever he planned. I cried out and struggled to break free, but he anchored me to him in a way that made my struggles worthless.

The wet heat of his tongue trailed over my neck to my jaw line. A low, rumbling hum vibrated off his chest as he repeated the tasting on the other side. I struggled to remain still from the sudden contact, but my body gave in with a sharp shiver that raced down my spine. He paused his trail at my ear to finally respond to a question I had already forgotten. "And what if I was?"

My only response was a breathy moan as my body gave in, melting to his form.

"Mortal!" His voice suddenly grew louder. "Wake up!"

I opened my eyes to the dim morning light peeking in and Erius shoving at my arm.

Well, shit. That was a good dream.

I blinked at him, clearing the sleep vision away. "What?"

"You whimper in your sleep. Did you know?"

I pulled my arm back, feeling the tight restraint of yesterday's clothing still wrapped around me. The blankets did little to help as they tangled with my loose flowing skirt, restricting me from clawing free of my own bed.

"No. I usually sleep alone," I reminded him as I struggled to untangle the blanket. It took a few good kicks before the cover loosened enough for me to climb free. I sat at the edge, waiting for my eyes to adjust and my mind to steady itself from the night. My hair flopped over my face, tangled from the night out of the cap. I groaned, knowing the work I'd have to put in to detangle it from whatever happened over the night.

When the van stopped spinning and I felt balanced enough, I gathered clean clothes for the day and placed them with a towel into the cabinet beside the shower. I didn't bother telling him to leave as I stepped in to undress. He was clearly respectable enough to not take advantage. I supposed it was my fault for assuming because he was a demon he would act like how we had depicted them all this time. He, in fact, had been a gentleman. I, on the other hand, had been a mess.

I should try and make it up to him. I was sure dealing with a drunk me pining for sex couldn't be all that comfortable for him when he was clearly not interested. He would probably enjoy some time further away from all the mortal interaction, and lucky for him, it was the end of the week.

Fridays usually meant a shopping trip and a drive up to Angeles Forest. I wasn't sure about camping with Erius, but groceries were definitely a need. Luckily the mini fridge ran on solar so I could do all shopping before work and just head back after without a pit stop. Maybe he wouldn't mind camping. Some space away from other eyes, privacy for me to see what more I could do. I think he would enjoy it.

But how to bring that up to him?

I dried and dressed in the shower while Erius took his usual place in the front seat. So long as he kept his attention out the windshield, we wouldn't have any problems. Once ready, I headed out to gather anything left outside and tossed it into the van. Disconnecting the hookups took a bit longer, but when all was said and done, the van was travel ready once again.

When I got back in, Erius hadn't left his place in the passenger seat, his attention still on the waves. I wasn't sure what it was about them other than being calming and nice to look at, but he looked at them as if he was waiting for a long lost love that had vanished at sea or something. That may be a bit dramatic for him, but there had to be something that was keeping his attention out there. It's probably another one of his *personal matters.*

I took my spot next to him and buckled in for the drive.

"Morning," I greeted, pulling from the lot. He tilted his head back to look me over. Considering I had all my clothes on, I was positive nothing happened, but his extra avoidance this morning was understandable.

"Sorry about last night." I shrugged. "But we gotta go shopping." With no answer, I turned onto the street and headed to the nearest super center. With it being only about five minutes from both the beach and shop, we arrived fairly quick.

I found a spot to park in the back and headed out with him right behind me. I grabbed a cart on our way in while he eyed it cautiously. I wasn't sure what he made of it, but he looked confused by its construction.

"These are communal?" he suddenly asked, watching intently as I began cleaning the handle with a sanitation wipe. I gave him a slow nod and he responded with a disgusted grimace.

"What do you use?" I asked, tossing the wipe in the bin and moving on. He didn't answer me, but this time I didn't think it was because he didn't want to. He was quickly distracted and began reading the packaging of some snacks the store kept up front.

I pushed the cart down the aisle, avoiding the new wondering gazes that found their way to the person beside me. Not that he cared or even appeared to notice. His focus remained on what items I put in the cart. Whatever I placed in, he pulled out to look over before putting it back in with a grimace.

"You can grab what you want," I snubbed to him.

The corner of his mouth kicked up to a half grin as he looked over the array of canned items. "This store would not carry anything of my liking," he reminded me.

"Oh, that's right, souls. Yeah, they don't sell those here. Sorry. You'll have to learn what your human form likes to eat," I teased.

His taunting grin fell as he looked over the shelved cans once more. "How are these kept fresh?" he grumbled as he picked up a can of maple baked beans.

"Fresh?" I scoffed, "Canned foods aren't fresh. They have preservatives in them, like—chemicals…That keep them sort of fresh but not really…It sounds really bad when you say it aloud." I struggled to explain but the horror on his face carved deeper into his features the more I spoke.

"We'll go get some meat from the butcher and some *fresh* produce," I said defeatedly. I placed all the canned goods back and headed to the butcher block.

Erius took great interest in the seafood section at the meat counter. The look of disgust soon faded as he glanced over the fish and crabs.

"You lot eat *ŭdh låb*?" The thick language came out smoothly in his deep voice that seemed to catch the attention of a small family passing by, and they just as quickly scurried away from him.

"Erius, I don't know what the fuck that is."

He pressed his lips flat as he thought of a way to translate it, "You would call it an ink fish, I believe."

"I do not call anything an ink fish—" I pulled my phone out and quickly typed in the name to the search bar. After a few seconds pictures of a squid began to pop up. I looked over the selection, finding the white colored sea creature resting on a mound of packed ice.

"Oh, squid? We had calamari on Monday. That's squid," I explained. That would explain why he enjoyed it so much. He thought over my words as the butcher stepped up to the counter with a not so welcoming scowl.

"What can I get for you?" he grunted with words that clung to my skin in a grueling way.

"Two pounds of ground beef, please." I pointed to the row in question. He nodded and wandered off to grab the meat. Every time I got anything from him, he seemed a bit standoffish, but this time speaking to him made my skin crawl. I considered grabbing some prepackaged meat, but he was already stepping back up with the package wrapped in brown butcher paper.

He held it out to me, and I reluctantly took it, my fingers grazing the plastic of his glove, and the quick connection was enough to flip my stomach. Raging heat covered me, locking my jaw and arms in place. Pressure began to build in my chest, taking up space for my lungs and making it hard to breathe. I dropped the meat on the counter and glared at the man. I wanted to jump over, but for what reason I was unsure. Anger flooded me, and if it wasn't for the burning pain crawling up my legs, I would have.

Instead, I spun around and darted from the counter, leaving the cart and Erius behind as my feet carried me through the store, across the lot, and back to the safety of my van before I had time to register what happened.

Once at my tiny home, I flung the door back and jumped in, slamming it shut behind me. I gasped for air, still struggling to breathe with the small space left in my chest. I sat on the floor with my back against my bed and head leaning on the mattress. Prometheus zoomed around me, trying to ensure I was well, but his meowing only seemed to bring more heat to my skin.

I tried steadying my breathing, counting to ten, doing that whole "five things I can see, four things I can hear" thing—but nothing slowed the climbing burn slowly making its way up my body.

The air around me grew thick enough to have me gasping for it. I fell back on the bed as the van began to spin around me.

First, I was stuck with this demon, I had no soul – no emotions, and now I was having anxiety attacks from touching people.

Great. All this because I summoned a demon and said a few wrong words.

No. this was because of him, it had to be. What kind of demon responds to a misspoken chant? One purposefully trying to sabotage me. We didn't even form a proper circle or have anything set up right for it to have even reached anything. And with how the book practically begged to be read, it seemed like he was just waiting to fuck up my life.

My skin continued to intensify with a sizzling blaze that started at my scarred arm and tore its way through the rest of my body. Blinding pressure filled my head, aiding in the spinning of the van. I gripped the mattress to keep from scratching myself out of the skin I felt trapped in. My muscles felt as if they were clawing to get out and feeling every bit of the pain with it.

After what seemed like hours, the door slid open and Erius stepped in with a handful of bags. He looked over me with an actual hint of concern.

"What the fuck is happening to me?" I snapped.

He set the bags down on the bed. "I can hardly answer that question being I do not know what it is that happened to bring all this on."

I scuffled up to my feet. "You don't know what happened? *You* are what happened! You're the demon—you should know when the summoning chant isn't correct." Fire continued to shred through me, racing up my arm and chest until it engulfed my eyes, blurring my vision to the point of mind trembling pain. The light felt as if shards of glass were pushed through my sockets to be embedded deep into my skull.

I cried out, throwing my hands over my face as I fell back onto my bed. Another shocking jolt shot through me as I landed on something unseen. My body flew forward, crashing into Erius as I struggled to see what was now attached to me. I spun around frantically, trying to knock it free when his arm hooked around my waist and anchored me to his chest. Still, I continued to swat at the long, fuzzy snake stuck to my skirt.

"Stop thrashing, Mina," he ordered.

I froze against him, shocked he said my name and the warming feeling it brought me.

A deep crease appeared between his brows as he looked over me, grabbing whatever it was I had sat on. The contact sent another shockwave through me, and I could feel every sensation his hand brought. I turned to catch a glimpse of it from the corner of my eye. He gripped the end where a blonde patch of hair sat. I followed the slithery thing down to my skirt where it tucked under the fabric. It wasn't a fuzzy snake at all.

"Is that a tail?" I gasped.

He grabbed hold of something above my head and pushed it back, tilting my head up. He gently tugged to the left, exposing my neck to him. I held my breath as his nose trailed down my jawline and for a moment, I thought I may be dreaming again because there was no way this was happening to me.

After several questionably deep inhales, I realized he was sniffing me like some animal.

"You still smell mortal. Faintly, but it is there."

"I still smell mortal. What the fuck does that mean?" I barked as he finally released me.

"See for yourself," he said, gesturing to the shower where I had a suction cup mirror. I ran over, throwing the curtains open to snatch it from the wall, but the reflection was clearly there, along with hands that weren't mine. They weren't even hands to begin with but claws.

It wasn't just my hands that changed or a tail that sprung free. It was my eyes, now as black as Erius's with a faint glowing golden iris. My nose, my beautiful nose, gone and replaced with a goat-like snoot.

Did it end there? No, of course it didn't. Growing from the top of my forehead were two spiraling ebony horns. Twitching alongside them were large floppy goat ears, all adorned with an odd fur that covered my entire body.

"I'm a goat!" I cried out.

"You are not a goat." Erius sighed, finding some odd amusement in my tail as it began to twist around his hand.

"No?" I grabbed my tail and pulled it back, wincing as I did. "Stop that!" I held it tightly while it thrashed about to break free.

Erius looked from his wrist to my tail before his eyes slowly climbed up to my face. "You shouldn't do that. Tails are delicate," he said with an amused grin.

"Like you care! You did this to me!" A feral animalistic hiss slipped from my lips.

He did his stupid eye thing as his grin grew wider. "I did nothing of the sort. I am an innocent victim."

"What am I?" I asked through clenched teeth.

His eyes raked over me with his stupid growing grin. "I am truly unsure. But I do know someone who may."

"Call them up then!" I order.

He laughed again, pulling a phone from his back pocket and shaking his head. "I will drive. You should stay back here," he said as he tapped the screen.

"Wait. Where are you going, I have work in an hour!"

"Do you know how to change back?" We looked at each other for a silent moment before he took a seat in the driver's seat. "Thought not. I do not suppose you want to go to work like this."

I opened my mouth to argue but I had nothing to protest against. He was right. I was not in the best position to be seen. With nothing else to do and the demon pulling the van into drive, I made a spot on the floor and put things away to try to take my mind off it. Not that it helped since I was working with claws and a tail that seemed to want to help with the process.

When I was finished, I sat on the bed to wait for him to pull back into the lot at the beach. But after ten full minutes of driving, I realized we were on the freeway.

"Where are you going?" I asked.

"Somewhere where you will have space to try and turn back. Or did you want to risk tearing up your van further?"

I looked around at the two torn trails in my ceiling and the mess scattered over my floor from the tail whipping about.

Again, he was irritatingly correct. I would need the day off and the privacy of the forest. I pulled out my phone to inform Andrew I would be out for the day. Luckily it wasn't ever a big deal for him.

Erius pulled onto the dirt path that led up to my isolated spot without direction while I sat on the bed. I ran my hands over the horns, fiddled with the tail, and examined my new clawed hands. The nagging feeling grew to a heavy rock in my stomach as more questions piled in my mind. What if I couldn't change back and I was this goat woman forever? I didn't think Erius would want to tow me along to his realm. He hardly wanted to talk about it or his life there.

We hadn't even broken this stupid tether, and now this.

Every slight noise hooked my ears which caused them to flick hard against the horns. The sounds of the forest seeped into the van, a much preferable noise than the highway, still loud and overwhelming but less jarring.

The calming quiet of the forest was my retreat, my safe space. A place away from the city to escape the noise. I shot a glare at Erius, the one at fault for first robbing me of my peace and privacy in the van. Now he had robbed me of my peaceful escape and beautiful human body.

The van pulled to a stop facing a cluster of trees, making it hard to see if he had found my usual spot for camping. Not that he gave me a moment to check as he stood and made his way back to me with a stern look.

"Did your friend get back to you?" I asked.

He looked down at me with his blank stare before turning to open the door. "Wait here. I need to ensure everything is clear," he finally answered.

"Where are we?"

"Where we met," he scoffed, stepping out into the bright afternoon.

"Nobody is ever up this high," I pointed out. Regardless of my words, he began his inspection. Not that I watched him for long. My attention quickly drifted to the beautifully vivid view of the forest, the shades of green and brown under the vibrant shades of blue that painted the sky. Each slight shift in the leaves created a sound that caught my senses instantly from the noise to the movement and even the faint scent of the fragrant oils released.

"Just sit down and wait," he ordered, the inspection of the site finished, but his sights soon fell on the tree line.

"There is nobody up here. What are you checking for?"

"Not mortals," he said without pause as he disappeared into the shadows of the trees. I looked around the familiar spot, not really knowing what he meant but figured I wouldn't argue.

I hopped from the van and wandered over to sit on the log around the firepit. My tail fell over my lap with an odd flick as it curled against my thigh. A voracious hiss ripped through my chest as I shoved it off me. The noise was startling, even for me, and my hands snapped up to cover my mouth in disbelief.

Oh my gods! I'm a creature! My thumb smoothed over the light bump in my lip, the new protrusion of teeth that had pushed through. I slipped a finger in my mouth, running it over the four fangs on top and the four on the bottom.

I tried to take deep breaths to calm myself in hopes that would change me back, but all it did was fill my nose with the strong scent of pine and firewood.

Slow, steady breaths. I can do this. I can calm myself. I closed my eyes and inhaled. Within a few moments I felt calmer, but the tail swishing in my lap told me that calming myself wasn't the way to change back. I slid off the log into the dirt and rested my head against the wood while I waited for Erius. There wasn't much I could do on my end, and he didn't seem to know too much either, but I know he had an idea of what happened. He had to.

The sun had tucked behind the trees, sending golden beams through the leaves and branches. My tail suddenly twitched up as the heavy scent of vanilla drifted by. I turned in time to see Erius taking a seat beside me. The heat of his hand slipped around my tail once again and it happily twisted around his wrist, an invasion that pulled his lips up into a smile.

"Is that not considered rude?" I narrowed my eyes on him and the tail in his grasp.

"Oh, it is." He chuckled.

"Then stop it." I snatched it away from him and his face fell, his eyes slowly leaving his empty hand to glare at me.

"Why do you like touching it so much?" I snapped.

"Your tail is the one who fancies touching me, Mortal."

Great, back to Mortal. I guess my name is only reserved for freak incidences.

"You seem to clearly enjoy it. Which is weird because you don't like me touching—"

He grabbed one of the horns and pulled down before I could finish.

"Stop inspecting me like some lab rat! What am I? What did you do to me?" I shoved his hand away from me, only for him to pull me back by my face. He held my gaze in his as he pulled me closer to him. I would say he was staring into my soul, but he took that.

"There is one thing, but I cannot be sure if that is applicable in this instance. You do not carry the scent...and you are alive," he explained as he continued to examine my new face. I stared at him wide-eyed, waiting for him to continue, but after a long minute, I knew he wouldn't provide one on his own.

"Please don't leave me guessing on that," I pressed.

"I think it is best I found out what you are before I give false information." He pulled a bottle of scotch from beside him along with two cups and began filling them both.

"Where did you get that?" I asked.

"The store," he said as if it were obvious. It was, but the bottle and cups were not out here when I stepped out.

"Here." He handed me a glass and shot back his own. I took it without question, I needed it. With a big gulp of the spicy drink came the trickling burn down my throat. I ignored it and shot back the rest, grimacing at the taste and releasing a full-body shiver.

Erius took the cup to refill, his eyes never leaving me. He handed it back, holding it out far so I had to reach for it. Delightfully, my regular human hand grabbed the cup.

"I'm back!" I cheered happily, celebrating with another long drink.

"You never left," he said flatly before taking a sip from his glass and looking over me. "You should learn to control that before you end up frightening your next client. Do you know what it was that caused it?"

I took another shot of the drink, thinking about the moment before the pain I felt in my eyes. "I was really mad right before."

"That may trigger it," he considered.

"I'm not a grumpy person." I shrugged innocently.

"No. That you are not. Well," he paused as he thought on something that brought a sinister curve to his lips. "You seemed plenty angry yesterday."

"And for good reason. People like that shouldn't be around." I shrugged and took another sip.

Erius looked over me, then the drink in my hand. "You now have the power to stop them. All you must do is learn to control it." His lips pulled up into a devilish grin.

"Are you suggesting I use your gifts for good now?" I asked with a thick layer of sarcasm.

His grin grew as he leaned back, taking a sip of his drink before speaking. "If that is how you choose to use them, who am I to stop you?"

I highly doubted he would ever stop me from doing something ill-hearted, even if it meant doing good in the end.

We finished what we had in the cups, and he poured another round. The quiet of the night and the crackling of the firewood was a bit too intimate for me.

Now I wouldn't say I was a lightweight, but I shuffled to a wobbly stand from those few cups.

"Mm, you're always getting me drunk," I slurred, steadying myself against the log.

"No. I think you just have a drinking problem," he said flatly, hovering his hand under my arm in case I fell.

I pushed his hand away, noticing the momentary hold he had before quickly releasing me. "It doesn't affect my life negatively," I countered.

"You traded your soul while drunk."

"Minor inconveniences." I shrugged, stumbling my way to the van for the speaker.

Prometheus was sitting on the entrance step, watching Erius as usual. The two basically avoided each other, and I hadn't seen much of my cat since Erius arrived. He was always hiding in his little cubby now that his spot on the bed had been momentarily claimed.

"Hey buddy," I cooed to him, stepping inside in search of the box. Without even a flick of his whiskers, he darted off back to his space to avoid me. Understandable. I probably smelled like the demon he already didn't care for.

It didn't take long to locate the speaker and once I connected my phone to it, I stumbled out to Erius's side on the log.

"Any requests?" I asked, but he just looked at me from under hooded lids with no response.

"Dealer's choice, I like it," I slurred as I flipped on my dance list and set my phone aside.

"How drunk are you?" he asked.

"Mm, why?" I tilted my head back to meet his gaze.

"Because there is a fine line between a drunken mortal and a poisoned one."

I narrowed my eyes to him. "Are you saying you poisoned me?"

A fang baring smile split his face, "If I wanted you dead, I would not need to poison you." He reached for my cup, but I pulled back and brought it to my lips.

"Charming," I giggled into my drink, taking another long sip when Erius snatched it from my hands.

"Hey?" I shot as the scotch spilled on me. "What the fuck?"

"Look at you. Positively drunk." He chuckled and his hand moved to brush off the droplets from my skirt and shirt, sending an electric jolt through me. I looked up to find him closer than before, close enough I could smell the scotch on his breath.

"D-did you spill that on me on purpose?" I breathed.

His smile widened with clear amusement in himself. "Why would I do that?" The smell of vanilla and mahogany mixed with whiskey burned my nose.

The song on the speakers switched to something more upbeat and ironically titled "Boo Hoo," perfect for dancing and perfect for slipping out from under his burning gaze. Using the log once again, I pushed up and brushed off my skirt.

"What are you doing?" he asked.

"I come here to relax and dance around the fire." I twisted about in whatever way I felt fit—I didn't think he knew what dancing was anyway.

"Are you going to dance for me, Mortal?" he said, suddenly at my side.

"Is that something you'd enjoy, *Mr. Goat*?" I teased.

He pulled his eye trick and cocked a smile as he spoke. "Immensely."

"You're drunk, aren't you?" I sidestepped from him, following the beat, and he was quick to match it.

"It would take much more than three glasses of watered-down scotch to affect me." He took another sip from the glass with his eyes still on me. "Dance."

His hand slipped around my waist as he pulled me close. With a deep inhale, his lips turned up into a devilish smile, moving with the beat of a song he did not know.

The night carried on with drinking and dancing around the fire until I was towed into the van. He sat on the edge of the bed, watching me as before. Burning hands slipped over my wrists and tugged me forward into his lap.

"What—"

"I just want to check something," he purred.

My breath was stolen before I had a chance to respond. His hand slid up my back to grip my neck while the other wrapped around my waist to hold me to him. With my lips brushing his, I could taste the vanilla that had been taunting me the last week, sweet and sinful all at once. The soft flutter of his lips swept over mine as he spoke.

"Wake up, Mortal."

The heat of his lips and body vanished, replaced with an empty cold. A dream. A fucking dream. A really nice one at that.

I squeezed my eyes closed in equal annoyance at the disruption.

"Why are you the way that you are?" I grumbled as my awareness of the soft pillow beneath my head became more apparent.

"You were whimpering again," he informed.

I groaned and rolled to my side, feeling the rough fabric drag over my bare skin. "What happened?" I shot. "Where are my clothes?"

"You don't remember?" He snickered.

I shook my head, unsure at what point my reality melted into a dream. If it even was a dream was still to be determined.

"You were drunk after three drinks. Then you put music on and started dancing. Very provocatively, it was… interesting."

I stared at him. "And you just watched?"

"You insisted I watch and insisted you were not that drunk." He paused for a moment, his gaze falling to the blankets I held to my chest. "I brought you in here when you began to remove your clothes."

My mouth hung open as I stared at him with wide eyes, unable to speak. I tried to recall the events of the night, when reality had ended and the dream began, if I could pinpoint the moment I started acting wild. But it was all so blurred together that I wasn't having much luck aside from sitting there looking goofy.

"You continued in here," he added with a slick grin. Maybe I was wrong about his gentlemanly qualities.

"Ugh—why did you let me do that?" I whined.

"You asked if I liked what I saw, and I said it was pleasant. You asked if I wanted you to continue and—"

"And you said yes?" I shot up straight, holding the covers to my chest. Not that it mattered since he got an eyeful last night.

"I said it was up to you if you wanted to do that." His eyes slipped down to my hand at my chest, his triumphant grin growing.

I tightened my grip on the blanket. "You were just passive as fuck about it, huh?"

"I would not say anything about it was passive." His voice was far too calm for the situation. Demon or not, I was sure there was some form of respect—at the very least he should understand harassment.

"So, you're a creep. I knew it."

He lifted a brow and pulled his lips down. "What is that?"

I snapped my mouth shut in disbelief at how little he actually knew about mortals. No matter, I'd be the one to tell him. "A creep? It's what you are. Watching drunk women undress."

"I was under the impression the dance was for me. It is what you told me at the start."

Fucking clueless demon. I glared at him with wide eyes. "You don't get out around mortals much, do you?"

He shook his head with a hard down curve of his lips.

"So, sex is a no, but watching me strip is perfectly fine for you?" I hissed.

"There is less of a danger with watching you," he said brazenly.

I bit back a scream as I stared at him with wide eyes. "Is that all I did?" I pushed out.

His brows pulled down as he looked over me. "You talked incessantly about how much you enjoy my human form."

Heat flooded my body again, not with anger, shame or embarrassment, but irritation that everything was so jumbled together I couldn't distinguish my dreams from reality anymore, nor control myself once it consumed me. Which was going to be a problem if we were trying to break this tether and fix whatever else it is that happened to me.

"Just get out so I can dress in peace!"

Part Two

"I think Hell is something you carry
around with you, not somewhere you go."
-Neil Gaiman

CHAPTER NINETEEN

Mira

I stepped out of the van wearing basketball shorts and an oversized t-shirt. Mostly because it was all I had that was clean. With everything going on, I completely spaced on laundry day, leaving only my emergency loungewear available. I guess if there was ever an emergency, it would be now.

The noise of the forest hadn't quieted over the night and the sky seemed a lot brighter than usual. I squinted through the annoying pain as I scanned the site for my demon friend.

Erius stood at the edge of the forest with his back to the camp. He glanced back at me from over his shoulder. A slight smirk ghosted his lips before he turned back to the trees. I wanted to be angry with him, but I literally had to teach him to eat more often. I couldn't expect him to understand the intricate levels of consent mixed with alcohol.

I crossed the dirt to his side and looked into the cluster of trees as he was. I didn't know what he was looking at or for, but I was sure he had some sort of plan for the day.

He turned to look over my outfit, an amused smile twisting his lips. "That is different from your usual attire."

"You've seen more than enough of me," I snapped.

His lips pulled up into a wide grin that displayed his fangs, smug with his accomplishments.

"What are you doing?" I forced my gaze back into the trees and away from growing questions that ran through my mind every time I saw them.

Why does he have so many? If he eats souls, why does he need teeth for tearing? How sharp are they? What would they feel like against my skin?

My body lit up from the thought, and I struggled to push down the feeling that began to rise.

He'd sooner rip a chunk of my skin off than anything else. I have to stop thinking about this. Monday cannot come soon enough.

"Are you squeamish?" he suddenly asked, a well needed distraction from other thoughts.

"You've seen the skull collection. Most of those came from this forest."

"Oh, good. No worries then." His eyes trailed down my body as if to reimagine what unfolded last night.

"Stop doing that thing with your eyes." I crossed my arms over my chest, not because I was embarrassed by what he may have seen but because the look on his face gave the impression that whatever he saw last night, he clearly enjoyed, and my traitorous body reacted accordingly.

"What thing with my eyes?" he purred as he did it again.

"You're doing it now, stop it." I spun around and headed back to the van to start breakfast before whatever adventures he had planned. His heavy footsteps trailed behind me along with his low, breathy chuckle.

Oatmeal seemed the most fitting and the quickest way to begin the day. Erius didn't oppose the meal and appeared to enjoy it. Probably another food item he was familiar with in his realm.

I wonder what it's called in his language. If it would even be translated to oatmeal or if it will be something like *wheat goop.*

I sat around the firepit to enjoy the small bowl in what I hoped would be peace and quiet. But no, suddenly, Erius wanted to be as far up my ass as he could while he sat beside me.

"You do not have to be ashamed of your dance last night, Mortal," he offered.

"I'm not ashamed." *I'm just sexually frustrated. Which is pathetic. It hasn't been any longer than I usually go.*

He didn't say much after that, eating and smirking to himself. He knew I was not ashamed. He was the one who told me I wouldn't feel such things anymore. I wouldn't doubt if he was altering my dreams, making me do all these weird things without knowledge, spending all this time acting as if he is being respectful but really dropping these fantasies into my head.

I wished I could say I was angry with him for it, but again, it wasn't anything to do with what should be but with what shouldn't be. I was more irritated he wouldn't just act on. Instead, he was just toying with me and my sexual frustrations.

I struggled to keep my attention on the oatmeal as I ate, which was hard because it was as if he knew I was trying to avoid him and did everything in his power to keep that from happening. If it wasn't his arm brushing against me, it was him purposely tapping his leg against mine while he ate.

When he was finished with his bowl, he took to watching me eat mine and when I was finished, he followed me into the van with a heated energy that crawled over me like tentacles sizing up its prey.

"What is wrong with you?" I blurted out after dropping my dish in the sink. "Why are you up my ass suddenly?"

He looked at me with wide eyes and raised brows, but a devilish grin began to slowly split his face as the tentacle like energy stilled around me.

"I am simply trying to see what it is that makes you tick." He leaned down to be eye level with me and tapped my forehead as he spoke.

"I think I preferred it when you didn't like touching me so much." I shook his hand off, hoping the lie sounded convincing enough. But the tight curl of his lips told me otherwise.

"What is it now?" I sighed after a silent moment of him staring.

"It would seem there is something I would like to test. Being a necromancer and all—if you can see spirits and reanimate the dead, you should be able to sense it and locate it. Specifically, a particular fungus that only grows off dead matter. In the Circles we call them *dàw shåkwìp*. I am not sure what you would call them here."

"Mushrooms," I inform.

"Yes, well, there are dead creatures out there. You are going to seek them out for me," he explained.

"Like a dog?"

He sighed heavily, closing his eyes and pinching the bridge of his nose as he spoke. "Will you ever not question me?"

"That depends," I said with a shrug.

"You should be able to sense death, even from remains that have died long ago. Raw death matter and spirits feel differently." He stepped into the thick brush of the forest. I followed after him, expecting him to explain more—such as what sensing death is supposed to feel like. But of course, he did no such thing.

"And how is that? How will I know?" I huffed, trying to keep up with his long strides.

"You will know it when you feel it. I wouldn't say it is the most comfortable sensation," he explained cryptically. I didn't care for surprises, and I certainly didn't care for ones that would cause discomfort.

"Will it hurt?" I asked, but all I got in response was a deep chuckle.

We walked deeper into the shade of the trees, further away from any marked trail I could see. I couldn't feel much other than the heat against my skin and the itchiness at my ankles from the irritating leaves and brush that rubbed against me. It was growing increasingly annoying the further we went.

"Ugh!" I groaned, taking a rest on a stump to rid myself of the irritant, my nails nearly shredding my skin in the process.

"What are you doing now, Mortal?" he shot from above me.

"My ankles itch from the twigs and shit," I hissed.

His hands covered mine to halt the assault I was placing on myself. "Stop. We are near something."

The moment he removed his hand, I returned to attacking my skin as he scanned the area around us.

"It will get worse the closer you get. I recommend not clawing off your foot just yet."

"Well, where is it?" I looked around, scanning the clear open area. "What is it?"

"Go find out." He leaned carelessly against a tree, crossing his arms with a heavy sigh. It was unfair how he could be so fucking rude yet look the way he did.

"*Go find out,*" I mimicked in a deep grumble.

I managed to pry my fingers from my leg, ignoring the begging sting as I stood and trailed off. In what direction, I was unsure, but the itching intensified either way.

Cutting right between two leaning trees, the itchiness seemed to subside not only in intensity, but it felt as though it was draining from my leg to my ankle, and from my ankle to my foot. The air sweetened, becoming fresher than what it had been, though I hadn't noticed then.

I can smell it and sense it, I thought to myself as I turned back, realizing quickly I was heading away from it. The sensation returned to my legs and flooded up my thighs with vengeance. The growing bitter scent of decay filled my nose and clung to the back of my throat. Not only was I getting closer, but I was able to gauge when and where to turn. The annoying crawling feeling covered my shoulders and arms, pulling me in the direction like a magnet.

The smell wasn't foul or rotten as I thought decay and death would smell. It was more of a bitterness, dry with a hint of stale bread— not pleasing, but not what I expected of a dead and decaying creature.

The bush I suspected the animal to be under was thick with leaves and hidden by the low-hanging branches of the trees nearby, a perfect, peaceful place to die, if I had to say. The twigs and rocks cut into my knees as I crouched down to get a look under the bush.

Tucked against the main branch, under some fallen leaves, sat a baby possum that must have lost its mother. Too small to have been on its own, it possibly fell off the mother's back. I didn't know too much about possums, but I reached out to try and grab it. My hand instantly became consumed by an icy chill that ripped from the tips of my fingers. Green vapor wrapped around the small body, pulling out a ghostly gas that dashed out of the bushes, passing by me as it fled into the forest.

I jumped up and quickly followed behind it. Ducking under low hanging branches and jumping over the large ones that had fallen. The glowing possum soul weaved around the bushes and trees in erratic confusion. It led me deeper into the forest, away from the camp, but I continued following behind.

Had the temperature not dropped so drastically, I may have missed that the crunching twigs beneath my feet had fallen silent. The songs and chirping of birds drifted to nothingness and the world fell still.

Goosebumps rose over my arms, sensing an unseen danger. I stopped chasing the possum to look around, trying to hear anything other than my own footsteps. Ice bit over me, stinging the scar on my arm and raising bumps over my skin.

I was suddenly yanked from the small path and thrown against a thick, rotting trunk. The loose bark of the tree cut into my back as a hand slipped over my mouth. The contact sent a shocking heat through my body and I pushed out a rumbling, muffled hiss against the invasion.

The smell of mahogany and vanilla filled my nose and gave me only a slight sense of peace in its familiarity, but it didn't keep me from struggling to break free.

With his hand over my mouth, Erius leaned over me, pressing his finger to his lips as his eyes drifted to something unseen. I squirmed with no luck, ready to demand an explanation when the already silent air fell more absent of its usual nature sounds.

The pleasant pine of the trees shifted to a strong rot that burned my nose. Soon after the stench, an ominous wet clicking filled the silence. It held no echo through the forest, only growing louder as it neared us. Erius kept his focus on whatever it was, caging me against the tree with his hand still clung to my mouth.

He lifted his free arm between us, melting the mortal skin away to present the swirling galaxy and sharpened claws. His eyes never left the source of the noise, and his body grew more tense as the clicking neared. I struggled to turn my head and see what it was that he was hiding us from, but he held me still with a low growl.

The creature crept into my peripheral a few yards from us. I tried to make it out with what little I could see between the two distant trees. A dark, lanky figure with white glowing eyes moved in the shadows, twitching and contorting along the path I had made. Its head snapped in our direction, filling the forest with more clicks.

Erius leaned even closer, caging me in what seemed to be a protective manner as mist began to swirl from his hand and twist around us. His body reverberated against me with a silent growl while the creature jerked and twitched its way closer. The glowing eyes snapping all around the tree we clung to. It was…searching for us, unable to see past the smoggy shield Erius called up. The claws on his hand grew longer as the darkness spread further up his arm to his elbow. His body tensed, locking around me the closer the thing came.

There were a lot of things pressed against me that took my focus from the creature that now stood behind Erius. My lungs squeezed, my eyes burned, and my body shook all at once. I looked up to him, his head turned to the side to follow the creature, but he was looking at me from the corner of his eye with a slick half-smile.

The monster twitched around, jerking its head from one side to the next as it searched. It didn't seem to notice or sense us with the cover, and after a while of moving around the tree, it tilted its head as if it were listening for something far away. I held my breath, not wanting to add to any noise it may hear, though I figured the mist shielded that as well.

After a few long seconds, the thing spun around to continue its search, contorting its body around each tree as it sniffed the trunks and branches. It spent ten minutes searching the area around us until it scurried over the hill and out of sight. With it gone, I thought the demon would let me go, but we stayed locked against the tree for a while longer, his hand still glued over my mouth and his body still pressed firmly against mine, keeping me from moving.

Erius sniffed the air with a growing smile before dropping his shield of smoke, but lingered when it came to releasing me, shaking both of us with his chuckle of clear amusement. How he found joy after having to hide us from whatever that was was beyond me.

"Look at you," he said with a chuckle, shaking his head.

"Erius, what was that?" I snapped, shoving against him for space. He stepped away with another musical laugh as his eyes fell to his leg. Something tugged against my back, pulling me closer to him and when I looked down, I found my new dreadful friend wrapped tightly around his leg. If there weren't other things taking my attention, I would have room to feel irritated about it. But clearly, there was more to his world than I had ever even considered, and now it was bleeding more deeply into mine.

"That," he said as he bent down and began unraveling my tail from his leg, "was a Watcher. A dense one, by the looks of it."

Ever so the all informant.

"Ok, now explain in a way I can understand," I pressed.

He straightened with a smile, my tail in his clawed hand. "I think it is time you acknowledge your world is no longer what you once knew it to be."

"What do you mean by that?" I asked cautiously.

"Watchers are creatures from the Circles, unseen by mortals and generally travel by night and shadows. It is uncommon for them to be out during the day." He looked around defensively and grabbed my arm again. "Let us get back to the van before more of them show up."

"How can I see them then?"

"Look at you. I think it is safe to say you are no longer mortal. At least not completely." He headed off toward the van. "Come on, let us see if you can switch back without alcohol."

I sat on the log by the firepit while Erius inspected me yet again, tilting my head back by pushing my horns while my tail continued to find a way to be near him.

"This looks to be triggered by emotions," he mused.

"I thought you said I wouldn't have those."

"I said you wouldn't feel fear and a few others. But you will still feel amusement. As I have mentioned, things like anger, satisfaction…sexual desire. You will feel all those strongly."

I grumbled under my breath at his words.

I knew that last time I was angry with him. This time, I wasn't angry or amused. I didn't even want to admit what I was feeling, or what I felt against my stomach.

I pushed his hand away. "Are we even safe out here? How are you so sure that thing won't come back?"

"There was more shade under the cover of trees. Here, we are out in the open with a few hours left of light. Besides, its scent cleared before we got back. It seems to have been the only one," he informed me, moving my head around once again.

"How can you be so sure when you said they don't even venture out like that often?"

"I have more experience with them during my time here to know their habits. They are creatures from my realm, after all," he explained. He didn't talk much about his time there, and now, I was growing increasingly interested with every slip of tiny information he gave.

"How often do you come here? To this realm?" I asked.

He looked at me with a narrowed gaze, the battle on whether to tell me clearly played across his face.

"I must spend ten years in this realm every century. I had just returned to my home two years back," he finally said.

And now he was back, stuck here again, way too soon. I'd

probably have a shitty attitude, too.

"Oh shit, I'm sorry. Why do you have to do that?"

His eyes darkened as he looked over me. "We all have our reasons, Mortal." His tone was low and withdrawn.

"What are yours?" I pressed, but he didn't answer. At least not with words. His body, however, was far more expressive or maybe it always had been, and I was just now noticing it. His jaw flexed as he turned back to the fire.

"Is it a personal reason?"

"Very much so," he pushed.

"Ok, well, how do you know its scent cleared?" I pried once more with a slight change of subject.

"Because it wandered off to the east and vanished, and since you cannot even control your forms, it would seem, *my little mortal*, that I have become your new beacon of safety."

"I don't like anything you just said," I groaned.

"Yes, you do," he toyed with a wicked smile, suddenly so happy to spend an even closer proximity to me. He flashed his eye trick with the grin. I couldn't even try to hide the flush that flooded my cheeks.

"Stop that!" I spat.

His smile grew as he shrugged. "Stop what?"

"Whatever that is that you're doing. Messing with me!" I tried to move away from him, but he scooted closer, caging me in my spot on the log.

"I am not messing with you," he said again.

"No? You're not giving me weird as fuck dreams? Stay out of my head!" I shuffled from under him and made my way back to the van. It was the only place I could go. Not that it got me away from him, but the fresh air was enough to clear my mind from his hypnotizing vanilla trap.

"I am not in your head, Mortal. Your dreams are all your own." He chuckled from behind me as he followed me in.

I sat on my bed, the only place to sit, and he took the space beside me, his eyes still glued on my horns. "Remember what I said about taking a picture," I huffed.

"Oh, but the real thing is so much better." He smiled.

I felt a rock form in my stomach and my blood felt like fire. Like clockwork, just to kick me when I'm down, here came the tail, resting over his shoulder like the traitor it was. I groaned out, not bothering to remove it because it would just find its way back to him like some lovesick puppy. I didn't think it could be any louder if it tried.

"You should embrace it. Your powers will be amplified."

I narrowed my eyes to him. "Yes, because being a shapeshifting goat with necromancy powers has been my life dream," I said with clear sarcasm.

His eyes slowly skimmed over me with a darkening hunger that wasn't unfamiliar to me from men—just the demon who supposedly doesn't like mortals. "You do not look so bad. A bit small, like a pet, really. But your form is not hideous."

"Whatever that means," I huffed. "How do I change back?"

He shrugged, his attention falling to my tail. "Try to calm down."

"I am calm!" I spat.

His brows rose in a sarcastic expression of surprise. "How did you change back last night?" His melodious laugh filled the van, distracting me for a moment from what had aided in my body's return. It was all so difficult to track. The last thing I remembered of the night was drinking scotch and having a decent conversation.

"I got drunk?" I shrugged. "I don't think it would be a good idea for me to do that again."

"That is wise. You should find other means to control yourself, aside from alcohol."

I glared at him with a click of my tongue to my cheek. "Thanks for that," I grumbled. "How do you do it? When you switch from your demon form?"

"I just think about it. The shapeshifters, though, they say it's a body reaction."

"Shapeshifters? Like bears, wolves, and dragons?" The only knowledge I had on shapeshifters was from my extended collection of monster fucking novels on my Kindle. Mostly bears, some wolves, and a few dragon stories, but that was my knowledge base.

His brows folded down with understandable confusion. "Why those creatures specifically?"

"No reason," I said, urging him to continue. I'd been living with a demon for a whole week and knew absolutely nothing about his life. Nothing about his world in general. I had all the information at my fingertips, and I had yet to access it. I rested my chin in my clawed hands and waited. "Go on."

"They can shift into whatever they want. They must think on it, though. But that is not what I believe you to be."

"And what is that?" I pressed.

He looked over me once more, his eyes growing darker. "It does not matter until we can be sure. But for now, you need to learn to control it."

"I think it is important! Is it what you brought up yesterday?" I urged again.

He dropped his eyes with a deep inhale. "There is a greater chance that you are not than it being the case. And if you are, we have other problems at hand than breaking the tether."

"Ok?" I urged again.

His gaze bore into me, the debate displaying clear across his face. With a deep exhale, he took my tail in his hand as he explained.

"We call them *Nipans*, a mortal-demon hybrid that can only be created. They are forbidden in the Circles. But, aside from that, I do not have the knowledge to create one and..." He paused for a minute, his gaze slipping over my tail and horns. "There has not been one known case of a mortal surviving the transformation, and as I mentioned, you do not carry the scent of rot as they often did."

"How would we know if you aren't even sure what you did to me?" I pulled at my tail tucked around his waist.

"I am not sure. But we will want to find out soon."

"Why?"

"Because, if you are and it gets out, we will be destroyed. It's...forbidden."

"Destroyed? But this was an accident." The heated irritation began to bubble in my chest again. First, I traded my soul for powers that somehow get me stuck with this demon. I lost my humanity, I was turning into a goat creature, and now I may be an illegal creation doomed to die! Talk about main character energy.

"The *Roshus* will not see it that way," he said calmly, far too calm for the information he just shared.

"The what now?"

He looked down at me with pinched brows. "We do not have time for me to give you a full history lesson. Just know, if you lose control in the wrong place and the wrong person sees you, *we* will be wiped from existence. So, let us try and control it, yeah?" He stood up and beckoned me to follow him from the van.

He walked the perimeter of the site before turning back to me with a devilish grin.

"What are you smiling for?" I snapped but before he could

respond. My phone began going off with notifications for both texts, missed calls, and calls coming in all at once.

He looked down at my pocket and back to my face as he waited. "Are you going to answer that?"

From the "I Don't Fuck with You" ringtone, I knew exactly who was calling and I didn't want to answer——but the buzzing and notifications did not let up. I pulled my phone out to find all four of my siblings had tried various forms of contacting me, from calls and texts to DMs in my social media which they had been blocked on, so their little brand-new accounts will also be added to that list.

I smashed ignore on the touch screen and violently scrolled through to swipe each notification to the delete bucket. When every single attempt was gone, I shoved the phone back in my pocket, a bit more irritated in my day than I was.

"You ignore those often when they are not your group of friends," Erius suddenly pointed out.

"Yeah, what of it?" I shrugged as heat began to flush my face again.

"Do you not care for your family?" he pressed.

I looked at him through narrowed eyes. He never wanted to give me any information about himself but wanted to play twenty questions with me. No sir.

"How do you even know they are family?" I snapped.

"I assume *Biological M* stands for your mother. The other four are listed as parasite, but I have a suspicion they are your siblings," he guessed.

The heat turned to fire under my cheeks and my hands balled to fists. "Are you reading my text messages?"

"No, I simply see the notifications pop up. Have they wronged you?" he pressed again.

"Like you said, some things are personal business and this, this is my personal, private business. Stay out of it and stop looking at my phone!"

I spun on my heels and marched back to the van, slamming the door behind me and scaring Prometheus into his hide again.

"Sorry buddy." I sighed, releasing the rage at the door like a coat. I flopped on my bed, ready to head home. Not that that would get me away from my new friend.

CHAPTER TWENTY

Erius

My mortal hadn't spoken to me the rest of the night and well into the morning. Instead, she talked to her cat loudly enough for me to hear her plans and displeasure with my invasion of her privacy. I did not find any interest in her personal relationships to read any messages, but it was hard to ignore several notifications popping up throughout the night and day with no response to silence them. It was as if she was waiting for something she clearly did not care to hear. It had burdened her deeply. I could taste it in her soul. Whatever it was had weighed heavily on her. Now, I felt she simply did not have the capacity to care, or she did not want to.

She stormed into the van, her cat racing in behind her. Her frequent failed attempts at a full change carved irritation deep into her brows. Not one successful formation was made through the many attempts. The most she was able to conjure up was her tail, which she did not care for in the slightest.

There was something we were missing about her previous transformations that we simply were not adding. If it was her frustrations that triggered it, how flustered must she be?

Mina's tail swung around behind her gracefully as she marched over to the cabinet that held the scotch. While she grabbed and poured herself a glass, her new appendage found its place around my wrist.

"Ah! Hey, don't touch." She jumped up, startled by the contact. She reached out to snatch it from me when I paused her, holding out my hand before gently unwrapping it from my wrist.

"You are going to damage it if you keep ripping at it like that. You should embrace what it snags onto." I handed it to her, adding a curve to my lips to show I meant no harm.

"Yeah, you'd like that, wouldn't you?" She took a drink of the scotch, glaring at me through narrowed eyes as she did. She didn't stop for a breath until the tail had drifted away.

"Ew. That feels weird," she said with a twisted grimace before finishing off the rest of her glass and slamming it down. "I'm ready to go."

"You should eat," I suggested. After so many attempts, successful or not, she had used a great deal of energy.

"We can stop for something on the way back to the beach. I'm not all that hungry," she grumbled as she took her spot in the passenger's seat. Her head fell back with clear exhaustion.

I slid into my newly designated seat, handing her a cold bottle of water as I did. She wasn't the healthiest of mortals, and frighteningly dehydrated. I was unsure how she lasted this long, clearly powered by the gross amount of bravery flooding her veins. She took it with a faint smile as I pulled off.

We headed down the lengthy dirt path that led out of the forest, leaving a dusty cloud to trail behind us. I did not feel up to hearing her lecture on how her old, clunky house could not handle speed and bumps, so I traveled at a gruelingly slow pace. Once the tires hit the smooth pavement, I pushed it as much as I figured she'd allow, making it to the freeway in under ten minutes.

We moved through the cars with surprising ease considering the size and ability of the van. It helped that there were not as many cars around as there were on our way up, making the drive home much simpler. I turned off at the appointed exit and moved to the left turning lane.

"Go right, there is a place to get food…please," she tacked on.

I switched over and followed the few instructions she had left until we were waiting in a car line. When we pulled up to the board, she instructed me to stop as she leaned over me. The sweet aroma flooded my nose as her loose curls swept across my chin. She managed to avoid touching me, placing one hand on the cushion between my legs and the other gripping the door for support.

I pressed my back against the chair as best I could to avoid the invading heat that began to swarm me, but then a voice called over a speaker and the mortal leaned forward, sending another wave of her essence out around me. She asked for a moment before turning to me. Her proximity did not appear to have the same effect as she looked over me with a blank expression.

"What do you want?" she asked, though her tone told me she knew. The heat of her breath fanned over my face. It was just as appealing and tantalizing but not what I should be wrapped up in.

"Whatever you are getting," I pushed out.

She rolled her eyes and turned back to give the order. The voice gave us the price and instructed us to move around.

Mina sat back to find her wallet while I pulled up to the first window. "Why don't you ever order something different than me?" she suddenly asked.

I did not care to carry out my imprisonment in this realm by exploring its lands. I kept to the hotel and the food it offered, which were familiar dishes from the Circles. Most of the mortal food tasted of garbage and fillers. I did not plan to explore their cuisines any more than I desire to eat them. Getting what she ordered was the simplest thing. Mortal women *usually* ate healthier. Usually. This one ate like an unattended youth when she was not out with her friends.

"It is easier," I say simply.

The window slid open, and a woman poked her head out to repeat the order and price. I nodded, pulling out whatever card I had in my pocket, turning it into a debit as I held it out to her. She gazed into the cab at the mortal and me with wide eyes.

For me, this was a regular occurrence. My mortal appearance is most appealing to them to draw them in and make them more susceptible to making deals. But I had noticed over the days that I was not the only one they find this captivated interest in. I waved the card to regain the woman's focus until she took it. With her eyes still locked on us, she slid the window closed and began chatting with her coworker about what she had seen.

"What is that? Why are people so speechless around you?" Mina asked, noticing the hesitation as I did. When I turned to her, she was looking over me with her usual expression of curiosity. The warm bronze color flushed her cheeks, sending a wave of her need my way.

"For the very same reason you enjoy this form. It is meant to be enjoyed by your kind," I explained proudly.

"Ok, relax," she countered.

Before she could finish, the window opened once again as the woman handed back the card and a bag that smelled of overly cooked beef and burned cheese. I placed the greasy mess in her lap and pulled off.

"Thank you," the mortal tossed back before we cleared the window. By the time I had pulled back onto the street, she was already digging through the bag for her food, filling the small space with its putrid scent.

Perhaps I was being too harsh. The fried squid, as she called it, was not bad at all and quite similar to a few meals in the Circles.

By the time we pulled onto the beach, she had finished her food and seemed to be a bit less heated by anger as she wiggled to the song that played over the radio. I pulled out the keys and sat back to eat. I supposed eating more than what I had been had been beneficial, but I had not been enjoying forcing everything down.

I should see if Alius could bring me something from the kitchens at the hotel. At least those were meals I knew of and their flavoring.

I pushed through the burger, forcing each rough swallow down until my body was full.

"Good, you're done. I need to shower. Since it's nice out and you've seen plenty of me. You can wait outside. Thanks," she prattled off, waving her hand at me as if to shoo me away. Her determination to hide herself was unneeded. Her mortal body was quite pleasant to look at and her new form was far from hideous. But in order to maintain the peace we had accumulated, I made my way to the door, perhaps a bit too slowly for her.

The moment my feet hit the sand, she slammed the door shut behind me with an over needed amount of force. She had a small setup near the front of her van in the sand. An overhanging cover was attached to the front roof of the cab and was anchored into the sand by two poles.

Bubble shaped lightbulbs hung on a wire clipped to the overhanging bars of the construction. Under it all sat a flimsy sun-bleached chair and a small table. She must have set it up while I ate, a bit differently than last week with a better view of the open ocean.

I took a seat and pulled out my phone to check with Alius and whatever news he may have. His sister, Vex, had a bit more knowledge in *Nipans*. She had a belief that without proper study of a true *Nipans*, there wasn't enough to go on to claim that they were created to cause harm. With laws in place keeping her from these studies, it was safe to say she would not be spreading such information around.

The dial rang through only once before Alius clicked on.

"I was just about to call you," he answered in a cheery tone.

"Has Dazron left?"

"Not just yet. But Vex has responded with immense interest in your mortal. She is compiling a few questions for Little Bird. Speaking of, how is she?"

I inhaled deeply at his questioning, filling my lungs with the overabundant scent of the mortal's lust as the faint sound of her soft, breathless moans escaped the walls of her van. My muscles locked as a shocking chill rained over me. The pain first flooded my mind before draining down to my dick. I never knew how reactive this body could be, though I never spent this much time around anyone during my time in this realm. I did not know this would be a desire I would need to pacify.

"She is well," I forced out, trying to maintain focus on the call but the smell of her only intensified as it spilled out from the van. The hidden whimpers mixed with an incoherent language as she continued in the privacy she thought she had. It would be a delight to watch if she wasn't so disproving of her nudity around me.

"I have to go," I blurted out, ending the call before Alius had a chance to question me. I released the tense hold and shot up from the seat.

I was under attack by her lustful scent, the mouthwatering distraction that had haunted me since the night of the deal. I didn't know what mortal would release such an emotion upon such a meeting. Usually it was fear or pride. Never lust. Then again, most mortals did not screw up rituals and get tethered to the demon either. I supposed someone had to be the first.

The sea and sand began to twist around me, lightening my head as the van seeped out the dazing toxin. It swirled around my arms and legs, pulling me up and over to the door where the cloud was more concentrated. My hand twitched, begging to grab the handle and head in, ready for the lecture I would undoubtedly receive, but if I could just bask in it for a moment, I would sit through such lashings happily.

I reached for the handle as the door flew open to the soaking mortal. Her scent fanned out as it was released in a massive wave. My muscles locked up as it rammed into me, heating my mortal skin and sending any amount of focus straight to my groin.

"I'm done," she said softly. A deep flush tinted her cheeks and shoulders, intensifying the scent further only to be made worse as she spun around.

My hands fisted as I struggled to keep myself from launching in the van after her, waiting until she sat safely on her bed before stepping in. I made sure not to stir the fragrance further, slowly moving around to shut the door. I leaned against it with my gaze on her as she began her hair routine. Her hazel eyes flickered up to me from the reflection, soft and curious for a moment before a slight darkness flashed over them.

"Can I help you?" She snipped.

A blazing fire covered my skin again, intensifying the pull in my pants. I shook my head and tore my eyes from her, forcing myself to sit in the front seat while she finished.

We ended the night with some movie that Mina fell asleep to before it had finished, as she did most nights. I looked at my watch and settled into position for what was now a nightly routine that this body did not oppose of. As with the last few nights, my mortal sought comfort from me by draping her arm across my stomach and her leg over mine. The first night I had thought it bothersome, but it gave this body a comforting warmth that was enjoyable enough to allow it to continue.

Her hand gripped my shirt as she curled into me, releasing a soft sigh before her body relaxed against mine. When I was sure she returned to the deepest part of her dreams, I rested my arm over her shoulder and drifted to sleep myself.

Dreams served me no purpose, and I had had very few over my years in this form. But all that seemed to plague my nights were dreams of the mortal. I had thought sleep would be a decent escape from her and how this body felt, but night after night I was forced to face this form's most favored quality of the delicate creature, qualities too ethereal to mar by my claws.

The dream vision of my mortal smiled up at me, her full lips as elegant and fragile as ever. A simple puncture would bruise the supple skin, yet my claws ached to slide over them, to feel the soft press of her flesh over me. I reached for the dream, grasping her and pulling her into me. She did not flee, which was not surprising even if it were not a dream. I traced the claw of my thumb lightly over her bottom lip, watching in delight as it trembled from the touch.

Not from fear. I would never get that from her, and it was no longer her anger I craved. It was growing too troublesome to deny any longer. Her lust and desires were far more captivating to witness. The dream mortal pressed against me with a soft gasp, her lips quivering once again. I could probably tear them to nothing if I were awake. My fangs would surely rip through them if they so much as grazed the skin.

But here I could allow my selfish desires to play out. I could satisfy my own needs, where she is out of reach from danger, and from me.

I pulled the dream up to me, crashing my lips with a desperation I was unaware of.

"Erius," she whispered, the confusion in her voice stirring me up.

I froze, my arms around her as I held her against me.

"Hm?" I pushed out.

"What are you doing?" she asked. Not that she sounded mad, but she wasn't joyous about it. I loosened my grip as she turned to face me.

"It is you that curled up against me, Mortal." Which was not entirely a lie. She had been the one cuddling up to me in her sleep most nights.

"You trying to take me up on that offer?" she whispered again.

I would have thought it an empty offer had her scent not bloomed out around us. I bit back the fire that raged in my chest, gipping the fumbling regard with all I could conjure to hold me in place.

"You are relentless. Go back to sleep," I pushed out.

"It will happen at some point," she said boldly. Shame had most certainly slipped from her.

"Sure."

She pressed herself against me as she stretched out, intensifying my own need with the senseless act. Her eyes grew wide as she paused. "You say no. But that is not what your mortal body says."

"That is not within my control," I admitted.

She scoffed at my answer and reached for her phone. With a quick look, she slammed it down and pushed herself up to her elbows.

"I have stuff to do before work," she groaned, wiggling free from my arms and off the bed.

It will happen at some point. Her words echoed in my ears, adding another layer of difficulty to my regard as visions of all the ways it could be safe for her. I supposed if I maintained this form, it would be no different.

"You can get dressed first. I'll be back," she informed me as she grabbed a small bag and exited the van. I took the time to dress and contemplate what to do with the mortal next. There were a number of things I could request her to try to get her powers up, but that, unfortunately, was not what wanted to fill my mind.

I had not gotten any closer to my answer by the time she returned, dressed for the day in a pair of stretchy tight pants and a top that covered only her chest. She gathered a rolled mat and pink box that she took outside without a word. I followed her out, assuming she had plans to go somewhere, but she simply tossed the mat into the sand.

Curious as to what she planned to do, I figured I'd sit in the chair and watch the waves but found myself entertained by her silent struggle to get the mat to lay flat.

When she had it to her liking, she placed the box on one end and sat at the other facing out to the ocean. Steady breaths began flowing from her, syncing with the motion of the waves to accommodate her breathing trance. I struggled to force my attention out on anything other than the stray curl sweeping over the curve of her neck, the illuminating color that flushed her dark skin as the sun hit it, or the steady rise and fall of her shoulders.

I tore my gaze from her to the pier full of mortals. The low clamor of their conversations did little to drown out Mina's soft exhales as they begged for my gaze to return. I dropped my attention to the waves lapping at the pillars holding the pier up, a failed attempt to distract myself. Keeping watch on her from the corner of my eye, I witnessed the most peculiar sight. Though most things the mortal did was peculiar, I had not witnessed this during her moments of silent reflection.

With reason, I turned to face the mortal as she lifted her hand up as if to wave at someone, but the beach directly before her was clear of any mortal or soul that I could see. As I searched the surrounding area, she stood from the mat and began walking off. Her cat yowled at the step of the van. Despite being able to jump free he remained inside, crying after her as if to call for her return. It was unlike him to remain in the van, often trailing after her during my time alone inside.

With curiosity balling in my chest and a growing desire to be near her, I stepped through sand, struggling to catch up without drawing attention to us. By the time I was at her side, she had stopped right before the shade of the pier. The sound of washing water beat against the pillars and sprayed us with the splashing sea, but she remained still. I leaned forward to get her attention, but her eyes were closed. Her arm lifted again, reaching for the shadows when the clicks of the Watchers began to fill my ears.

The smell came next and with a brief investigation, I caught sight of the death crawlers jerking and twitching out of the shadows as they crept closer. Their white glowing eyes locked on us, their new prey, with immense hunger. My body moved without thought, sweeping the mortal into my arms as I made a dash for the van at a speed that would remain unseen by anyone else. The moment my foot hit the inside of the cab, I tossed Mina onto her bed and threw the door closed. The bright distance between us and the pier should have been decent enough to keep them trapped there until night.

"Erius! What the fuck?" she squawked, rubbing the back of her head from the slight bump she may have gotten in my haste to get in.

"Do you have any other lights to set around this infernal thing?" I barked. There wasn't much time to explain the questions I knew were building on her end. Though it was something to keep an eye on, perhaps I can urge Alius to remove Dazron for the time to provide someplace safer for her, and somewhere more spacious for me.

I could not risk her falling into such…a hypnosis state with them surrounding us. I should have been more attentive to the creatures the first night their sound crept into the van and to the hallucination she had experienced. Now, she was nearly walking into dens of them, blindly led by whatever it was she was waving to, an invisible threat for me.

"We must maintain a level of brightness around the van at night," I said without waiting for her answer.

"Why? What happened?"

I held back a humorless laugh. Of course she wouldn't have an idea of what just happened.

"Watchers," I pushed. Hopefully that would be enough to urge her from this location—but given her general history of not doing what was best for her, I doubted it was even a concern.

"We can get more lights. I've been meaning to anyway. Do you think they can be detected by motion? I can get the motion detector ones and—"

"They cannot be detected by sensors of any kind. They are shadows," I interjected.

Her shoulders fell as she thought of other options. "I still need some. So, let's go."

The rest of the morning was spent picking out lights for the outside of the van and setting them up once we returned. I explained what I had witnessed and why we needed the lights after her incessant badgering on knowing. When everything was to her liking, she set up her mirror on the bed and began the ritual of hair and what she called makeup. I was beginning to grow an interest in the use of magic, altering her appearance in some way or another. She remained incredibly focused on it while she worked, so I didn't bother pestering her with questions.

"We should take the car so it isn't dark by the time we get back," she suggested as she began cleaning up. I agreed, as it gave me somewhere to wait until her clients showed up. I had gifts to sit in on, after all. This new form could potentially heighten her skills and I would love to see how she handled them. She was also drowning in shadows in that room, and with all the Watchers lurking around, it would be best if I kept her in eyesight.

We headed out to the car and off to her shop where she yet again requested I find something to do so her manager did not see me.

"I'll meet you at the pier when I'm off," she said as she exited the car and headed in. I listened to the traded greeting and following conversations until she announced she was headed for the room. I took that as my signal to sneak in from my usual way around the back. I pushed through the door, keeping as close to the wall and shadows as possible.

Dim light flipped on from a side room, stopping me in the hall as the blond mortal rushed out of the small office. The faint scent of summer drifted out of it, heating my senses with the familiar bloom.

My claws dug into my palms as the burst of rage rained over me. His scent had mixed with hers last week, tainting it for the night and well into the following day. It had been a displeasing alteration to her delicate scent, but now it grated against me.

I pushed my back into the wall, avoiding the bit of light at my feet while I waited for the simple male to returned to the room. It was not long before he marched back, closing the door and filling the hall with darkness once more. I took to the shadows that led upstairs, forcing my attention on my reason for being there.

I am only here to watch my gifts grow, I reminded myself.

I slipped into the room where my mortal readied her space. She pulled one of the bundled herbs out from the bowl that held about a dozen different ones. I covered my mouth and nose, ready for the attack she would soon feel, if she were a *Nipans*. She lit the match and held the flame under the dried rosemary. Smoke drifted up, circling her as it did with most dark energies. Within seconds, she began coughing and wheezing from the irritant. She looked at the bundle briefly before tossing it to the floor and stomping on it to snuff it out, choking and hacking up a lung in the process. I bit back a chuckle, fighting the urge to present myself with laughter that would undoubtedly lay waste to my throat the second the smoke hit me.

"You ok up there, Meems?" the other male called from the lower floor.

My mortal cleared her throat as she glared at the bundle. "Yeah—I just—sucked in—the smoke," she choked out.

"You gotta be careful with that!" he called back.

She waved her arms around the air, clearing the smoke from the room with her shirt over her nose. The smog slowly drifted out, returning the usual scent of frankincense and myrrh that clung to the walls. With breathable air now circulating, Mina worked over the small space in preparation for whatever reading was to come.

After a few moments, a woman stepped in and greeted Mina kindly. They shared a few words before getting to work on the reading with cards and pendulums and large crystal spheres.

The reading and client weren't much different from the last I had watched. They asked her questions, and the souls answered by either moving the pendulum or adjusting the bones, depending on the tools she used—nothing new to consider when it came to her ever-growing powers.

When it was over, I decided to head out and around early to get her. It had not escaped me what I walked into last Monday when I came, and I did not care to listen or walk in on it again.

I shifted forms, pulling the mortal eyes over as I stepped through the front door.

"Can I help you?" the blond pushed through his teeth. His

229

essence ran black at the first sight of me, seething his energy over the countertop and onto the floor. The corner of my lip kicked up at the bitter taste of jealousy as it coated my throat.

"I'm here for Mina," I said smoothly, fueling more rage into his dripping energy.

"You mean you are here for a reading," he pushed.

My smile grew. "I am not here for a reading."

"A spell then," he tried again, sparking true irritation within me. I held my smile as my gaze bore into him.

"My business with Mina is between her and I."

His essence flared out in a deep black ball, marring and twisting his features to the eyeless ghoul I knew was hidden within him. I cocked a smile his way, fueling his essence all the more.

"Andrew, it's fine. I have time for another spell," she called out.

The smirk returned to my lips as I made my way upstairs, my eyes still locked with his and the unspoken challenge he was placing.

When I reached the room, Mina hurried me in and shut the door. "What are you doing here? I told you I'd get you when I was off," she spat. Her cheeks darkened with the sudden flush of blood and a deep crease formed between her brows as she stormed around the room to clean up.

"I was bored." And this was far more entertaining.

"Yeah, well, be bored at the boardwalk. Haven't you had enough of me?"

"Had I interrupted something?" I poked again, the teasing smile tugging hard on my lips. It was clear she noticed as her face darkened with the frustration I caused, and they were mine to admire.

"Yes!" she blurted out. My smile widened, pulling my eyes from her to the door.

"Is he your mate? The blond one down there?" Though, by her offers, I did not think she had been claimed.

"What? No. Why would you ask—" She shook her head, her curls bouncing around her face as she did.

"He does not seem to enjoy my involvement with you."

She pressed her lips flat, looking over me with wide eyes. "He's been around you a grand total of thirty seconds. I'm sure he is just concerned that you are a *new client* coming in right before close."

Either she was incredibly naive, or she chose to ignore the mortal's feelings for her. "His essence was darkening by the second."

"You speak as if I know what the fuck you are talking about," she snapped. Her frustrations were one brand of entertainment, but this frustration flushed her face in a way I had not seen, and I could not help but laugh.

"I waited until your client left," I pointed out.

Her eyes widened further, sending another flood of blood into her cheeks. "You were listening?"

I nodded. "There is only so much to be done on the pier. I wanted to see how you conduct your readings now that you have a true connection to the other side."

Her mouth fell open with a slight twitch to her eyes. "Are you fucking with me right now?"

The terrors I would construct to watch these frustrations flash over her face all day. I chuckled again which only ignited her further.

"Stop laughing at me!" she ordered.

I stepped closer, my arms tucked tightly at my side to keep from grabbing hold of her. "Let us head back to your tin can before it gets too dark."

Chapter Twenty-One

Mira

I woke to the stabbing and tearing pain wreaking havoc in my lower stomach. The familiar and annoying ache of my monthly friend was the last thing I needed right now.

"Erius," I said stiffly, motioning to poke his side, but he was clearly already awake as he moved from me.

"Yes?" he pushed with an equal harshness.

"Can you get out for a second? Please," I asked as kindly as I could through the pain, hoping the tone would be persuasive enough. I was prepared for him to question me or argue against it, but to my surprise, he got up without a fuss. Black vapor circled his torso, leaving a dark shirt on him as he stepped out. I rushed to gather everything and jumped into the shower so that he didn't have to wait outside too long. It was only one in the morning. Definitely not the best time to be out, especially since he said it would be wise to stay inside after dark.

I washed off as quickly as I could while still being efficient in the matter. When I was done and out of the shower, I handled my personal business with a menstrual cup and finished cleaning up before welcoming the demon. I slid the door open expecting him to be waiting as he usually did, but the space was empty.

"Erius?" I called out, not too loud, but at a volume I knew he would hear. I scanned the beach, seeing no sign of him or anyone else, for the matter. He probably went to sleep in his car or found a patch of light somewhere. He clearly didn't go far or get taken away by one of those Watchers.

The silent air crept into the van, slowly quieting the washing waves to allow for the low clicking to take its place. I slammed the door but didn't lock it in case Erius decided to return. With all the light now around the van, I was sure they were all just waiting at the edge for the slightest flicker of the bulbs.

I crawled back into bed to endure the pain in a more comfortable position. Maybe it was best Erius stayed outside. I didn't need an audience, especially not one that would enjoy watching as I writhed in agony. I massaged my lower back where the throbbing began to take place while also kneading at my lower stomach to ease the discomfort.

Chilling pricks poked my palms as the feeling pushed through into my stomach, calming the affliction. I looked down to find my hands emitting the bright green glow as it wrapped around my waist, centering on the pained area. Heat radiated through next, calming the muscles further and allowing me to finally relax into the pillow.

I wasn't sure what power it was, but I was thankful for it. My cramps usually put me out the first two days, and something told me calling out would only add to whatever its been looking like to Andrew. Not that it mattered, I'm a free woman, I just don't want my routine ruined again.

The pain subsided, allowing me to sink into the mattress. A sense of tranquility rained over me, weighing me down in the comfort even further.

Unfortunately, sleep didn't hold me long as the van door slowly slid open. The cab rocked as weight stepped in, followed by the drawn out close of the door. He shifted the bed as he sat down without a word, and I didn't bother supplying any myself. Demon or not, I was sure he could grasp what was going on.

The bed moved again as he lay back. His leg folded up as it

usually did, pinning me in my tight space. When the bed stopped rocking and he had found his place, I thought he would drift back to sleep as quickly as he usually did. But the air around me felt tight, and I was suddenly hyper aware of his proximity to me. A concentrated charge lit my skin before a heated finger brushed down my arm, leaving a fiery trail in its wake. It slid back up just as lightly, sending a sharp chill shaking my body.

He froze as I slowly turned to face him, struggling with the blankets as I shifted over. "What?" I whispered.

He stared at me for a while with downturned brows as he cleared his throat. "Your skin," he paused to search his words, probably realizing how creepy it sounded aloud. "It is entrancing."

We looked at each other blankly, both a bit shocked by his statement. A ripple of ice white fluttered across the frost blue of his eyes as they bore into me. I pushed myself back against the wall but before either of us could stop him, his palm pressed against my stomach and slid over to grip my hip. He paused for a moment, looking over me as he contemplated his next move. In seconds, heat flushed my body as he surrounded me, pulling me into him and locking me down with his arms.

I pressed my hands against his chest, unsure if I wanted to push him off or allow it to continue. Not that I had time to settle on any option before his other hand reached for me again, shifting to his demon skin and claws as he collected my hands.

He kept me close as his body relaxed against mine, burning like a thousand suns over my skin. He didn't do anything more than trap me there while he trailed his clawed fingers over my arm. A low rumble rolled through his chest, reminding me of how Prometheus was when he's comfortable, purring and all that.

My demon was nothing more than a giant cat, when I really thought about it. His behavior since this past weekend had been odd in its own right. Now there was this.

"Is this some weird demon thing?" I asked.

He took a deep breath, lightly dragging his claws over my hip. "This has never happened before," he muffled against the top of my head.

"I find that hard to believe." In all his years coming to this realm, whether by choice or force, I doubted he hadn't been intimate with a human in some way or another. This couldn't be that much of a learning curve for him.

"I do not associate with mortals like this." He paused, his hands gripping me. I didn't know whether to believe him or not. He was a demon and a man, so I wouldn't put it past him to lie. Though I wouldn't really see the point in lying. We were all grown here, some of us more than others.

But if he was being honest, and I was his first experience with a mortal—I guessed I could make it worthwhile. I was sure I'd made it pretty interesting thus far.

"There is a first time for everything." I sighed, releasing my own hesitations to melt into him. My body instantly warmed with a comfort I had longed for since I was a kid, the feeling of peace and protection that ironically came from the very same one who has disrupted my peace, and the one I'd need the most protection from.

It was as if a match lit within me, a realization that set fire to my veins. I could live without fear; it was a weighing and painful feeling. But it would be my luck that adoration is a strong emotion to stay and latch to the very thing that caused all of this.

Logic would tell me to push away. But logic would have also told me not to summon a demon while drunk. And if there was one thing I knew about myself, it was that I was no listener of logic.

I inhaled his vanilla scent and exhaled it out, relaxing deeper into him as I fell into an instant dreamless slumber.

By morning, Erius was clearly struggling with his emotions and feelings that consumed him the night before. He sat at the front of the van, eyeing me with darkening eyes as if it was my fault he had suddenly got all handsy with me last night, leaving his little claw marks all over me like some feral cat.

I smeared Neosporin over the deeper ones, not anything that seemed threatening, but who knew what he used those things for? The last thing I needed was some wild infection.

I met his gaze with equal amounts of disdain. "Are you going to be weird all day? Or are you going to get over it?" I took a step towards him, mostly to put the cream back, but he moved away from me just the same.

"Wow! Really?" I shot. "I thought I was stuck with a demon, not a child. Get up." I grabbed my bag from the driver's seat and turned to leave the van with him keeping his little distance behind me, or what distance he could keep.

I opened the door to blinding bright light and the foulest stench of fish I had ever smelled.

"Gah!" I growled, stumbling back into the safety of my van. "There is something dead out there!"

"You did not see it?" Erius asked gruffly.

"The sun is overpowering!" I hissed out, cowering in the shade of the shower.

"And you asked if I was the child," he scoffed, stepping out into the brightness. His body illuminated under the glow as he walked around in search of whatever died to leave behind that smell. After several loops around the van, he returned with a shrug. "There is nothing out of the ordinary, and it smells no different than usual."

I gaped up at him, shocked he—of all people—couldn't smell it. I moved to the front of the cab to grab my sunglasses and dug through one of the drawers for an old face mask with a filter. I put both on as if I was going out to battle whatever felt brave enough to attack me.

Once ready for a second time with the shades and mask, we stepped out, Erius doing little to hide the smirk on his face.

"Don't laugh at me," I snapped, locking the van and marching off. Unfortunately, the glasses and face cover did absolutely nothing to shield the rays or stench. The screeching sound of tires against the asphalt jarred my nerves, but it wasn't until we were standing under the loudly buzzing stoplight that I felt that this was slightly unnatural from me.

"Erius," I began.

He looked down to me with a lifted brow, waiting for me to continue.

"If I am one of these Neapolitan things, how would those against it know?"

"You mean a *Nipans*. And they would not. Not here, anyway. In the Circles, it's the smell that usually gives away the facilities. That and the number of bodies and spirits being dumped in," he explained.

"You say a lot of them die?"

"Yes," he said flatly.

The light turned green, and we made our way across as more questions began to build.

"Has there *ever* been any that have survived?" I pressed further.

His face tightened as he thought but, considering the length of silence and the fact he actually looked to be thinking of an answer, gave me a bit of concern.

"Do you not know?"

"No. None have survived that I have heard of."

Great. Lucky me for getting drunk and summoning a demon. I should have just burned that fucking book.

The smell of fish shifted to a stale, moldy rot that pulled my attention from the path ahead. I scanned the road over to the sidewalk behind us. Living in L.A., there was always something to be seen on the streets, wild or not. But what I saw did not even seem human as people walked past it as if it weren't even there.

The same dark, bellowing shadowy figure that had led me off to the pier during my meditation. I never got a good look at what it was trying to show me, but by Erius's reaction and what he *did* tell me, it didn't seem as though the figure was too friendly.

"Whether you are or not, you still need to learn to control your powers," Erius said, pulling my attention back to our conversation. "Do you have any readings to conduct this day?"

"Um," I stammered, turning back to see the ghost before attempting to point it out to Erius, but it was gone. I turned back as we continued to the shop. "I don't think I do, but I'll have to check."

The clamoring noise of tourists shouting behind us rattled my mind and caused a pounding headache by the time we reached the door. I hurried to unlock it and pushed into the lobby with such speed that I crashed over the tables and chairs. The few magazines toppled over, and my sunglasses flew from my face to join everything else as it all crashed all over the floor. My nose fell under attack by the herbs and incense that had already been strong before.

The lobby filled with a roaring laughter, deep and ominous as Erius found humor in my discomfort. I turned to him, mistakenly sucking in a breath to cuss him out. Fire blazed down my throat. I clutched my neck as I fell into a coughing fit. Each struggle caused the demon to laugh more.

"Shut up!" I hissed dryly, tossing the fallen magazine at him.

"Are you alright?" he asked between his ghoulish chuckles.

"No," I choked out. "Everything is bright, and loud, and overpowering!"

His laugh and smile fell slightly, though he clearly still found joy in the discomfort. He helped me to my feet with a grin before clearing his throat.

"You should take the day off," he offered, assisting me in dusting off my skirt, putting a bit too much focus into my hip. My senses weren't the only thing overly sensitive. Each touch stilled a breath in my lungs, blazing my skin on contact. Something I couldn't keep allowing myself to get caught up in. Even if he did seem interested now, the tether had yet to be broken. What if all these feelings either of us have are purely from that? The tether that won't allow us more than a mile apart could be doing more than we thought.

"What?" I finally asked when he finished with his unneeded assistance.

"Take the day off. You will thank me," he said boldly.

Taking the afternoon off would be best. I'd rather be uncomfortable in the comfort of my van, not suffocating under these bright lights. But I still had to suffer until Amber or Jasmine got in.

I texted the group chat that I wasn't feeling well and that I was going to be leaving once either of them got in. After hitting send, I texted Andrew and took the risk of telling him I needed the day off. A gamble, considering the look he gave me when Erius and I left together.

Erius pulled out his phone and began typing something in before holding it to his ear while I struggled to keep my coughing under control.

"*Heů*," he said, speaking in that unknown language. "*Mich pà zhàzů ůzh.*"

His lips pressed flat at whatever was spoken on the other end, "*Hidh, mich ůzh tåk iez tou!*" There was another pause as he looked over me with furrowed brows.

"*Bůk,*" he said blankly. He gripped my hand and brought it to his nose. After a deep sniff of my wrist, he turned his attention back to his phone. "No."

Finally, a language I know. My phone buzzed with a response from Andrew.

That's fine.

-Andrew

Ouch, but I guess I can't really blame him. I just had to wait for Amber or Jaz to come in.

"What am I supposed to do until then?" Erius growled into the phone. "Just inform me when he leaves," he added before ending the call and shoving the phone into his pocket.

Struggling against the coughing fit, I made my way to the back wall to flip on the lights, instantly regretting it as the loud buzzing of the fluorescent rang in my ears and the odd brightness shocked pain into my eyes.

With a cry that likened that of a frightened deer, I smacked the switch and cut the lights out once again. The swift relief of the lights soon washed over me. I pressed my back against the wall and slid to the floor with a deep sigh. "What the fuck is going on?"

Erius walked over to me with a mixed expression of irritation and concern. He kneeled to meet my level and took my scarred hand in his. "It looks like I gave you a bit more then this here scar and power."

"What does that mean?" I snorted.

"It means you might be the first of your kind to survive."

My heart dropped at his words, pushing the last bit of air free. I stared at him for a minute, unsure if I should be mad at him or myself, or even at all. I should probably be scared, if anything—but none of that was my first concern. I was more interested in what this meant for us once this was all over.

The bell above the door rang as Jasmine and Amber both spilled in.

"What have you done to her now?" Jaz spat as they both raced between Erius and me.

"Jaz!" I snapped.

"Ever since you came, she hasn't been the same!" Amber added, rushing to my side as Jaz stepped between us and Erius.

"No, she would not be. Would she?" Erius droned with his eyes still on me.

"You guys! It's literally just my period. It's just a bit...different," I explained.

"And why do you think that is? Because he did some weird-freaky demon shit to you." Amber pointed to my arm for the main example.

Erius shuffled back to my side, ignoring the looks Jaz tossed at him as he pushed past her. He took my hand before turning back to them. "I am the best protection she has. Now, if you do not mind."

Before either could respond, we were already headed toward the door. They both clicked their cheeks as they prepared to jump in again.

"It's really alright, you guys. I promise!" I pushed out before he had me out the door and back into the uncomfortably bright sun. As we walked to the first crosswalk, Erius placed the sunglasses over my eyes.

"What—" I stuttered out.

"You dropped them." He had been nicer lately, but this was actually sweet of him.

"Thank you," I added as we cross the street. My attention wandered to the spot where the dark figure had stood earlier. I wasn't expecting to see anything, but there it was again, standing in the crowd. Though it didn't have eyes, I couldn't help but feel it watching me.

"Do you see that?" I finally asked Erius, nodding in the figure's direction.

He looked over and scanned the people but didn't seem too interested in what he saw. "The loud group of mortals?" he questioned. So, he didn't see it. A demon who didn't see ghosts or shadow figures or whatever it was.

Wonderful.

He didn't seem like he truly would care apart from asking what it was doing, which was nothing, and he didn't seem the type to care unless it's a threat that directly affects him.

"Never mind," I said with a sigh.

"If you are seeing things, please do not keep that to yourself." He groaned.

"You're so concerned all of a sudden."

He was quiet for a minute as we crossed the lot to the van, and I wish he had remained so. "I do not plan on being wiped from existence. But if we are, I suppose being kind to you is the least I could do."

His words echoed in my mind, freezing me at the door of the van.

"What?" I choked out.

He turned to me and leaned closer, speaking in a low whisper. "Your new sensitivities are common for the women of my world. I thought your ability to transform was a mere side effect, possibly. But truthfully, I am most certain you are a proper *Nipans*."

I stared at him, speechless, trying to make sense of all the information he has given me with little understanding aside from me being an illegal experiment in a world I am unfamiliar with. "So, we are going to be killed?" I asked, finally opening the door.

"Not killed. Wiped. But I do not plan on it. We have to first ensure it is what you are. We would not want a false execution over something that isn't the case, correct?" He didn't wait long for a response before continuing, "We will be seeing Alius again."

"When will that be?" I pressed.

"The moment it is safe for you to be there. For now, we should lay low."

"I thought you said nobody would know."

"Nobody will know unless told." He walked behind me, placing his hands on my shoulders as he faced me toward the pier in the distance.

"Look under the boardwalk, near the tides," he instructed. I did as so, squinting into the far-off shadows. The longer I focused, the louder the clicking became. A few Watchers jerked and twitched about the shadowy space, keeping far from the light.

Before I could say anything else, Erius tugged me into the van and slammed the door behind us, startling Prometheus from his spot on the bed and sending him flying into his cubby again.

The moment the door shut, the overstimulation stopped. The bright lights, the loud noise, the strong smell of fish all dissipated to the comforting feeling of home. I sat on the bed and fell back, exhausted and ready for a nap, but there was one thing left to ask.

"Should I be worried? Or scared. You don't seem too worried, so I want to know if I should be?"

"Being wiped from existence is not enough to give you a slight sense of it?" he grunted.

"You keep saying it like that but haven't really explained it. Are we going to die? Won't we just end up in these Circles you keep talking about?"

"Did I say we would be killed or did I say wiped? There will be no returning to the Circles. My soul will be shredded to nothing I am not too sure how they would dispose of you, being that I took your soul. Our essence, our light, our entire being will be wiped from the plain."

"Oh, that does seem bad," I said blankly.

"Try and remember the feeling of fear for this one thing and do as I say." He groaned, pinching the bridge of his nose between two fingers.

"I'll try," I hummed, nodding off to a quick sleep.

My nap couldn't have lasted too long, maybe thirty minutes or so before a chill caressed my arm.

"*Boja pi.* Young one," a voice whispered, spilling cool air over my cheeks. It sounded as rough as the language Erius spoke, but also different in a way I couldn't explain. I opened my eyes, not in my van but out by the pier, under the boardwalk by the tides, where Erius had pointed.

Over the washing waves and seagulls call I could hear the echoing clicking from the several creeping Watchers twitching about the shadows without noticing me. The cool chill swept over my arm, pulling my attention to my right where the faceless ghost stood. It waved its shadowy arm at me and turned to the Watchers.

I opened my mouth to ask what it wanted, but no sound came

out. I tried again with no luck and even gave a quick shout that went unheard. The Watchers continued to jerk about, sounding off their creepy clicks without notice of me or the figure.

This didn't seem too aggressive, nor did it seem friendly—at least it did not give off the feeling of either. Eventually, it turned to me again with a bow before heading off toward the water.

Whether it wanted me to follow or not, I headed off to my van. If I knew anything about lucid dreaming it was that I shouldn't interact with the people or, in this case, creatures.

The door flung open before I could reach for it, presenting Erius but in his demon form. He scanned the beach, taking notice of the figure at the far end. His lip curled and he snatched me inside, slamming the door behind us.

"Mortal," he called out, "are you awake?" Heated hands pushed against my arm to shake me up.

"Hm?" I hummed, opening my eyes to the demon at his usual spot on the side of the bed, leaning back without a care. He had a leather pouch in his hand that he placed between us.

"Eat that," he ordered with no other explanation.

I blinked at him, rubbing the sleep and confusion from my eyes as I gathered myself from the dream. When I made sense of my reality and what was going on, I turned my attention to the pouch.

I looked over the odd herb I had never in my life seen before. Spikey red-golden colored stigma sat at the center with several long golden stems and bulbs growing out, with yellow and green paper-thin petals that stuck out all around it.

"I'm not eating that," I said slowly.

"Why not?" He cocked his lips into a half smile and tilted his head with amusement.

I looked over the several bulbed flowers in the pouch once more. "What the fuck is it?"

"They are called *pozh zàg*," he said, pulling one from the pouch.

"Erius," I said blankly, "be fucking for real."

"It is an herb that will help with your…symptoms."

"What kind of herb is a *pozh zàg*?" I attempted to say, clearly failing as Erius didn't bother to hide the laugh.

"It's one the women of the Circles eat. It calms the senses from being overstimulated during this time."

I looked up at him with concern. This was all unusually kind of him, which could be him just finding another way to fuck with me. I narrowed my eyes at him, then the pouch.

"How do I know this isn't some trick?" I protested.

"Alius came all this way to bring it. If I wanted to hear you suffer more, I would not need to supply you anything. I would just turn that projector thing on and watch you squirm from that."

"Wow, thanks," I breathed, pulling one of the flower's heads from the pouch. The spicy licorice smell was only comforting because of familiarity, but I hated licorice.

"Do I just bite into it?" I quizzed.

"It can be made into a tea or cooked into food. The same way you mortals consume herbs." He shrugged.

"Hm, so we aren't all that much different, are we?" I muttered to myself as I placed the herb back and collected the pouch. Erius watched unmoved as I climbed over his obscuring frame to get to the small counter. I started the kettle of water and pulled out the only mug I own. While that boiled, I placed a flower bulb into the mug and drizzled honey over it to mask whatever flavor might attack my tongue.

The kettle sounded off with its screaming whistle that blared against my ears. I was not sure if it was his British accent, or the fact it was an herb from his realm, but making tea with him over my shoulder felt as though I was being challenged to make it properly. As I poured the water over the flower, I was anticipating a slew of *tsks* from him, but he remained silent.

As the cup filled and the boiling water penetrated the herb, I watched in amazement as the liquid fizzed to a bright golden color. The spicy fragrance bloomed into a delightful scent that filled the van, one that was most definitely not licorice.

I brought the mug to my mouth. Steam filled my nose and instantly calmed the attack that was in my nostrils. The sweet yet spicy liquid provided the same quick relief to the other senses while also leaving a very familiar effect.

"Is there a dosage I should consider?" I asked.

Erius looked over me and the mug in my hand with a slight curve to his lips. "One a day should be enough."

Chapter Twenty-Two

Mira

The plant did wonders in calming the severity of the symptoms down to nothing more than a nagging tug at my lower stomach. Sounds were back to normal, well, the new normal at least, and everything wasn't as bright. But Erius was still oddly obsessed with my skin and didn't let me out of his sight for anything other than to use the restroom, at which he still followed me up until the door.

All in all, I felt well enough to go out for lunch before heading to work and decided on a place I knew sold mini cakes. Regardless of if his human form actually aged, it was always nice to have a birthday celebrated. I doubted he'd ever give me the real date, so this would have to do.

We stepped into the overly sweet smelling lobby where pies and cakes lined a cabinet wall for pickup. Behind the counter sat a dozen different kinds of cupcakes and single slices of other delicious looking treats. I hadn't seen him eat anything sweet, but I couldn't assume he didn't. He did say my soul was sweet, after all.

I wandered over near the wall to look over the options, Erius hovering the whole time. A delicious fudge frosted double layer cake slice caught my eye, already pre-packaged in a clear container. Perfect, now for the distraction. I attempted to look around his blocking frame, but he practically mirrored my every move.

"What do you think is going to happen to me if you are a few feet back?" I groaned, pretending as if I didn't just spot the perfect chocolate fudge cake.

"If you have this strong of an effect on me, I cannot imagine any other creature of my likeness avoiding it. And they will move quickly."

I tried to hide the disgusted sneer. I'd had my period most my life and have never run into any demons or the like, until him. But before I could ask what that meant, an elderly gentleman approached us.

"Welcome, just you two?" the waiter asked, taking Erius's attention off me long enough that I managed to swiftly nab the cake container. Thankfully there was no door to fiddle with. I tucked it in my bag before he turned back to me and gave the waiter a brisk nod. As with most outsiders, he looked between us with the same questioning gape before leading us to a small booth in the far corner. I understood it looked like a date, but we didn't need to be seated as such.

Even in the booth, he was practically on top of me, consuming me in his overpowering heat and vanillic scent. His probing eyes scanned over me, causing him some sort of fuss as he struggled to keep his hands in his lap.

"You look uncomfortable." I began. "You know what you need?" I turned to pull the cake out of my bag and placed it before him. "Happy birthday," I cheered.

He looked from me to the cake with a slight hint of confusion. I pushed the cake closer to him, humming the tune of the classic song. Not that he looked too entertained by it, crossing his arms over his chest with his usual blank stare.

"It's your birthday," I repeated playfully.

"You remembered the date on that card?"

"Well, yeah. Don't you? Do you not usually celebrate it?" I offered him a fork and a soft smile. Clearly this was not something he did. Much like everything else. He must have spent those ten years collecting dust wherever it was he stayed.

"This form does not truly age, so I never found need to." He grabbed the fork and hesitantly took a bite.

"It's just chocolate cake." I laughed at his reluctance to enjoy a dessert, but that soon changed. The small ass taste must have sent him because he went back for more with enthusiasm. Poor cake never had a chance.

To my surprise, he ate half of it before sliding it over to me to finish off. The motion may have not seemed like much to him, just as this whole birthday thing, but it left a fluttery sensation that moved around my stomach. It may have not been a date, and him and I may not be anything more than…whatever we are to each other—but it starting to feel real, and I didn't know if I wanted it to end anymore.

It's just because I'm on my period. He's just having a reaction to it. That's all—don't look too deep into nothing.

I tried to push the feelings and thoughts back despite the fact he had draped his arm over the back rest of the booth, finding ways to caress my shoulder and twist his fingers in my hair. He wasn't at all shy about his new infatuation which may come to an immediate end at the end of the week. But for now he seemed to relish in every tremble he caused, bringing on more than a flood of emotions.

After the cake, I ordered some food to go and once it arrived, we headed out.

The walk to the shop was no different than the walk to the café, with Erius crowding my space, on the hunt for some invisible threat.

Hopefully he could manage to contain himself while I worked. If not for the cameras announcing Erius's presence, Antonio would be sure to open his mouth. Not that he'd mean to, at least. I didn't think he would, but he and Andrew were friends outside of work so the possibility of it just being a casual slip up was too much to risk.

"I need you to stay at the pier today. You've caused enough unnecessary drama at my job, and I don't need my boss breathing down my neck about fraternizing with clients," I said, turning to face him at the corner. He looked down at me without a word but the smirk on his lips told me he had some snark ass shit to say.

"What?"

The corner of his mouth kicked up, his eyes trailing off toward the shop. "Do you plan to hide me from that mortal forever?"

Ice spread across my face at his words, sending a sharp chill over my body. Forever? The fluttering returned to my stomach, sending my heart on an equally wild dance into my chest.

It was just instincts and he would leave the moment he can. He didn't even want to fuck, and if he wasn't going to let me fuck anyone else, forever might not work for me.

"I do not plan on being a demon's pet for the rest of my existence. Thanks, though," I argued.

His gaze dropped down before slowly climbing up my body to taunt me with his dazzling eyes and that weird thing he did.

"I wouldn't call you a pet. Pets are much more obedient."

I shot him a hard glare before spinning around to march off. The weighing heat of his energy lightened but never fell from me. I tried to wave it off as I entered the shop, but it was unfazed, clinging to me more like a second skin. I sighed, giving in to his little security measure, and headed to the computer to check clients.

I pulled out the displays and started the teas, set the incense upstairs, and dusted the crystals. I handled several groups of customers before Antonio showed up. He grabbed one of the free suckers we had for tasting and leaned against the counter with a quizzical expression.

"So, you and that new client?" Antonio poked with a toying grin. Nosy ass.

"I don't know what you are talking about," I lied as I looked over the empty list for the day, which wasn't a bad thing. I wanted to talk to the girls yesterday, and now I could explain everything that happened in person.

"Hey, man, when a coworker starts bringing someone who looks like they belong in the mafia around, I'm going to have questions." He laughed.

"Is that what you think?" I pulled out my phone, trying to ignore him, and texted the group to head up and come to my room once they arrived. Jasmine was due any minute for her shift anyway, but I wanted to tell them all together.

"So, you're not involved in any mafia heist?" he asked curiously.

"No, Antonio. I'm teaching him how to do readings. He's like— an intern," I lied, but it seemed to do the trick as he considered it. With that out of the way, I headed up to wait in my room. Normally I would pass the time with meditation, but after the last episode with the pier and the figure, I thought I would hold off doing that without some sort of supervision.

I did have my own questions for the universe and spirits that I had yet to delve into myself. At first, I didn't know how I would word them. Then I just didn't want to be given an answer I didn't want to see.

The easiest question to ask is if we would ever break this tether. But what if the answer is a solid no in all varieties?

Asking the spirits if I was an illegal hybrid seemed out of the question. I didn't know how their lines of communication worked. I couldn't even trust my own government to not be tapping my phone or other devices. What if bringing up the name brought on an "investigation?"

Let's keep it simple. I took a deep breath and sat on the floor with my deck in hand to focus on the question.

Will we break this tether? I shuffled the deck, repeating the question in my head before laying down three cards, face up.

The Devil

Death

The Lovers

I looked over the cards with a scowl before scooping them up to reshuffle. I didn't like anything about that answer. Mingling the deck once more, I reworded the question to "Will this tether ever be broken?" taking out us as a connection. I pulled three cards and set them down face up, yet again.

The Devil

Death

The Lovers

"Ugh!" I groaned as I scooped them up one last time. "I'll just ask something different."

What is *my* future path like? I screamed the question internally and pulled three more cards. With my eyes tightly squeezed, I flipped each one, holding my breath as I gazed down at them.

The Devil

Death

The Lovers

I slammed my hands down and mushed the cards about the floor with a growl. That cannot be my outcome—*our* outcome.

The bell rang, flooding the girls' cheerful voices into the lobby before I could begin to overthink everything. For now, I would keep this reading to myself. The last thing I needed was them asking me upon every gathering, nor did I need him avoiding me over a card reading that could, hopefully, mean nothing.

I collected the cards and wrapped them back up before the girls entered and witnessed my displeasure. Without greeting Antonio, they made their way up, their bright smiles shifting to concern as they caught sight of me standing in the doorway.

"Meems!" Amber greeted. "How are you?" She brought her voice down to a whisper despite the fact they were already crossing into the room.

"I'm—fine. I mean, I'm not hurt."

"Then what happened over the weekend? What did that monster do to you?" Jaz blurted.

I took a deep breath, gauging each of their expressions. We were all in this together. They lacked a soul just as much as I did. We all held some sort of power from the trade. It was just, I clearly got far more than expected.

"Maybe we should all sit down," I suggested.

They nodded and we all took a spot amongst the cushions and pillows. When we were all comfortable, I began to explain the events of the weekend and the following two days—what Erius had told me he thought I was and how we could be wiped from existence if anyone from his realm found out. I told them of the Watchers following us and the figure that almost led me into a den of them. Even the herb Erius brought that helped with my new and heightened PMS.

"And why can't he change you back?" Amber asked, despite my long explanation.

"He doesn't even know how he changed me in the first place and isn't even entirely sure if that is what I am. He says I don't 'carry the scent' of one."

"What do they smell like?" Mickey asked curiously.

"He said they smell bad or like death or rot—I don't know, he just said I smell faintly human but not bad."

"Can you show us?" Jaz asked as she perked up in her seat with a beaming grin.

I ground my teeth as I glared at her. Of course she would want to see it, just to pick at me about it.

"I want to see this tail of yours!" she added with her hands clasped in front of her chest.

"No," I said flatly. "I can't even control it, it just happens. Erius thinks it's because of anger or frustration, but I don't know."

I sat back in silence after that, contemplating who was next to share to get the focus from me. The room fell quiet as they waited, giving birth to a soft squeaking coming from Amber, or at least somewhere on her. I looked around the circle to see if anyone else notice, stopping on Amber herself, who did in fact seem to notice the sound just as she noticed me.

"What do you have there, Amber?" I said with a smile.

Her eyes widened as she looked around the room. "Nothing," she pushed, her face flushing a deep copper. I rose a brow and waited.

"Fine." She reached into her purse and pulled out a small bundle of leaves to present to us. We leaned in to get a better look of the various blades in different shades of green and brown.

"Um—you just carry around a bunch of leaves?" Jaz asked curiously, not noticing the gentle rise and fall of the pile. Each tiny exhale released the soft squeaking sound.

"It's breathing," I pointed out.

"*His* name is Fidget," Amber informed us as she gently stroked a finger over one of the leaves. The creature fluttered under the touch, lifting its petals up to present two big bug-like eyes.

"How do you know it's a boy?" Mickey asked curiously.

Amber's face flushed again as she looked down at the creature. "I've had to teach him to, um, use the restroom for himself. It was an odd discovery."

We all shared a disgusted but equally curious look.

"You made him?" I asked as she set him on the floor.

She nodded happily as she pulled out a small container of blackberries. "He loves these." She poured the berries out before the creature. Surprisingly, the pile of leaves rose and fluttered across the short distance, reaching out its two tiny arms as it dove right into the berries.

"I guess the demon isn't all that bad," Mickey began. "He stayed true to the deal, and he hasn't hurt Mina."

Jaz shot me a look through slit lids as a smile curved her lips. "No, he hasn't. He only made her some creature of Hell."

"Apparently, Hell doesn't exist." I shrugged.

They all looked at me with rounded eyes and hung mouths.

"Erius calls it The Circles, and it's sort of like the Underworld but not really. He didn't go too deep into it," I explained. None of us were religious so it wasn't a heartbreaking discovery, but in a way we all still found it fascinating.

We spent the rest of the shift discussing our powers while Jaz and I alternated between helping Antonio with customers. By the final hour, we were all cleaning up to close down.

The bell rang with a late customer that I figured was not here for anything in the shop. The strong scent of vanilla was hard to miss.

"You must be here for Mina," Antonio said brightly. "She's

upstairs."

Erius didn't say anything, but I figured he was on his way up.

"Does he always do that?" Jaz whispered from my side.

I nodded with my attention on the steps as he came into view, his usual blank expression replaced with the half smirk I was growing used to. I held my breath, fighting the sudden racing of my heart, more traitorous than the tail. My body flushed with a numbness that twisted my stomach and I thought I was going to be sick. His lips twisted up into that devilish, know-it-all grin he had, which didn't help the situation.

"Let me guess, you were bored," I pressed in an attempt to distract myself.

His smile grew, bearing his fangs for all to see. "On the contrary. Today seemed to be quite enlightening." He leaned down, and the sudden proximity of his heated energy lit my body on fire and dazed my senses from the heavy vanilla. I stepped back from the intoxicating cloud to regain focus.

"Whatever that means. Just wait downstairs while I finish cleaning and we can go."

CHAPTER TWENTY-THREE

Mira

Thursday sped by with no issues. The herb helped me as Erius said it would, though he seemed to be having more trouble controlling his own senses and weird demon urges. At least that was the excuse he gave. I think he just wanted a reason to cuddle which I find hysterical since he spent our whole first week together avoiding touching me unless he was dragging me around. Now he wouldn't leave me alone.

Thankfully, I should be ending it soon and he could go back to his usual stand-offish self. Being Friday, we were due to head back up to Angeles so I could practice my transforming in and out of my forms. I would prefer not to do it, but Erius insisted it would help me avoid changing unnecessarily.

Since my shift was with the girls, I told Erius he could come in as long as he didn't hover and stayed upstairs while I worked, and he did a decent job. I didn't know what he was doing to pass time, but every time I went in to at least make it appear as though he wasn't waiting for me, he'd just look at the books on the shelf. Between checking in with him and helping customers, Jaz insisted on probing me with questions.

"So you're going off to Angeles again?" she asked as we began setting away the jars of herbs.

"Yea. Erius wants me to practice for safety reasons. I think he just likes tormenting me," I teased, knowing he could hear.

"Have you heard anything about the woman meant to separate you, or have you given up on that?" she tossed with a more serious tone.

I snapped my attention to her, not missing the subtle sarcasm. "No, we haven't given up. I'm sure he's more than ready to leave. All he does is complain about my van and my distracting smell. We are just waiting."

She curled her lip at the statement. "Distracting smell? Do you stink?"

"I don't even know. I don't think it's bad, probably just annoying. He complains about it often enough. I'm sure if it was offensive, he would let me know." I scooped another cup of dried lavender into the second smaller jar. "He wouldn't hesitate to let me know I stink."

"How are you even sure he's doing anything about it?" she interrogated next.

I jarred off the herb for the front and slid the bigger one to her to take to the back, but she waited for an answer without motion to grab the jar.

"Because he's constantly talking to some guy he knows that has connections to the sorceress. And even then, he said she was the most powerful, but didn't have too much faith in her power as it was. Besides, I think we have other problems Erius is more concerned with."

"Oh, like you being part demon now?" Mickey poked from the front display table she was redecorating.

"Or that you two will be killed?" Jaz tossed next.

"Exactly. As far as breaking the tether goes, I don't think he cares too much right now. But I am sure it is still a concern." I began the sweeping while Mickey dusted the paintings and trinkets on the wall.

With the worry of the Watchers, I thought it'd be best Erius and I left early both to get to the site before dark and to draw whatever ones are around away from the girls. Erius mentioned the ones under the pier should be distracted enough by the beachgoers that they wouldn't leave that spot. As for what could be lurking in the forest itself, he said we should be well off as long as there is no hint of their scent.

"Well, if you are supposed to be an illegal creation, why is he trying to show you what more you can do?" Jaz pressed.

"Because, when it comes time for it, she needs to know how to protect and control herself," Erius said from the top lobby.

"You plan to have her fight?" Jaz shot up to him.

"If that is what needs to be done."

Mickey's body shook with a hard shiver as she looked up at him. Fear was clearly something she still held. I wouldn't say it was a prime emotion she felt, but she did not like scary movies at all. I was not surprised it would be an emotion to stay with her.

"Fighting?" Mickey said, swallowing thickly as she gazed up at him.

"Precisely." He flashed his fang-filled grin her way, which only sent her trembling back to stand by Jaz. The lobby filled with the irritated tapping of Jaz's nails as she glared at Erius.

"Stop that!" I shot to him, knowing he was trying to frighten her.

He made his way down the steps to my side, making sure to keep his little distance he wanted to maintain. Or tried to, anyway.

The heat of his body pressed into my back, and I was hyper aware of his struggle to keep his hands where they were. He was probably up in that room suffering this whole time.

Jasmine's eyes widened as she looked between us, her mouth dropping open for a second before she quickly collected herself. Given what she had said about her power, I'm sure she picked up on his odd behavior.

"What?" I asked.

She smiled and took the jar off to the back room without explanation and a faint shake of her head.

"Well, we should head out before it gets too late. Do y'all need anything before I leave?" I asked.

"No, go have fun!" Jaz called from the hall.

I looked to Erius who was already mesmerized by whatever it was he was going through, looking over me like some snack. Only for him, it was in both a literal and metaphorical sense.

"I'll try. See you later!" I called, waving bye to Mickey before leading him out the door and to the van.

We climbed in, Erius still up my ass the entire time while I put things away before we headed off.

"Why don't you drive and give yourself something to do?" I suggested.

He nodded with a look of relief while I settled into the passenger seat. I rolled my window down in hopes that would provide some comfort, if not for him, then for me.

By the time Erius pulled on to the dirt path, the sun was tucking beyond the horizon, providing enough light to see the evening beauty of the forest as we drove through. It was nice to be able to enjoy the sights coming up. It wasn't something I often witnessed being that I was usually the one driving.

The orange and pink colors that swirled across the sky fell beautifully upon the trees, beaming colorful light through the branches and leaves to create a dance of colors along the path we rode. Through the trees I could see the several occupied campsites along with open patches of wildlife roaming.

A mother deer and baby came to the path, waiting as we neared to pass through.

"Oh, look! A baby deer!" I mused happily. "Little baby Bambi."

Erius didn't seem to care about them one way or another as we drove by. From the side mirror I watched as they calmly crossed to the other side. It wasn't the first time I've seen deer here—rare, but not unexpected to see them from time to time. It was nice to see them so close to the busy sites.

We continued up the long path. The fires from the most used campsites dwindled behind us as he headed to my secluded site. It was empty and unused, looking exactly how we left it last week. Erius pulled into the worn-down space to park before turning to me.

I waited for him to get up first to keep from him being behind me. Not that my own hesitation meant anything; he did the same, sitting and waiting for me to move first. I squinted at him, holding back the smile that burned my cheeks.

"Is this your first time dealing with this?" I asked.

"Not at all."

"Shouldn't you be used to it by now? Aren't you thousands of years old?"

His brows furrowed at my words. "It is not something I can simply get used to," he pushed out.

"Is it like an animal instinct sort of thing. Am I in heat or something?" I teased.

"In a sense," he said slowly. "It has never been this strong."

"Well, lucky for us all, it should be ending soon," I informed him, news that clearly brought him a bit of relief, but it didn't change him being up my ass while I made dinner.

I forced him to sit across from me at the firepit to give us both space. He glared at me with either hatred or desire, I couldn't tell which. Either way, he looked to be in pain.

"Is it that hard for you?" I laughed.

"I'm sitting here in this spot. Am I not?" he pushed.

"Oh, crabby." I took a bite of the salad. "I think you just want a reason to touch me."

A gust of air swept past, and he was suddenly at my side, taking the bowl from my hand. "If I wanted to touch you, I would not need to drum up an absurd reason to do it."

"That's reassuring." I reached for my bowl, and he pulled it back further, placing it on the log. The scarred hand returned with claws and stars. The night sky crept up his arm to his elbow, spreading off in a web over his shoulder. He grabbed my arm and the scar lit up with a crackling sound, sizzling my skin to the new form of mine.

He exhaled, fanning the warm vanilla over me. "As I have mentioned, I do not normally spend this much time this close to mortals. I spend even less time in this form. I do not know what this body wants."

"Then change to the other form. Maybe that will help," I suggested blankly, my attention still on my hand in his. The stars and purple nebulas swirled around, circling my hand as if it were an obstacle in its way.

His fingers curled around mine, capturing them as he looked over the likeness as well. "I do not think it is that easy," he mused, pulling my hand to his nose.

My mouth hung open as I watched him, realizing what was happening. "Are—are all your forms having some feelings about me?"

His brows furrowed as he looked over me, keeping my hand in his grasp. "No."

We looked at each other, both knowing that it didn't sound convincing even for him.

"If that is your truth, you can live in it."

He dropped my hand with a blank stare as he reached around for my bowl to hand back.

"Thank you." I didn't want to make anything out of our new little discovery on feelings. It was probably only because we'd been trapped together in an odd version of Stockholm Syndrome. Once we broke the tether and he could go back to his home, I was sure it would be the only thing on his mind.

It wouldn't matter. It wasn't like I'd be hurt by it. I thought. The very thought did have an odd hollowing effect on my chest that I didn't care for—not a feeling I remembered, but one I just preferred not to have.

I finished the meal and wandered back to the van to clean the bowl, Erius close behind. I figured we might as well go to bed since it was getting dark, and it would be the absolute closest we got.

After my nightly routine, we climbed under the cozy, warm blankets. I tried to ignore him as I lay back, but the heat of his gaze dug into my side.

"Try and get some rest and don't be too much like a demon. Watching me in my sleep and all that." I sighed, closing my eyes and relaxing into the softness of my pillow.

Not that slumber came easily. Erius moved about more than usual, the discomfort reaching him even in his unconscious state, shivering and twitching about as if he were sick or in some horrible dream.

If it gives me a moment's peace.

I closed the small distance that separated us, tucking myself against his bare chest. I pressed my palm to him, feeling the shivering slow. His body wrapped around me, taking in whatever comfort it brought him as he continued to sleep soundly. Not that he was uncomfortable to be tucked up against. His heat and odd rumbling snore helped me fall into a deep sleep as well.

By morning, my monthly friend had gone and Erius was back to his normal distance. We headed outside for the day, a suspicious looking grin plastered hard on his lips.

"You never ran as I had asked that first day," he pointed out suddenly as we made our way to the edge of the forest.

"What?"

"I had told you to run as fast as you could. You never ran. Do so now." He gestured out to the open paths of the forest with his sinful grin.

I looked from the trees to him with a skeptical pinch to my

brows. "Why do you want me to run?"

"It will amuse me. We also need to see how fast your forms can travel," he explained, guiding me into the shade beneath the trees. Given his calm nature, I would guess the area was safe enough if he wanted me to go running through it.

"Why is that important?"

He looked over me, then back to the trees with a huff. "Since you cannot control your shifting yet, we need to be sure you can escape a Watcher. For both forms."

I blinked at him with a hung mouth, shocked that, at my age, I was being assigned to run.

"You just want me to run? Where to?"

"Anywhere your mortal feet carry you." He shrugged with a lazy wave of his hand. "Go on."

I lifted a brow to him, unmoved. This all seemed like more of some weird trap than to see my running speed. He did say it would amuse him before, so who was to say he wasn't just making me run for his entertainment?

"You can run on your own, or I can chase you and I guarantee I run faster," he threatened, his sinister smile growing as he took a step toward me.

"Ok, ok! I'll run. Damn!" I threw my hands up as I walked to the nearest tree, scanning the path I would soon take, where it led, where it ended, what obstacles lay across it to slow me down. With the clearest trail in sight, I took a deep breath and sprinted off.

I practically flew, surprised at the ease in which I could weave and duck through trees and bushes. Shades of green and brown passed by in a haze at my sides.

Wind pulled my hair back, whipping the free strands across my face and shoulders. My legs moved beneath me, blurring to nothing, a true freedom.

I cut through the trees and bushes with ease, making sharp turns I never thought a human body capable of. It wasn't long until my skin began to tingle, raising the bumps across my arms. My legs moved faster, pushing through the twigs as if to flee from something unseen.

I dug my heels into the dirt, skidding to a dusty stop to look around. The air around me was quiet and still with only the whooshing of my racing feet to fill my ears. The crushing silence crawled along, sending an electrifying static over my skin. My ears ached as I struggled to listen for any noise that the space was vacant of. Keeping clear of twigs to avoid the crunching sound on my end, each step echoed with an odd match to it. I took another. The soft press of my foot to the dirt seemed to ring off the trees.

With another step, I paused just before pressing into the soil. A soft snap echoed from behind me. The sound launched my body forward into a full sprint, blurring the surrounding greens and browns to smears as I sped through them. Heat flooded me, heightening my senses and slowing the world around me to better navigate through the forest.

I cut around a large fallen trunk and was immediately slammed into the rough wood as something pinned my body in place. A black mass covered me, blinding me from whatever held me down. I thrashed against the grasp, spitting out vicious, animalistic growls and hisses as I struggled to claw free. The more I moved, the tighter I was held down. The creature's chest rumbled with a responding growl, shaking my body to the bones. With another thrash, a tail slammed down at my side, curling around me to keep me captive.

My claws surfaced as I lashed forward in attempt to scratch the attacker, but it caught me before I could make a connection, gripping my wrist with claws that bit deep into my skin. Struggling did nothing but pull more defensive growls through my teeth.

I continued to thrash and buck at the creature until it pinned my hands above my head. The heated body pressed into me, pushing me further into the dirt as the bark of the logs dug into my shoulders. I struggled again as the creature brought its head down, tucking it into my neck as it inhaled deeply. When it pulled back, bright fangs beamed at me in a triumphant smile.

I blinked at the stars that came into focus across his skin, the exploding nebulas of red and yellow moved over his chest as he caught his breath.

"Erius!" I snapped, kicking, and pushing at his enormous body. "What are you doing?"

"That is interesting," he mused, releasing my hands from his grasp to examine the top of my head. He tugged gently to the left, pulling my horn to tilt my head to him.

"What? You chasing me like prey?" I spat as I struggled under him, but he refused to budge even the slightest.

"No. Your form came out at the first sign of danger. You may not have a sense for it, or fear, but your form does."

"Well, I would hope so. You've been stalking and chasing me through the woods!"

He looked around as if his actions had an obvious reasoning.

"Did you only tell me to run so you could chase me?"

"Yes," he said casually with his devilish grin twisting up. I attempted pushing him off again, and he pressed me down further.

"If you cannot control yourself or learn to protect yourself by the time we break this tether, who's going to protect you? We might as well just turn ourselves over to Tikara now."

His words clung to me, carving a hollowness in my chest as they echoed around in my mind. So much for all he said a few days ago about protecting me and forever and all that nonsense. We both wanted to break the tether, that much was obvious; we both had lives we'd like to return to. But hearing it aloud stung a bit. His world was so big and it was slipping into my smaller, less magical one and being able to change form in a sense meant I did not belong here anymore.

I did not want to.

"Who is Tikara?" I asked blankly.

He shifted his weight to rest on his elbow but never released me from the snare of his tail that had suddenly wrapped around my leg. He sighed, clearly realizing it was now information I should know.

"Tikara is one of the three demon priestesses of the major realms. She is the priestess of the mortal realm, and is currently the only one existing outside of what you would call a prison."

I looked up to him in awe. There was so much to learn from just that. A whole new world to explore and experience.

"I have so many questions."

"I would be more surprised if you did not." His body shook with amusement, building a heated friction that stilled us both, but he didn't make a move to break the connection. "Ask what you wish to ask," he muttered.

"What happened to the other two? What are their names?" I blurted out. I could feel him drag a claw over my horn as he thought on what to say. The odd sensation sent another shockwave through me that I didn't even bother to fight off.

"Chimeriea is imprisoned in the sixth circle of my realm. She is the Priestess of the Circles—not that she has much power over them anymore. But she still finds her ways amongst her followers."

"What did she do?" I pressed.

"She killed their eldest sister, De'Mordia. She was the Priestess of Spirit."

"Why?"

His face hardened as he looked over me, his hand finding its way to my hair. "It is said that De'Mordia caught Chimeriea creating the N*ipans,* a creature believed to eradicate the mortals and liberate the residents of the Circles."

"I was made to liberate souls from their afterlife?" The questions tumbled out with ease the more he supplied.

"No. The residents are those who are born in the Circles. As I have mentioned, it is not the Hell you believe it to be. It is not simply a place those go in their afterlife. It is a home to many you mortals have labeled to be monsters."

I narrowed my eyes, trying to make sense of his explanation. "I'm confused," I groaned.

"I could see how you would be. Just know it is Tikara who made the order to keep the creation of *Nipans* and their existence forbidden. It is her you should fear, or at least try to."

"Won't she know if she's the Priestess of this realm, that I'm here, transforming in and out of the form?"

"Ah, there we go, a sense of concern. No, she would not. She stays in her temple and cannot sense *Nipans*, though since you are the first to survive, I do not believe many would know or sense it either. I cannot even be too sure just yet."

Exactly. Nothing was known, nothing was for sure because I was the first, the worst sort of main character energy there was to have.

"Maybe I should change back then," I suggested, pushing at his large frame again to free myself. This time, he lifted off and allowed me to finally get up from the leaf-covered ground.

I shook the leaves from my fur and hair before we headed back to the van in our forms.

"Try and change without alcohol this go," he ordered as we stepped in.

"You say that as if it is so easy," I whined.

"It is."

I plopped on the bed, pulling my tail into my lap as to not sit on it. "For you, not me."

"And that is what practice is for. All the younglings must go through a term of training."

I glared at him with pinched brows. "I'm not a *youngling.* Please do not compare me to one ever again." I opened the fridge and began rummaging for something to make for dinner, hoping that'd be the end of it.

"Are you sure? In comparison to me, you are in fact, quite young."

I spun around with a sour grimace. The last thing I wanted to think about was our age difference. "Yeah, well. Guess what you get to do, Mr. Old-Ass-Goat? You get to cook dinner," I snipped.

Erius lifted his brow and tilted his head. "Are you sure dinner is what you want?"

"Yes, I'm hungry and I want to see if a shower will wash away this form."

"It's not filth on your skin." He sighed.

"It wouldn't hurt to try." I stood to head to the shower, only to be caught at the wrist. A shock raced up my arm, freezing me in place.

He released me just as quickly and cleared his throat.

"I do not..." His words stuttered off like he was trying to find the right ones for whatever it was he wanted to say.

It all clicked together. Silly me.

"Can you not cook or something?" I asked.

His face instantly fell. "Take your shower," he grumbled.

"Ok." I turned my back to him and stepped behind the curtain to undress. Not that that was made easy since I struggled to pull the top over the horns due to how they twisted. Even more, my tail kept pulling back the curtain, and I had to manage that while fighting with the top as I struggled in the space that was now too small for me.

I can't imagine Erius squeezing his tall ass in here.

"Ugh!" I groaned. With one arm tangled in the shirt around my horns covering my eyes, my other hand fought blindly with my tail.

"Are you ok?" Erius asked, his voice a lot closer than I expected—tits out, pants around my thighs in a last-ditch attempt to control my tail.

"Erius?" I breathed.

"Yes?" He said slowly, the smile hard on his voice.

"Is the shower curtain open?"

The sound of his low chuckle mixed with the clanking of the spoon in whatever he was mixing. "Wide open."

"Ugh!" I groaned again, struggling to pull my arm free and close the curtain.

"Would you like help?" He laughed.

"No! I would like you to stop looking!"

Rough hands closed around my arms to hold me in place. "Just hold still," he ordered in a deep voice that locked my muscles and melted my mind all at once. The heat of his body pushed against my fur-covered skin. The tips of my nipples brushed against the cool silk of his shirt which only lit my skin up further. I sucked in a sharp breath as his hands worked with the fabric around my horns.

"How did you even do this?" He pulled me one way then yanked the other. "Here we go."

The sound of shredding cloth filled the small shower space as he tore the shirt off. Now free, I immediately covered my chest.

"You know, here, we call that sexual harassment," I grumbled.

"Have I harassed you in any way?"

"Peeping. It's creepy, and don't give me any of that 'your tail didn't mind' or any such nonsense."

"I am not peeping. There isn't anything to see. Your form has you covered in this fur," he pointed out. I looked down to find that he wasn't wrong. I felt naked but visually, all the mortal private bits were covered.

"I don't have the shampoo for all of this!" I was not sure why that was the first thing to come to mind, but I figured body wash wouldn't work the same.

"I do not think mortal shampoo works on goat fur," he jabbed, as if to read my mind.

"Shut up!" I barked, ripping the curtain closed to finish undressing and complete my shower. His stupid chuckle filled the cab, followed by the door opening.

CHAPTER TWENTY-FOUR

Mira

The shower hadn't done shit, other than add a shine to the fur. My fur, tail, and claws all remained. I spent what felt like an hour drying off so I could get the damn shirt on without drenching it and still struggled to get it on over my horns. As for my bottoms, I had to situate my tail through the leg of my pants with the loosest fabric I could find.

I stepped out in shorts and the top, finding Erius sitting in front of the pit stirring the stew I had been smelling for the last thirty minutes. I was not sure why he settled on beef stew, but the heavy scent of it lofted around the camp. I would not say it was mouth-watering; it smelled more like regret in appointing him as chef for the evening.

But my stomach twisted nonetheless at the smell, and my legs carried me over to his side. With a quick glance over his shoulder, he grabbed a bowl from beside the pit.

"I see the shower did nothing," he mused with a smug smile.

I glared at him through narrowed eyes. "Clearly not," I grumbled, taking a seat on the log and folding my arms over my chest.

"I told you it was not filth upon your skin." He handed me the bowl with a single scoop of the thick liquid in it.

"Are you rationing the food for some reason?" I asked.

He leaned over me with another smile, his eyes dropping to the bowl in my hands. "You should taste it before you waste it."

I pressed my lips flat as I glared at him. If he was so worried about the taste, he could have just said he can't cook. Why waste our food?

"If it's bad, you can just say that," I breathed, pushing the bowl to him.

He gently pushed it back with another teasing grin. "Oh, it tastes fine to me."

My face pinched, pulling my brows deep over my eyes as I looked over him and then the food. "Why wouldn't it taste fine for me?" I quizzed.

Erius shrugged, his eyes still on the bowl. "Just take a bite," he urged, a tad too happily. The teasing grin never softened as he watched me.

"I feel like you did something to it now."

His smile grew even wider, showing his fangs, "I would not dream of doing anything malevolent to your meals, Mortal." His gaze dropped to my tail as it wrapped around his wrist, lighting his face up with another pleased grin as he tended to the invader.

"Besides, if I killed you, your tail would have no one to cling to."

Well, yeah, I'd be dead—how is that supposed to provide comfort?

"Go on, then," he urged again.

With a low grumble, I scooped up the stew and sipped it down, regretting it instantly. I spat out the overly salted liquid. "Why does it taste like that?" I shrieked. Not only was it too salty, but the meat tasted as if it had been left out in the sun for days to rot.

Erius took a bite with no issues. "That is how all mortal food tastes. For demons."

I watched in shock as he took another scoop down without flinching.

"Does it not taste bad to you?" I burst out.

He looked at me, his smile splitting further across his face. "Would you like me to join you in this form?" he suddenly offered. I looked over him with a heated gaze.

"I wish you wouldn't," I responded dryly.

Stay in your uncomfortable human form and suffer. "If it tastes so bad, why are you eating it?"

He shrugged again, stuffing another spoonful into his mouth. It probably didn't even bother him in the human form and he was just fucking with me again.

"Ugh, what do demons even eat?" I groaned.

"We eat prey."

As if that explained anything. Sharks and lions eat prey—that doesn't make their choice of food the same. "What does that mean?"

He paused for a moment, looking off into the woods, a mischievous grin teasing his lips, "You know that cute deer you pointed out to me?"

I could feel my stomach twist in disgust and horror. "You ate the deer?"

"What was it you called him? Bambi, right? Was that his name or the type of deer you have here?" he asked casually.

"You ate the baby deer?" My eyes rounded and mouth fell open in disbelief. I would have never pointed the poor thing out if I knew he would eat it later.

"Wait until you catch the scent of one." He cackled with the sinister twist to his lips.

"You're lying!" Not that I had ever caught him in a lie to determine when and if he was. I didn't think he would joke about it.

"Only slightly." His shoulders shook with his usual chuckle at my expense. "We all eat different things to sustain energy. Some eat children, some survive on blood, some eat souls."

I tried to regain composure but the thought of anyone, demon or not, eating babies twisted my stomach to knots. The image of Erius eating babies flooded my mind instantly.

"What do you eat?" I inquired, my voice a bit softer then intended.

He stared at me for a moment before taking another bite.

"That bad, huh? Is it babies? Our cute little innocent human babies are what you eat?" I shot, hoping I was wrong.

"No! Is it not obvious?" he barked.

I shook my head in response, releasing the breath I had been holding in anticipation for his answer. It provided slight relief.

"I eat souls. I ate yours... I ate your friend's."

That made sense, but I honestly thought I was making jokes all those times I mentioned it. His lack of correction should have tipped me off.

"What did you think I did with them?"

I guess I never thought about it. I just figured he collected them, maybe.

"What did mine taste like?" I blurted out. He had mentioned it tasting sweet, but a lot of things are sweet. Did it taste like a cinnamon roll or a sugar doughnut? Maybe none of those things from this realm at all.

We looked at each other awkwardly for a moment before he spoke in a low voice. "I do not think you would understand the words I have to describe the taste of your soul."

"Ew, that does not sound pleasant." I scrunched my nose to him, not really wanting to hear more anyway. "What do I eat, then?"

"You will know when you come across it. Trust me."

I looked down at the stew and set it at the edge of the pit. Whatever this form ate, it most certainly wasn't that. I stormed back to the van and sat on the bed. The pain in my stomach began to climb up my throat, setting my mouth on fire as if acid was flooding it.

Erius entered and sat beside me, and like clockwork, in came the tail, resting over his shoulder.

"Traitorous snake," I hissed to it.

"Why do you hate it so much?" He chuckled, taking the new limb in his hand.

"Why do you like it so much?" I countered, mimicking his voice.

"Someone has to."

I pulled it back into my lap. "I don't hate it. I just—I'm not used to it. I can't control it. It's always on you, and I don't know why. Everything is still so loud and bright." I shot the issues off without pausing.

"That's because your senses are heightened. Are you feeling irritable?"

I nodded.

"It's because this form needs to feed. It grows weaker by the minute."

"*Feed?*"

"We need to find out what you eat." He smiled down at me, taking my tail back in his hand. We watched as it snaked around his arm, widening the smile on his face.

Erius stood with his hand out, waiting for me to join him. I hopped off the bed and took my new place at his side and we left the van.

"Stay by me," he instructed, heading off toward the woods once again. I know we were looking for what it was I ate, but how did wandering the woods help us figure that out?

"What about Watchers?" I poked.

"I am keeping an eye out for them. Do not fret, Mortal. I will sense them long before you." His explanation didn't help me feel any more comforted.

"Can they sense us? Is that why they are under the pier?" I questioned, following him deeper into the darkness he had warned me about.

"No—they are attracted to anything. That is why they are dangerous to even those in the Circles." He kept his head high as he constantly scanned the thick trees around us.

"How will I know, and how will we find it in the woods?" I quizzed.

He abruptly turned, his hardened features fixed on me. "Do you remember what I told you we eat?"

I nodded again.

"We will look at those options first." He pointed to a cluster of distant dots of light, no doubt fires from other campsites and families.

"You want to see if I will eat a baby?"

"Is that all you heard?" He scoffed. I looked at him blankly. It stuck out, so of course that's my first concern.

"You may eat souls; you may eat dreams and leave them with nightmares. There are other things that will provide you nourishment."

"Nourishment?" That wouldn't be the word I would use, but ok.

The wicked smile flashed his face as he cocked his head toward the camp. I wanted to protest, but the ache in my stomach was growing exponentially more painful as time passed.

We pushed through the thickness of the trees to keep off the main hiking paths. The creatures that scurried about the day were now reduced to the creepy crawlers of the night. The low chirping of the nearby crickets overpowered the faint laughter and chatter of the distant camps.

Shadows covered and cloaked every inch of the forest, but it was all still so clear and vivid as if the sun had a filter over it.

"Whoa," I breathed in amazement. "Is this night vision or something?"

"Or something? What else would it be?" Erius asked. I was pretty positive it was to himself, but it was clear as day, as everything else had been with these big goat ears. Every slight noise caused them to flick against my horns as they tried to shift in the direction of the sound, an even more uncomfortable feeling than having them all together.

I paused by a tree, fussing over the ears to try and find a comfortable way for them to rest.

"What are you doing now, Mortal?" Erius sighed,

"My ears are huge and uncomfortable. They keep whacking these horns," I grumbled as I fussed with each one. "Ugh, how do you control yours?"

He turned to me with a wicked grin. "Let me show you." His voice was low, deep, and alluring, but at the same time, it sent a sharp chill down my spine.

Black mist fanned out around him, engulfing him in the vapors, but his transformation was vividly clear. I stumbled back into a tree, watching as his body changed. The fair skin slipped away to reveal a universe embodiment. Purple and blue gases swirled with the millions of tiny stars sprinkled about him.

Claws grew from his fingers, horns twisted from his head, and a thick tail slammed to the ground alongside me. His body grew, pushing the low hanging branches up until they snapped from the pressure. Big, bulky, and naked—always fucking naked.

He sat down in the small open space with little room to hide. His glowing eyes gazing down at me like two big full moons in the night sky. It was a decent reminder that he was definitely not human, with a form that—I can't even begin to describe because of how well he blended into the night sky and shadows around him. Almost like he wasn't even there, but with my new vision I could make out the faint outline of his massive form.

He could say he wasn't a goat all he wants, but what was I looking at right now? A ginormous goat-like skull with hooved feet and clawed hands.

"Erius!" I cried out, trying to avoid what was at eye level with me. I followed the length of his tail, the swirling stars and colors looked almost tangible. "What form is this?"

"My true form." His voice echoed in my head. Telepathic communication was not something I'd considered he'd have. It was more than hearing him; it engulfed me, the words flowing through my body like a slow-moving current.

"How many do you have?"

"Only the three you have seen," he echoed again.

But I specifically remembered a fourth forms used to gain my trust in the beginning. "What about the goat?"

He crossed his arms, turning his head from me with a flick of his ear. "You saw what I wanted you to see."

My body stiffened at his words as my mouth fell open. "But—I scratched your head," I said, gasping.

"Yes. You did, and it was pleasant," he mumbled, unfazed.

I looked at him blankly, not sure how to proceed while trying to imagine how that must have looked. "Why are you showing me this one?" I finally blurted out.

"Holding the human form becomes uncomfortable after a while."

"Oh. Are clothes also uncomfortable for you, or do you find any excuse to get naked?" I tossed to him as I placed my hand on his tail for distraction. I knew my hand would be stopped, but it still amazed me when it did. It was a surreal feeling of touching the universe through glass.

"Clothes are a mortal construct," his voice rumbled. Of course they were.

I looked up to him with a raised brow. He was closer, leaning over me with his massive head.

"Why are you so big?" I pressed.

"I told you. You are quite small—even for an average mortal. I am no larger than my kind grows to be."

"And what is your kind? Are you the universe personified?"

His body rumbled with a low chuckle. "No. I am not."

"Well, can you control your size? My neck hurts, and stealth is not your friend in this location," I advised.

He shook his head and without a verbal response, shrunk down to match his mortal size, or better yet, his "second" form, which was just a small humanoid version of his main one.

"Better?" He grumbled.

I kept my eyes up to his, forcing my focus from falling to his dick as he stepped closer to me. "Mmhm," I hummed.

"Do not strain yourself, Mortal." He chuckled, snapping his fingers. Black vapor swirled around him, leaving him in his usual black button up and pants. His tail was free to whip and move about behind him, so I could only assume he had fitted attire for his demon form as well. Why he wouldn't wear it was beyond me.

He stepped closer, pinning me against the tree as he caged me in with his arms. I inhaled deeply as he leaned down to be eye level with me, but I averted my attention from looking him in the face. Not with him this close.

"You seem nervous, Mortal," he snickered, running his free clawed hand down my cheek.

"Not at all. Why—why would I be nervous?" I stammered, still avoiding his eyes.

He pulled my face towards him, brushing his nose to mine with a deep inhale.

"Steady your breathing and focus on what is around you. The sounds, the smells—you cannot always rely on your eyes," he explained. The heat from his claw sent chills over me. If he wanted, he could crush my skull like a grape in one squeeze. He tilted my head up and leaned even closer. With a sharp breath, my body locked in place. All but my tail, which seemed to wrap around his and oddly, the contact felt otherworldly enjoyable. I bit back a moan that threatened to escape as his tail seemed as equally thrilled in mine.

"Close your eyes," he whispered, fanning his vanilla scented breath over me.

"Why? What are you going to do?" I pushed through a heaving chest.

Erius's hand slid down to my neck, resting there as his eyes narrowed on me.

I wasn't nervous. Not in the slightest. I was, however, highly turned on. Wiggling under his grasp, I clamped my thighs together and shoved my back into the bark of the tree even further.

"Again, Mortal. If I wanted to do something to you, I wouldn't have you close your eyes. I don't need absurd reasons to do what I want; I will simply do them. Now, do as I say and breathe," he ordered once more, looking down over my body. A slick smirk twisted his lips. "And try to calm yourself. It's distracting."

"What is it that I am doing that is so distracting?" I argued.

A deep growl emitted from his chest, rumbling his body against mine. "For one, you're incessant need to question me on everything," he breathed.

I smiled. "It's a gift."

"Close your eyes and take a deep breath. Please," he instructed oh so kindly.

"There. Wasn't so bad," I giggled, doing as he requested. The moment my vision was cut, everything around me was amplified as he had said it would be.

The sounds, the smells, the feelings that circled us—but mostly I felt him still pressed against me with his hand on my chest and the heat of his breath fanning over my face with every steady exhale. I parted my lips, taking it in as if my very survival depended on it.

His lips brushed against mine ever so gently but still, I sucked in a sharp breath.

"Remember to breathe," he whispered.

Again, I did as instructed, taking in a slow, steady breath as a heavy gust of wind blew past us. At first it carried nothing but the scent of pine trees and dirt, but the second time the wind picked up, my body stiffened, locking in a way much different than how it reacted to Erius.

The fur over me shot up and my tail whipped behind me as if to snap to attention. The scent that carried with the wind pulled my focus in its direction. The tantalizing smell of sizzling grilled steak clung to the back of my throat with an intense, drying blaze.

I ripped from Erius's grasp, unconcerned with whatever it was he was trying to do. The only thing that mattered was whatever food was setting fire to my mouth with every inhale.

Another gust of wind from the east brought on another cloud, giving hint to its direction. I darted off, following the trail, pulling me as if I were on a fishing line. It wasn't until the cloud grew, that my mouth began filling with a burning saliva that dripped down my chin.

The heavenly scent became more concentrated near a small campsite surrounded by thick bushes and overgrown trees. I crouched in the nearby brush to see what crafted such a delicious fragrance. I could almost see the cloud of it, the faintest shade of forest green lofting around the entire site like a low fog.

I lowered myself to the ground, waiting for whatever it was to be brought out. I only needed a few seconds to grab it and be off into the darkness again.

The tent door unzipped, falling open to present a burly sized man. He held no food in his hands, nothing in his tent and no cooking happening on the fire. The scent hit me again just as the realization did.

It was not food I smelled it was a whole ass human. My mouth filled with burning venom as my muscles released the tension. I shot forward, swift and silent as I covered the man's mouth and ripped him from sight. I didn't give him a chance to scream or really any time to realize what was happening to him.

I placed my hands on either side of his head and whipped it to the left, filling the silence of the night with an echoing snap. The body fell with a loud thud, sprawling out before me. A numbing sensation took over, putting my mind in a sort of auto pilot trance.

Dropping to his side, my claws gripped at his plaid button up. With a flick, I tore open the shirt, sending the buttons flying into the night. He wasn't an unfit man, just an unsuspecting one.

I didn't need to pause and figure where I would start first; my new form moved for me. His skin tore instantly as my claws plunged in, slicing him open to display my prize. Warm crimson spilled out in a dark mess over the dirt.

The scent strengthened, creating a bouquet of smells that watered my mouth and hardened my stomach as it begged for a taste. I brought my clawed fingers to my lips, not hesitating once the scent wrapped around my nose like a warm hug. I licked the liquid clean from one clawed hand, while the other dug for something more solid.

Everything I touched was warm and slick, slipping from my grasp as I fished for whatever it was I could even grab. I dove my other hand in, gripping the meat with my claws rather than my hands as I tore it out. It pulled free of the man with a wet snap. Warm blood covered my hands and dripped through my fur.

Without bothering to examine what I held, I brought it to my mouth and tore a chunk from it. The taste was far better than the smell, indescribable in a sense, but with a very close likeness to a crab broil.

Don't get me wrong, I was highly aware that was not what I was devouring. But still, it was delicious, and I managed to polish it off in seconds.

I dove my hands into the open pool and fished for something else, not caring of what it was as I gripped it with my claws, tore it free from the body, and shoved it in my mouth. I continued like this until there was nothing left but a blood-filled cavity. Surprisingly, I didn't stop there. Cupping my hands, I dunked them into the warm, thick liquid and brought it to my lips.

"Mina!" Erius called out. His tone was neither upset nor

shocked, but it was definitely demanding.

I shot my head up in the direction his voice came from. The glow of his eyes and soft illuminance of his odd galaxy skin lingered a few feet from me.

I looked down over the mess and the filth smeared on my clothes. A slow realization of what my form eats finally had its moment to fill my mind.

"Am I a monster?" I cracked.

Erius stepped closer, his eyes on the body with a look of satisfaction.

He leaned down, offering his hand to me as he spoke. "No. You are a predator."

CHAPTER TWENTY-FIVE

Mira

"Are you ready for your next lesson?" Erius asked. We stood over the hollowed body of the man I just devoured, my fur still slick with the blood I could taste on my lips. Despite completely slaughtering the man, I felt much better. My throat was no longer on fire, and everything was far less intense but still not like my mortal senses. They felt more tuned in, if anything.

"Yes," I said, curious as to what he would show me next.

"You did not eat his brain, so that will be helpful."

"How so?" Surprisingly, talking about the disposal of a body wasn't as stressful as I always figured it'd be.

"With your gifts, you should be able to make him move. If you can't, it will just look as though a bear attacked him."

"And ate only his organs?" I countered.

"Hmm," he hummed as he reconsidered what to do. "See if you can control him. We will move on from there."

There was nothing else we could do but try. It was not like we had the availability to report it. I looked over the body, focusing my mind as I had before, feeling the energy drift from me as if it were an extension at my control. The phantom cool stiffness of the man's skin lined against me, making the connection I needed. The sickly feeling that had brought me to the man began to stir up an unfamiliar disgust over him. When it all happened, I didn't stop to think or take the time to care and question who he was. But now, I couldn't help but feel it was deserving.

His finger twitched as my control gripped around him. I extended the grasp out to his arms and down to his legs, feeling the entire body out as if it were a suit on my skin. I shuddered uncontrollably at the sensation, shaking free the itchiness that consumed me as I urged him up to his feet.

It took several attempts to get him sturdy in his stance and then another few minutes to accomplish a distance of five feet.

"Now what?" I asked, my words and movements transferring over to the body so that a haunting moan escaped him. Erius and I stared at the walking cadaver with wide eyes.

"I can make them talk?" I whispered, the man following along with a low gargling breath.

"I would not call that talking. But it appears you can take full control. Quite well, actually," he said passively as he inspected the droopy dead man. It wasn't the first time he praised me, but it had the same warming effect as the last time. Only this time, my tail decided to swish from one side to the next, happily displaying my need for it.

"Well, what do we do with him?" I asked again as I swatted at my new appendage to stop ratting me out.

Erius let out a pleased chuckle before looking to the ground between us, sending his black vapor over our feet like a fog. When it cleared away, it left a decent sized hole in the earth.

"Place him there," Erius suggested.

Focusing on the grave, I urged the body over to the edge with one single thought. It lugged itself over, dragging its foot until it came to a wobblily stop over the hole. I envisioned him falling face first into his new grave, and that is exactly what he did. His body released from mine, collapsing into the pit and sending a dirt cloud up.

The disgusting, creeping feeling that had drawn me to him slipped from my skin, leaving a curiousness as to why. What was it about him that caught my form's attention?

Before Erius could cover the hole, I hopped in to dig through the man's pockets. Once I found the leather fold of a wallet, I hopped out.

"What do you have there?" Erius asked as he filled the plot and muffled the dirt and leaves over it.

"Research for later. Right now, I want to get clean. Maybe have a drink," I said, shoving the wallet into the pocket of my shorts. We checked the campsite the man had constructed to ensure he was alone. The entire setup looked as if he had been long-term camping for some time. He even had a counter he was building that looked to be the beginning of some sort of wash table.

When we were sure he was alone, we headed back to the van in near silence. Mostly because I got stuck picking chunks of meat from my fur and teeth.

By the time we got to the camp, our fire had dwindled down to embers. But instead of feeding the flames to keep the light around camp, Erius followed me into the van, changing to his mortal form.

"Oh? Are you changing with me?" I asked sarcastically.

He pulled out the bottle of scotch we had from last week and poured a glass that he handed to me before pouring one for himself.

"I'm sure you do not want to clean all that fur out," he teased as he took his first sip.

I looked down over my blood drenched fur. The dark chestnut color was stained in crimson. I took a quick sip, knowing he was absolutely right. There was no way I would be able to clean this as-is.

My body shivered as the spiced drink burned down my throat, shifting me back to my mortal form. The sticky blood coated me more noticeably, looking as if I bathed in it.

Erius looked over me with widened eyes. He rolled his sleeves up past his elbows and grabbed a rag to soak. "Sit down."

I didn't bother arguing with him. I just leaned against the counter near the bed. I wasn't about to get blood all over the sheets.

The damp heated rag pressed against my cheek as he began cleaning the sticky liquid from my face. I scrunched my face as I looked at him, confused by his actions but not really wanting it to stop.

"What are you doing?" I blurted.

"Some of this blood is your own," he explained.

"How?" I managed to push out as he moved from my face to my neck and shoulders, soaking the rag with blood before rinsing it out in the sink to repeat the process. He cleaned and inspected a part of my shoulder where I assumed my injuries were, but I felt nothing.

"When you ripped away from me," he continued to explain while wiping away the collected blood. The slight sting of the claw marks alerted me to the sudden wound I wasn't aware of.

"Do you feel alright?" he asked, holding my face still. I felt fine in means of my senses, but my body and mind were wired in more ways than one, and it felt as if all that energy I had consumed needed to be burned off somehow.

"I could go for a jog." *Alright, maybe something is wrong with me.*

Erius smeared the rag over my chin before tossing it into the sink for what I hoped was the final time.

"I mean, you devoured human organs. You don't feel anything? No guilt or remorse?" he pried.

I tilted my head, a bit confused. He was the one who said I wouldn't have emotions without my soul, yet he always seemed surprised when I didn't show any.

"Should I?"

"I suppose not," he said with a shrug. "Did you enjoy it?"

I fought a smile I could feel teasing my lips. "What did it look like?"

"It looked as though you had never tasted anything more delicious."

"Then, there you go. My form eats people. Are you happy?" I snipped. It was better than eating innocent babies, I supposed, and I wouldn't even know how one would eat a dream and place nightmares in its place. Dreams didn't even sound appetizing or filling; It sounded like I'd be eating a bag of air.

"I am happy we know how your form eats. Like a slob," he teased as he rung the discolored water from the rag. The cloth smeared against my cheek again as he continued to scrub more blood free.

I waved off his hand. "Alright, that's enough!"

But he gripped my jaw and continued like it was nothing. It lit my skin to an uncomfortable degree. The longing ache crawled its way back to the pit of my stomach. I squeezed my thighs together to fight the gripping need that began to grow in the worst moment.

His hand tightened around my jaw and his gaze bore into me. The purring returned to his chest with a look of confliction carving his hardened features. "Mina, must you do that now?" he growled with a scrunch of his nose, the sound only stirred the feeling further.

"I'm just standing here!" I struggled to say.

"Oh, please." He tossed the rag in the sink but kept a firm grip on my jaw. "Your pheromones say differently."

My eyes widened at him. "You can smell that?"

He leaned into me, casting his eye trick as he spoke about his little secret with pride. "Every time."

I tried to fight off the pounding of my heart, figuring he could hear that just as well. "Every—time?" I repeated.

"Every time," he echoed with a sinister grin.

"That's not possible…" I stammered, knowing that it was the most possible thing with all else going on. Just not a convenient one. I don't know why I hadn't considered it when he told me he could smell rain from so far. All this time… Every time. I'm probably just some horny smelling mortal to him.

"I am a demon, it is what I do," he assured me with a devilish grin.

"Well, stop it!" I snapped, reaching for the rag to finish cleaning the blood from my arms and chest.

"I cannot stop it; it is my sense of smell." He stepped closer, closing the distance he had given us to cage me in.

"Well, then stop sniffing *me*," I countered, clearing the blood as best I could before tossing it to the trash.

"I do not think you really want me to stop," he purred, locking me in place as he caged me between him and the counter.

The wild thundering of my heart was loud enough for me to hear, rocking me as if it were trying to break free. The overwhelming power of his entire being encompassed me, demanding my attention on him as if he called for it. The frost white flickered an icy blue as he locked his gaze on my mouth, causing my bottom lip to tremble as I watched him. Anticipating the inevitable, I tilted my head back with a faint grin.

"And what if I don't?" I breathed. "It wouldn't matter, because this is as far as you'll allow yourself to go." I lifted on my toes, using the counter for support as I brought my lips a breath away from his.

"Just sniffing me," I toyed.

A deep chested groan rumbled against me, and I was hyper aware of the sudden dampness in my panties. His gaze clung to me, determined and hungry with a darkness I had never seen. Before I could think to move and lower myself, his hands moved from the counter to me, holding me in place beneath him as the fight raged in his eyes.

I sucked in a breath, waiting while his hand roamed my stomach and hips, stopping at the band of my shorts. He paused there, fighting with himself over something we both clearly wanted. There wasn't a need to fight it anymore. If anything, we could just get it over with and do away with all this intense sexual frustration it caused.

I smoothed my hands over the buckle of his belt, prepared to unfasten it when he stopped me with another bone rumbling growl. He slipped his hand under the band, dipping further until the heat of his fingers brushed over my clit. Fire flooded my body as I sunk back with a weak nod for him to continue.

Would it be wise to fuck a demon? Probably not, but I sure as fuck wanted to. I rolled my hips against his hand, urging him to finish what he started.

Erius snickered, plunging two fingers into me without warning. I arched into him as a throaty moan escaped me.

"Look at you. Soaking wet," he groaned, his eyes locked with mine, refusing to let me look away.

He started slowly, circling his thumb over my clit as he pumped into me. My soft whimpers turned to sharp gasps as he began to speed up. His lips brushed over mine, along my jaw, and over the curve of my neck. It was as if he wanted to kiss me but was hesitant about it for some reason. Kissing would probably make it too intimate for him, and I didn't think he was looking for intimacy right now—I knew I wasn't.

Each pump drew me closer to an edge I never knew I'd find, a fire that lit at the pit of my stomach, ready to burst as the tension continued to build. I gripped the hand that held me, dropping my head back as I fought against the moan clawing to break free.

"Do not be silent now. I want to hear you," he groaned into my ear, breaking the little hold I had on control. I clung to him, ready to give in to the bursting pressure when he stopped and pulled back to look over me. A devilish smile pulled at his lips. "Not until I say."

I stared up at him, struggling to hold myself together as I nodded again.

"Use your words," he ordered darkly.

I didn't think I'd have the energy to speak, not with how jittery I felt. I swallowed thickly.

"Ok," I panted out.

He began working into me again, slowly before gradually rising and pulling out whatever sounds from me he wanted. His lips brushed over mine with less hesitation as his tongue swept over my top lip with a satisfied groan. My body locked as I struggled to fight off the pleading orgasm. I suppose I didn't have to follow his order, but I wanted to, and the look on his face when I did was more than enough reason.

He stared down at me with an odd flush that slowly began to present his true skin. His dark gaze hung on every rise and fall of my chest. "Come for me," he breathed.

Finally, I let my body release the hold. I cried out, dropping my head back as his fingers continued to pump into me. The wet warmth of his tongue slid up from the hollow of my neck to my chin, stirring another heated flood through me.

"Good girl," he purred against me.

My heart jumped to my throat at the words. I rolled my hips against his hand, ready for more and already at the edge of a second finish. His dick flexed against my leg, reminding me I wasn't the only one with a need. Dazed, I reached for his belt, unfastening it with clumsy fingers. He continued to work into me while I tugged at his button until it fell loose. With my eyes still on his, I slipped my hand down and gripped him. He paused for a moment, the frost blue of his eyes flickering to the snow white and back.

My eyes widened as I pulled him free, feeling the weight and girth in my hand. He smiled down at me and began pumping into me again. I slid my hand up his length, stroking him slowly while watching his mortal cheeks flush the dark night sky across them. He paused for a moment, thrusting into my hand with a deep, labored groan. I stroked against his movements, enjoying the tremble that shook him. With another slow slip, his dick throbbed, growing and changing in my palm. I slid my hand up again, feeling several notches along the bottom of him.

He grabbed my wrist and pulled free from me as a low growl rumbled through him. The flush of his demon skin spread over his face in a slow transformation. With another rumbling groan, he pulled my hand off him and spun me around. I looked back at him over my shoulder as he tucked his fingers into his mouth, tasting me as he said he would.

I attempted to turn but he gripped my waist with one hand and kept my head facing forward with the other. When he was sure I wouldn't move again, he began fussing over his belt and pants before moving to my shorts and pushing them down as far as he needed. There was no warning before the heat of his cock pressed against me. I gasped out, arching into him as I pushed back. His hands gripped me tighter, anchoring me in place.

"Do not fucking move," he ordered. It was the first time I had heard him cuss at all, and it kind of threw me in a way that only turned me on further.

"I thought you said you weren't going to have sex with me?" I teased.

I was half ready for him to wake me up, for this all to be a dream, but the heat of his breath brushed over my ear, filling me with the vanilla scent no dream could match.

"I'm not going to have sex with you, my sweet mortal," he said breathlessly. "I'm going to fuck you." He pushed forward, filling me instantly.

I cried out at the slight sting but continued to remain as still as he was. A low rumble moved through him while his grip grew tighter. I fought the urge to move against him, unsure what battle he was clearly dealing with himself.

"*Fuck,*" he groaned, pulling free from me. I gasped out in protest, turning to him when he stopped me. The heat of his breath moved over my neck as his lips brushed against my ear.

"Listen," he said in a deepening voice, "no matter what you hear, do not turn around."

"Why?" I panted.

His body seemed to grow around me, tightening the enlarged grip around my neck and waist while something began to wrap around my wrists.

"You must remember what I am, Mina," he said in a deep, gravelly tone.

I nodded softly, taking his words for what they meant to be. He held me still with one hand as he lined himself up to me with the other. I cried out at the new size and feeling of each notch as he slowly pushed in.

"Relax for me," he grunted, lightly dragging his claws down my back. "I will be easy."

He paused, giving me a moment to adjust to him before continuing until he was completely buried. Once he was sure I was comfortable, he slowly pumped into me. He pulled my wrists back, wrapping what felt like his tail around them. Once his hands were free, he used one to hold me in place while he dragged the claws of the other over my shoulder and down my arm. Chills shook my heated body and I rocked back, rolling my hips against him as he thrust forward.

His clawed hand slammed down on the bed, and I froze, knowing I'd probably get scolded for it but honestly, I wouldn't mind it. Instead, he pushed me down until I was flat against the bed and held me tightly in place as his speed picked up.

The small space of the van filled with the sound of moans and screams that were not of my own voice. But none of it seemed to bother him as he continued to fuck me at a frantic pace.

The rough, breathy groans that escaped the demon only pushed me further over the edge. He didn't give any order to wait on his word, not that I think I would have been able to. Anything out his mouth in this form had me weak enough.

"Are you going to come for me again, sweetness?" the demon purred darkly, quickening his thrusts as he ground deeper into me. The shockwaves gripped my body, sending trembles through my arms and legs as I convulsed around him. My screams mixed with the ones that circled us, taking my moans and sounds to repeat back in a near haunting way. But he did not stop as he pulled me into each thrust. I cried out again, rocking back as he continued to drill into me without remorse.

"That's a good girl. Give me another one," he ordered. Each thrust was more primal than the last in the most fantastic way.

My mind numbed over with the flood of pure pleasure as I came again. Never in my life had anyone managed such a feat and still, he wasn't finished with me.

His tail continued to restrain my hands behind my back as he pulled me up again. He covered my eyes with his clawed hand, blocking out whatever began swirling around us. His nose trailed over my shoulder and neck again with heavy heated breaths. The sharp point of his fangs grazed over my skin, pulling a trembling chill through me.

Some biting wouldn't be so bad, and I throbbed at the very thought. A feral growl tore through him at the feeling, jerking into me as his teeth pressed against my skin. I tilted my head to the side, opening my neck for better access. The anticipation burned my skin where his fangs rested.

The screams around us continued as the van rocked violently. He paused, digging his claws into the softness of my hips.

"*Fuck*," he pushed through clenched teeth, ripping himself from me. He held my head in place, still blocking my vision for whatever reason. I'd already seen all his forms; him fucking me in one wouldn't frighten me any.

I tried to steal a quick glance at which form he was trying to hide, but he held a firm grip.

"Wait," he panted. The hand at my neck shrunk and the tail unbound my wrists. The energy felt light again, though I hadn't realized when it began to feel weighing.

Erius released me, stepping back as he situated himself. I pulled up my shorts and turned to him. His wide eyes on me in disbelief of what he did, rubbing at his jaw in what looked to be a discomforting way.

"Are you ok?" I asked.

"I am fine." His words were clear and direct, though that was not how it felt. Maybe I should have considered what would happen after. We still had to live with each other after all, and sleep in the same bed. He kept his eyes on anything else but me as his hand clung to his jaw.

Did I head butt him by accident? I don't think I did; I would have felt it.

Despite it clearly being a consensual act on both our parts, it looked like he feels awkward about it. Luckily for me, it appeared to be an emotion I didn't have. It just sucked ass that he does. He was the weirdest demon I have ever met despite being the only one. I just figured they wouldn't be so...modest about sex.

I nodded, not wanting to make anything more of it and climbed into bed, grabbing my bonnet off the hook as I went. Erius remained clothed as he took his place at my side, his eyes on me.

"You don't have to be weird about it." I sighed.

"I'm not," he said gruffly, but it wasn't too convincing for either of us.

"Oh, ok then," I said, slipping under the covers, our gaze still locked on each other.

Well, this just got harder. Maybe it was my fault for assuming it would be like any other hookup. It was far from that, and I didn't think I would be able to enjoy sex with a human man ever again.

Mind-blowing demon sex or bland, unseasoned mortal sex? I think the answer speaks for itself. But I couldn't fucking let him know that. He wouldn't even care either way, and he most certainly would rather go home. It would be better for us both if I just remained passive about it. If I didn't make a big deal of it, there wouldn't be a big deal.

I turned around to face the wall and forced myself to sleep. Not having feelings felt strange because I did feel something. If anything, I felt like we could go again. We could go all night.

Lust, the feelings I was having, were purely sexual. But knowing I will probably never experience that again, especially once the tether is broken, it felt empty, and within that emptiness was pain, straining to feel something. A pain I had never felt before in my entire life. It wasn't hurt from rejection or loss; it was something entirely different and completely new.

I wish I could say his demeanor changed by the following morning, but he was more distant than ever, going as far to avoid eye contact with me and if he couldn't even look me in the face, there was no way he would want to show me anything. I figured it'd be best to pack up and head back to the beach for the day. I had shopping to do anyway, and he could sit and mope about it all in the van alone.

We packed what was left outside and cleaned up the space, all while he continued to avoid me. I thought he would sit on the bed during the ride back, but surprisingly, he took the passenger's side. *Unsurprisingly*, he spent the ride glaring out the window.

We drove back to the city in silence. I wouldn't say it was awkward, though if I had any feeling I probably would have felt as much. The heavy energy that filled the van last night still weighed against me despite the windows being down.

Erius kept his focus on whatever passed outside his window the entire time, but we were coming up on the exit, and with the exit came a place to stop for food.

"Are you hungry?" I asked softly.

He didn't answer, so I just took that as a yes. If he was just going to be stubborn, and not admit he'd enjoyed himself, then that was on him.

"Erius, we had sex, we didn't get married. Do you want food? Because I'm stopping either way," I asked again.

"Yes," he said without turning from the window.

"Oh, sassy. You don't have to make this weird, you know. I'm not new to casual sex, and if it was the only time, then it's not a big deal." I shrugged, but still, he kept his attention out the window.

Ok, make it weird, then. Honestly, thank the gods I didn't have emotions, because this would suck. I would probably even have been in tears. But I don't even know, maybe I was reading it all wrong.

I took the exit, pulling into the Taco Bell at the light. Asking him what he wanted would probably end in being ignored or told he'd just get what I'm having. I ordered the party box and two large drinks that way he had options and I didn't have to bother him.

I drove around to the window and I handed off the money. The man staring at us a little longer than I felt comfortable with.

"Hi," I snipped. He blinked at me with a hung mouth as he searched for his words. With movements as slow as a snail, he turned and grabbed the box, pushing it out the window with the mindless gape still stuck on his face. I snatched the bag, and the delicious smell of the tacos drifted out as I pulled it through the window and set it in my lap. I grabbed the drinks next and handed them over to Erius.

Once everything was set, I pulled off and parked in a spot in the empty lot. I took what I wanted from the box and set it between us, not bothering to request my drink. He would have ignored it anyway, so I leaned over and took it, ignoring his slight shrink from me.

Back to being an untouchable, I guess. Better to leave him alone and just enjoy my food before we headed back to the beach. A long walk on the sand and what little distance we could have would be good. A moment out of his entrancing energy to gain a clear mind. Everything had been so muffled and consumed in him lately, I hardly felt like I was me anymore. Just a fucking shell of a human. When you lack a soul, that was basically what you become.

An emotionless husk in the wind.

We ate our meal without a word and drove back to the beach in an even deeper silence. Since we weren't speaking—well, since he is not responding—I didn't feel it necessary to inform him when I grabbed my bag and headed out of the van. Prometheus was quick to follow me as I trudged barefoot through the sand. The calming sound of the crashing waves and the feel of the cool sea mist against my skin instantly brought on the calmness I had missed.

The warm sand between my toes countered the breeze that drifted from the ocean. It was like stepping into a cool shower and washing away the thoughts that riddled my mind. I could finally think clearly, undistracted by the energy he carried. I could feel more than the need for sex. A relaxing tranquility that I hadn't felt since his arrival settled in me.

I found a spot in front of the van but closer to the tides to sit. Prometheus curled up in my lap, snuggling against me in a way that told me he had missed me. It had been a whole week since I really cuddled with him or had any delusional conversation, too focused on the demon that now invaded our space. A demon Prometheus did not seem to care for. Not that I thought he would care for very many other demons out there, but it must not be very comfortable for him either.

"I'm sorry I got us into this mess, baby boy. I'm sure it will all be over soon and we can get back to our semi-normal lives. Sound good?" I held him up as I spoke. His pupils widened and gave him that cute wide-eyed cat look. "Yeah, you forgive me." I laughed, pulling him in for more snuggles.

After a few moments I set him down and let my head fall back, taking in the rays of the sun and closing my eyes. Within a few steady, centering breaths, I found peace. Thankfully, meditation seemed much easier to fall into now.

The calming waves and the crying seagulls fell eerily quiet around me, not a normal silence but one where you had to struggle to find sound, to hear any small noise in the painful strain of stillness. I opened my eyes. The ocean and tide still swayed calmly, and seagulls flew overhead. All was normal aside from the complete lack of sound. Prometheus hopped from my lap and sat before me with a soft flick of his tail.

"These are starting to get a bit weird," I told him.

He tilted his head, meowing loudly, the only other sound besides my voice. It was reassuring for a moment, a split second of familiarity torn away as my beautiful cat morphed into the shadow figure that had been drifting in my meditations.

"Oh, it's you again. What is it now?" I asked aimlessly. The figure leaned its odd-shaped head to the side, waving its arm-like appendage out for a faint wave.

"Yes. Hello. How can I help you?" I say flatly.

It reached its arms out toward me, gesturing for me to touch it.

"No thanks." I shook my head, tucking my hands into my sides. It gestured its arms again with a low groan.

"I said no," I snapped. The charging energy lifted the goosebumps across my body the same way it did when Erius began chasing me. It twisted and jerked for a moment before completely freezing. The tilt of its head changed before it washed away with the incoming tide.

The moment it was out of sight, the sounds of the world flooded my senses once more—the loud call of the birds, the rough washing of the water of the sand. The conversations of a few passing beachgoers added to the noise that crowded my mind.

The setting sun cast the beautiful golden glow over the puffy clouds above. Shades of brown and orange twirled about to create a painted picture in the sky. I inhaled the peaceful view, closing my eyes once more.

"Mortal?" Erius said from behind me. Tranquility and peace interrupted.

"Oh, you're talking to me now?" I kept my attention on the sky. He was quiet for a moment, whether it was because he was thinking of how he was wrong or thinking of an excuse for his behavior, it was unclear.

"It is near dark."

Oh, well, that made sense. I tilted my head back until I could see him. "Thanks."

He watched me as I got up with Prometheus in my arms and marched off. I didn't bother to wait for Erius or even look back at him as I headed to the van.

The door was already open, and I found blankets scattered across the small space on the floor. I tossed the cat and dusted off the sand from my feet before stepping over the makeshift bed. He wasn't just ignoring me, he was full-on avoiding me now.

The heat of his body pressed against my back as I studied his uncomfortable looking space. I spun around to face him, fed up with his childish ass. You'd think a demon wouldn't give a single fuck about sex. But no, this one was super particular about it.

"What's wrong with you?" I snapped.

He blinked at me with widening eyes and pressed lips. I mimicked his expression of dumbfounded shock and waited but got no reply.

"You're avoiding me."

"I am not avoiding you," he tried to say, but his words were muffled by whatever he had in his mouth. He rubbed at his jaw with discomfort and turned away from me without another word.

"What was that?" I asked.

"Nothing," He pushed through his teeth, a bit clearer since it was one word, but I knew the mess I had just heard. Lucky for him, I didn't feel like pushing it tonight.

CHAPTER TWENTY-SIX

Mira

The following morning wasn't much different from his silence. I guessed it wasn't completely the same. He watched me intently as I fixed my hair and makeup. Again, he felt it ok to try and watch me dress, but I shoved him out of the van, all while remaining perfectly morose and straight-faced.

I pulled on the lace cover dress and slipped on a pair of black wedge boots. Before grabbing my bag, I adjusted the bralette and matching shorts under the lace and turned to my cat.

"I shall be back, my sweet king," I cooed, pulling my bag over my shoulder. The door opened with its loud whooshing noise, presenting Erius, whose attention was out on the water. We could play this game, if it was even a game. It was insanely clear he was avoiding me. Whether he felt disgusted with himself or not or whatever, it didn't matter, and it shouldn't matter.

He would be gone in a short time.

I closed the van door, clicked it to lock, and began the walk to Martha's for brunch. The girls were going to miss it, but I desperately needed the weekly start and Monday mimosa. I had also been craving their strawberry French toast for days, and I'd be damned if he ruined that. Not that I would know; his footsteps were silent, and I wasn't going to turn around and check if he was following.

The mid-July heat baked down on my skin, but the distinct scent of summer and beach waves filled the air. I tilted my head up to the clear blue sky. The humidity wasn't too high, making it a far less sticky venture but bringing more of the heat in its place.

It was most ideal weather for my favorite garden to be in full bloom, just a street up from Martha's but still on the way sat a corner loaded with the brightest sunflowers filling the sidewalk with its golden dust and sweet scent. A small chunk of normalcy to brighten my day.

I pressed the button at the light to cross instead of making the right turn that led straight to Martha's. The heavy sensation of Erius's presence pushed against my side. Not bothering to look up at him, I kept my eyes on the light, waiting for it to turn.

On second thought, I don't like this. Not at all. I liked to talk. I liked to laugh and have fun and he had the biggest stick up his ass I couldn't even pretend. I balled my hands at my sides, fighting the words that bubbled up to burn my tongue.

The light finally turned green, and I marched across, not pausing or waiting or slowing my stride, ready to be under the pleasant aura of the flowers if his dark, gloomy cloud didn't shrivel them away.

As I turned the corner, a hand wrapped around my arm and yanked me back. I came nose to nose with him, the pleasant vanilla locking me in place.

"Why are you running from me?" he growled in his deep demonic voice. I blinked at him, a bit confused. I didn't think I was running. Maybe walking fast, but not running. Certainly not from him.

"I'm not," I said blankly, fighting the flame that raced to my core.

"You're walking fast," he pointed out, his eyes taking in my whole being as they swept over me.

"Yes. I'm hungry." I turned away, ready to head off and see the flowers when he pulled me back once more.

"I do not like it, stop," he ordered, his hand tightening around my arm.

"You don't like—that I walk fast or…that I'm hungry?" I asked, dumbfounded by his sudden demand. My words settled on him as he chewed them over in his mind. His hand loosened and his face fell as if to realize all he had just said.

I looked at his retreating hand and then back at my arm with a lifted brow. "You good?"

He nodded, a new look of confusion touching his face. Not that there should be anything to be confused about. Not at his grown age. Yet here he was like a lost lamb searching for meaning.

I turned triumphantly and sauntered away from him, just to taunt him more now that I knew. He should have just continued to ignore me, saying entirely too much without saying anything at all.

He closed the distance between us enough for me to feel his energy wrapping around me, not just pressed up against my skin as it usually did. It wasn't restricting but oddly comforting as it twisted over me like weightless silk, invisible but not absent.

I glanced back over my shoulder, expecting to see his dark expression, but he looked to be in deep thought. I still didn't know much about demons, but I wouldn't expect them to be so confused all the time.

The scent of the sunflowers grew heavy as the flower heads began popping into view. Stretching out over the sidewalk were a few overgrown stalks curved and weighed down by the large disc of sun-dropped petals. Something about them made my cheeks burn with the enormous smile they brought to my face.

As we came under the far-hanging plants, I lifted my hand to grasp one and pulled it close, inhaling the calming fragrance before releasing it once more to spring up with the rest of them. I walked a bit slower, bathing in the fragrance of the flowers to hopefully catch even the slightest hint of the natural scent on me.

Ending the beautiful trail was one that was not in as lovely a condition as it hung down. It had snapped at the stem, left to sway in the light breeze. I gripped it near the wound and gave it a firm twist until it released. A new flower to brighten my dark van.

At least I can still feel joy. I buried my nose in the disk, taking in the beautiful scent before tucking it into my purse, keeping the head and petals out to avoid crushing them.

We continued to the next the light, joining a small crowd of tourists that didn't really appear to be waiting to cross, just taking up space. One person was smoking a joint off to the side as if they were trying to hide it, but not really. I ignored them and headed for the button. As I reached my arm out, Erius shot in front of me and pressed it. He turned with down-curved lips and a furrowed brow. His hair fell over his eyes, but I caught the slight shift in them.

"What is wrong with you?" I pushed in a low tone. He inhaled deeply through his nose, glancing up at the small group and back to me.

The light turned green, signaling for us to cross, and I headed off without waiting for a response. He returned to his steady pace as he drifted back a few steps behind me, his energy never slipping from the cloak like cover over my body as I headed to Martha's.

I only waited for him once I got to the door and when he finally caught up, he raced to open it before I had a chance, all while still avoiding eye contact.

"Thanks," I said slowly, passing him to enter the small lobby. Amy stood at the podium, her eyes wide as she looked from me to Erius.

"Hey, Amy. Just two today," I advised her. I offered her a kind smile and waited, but she didn't seem to notice I had even spoken.

"Amy? Are you ok?" I asked. She blinked at me for a moment, her face twisting from curiosity to confusion.

"Oh, sorry, Mina. Yeah, come with me," she stammered, grabbing up two menus. We followed behind her as she led us out to one of the private booths on the patio, a section blocked off by white fences that provided both shade and a decent amount of privacy with only the main street to see. There were three tables in the section, all with no more than two seats. But what made it extra special was the access to the TV and music they had set out.

We sat in the chairs across from each other and, despite his best efforts, his eyes raked over me, taking in every bit as if to relive the other night.

Amy set the menus down with her welcoming smile, but her eyes danced between us with caution. "What drinks can I get you two started with?" she asked, pulling out the pen and pad.

"I'll have a coffee," I said, looking at Erius.

"Water," he finally said. She wrote it down and was on her way.

I looked over the menu, already knowing what I wanted to eat. Erius did the same, looking over a few items with great intensity.

"You brought me here to feed me chicken embryos?" he suddenly asked.

"They have pancakes," I countered, pointing to the bottom corner of his menu. "See? Different kinds, too, and look. Stuffed French toast."

Amy came back with our drinks, placing a bowl of creamers in the center of the table for my coffee.

"Thank you," I said.

"No problem. Are you ready to order?" she asked with her pen ready.

"I think we need just a little more time." I looked to Erius as he still eyed the menu and its offerings.

Amy nodded with a smile. "I'll be back then." She tucked the pen away and headed inside.

I turned back to Erius, his eyes on the menu. "I'm having the stuffed French toast. Maybe you'll prefer the salad," I suggested.

"Why would I prefer the salad?" His tone was smooth and relaxed, not like how it had been earlier when I was apparently running from him.

A smile spread across my face. "Isn't that what goats eat?"

He glared at me from over the top of his menu. "For the last time, I'm not a bloody goat."

"You were nicer as a goat." I shrugged, reminding him that he let me pet and rub on him for a good minute like we were in a petting zoo, despite the fact it was just the visual he gave me.

"Why did you take on the appearance of a goat anyway?" I questioned, adding sugar and creamer to my mug.

"It was…easier."

"Easier than just being a human?"

"Would you have felt safe if I walked up to your camp like this? In the state you lot were in?"

I guess I would have been more standoffish if he walked up. Then again, I may have thought him to be a drunken hallucination. I shook my head slowly.

"I doubt my regular form would have given you comfort either."

I couldn't say it would have been acceptable or not. Definitely not by Jaz and them. But I wasn't too startled by the demon standing in the firepit, so I don't think one stepping right up to camp would have frightened me either.

"Isn't that what you basically did, though? When I brought the carrots out?" I reminded him.

He considered my words as a soft smile slowly creeped on his

294

lips. "I suppose you are correct."

Of course I was. I'd been nothing but correct since this all started, save for maybe fucking up the ritual. But I'd just keep all that to myself. Who knew if it would send him into another spiral of internal questions. He clearly wasn't the type to announce when he was going through it, and I didn't want to give him anything more to worry about.

Amy finally popped around the corner with her pen and pad at the ready. "Are you all good to order?"

"I am," I shot quickly. "I'll have the stuffed French toast. That's all for me, thank you."

She wrote the order down and looked to Erius.

With his eyes still on me, he grumbled, "Just a salad." And I fought the laugh that burned in my chest.

She wrote it down and was off once more, freeing me to release the chuckles. "You didn't have to get a salad."

"It's light," he admitted.

I laughed again at the thought of a demon being concerned with something so normal.

This. This was much easier than ignoring each other, especially over something we'd both agreed to.

"Erius?" I began.

"Mortal?"

"Are you done avoiding me, or are you going to be mute once we leave here?"

He took a slow drink of his water with his eyes on me. Taking his time, he placed the cup down before providing a response.

"I was not trying to avoid you," he spoke each word carefully.

"What would you call it then?"

He dropped his shoulders with a heavy sigh. "It is difficult to explain, and I would prefer not to."

I glared at him through a narrowed gaze. Everything was either too difficult to explain or he just didn't want to. But if I was what he thought, he needed to learn to trust me with information, because I was going to need all I could get.

"You act like you committed a sin. What kind of demon doesn't approve of a little sinning?"

His lips twitched up. "Sins are a mortal construct."

"If you say so." I sat back and folded my arms over my chest, trying to think of something to talk about and pass the time since he was being responsive.

"Well, what was all that screaming and noise the other night?" I interrogated. He looked up from his drink and finished his sip before placing the cup down with a devilish grin.

"Did you expect sex with a demon to be just as your regular encounters?"

I couldn't really argue with that logic. He definitely wasn't in his mortal form for most of it. "No, I guess not. Does that happen all the time?"

"In those forms, it does." He flashed me his cocky grin before finishing off his drink. I couldn't help but imagine a second round in his demon form, but facing him so I could actually see it all. Before the fantasy could build up too much and expose me, I picked something off topic to discuss.

"So," I poked, breaking the brief silence, "what did you do in The Circles? I mean, did you have a job or something?"

For a moment I didn't think he would provide an answer. He kept his eyes on his glass, then the road, anything but me. But finally, his attention landed on my mug of coffee. "What I did in The Circles is the reason I am two parts less of myself."

I swallowed thickly, my mind going back to the two healed-over gashes on his back. "Two parts less?" I asked slowly.

"Do not pretend as if you have not seen the scars." His eyes flashed up to me, shifting from the regular human shade to the demon frost blue and back.

"I have, but that doesn't mean I know what was taken. I thought it be rude to ask what they were from."

He leaned back, narrowing his eyes on me as he spoke. "There was a time, some centuries ago, when I had wings."

"Wings?" I was not expecting him to say that, but given their size and location, I should have figured that was what they were from.

"Yes. Large, and glorious. As black as obsidian." His eyes unfocused as if to lose himself in a memory of it all.

"What did you do?"

He blinked rapidly, torn from the memory. He began to look at me through darkening eyes. "Something bad enough to cost me my most valuable assets, but not horrific enough to wipe me from existence. That is all you need to know."

I stared at him speechless with my mouth hung open, unsure what to say. I didn't know if an apology would mean much to him and, despite feeling a bit sorry that he had to endure literal disfigurement, I was happy he shared it with me.

After about twenty minutes or so of extremely light conversation, Amy came with our orders and set the food down in front of us before scurrying away once again. I took a bite of my French toast, adding a little dance of enjoyment to the sweet treat.

"Is it that good, Mortal?" he questioned, eyeing my happy food dance. Without answering, I cut him a piece and offered it to him. At first, he looked confused, but leaned over and took the bite off my fork.

"You could have just grabbed it." I sighed. It wasn't that big of a deal, I supposed. We shared more the other night.

I went back to my food while he poked at his salad. The silence soon became too uncomfortable to bear, so I began digging through my purse to clear it out, finding the wallet of the man from the weekend. I looked up to Erius, whose attention was out on the passing cars, giving me the privacy to indulge in my prying. I was curious about the man I made a meal of, mostly to find out if there was anything in his life that gave hint to why. Not that I had much to compare it to, but I was sure something would stand out. Maybe it was the blood type, not that most people carried that information around with them in their wallets. But there must have been something more appealing about him.

The worn leather crinkled as I opened it, making a weird stretching noise that old, fake leather made. I looked up to Erius to ensure his enhanced hearing didn't catch it. He probably didn't even care if he did. He continued to watch the passing cars, unbothered.

I went back to searching, not finding much inside apart from his ID and less than five dollars in cash and change. Not that I expected much; I really only needed a name to find the rest. With another quick glance at Erius, who remained distracted by his food and passing cars, I pulled free the ID to investigate.

Charles Black.

I tugged out my phone and tapped it into Google. Several links popped up to various social medias and a multitude of men with the same name. I looked back to the picture and proceeded my search based on that until I came across a news article from five years ago.

String of homeless found burned to death along Dallas interstate. Suspect Charles Black under investigation.

I stared at the picture of the deranged man in the article and back to the photo on the license. Same nose and eyes with the same dark, soul stealing stare. In the ID he had longer hair and a shaved beard, but it was most certainly him.

"What are you looking at there?" Erius quizzed suddenly.

I looked up to find him eyeing the ID in my hand. I figured telling him wouldn't hurt. I hadn't much to make of it yet other than he wasn't a good man and probably wouldn't be missed.

"I wanted to see if there was reason why I went after him. But all I found was this." I slid my phone and the ID over to him.

He looked over it briefly, his brows pulling down over his eyes before he slid it all back to me and pulled out his own phone.

After sending off a lengthy message, he shoved it back into his pocket and returned to looking out to the street.

"Are you going to fill me in on that?" I pressed.

He shook his head and took a sip from his drink. "Perhaps tonight when I can think of how to test my theory," he said after a moment.

"And what is your theory?"

"I think I will wait on telling you until after I have more information." His phone went off, but he kept his eyes on me.

"Oh good, you can do that while I work," I tossed, knowing he was waiting to read the new message until then.

He looked over me, his eyes lingering on my dress. "Are you trying to keep me hidden from that blond male?" he asked, though it almost sounded as if he was doing that weird chest growl as he spoke.

"What? No, but I am sure he wouldn't be too thrilled with you hanging around while I worked my readings. I need you to do something other than follow me around."

His jaw flexed as he watched me take a bite of my food. I didn't know asking him for space would upset him so much, especially after the other night.

"Fine, I will stay on the pier," he grumbled,

"I'm sure you'll enjoy two hours to yourself." I pulled my bag to my lap and dropped my phone in. The sunflower I had placed in the bag earlier moved about as I shuffled things around.

"What are those?" Erius suddenly inquired. I looked up at him with a raised brow, is eyes on the flower.

"You come to this realm often enough, but don't know what a sunflower is?" I countered.

"I do not spend the time investigating flowers." He kept his attention on the flower as if it were going to grow a head and attack us.

"Well, what do you spend it doing?"

"Not… *this*," he said flatly. I don't know what *this* entails in his mind. Walking? Smelling flowers? Eating? Gods knew he wasn't eating very much in this form before me anyway. Or, and the much more likely reason, "You mean hanging around mortals?"

"Amongst other things, but precisely," he said with a smug grin.

"You're irritating," I teased, but his attention was still on the flower. "Here." I held the plant out to him. "Smell it. It's said they bring happiness. You need it."

"I am plenty happy," he scoffed.

"Are you?" I waved the sunflower at him. "Just smell it."

Erius narrowed his eyes but leaned forward, burying his nose into the disk. He flashed his gaze back to me as he pulled away, scrunching his nose at it.

"I take it demons don't like the smell of pretty things." I sighed, putting the flower back in my bag.

"You have much to learn," he tossed out. His eyes grew dark as he leaned back in the chair. His knuckles grew white as his hands fisted on top of the table at whatever clearly enraged him.

"Are you ok?" I asked, tapping his hand.

"Mina?" Andrew's voice came from behind me, deep and surprised.

Erius flashed an irritated glare my boss's way, his eyes flaring to frost blue. As much as I didn't want to turn around, my body spun as if my life depended on it.

"Hey, Drew!" I greeted, a weak attempt at defusing the tension.

"Hey," he said nervously. "I thought that was you." He looked from me to Erius with pressed lips.

Great. Not that I expected anything from him tonight, I just didn't need anything to become awkward at work.

"Was there something I needed to do with the shop?" I knew the answer was most likely nothing, but there really shouldn't have been any other reason he would come up to me outside of work when I had made it clear I didn't think it was a good idea.

There was only one reason he came over here, and it hadn't shit to do with anything important regarding work.

"No, not at all. I was just out for my morning run." He shrugged. I didn't run often, but a fancy button-up and slacks weren't the usual options for workout attire.

"Oh, ok. Well, enjoy it," I offered. I wasn't here to argue.

Erius snickered under his breath as I turned back to him, his eyes on his salad, a pleased smirk on his face.

"Stop," I hissed in a low voice. I was positive Andrew did not hear it as his footsteps retreated from the fence, but Erius snapped his head up to me, his smile growing wider.

"He is not very bright," Erius snickered.

"He's under pressure!" Granted, my boss was under pressure juggling his sick mother and running the shop. But more than likely, in Andrew's mind, he just saw me out on a date.

When I arrived at the shop, Andrew was in the back office. He didn't call out to welcome or greet me, despite the fact I could have been a customer. I was sure he just saw me on camera and was sulking because he saw what most certainly looked like a date from the outside, something he has been practically begging for, and something I kept insisting I was not ready to do. I had put off lunch and dinner dates with any and all excuses I could muster. Yet here I was, sharing my breakfast with "the new client." There was no way I can dance around the fact I was out having brunch with Erius when Andrew already questioned me. Not that he has any place to question me about whom I was seeing or if I was seeing anyone. I told him no, and that should have been all that mattered.

The night went by smoothly with just me and Jordan working the front while Andrew stayed in his office, coming out once or twice to fiddle with the computer. Not that it seemed like he was doing anything other than shooting a mix of hate-filled and sorrowful glares my way.

Ten minutes before closing, Erius strolled in and for once, it was a relieving sight.

I swept up the mess I was working with and looked up to him. "I'm almost done."

"I can finish up, Meems. I don't mind," Jordan offered kindly. I was not too sure why. We weren't extremely close. But he clearly wasn't too close with Andrew either.

I thanked him and grabbed my bag before meeting Erius by the door.

"Hey," I greeted with a smile like a silly little schoolgirl. Catching myself, I pressed my lips flat and headed out the door. I could hear Erius's low chuckle while we stepped out to the sidewalk.

"Are you hungry?" he asked between his silent snickers. I hadn't really thought of it, but I was. Even the question brought a fierce growl to my stomach. I froze and looked up at him, knowing he heard it so my answer wouldn't matter.

"I thought as much. I was thinking about what you had shown me earlier and I wanted to test some things," he said grimly.

I looked over him with widening eyes, curious as to what he planned and theorized.

Chapter Twenty-Seven

Mira

We parked across the street from the California Medical Facility, a hospital for inmates that had medical needs that outweighed those in which the prison doctor could provide. It had started pouring rain on our way over, and for whatever reason, Erius considered that lucky.

"Why are we here, and why is it good that it's raining?" I inquired as I sat back in my seat.

"Because the rain will aid us in entering with a bit more ease, and it disorients the Watchers. They hate water. As for why we are here, that is to test my theory," he explained, his glowing eyes scanning the lot. Not sure if he knew what inconspicuous meant, but a man with glowing eyes was not it.

"And what is your theory?"

"That your form hungers for mortals tainted by their dark

essence. You lot call them criminals," he explained.

"Ok, but why are we at the medical facility?" I pressed again.

"We can go to the prison if you would like. More guards and less time to feed." He shrugged and went back to looking out the window.

My stomach hardened as I gazed at the distorted buildings in front of us. I shouldn't have been considering it or weighing the option of having fewer guards to deal with as opposed to more. It should have been strange to me to be even sitting in a car with a demon casually discussing the best course of action when it came to hunting humans. But here I was.

"Erius, some of these patients couldn't help what they did," I pointed.

"And if I am correct in my assumption, you should be able to weed them out and leave them unharmed."

I looked out the windshield again. "But what if I just kill everyone?"

"Then you kill everyone. You must understand that even if we are unsure of what you are, what we can be sure of is that you are not mortal. In fact, you eat them. I believe it is time for the predator to stop caring about the feelings of its prey and just hunt," he said darkly as he leaned over me.

"Just try and focus on what you smell and let your senses carry you." He chuckled, leaning back to continue scanning the distance between us and the door.

He wasn't wrong, I guessed. If I was going to do this, then I needed to suck it up and just do it.

"What are we going to do about the guards then?" I finally asked, settling into my decision.

His lips curved up into a triumphant smile. "Leave that to me. You simply need to stay in my shadows until I return. He looked to my neck at the raven skull. "You should use that to your advantage. Come on." He exited the car and slipped into the darkness, gone from view in the misted winds and large drops of water. My sight may have been better, but the weather and darkness still brought its usual challenges.

I walked around the car to his side, my hair and clothes already drenched from the rain. I looked around at the spreading darkness over the pavement. It blotted out the dim lot lights as they surrounded me and cut the heavy pounding of drops and rushing winds out to submerge me in silence.

"Send out your raven to guide you," an echoing voice instructed.

I could feel the warm press of Erius's hand push against my back. I turned, expecting to see him, but was met with an empty darkness, vacant of light of any sort. When I turned back, the only thing I could see was the fading buildings across the street.

I held the skull between my hands, casting a green light to illuminate the space around me. It was as if I had been placed in an empty black room with no light source, no furniture. Nothing on the ground but endless despair.

For those who could feel it.

I brought my focus back to the skull, sending my raven high into the air with an illuminating glow. It shot forward, lighting a small path that led to a white metal door. With his invisible hand still pressed against my back, Erius guided me through the entrance as it creaked open.

His shadows spilled in violently, racing down the halls and pushing into every room. Lights shattered to the ground, sending bright sparks out to the darkening floor. Screams filled the silence as people began darting around the front counter to escape.

I stepped through the door to get a better view of the scene, my nose filling with an overpowering scent of cooked meats of all sorts. I dropped my head back, taking in the scent as my body began to ignite.

I was pulled from myself by a rough hand gripping my arm and yanking me forward. I jerked back with ease, causing the intruder to fall back. Their wide, fear-filled eyes locked on me as a scream ripped from their hung mouth. My tail whipped out, striking at the man and sending him further back.

The raven cried out from the hall to my left where the delicious scents were more concentrated. While Erius seemed to be herding the guards, doctors, and nurses to one wing, my raven and I ran down the other. I dodged and slid around human obstacles while my raven raced ahead, strategically plucking at the eyes of guards with weapons. I made a sharp turn right and stumbled into a room lined with hospital beds but no patients. Wrist and ankle straps stained in blood were attached to each and every gurney with sheets just as distressed, while pills and empty bottles lay scattered across the floor and on some of the beds.

I didn't pause to investigate much further as I ran through to the other end where the smell continued to grow. My raven cawed angrily as it pecked at the door to get to the other side. With a deep inhale, it was clear the one with the scent was there, trapped and waiting.

One forceful kick was enough to dislodge the door from the lock as it crumpled around my foot. I clawed at the metal still connected until it gave away with a metallic scream. The door squeaked open with an eerie echo to announce my presence amongst them.

Three men of various ages cowered in the corner. They gawked up at me with trembling mouths as I stood in the doorway. My shoulders rose with each deep inhale I took, savoring the scent and sight.

I hadn't realized it before, but fear was such a silly thing to have. It was easy to spot and enjoyable to witness. However, it was useless once you got down to it.

A heated hand pressed against my back once again and when I turned, Erius's star-filled skin greeted me. He looked over the men with a half-smile before turning my way. "Good. You found them. Now, try not to make a mess of them."

My eyes widened as I realized what he meant. He was sorting them out, herding them into different areas of the facility to allow me to track them down. I would have been upset about it if I didn't feel the spark of excitement filling my chest.

I stepped forward with extended claws, and the men immediately fell into a fit of screaming and hollering. The blearing sound sent my poor ears into a twitching fit, and even my tail had a jerking reaction. I turned to Erius who was closing the door, his shoulders shaking from his laughter. When I looked back to them, their screaming intensified.

"I haven't done anything," I shouted, which only frightened them all the more and sent Erius into a raging laugh.

"Do you expect them to sit quietly? Look at you!" he pushed between laughs. My chest rumbled out a growl as I lunged forward, snapping each man's neck to silence them and give me peace.

"Well, how very anticlimactic." He sighed, pinching the bridge of his nose the same way he did as a human. He walked over and kneeled beside the lifeless bodies to inspect them.

After a moment, he reached into the first one's mouth and pulled free a glowing blue orb. I thought he'd bring it to his mouth and eat it how one would normally eat something. I mean, that was how it usually worked. Instead, he closed his hand around the orb, absorbing it into his palm until it created another bright star in his skin. He proceeded to do this with the others. Though it was amazing, and I had questions, my stomach rumbled and my mouth watered at the tantalizing smell that came from the men.

I gripped the ankle of the one in the middle and pulled him closer to me, freeing his torso as I did with my first kill, and like with him, I made this man's body a soup bowl. This seemed to be my process as I consumed the following two men. The whole event didn't take long, not that I would know exactly how long I spent with them. But given the fact Erius's shadows still cloaked the walls and floor, along with the continued screams of the patients and convicts, I would say it had only been a few minutes.

Half expecting Erius to comment on the mess, I turned to find the room empty with only the green glow of my raven.

My clothes were soaked in the deep wine-red color that spilled free. The bodies lay dismembered and tossed about in a way that it was hard to tell there were three men—if they had been men at all. Their blood covered the floor and splattered wildly around the walls, a scene right out of a horror film.

My stomach continued to rumble as hunger clung to me and my mouth burned for more. Screams still rang off the walls, and though there were fewer than before, the cries didn't stop. Along with the terrors from the people came a very upbeat club song that blared through the intercom speakers.

I stepped out to the hall where the darkness wasn't as consuming, allowing the flicking bulbs to shine through. With the flashing lights and screaming, it looked more like a rave of some sort was taking place rather than a literal slaughter of life. But hey, it added to the excitement.

"Take me to Erius," I commanded my ghostly creature. With a squawk, it took to the air and led me through the haunting darkness, following a raging wail of screams and cries. The raven crowed as it zipped down the corridor. Its green vibrance guided me as we raced through several more halls until finding another door. A smoked meat scent lofted out, gripping my muscles as I ripped the door open and stepped in. Two more men sat cowering under a bright light while darkness circled them in all directions. Glowing eyes flickered from the far back with a snicker.

"I thought you were supposed to be practicing manners," Erius scoffed as he pushed off the wall.

"Blood is messy!" I spat.

"Yes, there are ten units in most mortals. You must learn how to not spill so much of it," he instructed calmly.

The men in the middle of the room continued to shake in fear as our conversation continued.

"I can't control blood, Erius!" I snapped to him before looking back to the men, considering ways to drain them without a mess, but waiting for a body to drain might take too long. I looked back to Erius. "You show me."

"I do not eat organs."

"You don't have to eat them. Just show me how to get them without this so-called mess."

"Just kill us already!" one of the men shouted in a shaky voice.

I snapped my attention to them, unsure which it was. "Shh, criminal," I hissed before returning to Erius, waiting for the presentation.

A low growl reverberated around the room as he kneeled to one of the men. He looked him in the eye with no expression until his body settled and his breathing calmed. When he was just blankly staring into space like an empty vessel, Erius placed his finger on the man's chest where his heart would be.

The convict's body slumped to the ground and the other inmate scurried away from it while still being sure to stay within the light.

"That explains absolutely nothing," I huffed, walking over to the other man. I grabbed his arm and towed him back to the center.

"You told me to show you, not explain." Erius shrugged.

I gripped the man's head between my hands and flicked it right, snapping his neck as I had with the others.

Erius watched the body fall to the floor, unimpressed. "I'm sure you will find more imaginable ways to end them." He got to work pulling his souls before aiding me in a cleaner extraction. which didn't seem much different than my way, as he still had blood smeared all over him.

"What did you do with the guards?" I asked, licking the blood from one of my claws.

He licked his thumb just the same before answering. "I left them in a state of delusion. Along with the rest of the staff. I did manage to have one supply me with files of every patient on this floor." He pulled a thick as fuck accordion file folder from behind him. Where he was keeping it this whole time was beyond me. He probably turned it to mist.

Throwing it down between us, we began searching through the thinner, numbered folders. File #354, #251, #987, #333, and #199 were pulled and set before me.

"What are these?" I asked, already knowing the answer.

"The files of the men you have chosen for your meal." He began opening each folder, grabbing one at random to inspect more closely. As he flipped through the pages, I pulled #251 for my own research. I found his name was Lance Brew, age twenty-eight. He was in the medical facility due to prolonged COVID symptoms though it appeared his last high fever was several months prior. As for why he was an inmate, it didn't specify further than saying "High Caution." I tossed the folder and picked up the next, finding the same spot filled out with the same status.

"What does 'high caution' mean in this absurd facility?" Erius grunted as he tossed the last folder down.

"Did those three say that?" I asked, and he simply nodded.

He looked at the men's lifeless bodies and then at the scatter of files across the floor. Bloodied, inhuman prints covered the sheets and folders. "Based on the commonalities, I would say my theory is correct." He waved his hands, sending the files into oblivion. The stars in his arm spread out across the rest of his body, fading into constellations and nebulas that only added to the beauty of his skin. We looked over the mess at our feet, less blood than in my last room, but not by much.

The screaming and music still boomed through the speakers. The light above the men began to flicker along with the rest. Erius's bloody grin grew between each flash as he neared me. "Have you finished terrorizing these ones?" he asked.

I was full and content in more ways than one. With the info of what this form ate, I felt more confident I wouldn't just go on a killing spree of innocent people. But now I had an inner tracker for people that were so rotted from evil that it had the capability of sending me off at the very smell.

"I have. Do we have to hide these ones? It looks like a lot of cleaning."

"No. But it would help if you were cleaner in your attack." His tail wrapped around me and pulled me closer to him, wrapping me in his shadows with a cool breeze. Before I knew it, we were sitting in the front seat of his car, my green raven speeding toward us from the facility. It burst through the glass without breaking it and flew right into the skull around my neck. The bone heated up for a moment and slowly faded as the glowing died down.

Erius looked over at me and my blood-soaked clothes and an overly pleased grin. "Let us get you changed back."

Chapter Twenty-Eight

Mira

I didn't remember any dream, nor did I remember when we got home or how I got cleaned up and in bed, a usual feeling after a night of drinking. However, I felt more refreshed than I ever had. Erius, on the other hand, thought it be best to keep an eye on me and since it was Tuesday and I'd be working with Amber and Jaz, I figured him having a "reading" today would fit since he was, for all intents and purposes, a client learning to read tarot.

He sat at a table in the apothecary lobby, drinking tea, which seemed fitting for him. With few customers to help, I spent most of my time searching up the names of the five men from the night before. Erius didn't think it wise when I had brought it up that morning, but I felt there was a bigger connection between all of them other than they were just criminals with bad reputations.

How cliché.

Unlike my first victim, these men didn't have any articles written about their crimes. Just what was public record. Which, again, they had something in common with those. Most of the crime descriptions were redacted for being "too graphic" for public attention. Whatever that meant.

When Jaz and Amber finally arrived, Erius excused himself to wait in the room which I think was best for everyone.

"So, how was your weekend?" Jaz asked with a probing gaze. After she explained her gifts, she should know exactly how my weekend went.

"Fine," I said flatly.

"Yeah, what did you and the demon do? You were awfully quiet in the chat," Amber tossed in, clearly unaware of what Jasmine knew. Her smile grew as she waited for me to answer Amber's question.

"Um, a lot happened, and my phone was usually left behind," I tried, but Jaz fell into a fit of laughter.

"Oh, I bet!"

Amber looked between us with confusion before the realization quickly dawned on her. Lighting up her eyes as she stared at me. "Meems!"

I mean, if they thought that was wild, wait till they heard about my new diet. However, I was not too sure they would take it the same. Their fear left them later if it even left at all. Who knew what other emotions still lingered on them. Maybe that was a conversation for another time, as was the other one.

"It's not a crime," I push flatly.

"Gods, you even sound like him now!" Jaz snickered. We laughed as Amber got to work with the teas and our conversation switched to less personal affairs such as Amber's little friend.

"How's Fidget?" I asked.

"Nice topic change. He's good, actually." She turned to pull him out of her bag when the entrance door swung open. Andrew stormed in straight toward me with a heated gaze. A black vapor spilled from him as he stood over me.

"Mina, can I talk to you privately?" he asked through clenched teeth.

I looked back to see Jaz coming to the realization while Amber looked as if she were ready to march between us. I held out a hand to her and nodded to Andrew.

"Sure." I made my way around him to the office as he followed close behind. With Jaz and Amber here, I figured he'd shut the door. Not that it mattered for Erius. But he marched up to me with a harsh scowl, putting everything on broadcast for all to hear.

"Mina, what are you doing?" he barked.

I backed up into the desk, trying to keep a distance in case my form decided to come out. I had yet to be aggressed upon in this fashion, so I was not sure how my body would take it. I was already pissed he'd even come at me about it.

"Um, Andrew. I don't think this is the right time. I—"

"And when is the best time, Mina? Ever since this new client showed up, you've been blowing me off," he argued. His words touched on every nerve in my body, igniting me with the long overdue irritations of his constant attempts. I pushed off the desk to step around him. There was no reason to put him down gently anymore if he was going to make a big deal out of it.

"Blowing you off?" The rippling sensation bubbled up at my skin, ready to shift at any sign of danger. The smell that radiated off him wasn't like that of the criminals, nor was it anything pleasant. It was sour and foul, like rotten milk, and it grew more unpleasant the more he spoke.

"You told me you didn't want anything serious, but you look pretty fucking serious with your 'new client.' Who is he?" The grim energy that seeped off his skin felt thicker than sludge, creeping around me but unable to make contact.

"My client, Erius?"

"He gives me bad vibes, Meems. And you parade him around here to make me jealous!"

No shit, he's a demon. I'd be more surprised if he gave him happy warm feelings. A stinging ache filled my palms from my nails digging into them at his accusation. Feeling jealous was all his own insecurities, and I couldn't believe it took me this long to see it.

"Make you jealous? Andrew, you sound like a fool. I liked having sex, that was literally all we were doing. Did you expect me to be fucking you in the supply closet well into my thirties? I don't think so." I pushed past him to escape the cage he had created with his body. As I squeezed between him and the desk, he grabbed my arm and yanked me back until I was nose to nose with him. The putrid smell of dark energy seethed from him as he glared down at me.

He may not have been a criminal that matched the scent of my form's usual prey, but he wasn't a good person in his soul. Maybe I wouldn't kill him, but a broken leg and wounded ego weren't lethal.

"You and him both have these matching tattoos—"

"Andrew!" I warned with a jerk of my arm before giving my final warning. "Let go!"

The pressure flooded my mind as I fought the urge to change. I yanked back again before black vapor spread over his hand. In seconds, Andrew was screaming out in pain as the sound of crunching bone filled the small space.

Gasps filled the room as the girls spilled in to see what was going on as well. They stared wide-eyed between the three of us trying to make sense of it all.

The demon leaned down with a feral growl as his glowing eyes locked with Andrew. "You will never touch her again."

My frightened and wounded boss trembled before Erius sent him flying back. The crash to the floor did him no favors as he landed right on the fucked-up arm.

Before I could scold the action or decide if it turned me on, Erius swept up the arm Andrew had grabbed, inspecting it with great care before towing me from the office and through the lobby without letting me say a word to Jaz or Amber. They followed us out, unsure if they should stop Erius or scold Andrew. By the time he was pulling me through the front door, I figured I wasn't working today.

"Erius!" I protested.

"We are leaving," he said, opening the car door and pushing me in. He slammed it shut before I could ask anything about it, making me wait until he was sliding into his seat.

"What was that about?"

"Put your seatbelt on. Please," he grunted, throwing the car into drive.

"Erius!" I barked again. Of course I wanted an answer. I mean, him grabbing my boss for grabbing me makes sense, but he was acting as if we were fleeing a predator. Andrew wasn't going to do shit else but fire me.

"We are going to the Four Seasons," he huffed before throwing the car into reverse.

"All because he grabbed me?" I shot. The tires squeaked against the asphalt as he sped out of the lot.

"No. He has a broken arm because he grabbed you. We are

leaving because I spoke with Alius."

With so much to unpack, I wasn't sure where to begin.

"Did he hear from the sorceress?"

Erius paused and looked at me as if he had forgotten all about us waiting for her. "Oh, no. I was waiting for someone to leave before taking you there to wait it out. I have been a bit tired of your small van," he explained.

"Well, I need my small van! Prometheus is there and all my stuff," I cried out.

"Yes, of course. We will go get your cat and whatever else you need."

"My entire van!" I protest.

He leaned over the seat as his eyes slowly swept over me.

"Fine."

"Thank you. By the way, you can't just break people's arms for grabbing me. I had it under control," I assured.

He gave me a skeptical look, weaving between the cars before us without even looking. Normally I would be horrified, but I was just irritated he was showing off the way he was and not supplying me with easy answers and explanations.

"I have given you the gift to rip the flesh from bones of those who disrespect you, and you choose to squander such a talent," he huffed with a shake of his head.

Well, that was news to me because I didn't know he gave me such a power. I didn't think I would have used it in this case even if I had known.

By the time we pulled into the lot where my van sat, I had over fifty messages in the group chat asking me what happened, why Erius broke Andrew's arm, how the cops were at the shop. Of course the cops were called——someone was assaulted. I told them I would message when I could, but the cops were the least of my worries at the moment.

We left the car and jumped in the van, Erius taking the driver's side. I made sure everything was put up and ready for his reckless driving and took my new spot as the passenger. He pulled onto the main street, going the actual speed limit for once. He took longer than normal at each stop and followed every road rule with patience, dragging out the time it took to get to the hotel after rushing me for whatever reason.

"Who are you hiding from?" I finally asked. It had been excruciatingly clear he didn't care for my van, yet he had forced himself to deal with it all this time to just wait for someone to leave. *Sounds like hiding to me.*

"I am not hiding from anyone."

"Then why were you waiting for someone to leave?"

He pressed his lips flat, his jaw flexing as he stalled some more, but I didn't back down. "So, you *were* hiding?"

His shoulders fell with a defeated sigh, but he kept his attention on the road. "It was someone I owe some things to," he finally said.

"Oh, like money?" I was not even sure if they have a currency in his world. He understood the concept of it so there must have been some form of it where he was from.

His lips kicked up into a smile. "Yes, like money. Only more valuable to him for whatever reason."

"Why haven't you just given it to him?" I probed some more.

He broke away from the road to look over me. "I have not found reason to part with it, and I tend to keep things I am fond of."

"So, risk my life because you are fond of an item. That's generous of you. Whatever it is must be valuable. Can I see it?" I asked curiously. I wanted to see what was worth risking our lives for and what had him in hiding.

His gaze raked over me again before he fixated it back on the road. "When it is safe to do so."

I was quiet the rest of the way, thinking up more questions to throw at him once we arrived. Like why is a demon staying at the Four Seasons of all places? Why are demons conducting deals in a busy mortal hotel and not, I don't know, the cemetery or such places?

He managed to get us there in under thirty minutes, which was decent. As we had the first time, he pulled the van all the way to the top before throwing the gear into park.

I stood to collect some clothes and whatever else I would need for the surprise stay. "How long are we going to be here?"

"I'm not sure." He paused me before I could reach the bed, looking over me as if to realize something. "We will have to do something about your scent."

"My scent? Well, I'm not sure how else you want me to smell—"

Before I could get out another word, Erius was shoving me into the shower, crowding me in the tiny space.

"Erius!"

"Don't move," he ordered. I squirmed against the invasion as he tucked himself against me, burying his face in my neck.

"What are you doing?" My fight slowed as my mind and body welcomed the touch.

"You need my scent on you before we go in." His voice was deep and gravelly, vibrating through him into me. Warm, soft lips grazed the hollow of my neck as he moved around, trailing my jaw down to my collarbone. Every switch in direction was met with a short pause as he exhaled the vanillic scent, burning my skin and inflaming my need to have him inside me again.

His hands slid down my arms, lifting them above my head and pinning them there. Body to body, heat consuming energy, and the heavy smell of vanilla locked me in place.

"Breathe," he whispered, grazing his fangs along my skin as he exhaled over me, moving from my collarbone down to my chest and over my breasts..

"Erius, this isn't fair," I panted weakly.

"You do not know the meaning of fair," he groaned against my skin, spilling more of his scent and heat over me.

I gasped out, struggling to control the whimpers of straight pleasure that pulsated through me.

"Erius, please," I whined, not sure what I was pleading for. For him to stop, to continue—I did not know, but what I got was mind-numbing bliss.

The soft heat of his lips brushed over mine as he continued, but still, never connecting as he so clearly wanted to. He came around to my cheek, the tip of his tongue gliding across the corner of my lip before he pulled away.

"There, every inch of you smells of me. Even your breath," he laughed, pushing off the wall. "Grab your things, and your cat. We will stay here for now."

PART THREE

Chaos is an angel who fell in love with a demon.

-Christopher Poindexter

Chapter Twenty-Nine

Mira

I struggled to balance Prometheus's crate and my duffle bag in my hands while trying to exit the van. Erius followed behind with empty hands and an amused grin.

"I'm so glad my struggles are your entertainment," I huffed, stumbling out the door.

"Set that down," he ordered. I needed to search for my keys anyway, and I hadn't a free hand to do so. The moment the bag and crate touched the floor, the black vapor whisked them away before my eyes.

"What did you do to my cat?" I shrieked, stumbling forward to the empty spot my baby had just been.

"He is safe, as are the rest of your things. It would be best he isn't with us when we walk through. You should also keep close to me and not wander."

"I don't like half ass demands, Erius," I groaned.

He responded with a slick grin and casually slipped his arm around my shoulders.

"What is this? What are you doing?" I hissed, still sensitive after his performance in the shower. His body shook with a silent chuckle as he guided me to the elevator just like before. Granted, this time he was much more friendly.

Even on the elevator, he stayed close, never dropping his arm from me. He buried his nose in my hair. I didn't know if he was sniffing me or if he was about to do some weird mind control trick, but he didn't allow me to move.

"You're awfully handsy today. Did breaking my boss's arm send you into some territorial demon state?" I tried pushing him off to give me some air, but he remained locked around me.

"I need as much of your scent on me as you need mine on you," he purred again. "There are going to be a lot of things your mortal eyes won't be used to. This is not a place where laws from my world are held highly, and mortals are not aware when they enter. So please act dazed." He rushed the words before the doors slid open and I gave a faint nod.

We moved through the bright lobby, walking right up to the same check-in counter with the same blonde woman. I kept my attention forward, keeping a blank stare but I could make out the people around us. No one seemed to take notice, so we were still in the mortal part of the hotel it seemed.

"Hello. Welcome to the Four Seasons, how may I assist you?" she asked kindly, her eyes shifting from me to Erius.

"*Bach zhoi*," he said in the rough language.

As soon as the words left his mouth, the woman's eyes fell blank and vacant. "Right this way," she said monotonously, as if her very essence was sucked from her and replaced with a robotic zombie. She opened the side door and ushered us behind the counter as casually as if we worked there.

Erius pulled me closer and leaned down just far enough to whisper more words of warning. "Remember what I said. Do not speak, no matter what you hear me say."

We followed the woman through a door in the back that took us down a long hallway. Opposite us sat an enormous red door, but the fluorescents were so blindingly bright I could hardly focus on the door as the loud buzzing rang in my head. Squeezing my eyes shut wasn't enough to block out the light. I turned into Erius, tucking my face against his side, a last attempt that did a better job, but not by much.

His body shook with a silent laugh as he tightened his arm around me, taking advantage of my confused discomfort to be entertained.

We came to an abrupt stop, and I assumed we were finally at the door.

"Have a wonderful evening." The woman's voice drifted further as she departed from us with the echoing clack of her heels against the tile floor.

"You can open your eyes now," he whispered. I did exactly that, finding the lighting to be far more bearable.

Erius fisted his hand against the red metal three times before returning to wrap his arm around me once more. There were no other markings or indications on it other than the small hinge door styled peep hole.

He gripped my chin and tilted it up to hover his lips over mine. I wouldn't say it was a kiss so much as him just sensually breathing into my mouth. The tip of his tongue slid across my upper lip, and I trembled under it. He cradled my head, keeping me in place as he drank in every breath I made.

The door to the peep hole swung open, and a man cleared his throat with an irritated gruff. Erius pulled away to greet him, keeping his hand firmly on the back of my head.

He spoke to the man in the strange language for a moment before the eyes behind the door danced between us, never softening from the hard glare. The small door closed with a bang, followed by the clicking and clanking of locks being undone. Hot, musty air escaped as the entrance cranked open. Erius pulled me in, walking swiftly through, but the man was gone, leaving an empty space behind the door as it closed behind us.

We stepped into another long hall lit by blue neon and black lights. Walls jutted out in odd disfigurements, making it look more like a fun house than some secret hotel. The pungent smell of sweat and alcohol stung the back of my throat while loud, pumping music blared from behind a thin black sheet—very much like a mortal club aside from the creepy bouncer and entering décor.

Odd sigils painted in neon colors covered the bouncing sheet we neared. Sounds of screams and monstrous growls rang through, mixed in with the pounding music. I grabbed Erius's shirt, tilting my head up enough in hopes he'd hear me. "Where are we?"

"Remember what I said," he reminded me.

The mortal appearance he had been holding onto slipped away, revealing the other familiar form. The tail I hadn't had much time to look over wrapped around my waist and reached to twine around my right wrist as well.

He kept me close with the tail, tightening the arm around my shoulder for added barrier before pulling me through the tapestry into a crowded club. At least, that was what it looked like. Aside from the loud music and strobe lights, people, creatures, and all sorts of glowing eyes danced and moved about the floor.

Mirrors and black velvet surrounded me all around with every inch of the room sparkling as if we were walking inside solid obsidian. In the center of it all sat a rounded bar with crystals and diamonds suspended above the shelves of uniquely crafted bottles.

Dozens of glowing eyes turned to us, whether for a brief moment or a complete stare down. Not all looked to be entirely hateful, but the grip on my shoulder never laxed the deeper we went.

Some of them looked human, sporting glowing eyes. Many, however, were unworldly. Horns, fangs, and tail. Big, burly fur covered beasts. Creatures I had only ever seen in sci-fi movies surrounded me in every direction.

We walked around the bar and through another large crowd until we found ourselves at a table that looked very much like a blackjack table you'd see in a casino.

"Azal?" a large man grunted, dealing out a few painted bones to those around the table, each bone painted either black or white with an odd sigil. So, maybe not like blackjack at all, but definitely some sort of gambling.

"Where is Alius?" Erius asked.

"In his office." The man looked us over for a moment, his gaze falling to the tail at my wrist. "Where did you get this one?"

This one? His words dug into me as I remained unmoved as instructed. Though my mind was reeling with more questions and that annoying ball of irritation began to bubble up in my chest. How many other mortals had he brought here?

Erius pulled me even closer, tucking me under his arm as his tail constricted me.

"Let him know I am here," he instructed the man, ignoring the question. The tender nodded and picked up the phone hanging on the wall behind him. The few at the table turned to get a look, eyeing me with interest and confusion. Some had eyes just like Erius's, but along with the frost blue, there were some whose eyes were a deep glowing red.

They were the ones who looked more irritated in their interest as we waited for the man to get off the phone.

"He will meet you at your door," he instructed blankly as he hung the phone back on the receiver, his deep red eyes burning into me. Erius tugged me away without a word in return, shuffling me toward a dimly lit elevator lobby.

I waited until he hit the button, before tossing my questions at him. "What did he mean by that?"

"What did who mean by what?" he attempted.

"That guy – when he asked 'where did you get this one?' How many *'this ones'* have you brought here? And who the hell is Azal?"

He snickered. "I am Azal, Eriusazal. It is what they call me here, and you are the only one. Bartholomew gets confused with his patrons and their stories," he pushed.

I didn't feel he was being completely honest if he was being honest at all. The man seemed well aware of him, he addressed him by name, and Erius said he spent most of his time in the hotel when he had to live out his ten years sentencing. Ten years was a lot of time in the mortal realm doing nothing but supposedly staying in a club hotel. It was not my business if he was fucking mortals before, I just didn't see why he'd lie about it. We could have been doing it this whole time if he wasn't such a grump.

The lift arrived before I could toss out another question and I figured I'd just leave it at that. If he wanted to lie, that was his own business.

We stepped in and he finally released me to press the highest level on the dash before turning, placing a hand on either side to cage me in the small corner. In this form, he was completely consuming, pressing his weighted energy over me.

"You did well. Thank you for remaining calm." His voice was a rough growl that rattled though my bones to light the flame deep within me. I squeezed my legs, knowing that it wouldn't help.

His lips kicked up into a bright smile. Green and blue nebulas swirled over his cheeks. "Try and control yourself. I am not the only one who will find that…distracting."

"I'm starting to think by distracting you mean enjoyable," I whispered.

His grin widened but he didn't entertain a verbal answer.

The elevator stopped and he grabbed my hand to lead me off, towing me through the wide and obnoxiously high-ceilinged hall until we arrived at a large door.

"Azal!" a voice called from behind us. We turned to find Alius trotting our way with a red card in hand and a cheerful grin spread over his face.

"I see you haven't lost your temper yet," he said as he reached us. His eyes widened, looking over me from head to toe, ensnared in Erius's tail like some trapped prey.

"We need to talk." Erius took the key card and swiped it over the lock. He pushed it open and guided me in with Alius close behind.

We stepped into an enormous entrance hall that was awfully spacious for a single mortal sized individual, but considering the size of one of his forms, I would say he didn't spend his time here as a mortal. He pulled me through a gap in the wall at our right, flipping a switch that illuminated what I could only assume to be a kitchen. The sight was nothing short of amazing. Luxurious, even. A commercial-grade kitchen with all-black appliances and a sink deep enough to bathe in for a demon who hardly ate.

"Whoa," I breathed. "Do you live here?"

"Yes and no. It is mine in a sense," he said cryptically.

A wave of meows moved around us as Prometheus ran to me, zipping around my feet with excitement.

"Yes, there's so much space!" I cooed as I bent to scoop him into my arms.

"So, have you decided you no longer want to break the tether?" Alius assumed proudly.

"That is not why we are here. What have you heard from Vex?" Erius corrected.

Alius looked over us, his smile falling. "I think it be best if we speak alone," he suggested.

Erius looked at me before responding, pulling me from the kitchen into an even bigger room set up with a sizable leather couch and theater sized TV screen.

"Oh! You got money," I gasped as he guided me to the couch. My attention was far too focused on the high up rafters and glass wall that looked out over the ocean to care about being excluded from a conversation I clearly should be involved in. But I was tired, and I didn't care to listen or try and follow along with shit I most likely would not understand.

"Wait here," he ordered before returning to his friend. I leaned back with Prometheus in my lap, running my hand through his fur. Unfortunately, their conversation carried into the living room and I was forced to hear it all anyways.

"We do not have time for questions—what *does* she know about them?" Erius asked him.

"You wanted me to seek out my niece to break the tether, and you turn the mortal into the unthinkable," Alius said in a sarcastic whisper.

"As I mentioned, it must have happened with the tether, and it was out of our control," Erius explained. There was another long pause before Alius finally spoke.

"Why do you think she is not a *Nipans* again?" Alius inquired, clearly discussing a conversation that was had over the weeks.

"She doesn't share the scent you described," Erius added.

"Of death? Does she look to be dying to you? Does she look like the transition isn't taking?"

They both were silent for a moment before Erius finally spoke up again. "Nowhere did you insinuate that the smell was due to the fact they were bound to die."

"I thought it to be a common assumption," Alius said.

"Can your niece change her back?"

Again, stillness fell over them for a few seconds too long before someone spoke up. "Erius, I know as much as I have shared with you, which is the same I shared over the last few weeks. I can only move as fast as the serpents will allow. Her's are on watch, as you know," Alius explained. I wasn't sure what they used snakes for—just another question to bother Erius about later.

Their words shifted from English to the unknown language as they spoke of an obvious secret they didn't want me to know about.

"Don't let anyone know what she is. She is mortal where all the others are concerned," Alius instructed as they exited the kitchen and made their way to the couch to kneel before me. Something about the gesture to be at eye level with me seemed condescending.

"Hello again, little bird," he greeted.

"Yeah…I still don't like that. I like it less than mortal, in fact. It implies I'm small and weak." I leaned forward with narrowed eyes. "I'm no weak bird."

"But you are little," Alius pointed out. He turned to Erius. "How big does she get in the other form?"

"Not much. Maybe a foot taller than what she is now." He shrugged.

Alius rose a brow and turned back to me. "Interesting. Well, no harm will come to her. But I would advise you keep her human if you plan to leave the safety of your walls."

"I will see to it she tries," Erius said, knowing my grasp on full control of my changing had yet to be mastered.

"I am right here, and still a very big part of this conversation," I interjected.

Alius rose with a smile and nod, though I couldn't help feeling patronized by it. He parted with a wave, joining Erius as they made their way to the entrance. Their conversation ended with a quick goodbye and click of the door.

"What if this can't be fixed? Even the tether. What if she can't break it? What are we supposed to do then?"

"Honestly, Mortal." He held his hand out to me. "I am not too concerned with that at the moment. We have bigger issues, it would seem."

I took his hand, and my cat jumped off my lap to finally explore while Erius led me up the stairs. We entered a loft-like bedroom with a large bed in the center facing the floor-to-ceiling window that overlooked the L.A. skyline which was odd. I thought we were in the basement. At least that was what it seemed like. At the end opposite us sat a darkened balcony. I couldn't make out much further than that.

"Bathroom." He pointed to a dark room with no door. "Bed. Make yourself at home."

"What? Where are you going?"

He pulled a remote from the nightstand drawer and clicked a button that revealed a projector screen against the glass. After a few more cautious clicks, he handed both the remote and his phone to me.

"The movie thing is new. Do what you want with it. And please put your information in this. I am going to get you food."

I took the phone and dialed my number under Mortal, just for fun and handed it back to him.

A faint grin ghosting his face as he looked over the name. "I will be back," he said before turning and walking downstairs to leave.

I kind of felt stupid just standing there staring at the top step, but I wasn't too sure what else to do.

First things first, I needed a shower. Then I could be nosy and look around. *Yeah, that's it.*

Prometheus hopped up onto the first step and flicked his whiskers at me.

"I know, I know. It's all very flashy for a demon. Expensive, too, but it's nice! Definitely better than the van," I prattled to the cat as I walked to the doorless bathroom.

I slid my hand along the cool tile wall until I found a switch and flipped it, illuminating the room of all-out luxury.

"What the fuck does a demon need all this for?" I whispered, eyeing the full walk-in shower with tiling, the large black crystal carved tub that most certainly covered knees and shoulders. The left side of the wall was all mirror and counterspace, while the right wall continued the floor-to-ceiling window.

Prometheus meowed.

"I'm sure it's tinted. Besides, I've never seen this part of the hotel. I thought we were lower than the lobby." I made my way to the shower glass door. Two shower heads came straight down from either end of the ceiling. Along the dark tile walls were what I believed to be water jets.

Why the fuck would he choose to stay in my van when he had all this?

I pulled the door open and walked to the odd screen on the wall. With a tap, it blinked on and pulled up several options for pressure, rain style, temperature—something from the future. Or maybe I was broker than I thought.

I tapped in the options and pressed continue. The screen flashed once more to pull up a new page, a diagram of the showers with each shower head, one labeled under Erius and the other labeled under Ennaza. I wasn't sure who that was, but it sounded like a woman's name.

A heated spark zipped through me but honestly, I was not sure if it was an emotion or not. If I should feel something or not. Guilt, anger, sadness, maybe jealousy. I was not too sure, but I clicked Erius. I didn't want to fuck up any more of Ennaza's shit, and I didn't even know who or what she was. She'd probably kick my ass into the underworld.

The shower switched on to pour the water down in a light rain like fashion. Thunder cracked above my head from speakers that blended into the tiles with lights flashing in sync.

"Wow it's the whole experience," I breathed. With all the space available, I undressed and left my clothes in a neat pile in the corner where water was not reaching.

Now, to enjoy the most surreal shower I would ever experience in my life. I walked under the head. The heated water saturated my hair and trickled down my body. The lights flashed and more thunder cracked through the speakers. Luckily, Erius had a shelf stocked with body washes, conditioners, and shampoos, all of which looked to be brand new and unopened.

The lights flashed again as I reached for the wash. When they flickered back, a dark shadow lingered in front of me, blocking my hand from the shelf. It bellowed, rattling its surface like ripples in water but made no other motion or movement. I stared at it blankly, annoyed that this is all it ever did—why not speak? Why not give me something other than following me around or leading me off to Watchers?

"What are you?" I asked under my breath. It didn't answer, not that I expected it to. I didn't know what I was expecting, but it certainly wasn't the thing lifting its *hand* up to me.

I looked over it as it lightly swayed its appendage from side to side.

"You want me to touch you?"

The shadow swayed its hand again, urging me to do the same. Maybe that was its form of communication. I hadn't tried pulling out my cards or pendulum to speak with it. Then again, it usually approached me when those things weren't available.

I dropped my shoulders with a defeated sigh. "Fine. Let's see then."

My palm pressed into the figure, consumed by the icy black chill that shot up my arm.

In a blink I was no longer in the shower, no longer naked, and no longer soaking wet. My hair was freshy done up, pulled up until it was a weight on the top of my head. The feel of smooth silk moved across my stomach, chest, and legs but my arms were free.

The chilling room held nothing to be seen aside from a yellow glowing outline in the shape of a crappy circle, the only light to guide me.

Though I was unable to see, I could feel others around me. I could hear their soft whispers of concern and worry. A hollowing feeling sunk into my chest, creating a heavy weight in the pit of my stomach. I felt nauseous but hungry all at once and my body was overheated, yet I couldn't fight off the shivering that consumed me.

Fear that I thought had been sucked away from me, had burrowed deep, creeped back in.

A thunderous roar shook the space, rattling the weak sliver of light to near nothing. Another howl bellowed through the rocks that silenced our whispers to listen for the final blow. From what, I wasn't sure, but when the floor quaked again, the sound of a thousand bombs blasted, cutting out the sliver of light and casting a sheet of pure darkness over us. Haunted, blood-curdling screams carried over the tremors, sending the mysterious group into an uproar. They ran around blindly, shoving me forward and back until I lost my footing and fell.

"Mina! Wake up!"

My body jerked from one side to the next, shaking my vision into focus. I stared up at Erius, confused again. Back to being soaking wet, and just naked in this man's arms.

"Showers are personal, Erius!" I snapped, waving him off. I looked to the corner where the shadow had been, but the space was empty. The sounds of thunder, water, and the fake flashing lightning had been cut off. I looked back to Erius who was wide-eyed and paler than I had ever seen.

"Something weird just happened," I muttered.

"I'll say." His eyes swept me from head to toe as he tried to take in whatever it was he just witnessed.

"Can I get dressed before I ask what that may be?"

He waved his hands, draping me in a fitting fuzzy robe, white and way too small for him, and not the style I would think he'd care for. He pulled me out of the shower and began searching for something under the counter. I just leaned against it and waited.

"So, what's going on?" I poked.

He stopped his searching to look over me. "You tell me. What just happened?"

I looked around the shower again, perhaps now would be the time to tell him. I was just unsure how to start. Probably would be best to start with the most recurring thing. "Do you remember when I asked if you saw something the other day?"

He thought for a moment before nodding.

"That wasn't the first time I had seen something, or maybe it's a someone. Whatever it is, I have seen it since the morning after we met. At first it was just standing in the distance, but then it led me to the Watchers under the pier. Now, it's giving me visions."

His brows pinched, creating a deep crease between them.

"Visions? Of what?"

"I'm not sure exactly, everything was dark. And people were scared—"

"You were not alone?" he interjected again.

"No. And before you ask, I couldn't see anyone." I continued to lean against the counter, watching as Erius began to pace back and forth, muttering to himself.

It was all very strange, but I hadn't truly been injured in any way and the visions hadn't harmed me yet.

"It's probably just a side effect like everything else," I hummed, growing more bored of the conversation the longer we sat on it. He said he was getting food, and I was hungry.

"All I know is that when I walked up here, you were standing in the middle of the shower staring blankly at the ceiling, mumbling ancient tongue," he prattled on.

"Ancient tongue?" I repeated as I examined the fuzzy robe sleeve.

"A language that was lost long ago in my realm. There is no reason for you to know it."

"There is no reason for me to do a lot of things. It doesn't seem any stranger than me being a Neapolitan or whatever." I shrugged and held out the sleeve of the robe. "Is this Ennaza's? I don't think I want to intrude on her stuff, and this seems a bit out of taste for you."

His eye twitched a bit as he stared at me with a dumbfounded look but didn't answer.

"Her name is over the shower head option," I added.

"What?" he snapped, his brows pulling down.

"Her name. It's on the left shower head option," I repeated, pointing back to the shower over my shoulder.

Erius stormed past me and marched in, headed right to the screen pad on the wall. He angrily tapped at the screen, curving his lip when he got to the page for the layout. He dialed something in with a few more clicks before returning.

"The robe is yours. Everything was restocked when we got here. Now, if you could have just an ounce of concern, tell me what you saw," he demanded.

"I didn't see anything, I just heard shit. Loud banging and dinosaurs going at it. That's what it sounded like. Anyway, there's my answer. So, is Ennaza your mate?"

"I need you to focus." He stepped toward me, ready to cage me in place again, but I slid to the right and out of reach.

"I don't want to cause any problems being here," I said smoothly.

His brows pinched at the center as he looked over me. "Problems?"

"Ennaza. I don't know who she is, but it sort of seems like things are preset for the two of you, and if she's your mate…" I was cut off by his low chuckle.

"Ennaza is not my mate. If she was, I wouldn't have drug you through the lobby for all to witness. You can say she was to me what that blond mortal was to you. Now focus."

"Erius, what is there to focus on? Enlighten me," I began. "From the little you have told me we are on some hit list. You nearly broke my boss's arm. I'm positive I don't have a job anymore. I'm in some underground, black-market hotel. I'm apparently an illegal combination, and on top of it, I'm being followed by some weird, bellowing shadow that places me in trances. There is entirely too much to focus on right now, and I'm just trying to enjoy whatever amount of time I have left."

His jaw set, unmoved, unresponsive as always. After a moment of unhinged glaring, he pulled out his phone and began typing away. There was no point in arguing against that.

"Well, come along. The food is downstairs," he advised.

"Oh, what did you get?" I asked happily. The thought of food twisted my stomach to knots. I hadn't eaten since breakfast, and now I was starving.

He rose a brow and shoved his phone back in his pocket. "Whatever they had downstairs." He turned and headed from the bathroom, and I followed behind.

The delicious smell of burgers and fries filled the air as we descended the steps. Erius guided me into the kitchen, a room oddly suited up with chef grade appliances and enough counterspace to skin a deer.

"Why do you have so much modern shit?"

"Believe it or not, mortal, demons like flashy things, too." He turned to me with a smug grin and pulled a to-go box out.

"So, you *do* have money?" I teased again.

"Money is a human construct."

"I will just assume everything I am familiar with is a human construct."

"Yes, and now you are in my world, where this," he gestured toward everything around us, "is the only human familiarities that you will find."

"That's comforting. How long are we staying here then?" I pulled open my box to be greeted by a full-size cheeseburger and a side of limp fries.

"Until it's time for us to go," he said with a lazy shrug.

"You are so cryptic. It's starting to sound like I'm a prisoner."

"You can leave the suite as long as you stay near me when you do. It's safer for you that way." He quickly took a bite of food. Now I had more questions he clearly wanted to avoid.

"What does that mean?"

I waited patiently for him to chew his food, though I think he was taking longer to taunt me. He swallowed thickly and glared at me as if the answer was an obvious one.

"Mortals are not generally treated well here. As I mentioned, laws from my realm are not held too highly. Magic has been placed to keep it hidden not only from you mortals, but from anyone not in possession of a key or escort. What others do with their mortals are not my business, but it ranges vastly. From using them as meals to the few who find other entertaining uses for them," he explained darkly.

I narrowed my eyes at him as heat began to flush over my cheeks and ears as I thought back to what the bar tender had said. "And yet, you brought me here."

"You are safe as long as I am by your side and you are covered in my scent," he said with a smug grin. Oh yes, the going nowhere fourplay.

"Are there other ways you can do that?" I tossed.

"I don't think you are understanding the reasons as to why my scent would be all over you. Why that is relevant for your safety." He walked around the island and leaned down over me. "While we are here, *you* are my mate. So, are there other ways? Absolutely, but I'd like to keep it light."

"What do you consider light?" I asked, fighting the entire body reaction I had at the words *"my mate"*

"Whatever I can control. Eat, so we can sleep."

I figured he would only continue with the vague answers, so I finished my food and he ushered me upstairs and to the side of the large bed. He guided me down to sit before taking a step back to unbutton his shirt. I guess that was one way to cover myself in the fragrance that was him. Heat flushed my face as I continued to watch.

His shoulders shook with a deep laugh before his body grew as it did that day in the forest. Instead of a mix of purple and blue, the atmospheric gas twirled a deep green with the stars a bit brighter than the last time. The large, thick tail hit the floor with a thump.

I tilted my head to the side as I gazed up to him. "You're going to sleep next to me like that?"

"This form will leave a more potent scent on you," he rumbled as he climbed into the bed, making it squeak under his massive weight.

"All big like this?" I quizzed.

He shuffled under the thick blanket and waited without a word.

I joined him, laying back in the small space that kept me close. His arm curled over my body. His tail was next to follow as it wrapped around me to pull me even closer to him, a protective cocoon of dark energy. My body flushed with heat, sending a flood of need over my skin, and I was sure he sensed it with how his body reacted.

Each exhale fanned over me, encasing me in the vanilla, which I was beginning to think was the scent he's been covering me with. Which was absolutely fine; better it be a sweet scent than an offensive one.

The stars danced across his skin, mixing with the colorful nebula that swirled around him. Even if he is just the night sky in a monstrous form, he was still the most gorgeous thing I had ever seen.

A soft purring shook the bed as my big, cat-like demon cuddled against me. The vibrations with the added night sky at my side felt as if I was drifting aimlessly amongst the stars in the galaxy. Safe, comfortable and relaxed, my mind instantly drifted to sleep.

CHAPTER THIRTY

Mira

Surprisingly, Erius slept a lot more calmly than he had in my van which was understandable considering this bed had far more space and he was in his regular form, so he was probably more comfortable.

I stretched, pulling myself from his side to try and slip out, but he didn't leave me much room here either. His tail twitched, flicking from one side to the next as it shrunk down and slipped away from me, untwining me from its captive embrace to return to its owner. I followed its retreat to the heavy presence it was attached to. Stars drifted over his shoulders at a slow pace while the other odd mixes of colors began to surface.

My gaze climbed his captivating body up to the ebony horns and messy hair. I didn't think something so simple and normal would set me off, but my skin flushed with the returning flutter to attack my chest, a need he instantly noticed. I wished he had never told me he could smell it or sense it. It was none of his business, and I liked when it was my secret to me.

Green and blue nebulas soon began circling his shoulders and chest before shifting to a clash of yellow and pink clouds, an interesting shift that seemed to happen often enough with his own emotions.

"Do the colors mean something? I mean, is the change emotion based?" I asked mindlessly.

He looked down over his chest, viewing the shift as I did. The flat press of his lips curved up to a half smile. "In a sense."

The fight to remain composed was an unsuccessful one, but texts began to flood my phone to distract me. I was sure all of them were regarding the day before and probably telling me what I already knew. I snatched it from the dresser and opened to the twenty-one messages waiting for me in the group chat, all confirming what I assumed. I'd been fired. On top of that, I was not allowed back in the shop, which did hurt a bit. But again, that's understandable.

Since I wasn't allowed back in and everything from the altar to the shelves in that room were mine, they offered to pack it and bring the smaller things to me while Jaz offered to store the bigger things at her place. With everything planned, I sent them my location and told them I would check in with them when I could.

Erius drifted off to the bathroom to shower, leaving me in his ocean of a bed. I couldn't say I was surprised, and I didn't expect to work there forever. But it was a part of my life I wasn't ready to close just yet. A lot of aspects of my life had been closed before I felt ready. All I had left was to find open ones or open a few myself.

I looked out over the skyline and on to the ocean. My life was no longer what it was, and even if we broke this tether, even if we could somehow find a way to take the demon out of me, my life would still be massively different. I couldn't imagine walking around knowing demons existed, knowing Erius was out there, and a full world to go with him, and just existing in a normal, mortal life. It didn't seem as if the world I grew up knowing was right for me anymore. Not that one looking to wipe me away was any better.

"Are you alright, Mortal?" Erius asked from the bathroom opening. He leaned against the side wall, propping himself up with the same arm he used to comb back his thick hair.

"Yeah, I'm fine. I lost my job, I'm tethered to a demon, I can change to a goat, and I'm going to be executed for it. I'm just fine. Great, even," I said, hoping the sarcasm was thick enough for him.

He walked over to me, hooking his finger under my chin to pull my attention up to him. I sucked in a sharp breath, forcing my focus on anything else other than the loud beating of my heart or the sudden gush of heat to my center.

"Why don't you get ready and meet me downstairs?" He dropped his hand, taking the comforting warmth with him as he left the room before I could ask why.

There wasn't much left to lose, and no point in sitting in my own pity about it. I hopped from the bed and tossed on a black sundress adorned in sunflowers for a pop of color. I moved to the bathroom to complete the rest before heading downstairs as Erius commanded.

He stood looking out the glass wall with his hands stuffed in his pockets. All his clothes seemed to be fitted well for his form and matched the same I usually saw him in, but with slight alterations to his pants. The serpent-like tail was free to sway behind him, having a slight disruption to the flow as I stepped down.

I made my way to the couch without announcing myself and sat by Prometheus who was sprawled out on the cushion, enjoying the comforts in the home of a demon he hated so much. Gentle purring vibrated through him as I began running my hand over his soft fur.

"Good morning, my baby," I cooed to the cat.

Erius turned at the greeting, his gaze shifting from Prometheus to me. After a long, silent moment, he stepped over to me with darkening eyes that remained locked on the dress.

"You are lovely," he said kindly, a peacefulness that soon ended once he was before me as he kicked out my foot, spreading my legs to kneel between them.

"Now sit still," he ordered.

I attempted to move away but his hands clamped down on my knees while his tail locked itself around my ankle, I pushed myself up to find a more comfortable position.

"It does not make this any easier when you squirm about like that," he warned.

"Is there another way to do this, maybe one that'll last longer?"

"There is, but that involves something a little more permanent."

I looked at him from under furrowed brows. "What are my options?"

Claws painlessly raked up my thighs, hiking the dress up to my waist. His body pressed against mine as he buried his nose in my neck.

"There are a few," he said in a dark voice.

I would have asked what those options were, but my mind fell numb under his touch. The hard press of his dick pushed against me, sending an electrifying jolt through my body. I arched against him with a gasp that stilled us both.

"Even fewer that call for your clothes to remain on," he muffled into my neck. The soft brush of his lips mixed with the consuming scent sent my mind spiraling into oblivion. Heated hands continued to climb up my stomach, tugging the dress up with.

His chest rumbled with a low purr. It all began to make sense as to why it had to be such an intimate experience and why I was *"his mate"* while we were here. The concentrated breaths left my neck to travel over my chest to my bare stomach before hovering over my waist.

I gasped out, arching into him as he continued to move over my stomach. The heat of his breath covered me before the warmth of his tongue replaced it. I shuddered under the contact as his tongue slid lightly across my lower stomach. I arched into him again, struggling to hold in the moan that wanted to break free. He moved lower over my panties until the heat of his breath and lips found my clit.

Unable to hold back, a hitched breath caught his attention and he paused, his claws digging into my skin. His head snapped up, ripping away from me without warning. I tried to steady my breathing as I glared up at him. We were going to have to find a place to draw the line with that if it was never going to go any further. I didn't think I could live in a constant state of arousal and no sign of relief, at least none that was private.

He cleared his throat and pulled my dress back down. "We should go."

I wanted to protest, but I was a bit too dazed to even catch my breath let alone argue for him to continue.

"Go where?" I asked blankly.

"To eat. There is nothing in the kitchen."

I looked to the commercial grade appliances and French door fridge with a raised brow. "Why do you have it then?"

"It came with the flat." He shrugged and turned to leave, his tail snagging my wrist as it tugged me to his side. "Do stay close."

His hand slipped around my waist as we stepped out into the overly bright hall. Along the way to the elevator, Erius kept his head on a constant swivel as if we were being hunted.

"If it's so dangerous for me, why are you taking me out?" I asked.

"I swear, you do not listen. As I said yesterday, Mortal, it is only a danger if you are out without me. My scent on you as-is will only go so far, and some may look to challenge it."

I shot my gaze up to him as we stepped to the elevator door. He reached out, pressing the down key with his claw as if what he said was normal for me to hear.

"As-is? Challenge it?" I sputtered out.

The door opened and he pulled me in, pressing me up against the corner as he did before. "To everyone here, you are a mortal in a world of demons and residents of the Circles. Why would you think you'd be safe alone?"

I didn't have a response to give. The feeling of fear was gone, and I had felt nothing but a sense of safety. Then again, Erius had only been away from me a total of three times. I hadn't had a moment to feel safe alone.

The doors opened again, and Erius led the way through the odd halls and lobbies the mortals didn't have access to. Not that I had seen anyone who even looked remotely mortal. Even the most human-looking creatures had something different about them that was certainly not mortal. Many had either red or frost blue eyes, and those that were undeniably not human looked more like creatures you'd see out of some fantasy book.

No matter what they looked like, they all paused to stare as we passed, whispering in different languages to each other. I was sure Erius could hear it, but he didn't react apart from where his hand was placed. If not my shoulder than around my waist, but it never parted from my skin.

We turned the corner to an opening with a podium manned by a creature with moss green skin and protruding bottom fangs. His eyes moved from me to Erius with a twist of confusion.

"Eriusazazl," the man greeted.

"*Pà how,*" Erius said.

The man froze for a second as he looked back to me. "*Pà ka how?*" he repeated slowly.

Erius nodded, pulling me closer to his side. With an odd look of curiosity, the man grabbed two average-looking menus and led us through the busy dining area.

"What did you say?" I whispered to Erius.

"I requested a booth," he informed without whispering, which garnered another look of shock from the man leading us.

We stepped into another room with several caged booths lining the walls, no tables or chairs, leaving the floor spacious and open.

The man ushered us to one with deep burgundy cushions and set the menus down. I slid in first, followed by Erius, and once we were situated, the man closed the booth.

"What the fuck?" I breathed as I looked about the dimly lit space. "Why is it like this?"

"For privacy," he said as if that were an obvious fact.

I pushed away a few inches from his new obsession with being on top of me. He chuckled and pulled open the menu to place between us to display the wide range of food selections that I couldn't understand.

"Go on and pick something then," he snickered, something that would have been easy if I could understand the language.

"I can't read this," I protested.

A deep laugh rumbled through his chest, dark and menacing yet full of joy and amusement. He pointed to an item on the menu that I would never in my life figure out. The language was not only different, but the writing and text was nothing I was familiar with.

"Ok, what is that?" I asked.

"*Creamǔ mùdh låb zìl*. It is a stew," he said a bit too cheery.

"What does this stew have in it? *Creamǔ* sounds like creamy. Is it a creamy stew?" I guessed.

Another menacing chuckle broke through him. "Close. It is creamy barracuda stew."

My stomach dropped and my lips twisted to a sneer of disgust. "Erius! I have never had, nor will I ever want to try, barracuda. Point to something else."

His smile widened as he pointed to an item just below the first. "*Jìk bush jǔp* is roasted meat."

"What kind of meat?" I whined.

"You lot call it steak, I believe. We do not have a name for the creature or the meat it offers."

"It's a cow," I say mindlessly as I looked over the odd writing and words. The meal sounded the most human, and I didn't want him to read off every option to me like some child.

"I'll have the roasted meat," I said hesitantly. He laughed again and closed the menu. "What are you getting? Sauteed souls?"

"I eat more than souls, Mortal. I just did not want to disturb you with it."

The list he had already given me echoed in my mind again. "How kind of you."

Three heavy knocks rattled the booth's doors. Erius leaned over to crack it open, speaking a few words to the new individual as they looked in with wide eyes. Even here, people had a problem with staring. From the few words I just learned and how the person was jotting it down, I figured Erius was giving the order. When they were done, they looked back in at me one last time before Erius shut the barrier on them.

"Why are they all looking at us like that?"

He leaned back over me with softening eyes. "They are not accustomed to seeing me so near a mortal, least of all one such as yourself."

Such as myself? What the hell is that supposed to mean?

"What's wrong with me?"

He shook his head with a growing grin, brightening the stars that drifted over his cheeks and nose. "You smell... *pretty*," he said with an odd expression.

"I smell pretty?" I repeated.

He twisted a curl around one of his claws as he took a not-so-subtle inhale of my scent. "That is the word you used to describe that flower."

"The sunflower?"

He nodded. "As pleasant as it is, it has been increasingly distracting."

I stared at him wide-eyed and speechless for a moment, recalling all the moments he had commented on my scent. The only other time he seemed to enjoy it without complaint was when I was under attack on my period. Other than that, he had avoided it. At least it seemed that way until recently. Granted, I should have considered how I was feeling every time he pointed it out. All this time I had thought it was distracting because it was offensive or annoying in some way, but it was distracting because he was attracted to it.

"Ok, well. How do they know you don't hang out with mortals? And why is it so odd that you are?" I pressed next.

The colors swirled across his cheeks until a clear night sky gazed down at me. "Just know that it is not something I am known for."

His body lit up like a furnace, but the heat was not consuming as it usually was. It crawled over my skin as the question bubbled on my tongue.

"Does it have to do with you losing your wings?"

His face fell hard, clenching his jaw as red nebulas began to surface. He sat back, pulling his hands to the table. Words or not, he provided a clear answer.

"You don't have to tell me," I began.

"I was not planning to."

"Do you ever? Plan to tell me, I mean?" I probed.

"No. It is much too long to explain."

I didn't care how long it took to explain, I wanted to understand. It wasn't as if anything he said would frighten me from him.

"You'll tell me when you're ready," I said matter of fact, just like when I told him us fucking would happen. Sooner or later, he would tell what he did to lose his wings.

The booth screen rattled with the heavy knock of our waiter. Erius did the same as before, opening it enough to pull the platter in and sharing only a few words. He thanked them, or at least I think he did, and closed the booth once more after they rushed off.

The familiar smell of heavily seasoned steak filled the space. Next to the average-looking steak sat a slab of meat that I did not recognize, but it smelled amazing and came with a side of familiar sautéed spinach.

After we ate, Erius mentioned a shop with some things he thought I might find interesting. He dropped some square golden coins in the waiter's hand before leading me through the labyrinth of halls. Most everything in the weird underground lobby was connected by even stranger corridors. The last hall took us to a grand court that somehow sat outside, apparently unseen by the world outside of it.

We entered a small-town center with little shops and food carts. The only thing that set it aside from my world was the occupants. Aside from those I assumed to be demons as Erius was, there were creatures that looked to be a mix of hyena and human. Other creatures I had no other explanation or description for aside from orc, which all was based on knowledge of *Lord of the Rings* and other fantasy works.

Unlike what I had ever read or seen, they were the kindest ones and didn't have as big of an issue with staring us down. If they did, they were much better at hiding it.

Eventually, we came up to a shop with stacks of old, tattered books stationed out front, some neatly towered while others had clearly toppled over without anyone to care for them. Sage and sandalwood drifted from the open door with soft folk-tuned music flowing out. Not too different than many of the spiritual shops I'd roamed before.

"Welcome to Night Shade. Call out if you need anything," a woman greeted from the back as we entered.

"Thank you," I called back. Not everyone seemed to speak the language or at least, they chose not to.

I looked at the crystals and herbs before venturing deeper. As I wandered around the cluttered shop, my skin grew itchy, a new alert that I was nearing something dead. It wasn't long before I located a shelf full of many kinds of animal skulls. Well, they looked to be animal skulls to me—fox and wolf skulls to be exact—but there were those creatures out there that would have a very similar skull.

"What are these from?" I asked Erius.

"Those come from a creature known as an *uawd*. They are similar to the dogs of your realm," he said with a faint smile.

I turned back to the shelf, examining the hefty bone that looked nothing like that of a mortal world dog. The bridge of the muzzle ran flat from the forehead to the nasal sockets with a slight dome to it. The area was visibly thicker with a number of hairline cracks and a few crushed spots. Holes of an unknown source or cause dimpled the back crown of the skull. Lastly, the teeth were three times as big and as sharp as that of any normal dog.

I lifted it from the shelf to examine further, brushing my fingers against the coarse bone, instantly zapping the fierce energy into every nerve throughout my body. With a deep breath, I centered it in my chest, holding it there until I felt well enough in control to grasp the skull fully. My arms shook from the energy that flooded me, but I held firm as I looked over it.

"Do you want it? It's a decent source of power. Better than that fox and raven you have packed away."

"I didn't bring my wallet, and something tells me my mortal American dollars will not work here," I grumbled.

He reached across and took one of the skulls. "Go grab whatever you want," he said with a sigh and a soft curve to his lips. I didn't know what all was in the shop, but I wasn't about to argue either. I could just pay him back if he's offering. I spun around and continued to look at the selections, scanning another shelf of books along the same wall. Some were written in English but most used the other language.

"What is this language?" I asked, pointing to a book written in that text while also pulling out one of the few I could read.

"It's Demric," the voice from earlier said.

I turned to my left, finding a woman of the deepest ebony skin and gold, glowing lines that decorated her face in an intricate pattern. Her clothes were just as beautiful, draping over her until they fell in a dark puddle of fabric at her feet.

She did as most, shifting her gaze between me and the demon at my back, a hard look of concern painted her features. Not a reaction many of the others had when they looked at us, curiosity and maybe disgust but never concern, not that I had seen. It was clear she tried to maintain indifference as she struggled to compose her face.

Erius moved in front of me, grabbing a book from the shelf as he stepped to her. "Do you have these two in the mortal American dialect?"

While he spoke with her, I moved back to looking over the books, one in particular with soft gold foiling on the spine. In English and read in bold text were the words *N.S Records of the Circles, Priests, and Priestesses.* I was not sure what N.S stood for, but I grabbed the book and tucked it under the other one.

"Here," the lady said to Erius, handing him two newer-looking books with one titled *Death Magik'* and another titled *Anatomy of a Tail.* I made my way over, having seen my fill and also not wanting to end up owing him hundreds. Three books and a skull, even in the mortal world, would be pricey.

"Who's that one for?" I asked as I nodded to the tail book. Erius chuckled but didn't give a full response. I looked to the woman as she moved back to an old-style register, her eyes still on us.

I set everything on the counter. The woman still glared at Erius as he pulled out a small jingling pouch. He took out whatever was inside and dropped them in the woman's palm, gold coins like the last but these were shaped like a crescent moon and seemed to be well worth something as she stared wide-eyed at them.

She placed all the items in a paper bag and pushed it toward me with a sympathetic grin. "Stay safe," she said grimly.

"I will, thank you," I said in a cheery tune. Hopefully it was enough to hint that I wasn't in any danger that she may have thought.

Erius grabbed the bag up in one hand and took mine with the other, towing me from the shop and back onto the busy path.

"That book better not be for me!" I snapped instantly, sending the demon into a fit of laughter.

"It will help you with your tail," he said between chuckles.

"I don't need help with that!" I hissed.

He turned with a lifted brow and wide smile, his shoulders shaking in his joy to patronize me. His tail wrapped around my wrist and tugged me along until I was at his side again. He lowered his voice so only I could hear, drawing me closer to him until his arm was securely around my shoulder. "You have no understanding of your tail, and this will explain it." With a quick scan of those around us, Erius tucked me under his arm once again. My heart set off pounding against my chest with the added flutter that hit my stomach. I squeezed in closer to him, taking in as much of the new comfort as I could.

"We should get back," he offered. Without waiting for me to respond, we were off again, headed back into the hotel. We did not stop until we were at the elevator doors waiting for one to open.

"That was all, very interesting. Thank you," I said happily. Two weeks ago, I would have never thought we would have an enjoyable time together, but here I was, having a better day in a new world with him.

He looked over me, drinking me in with his gaze. His brows pulled down with a sudden mix of perplexity I hadn't seen. Before I could ask, the elevator pulled open and he towed me in, selecting the button to the highest level before pressing for the doors to close. I was not sure what he was in a sudden rush for but the longer the doors took, the tighter his grip grew.

When they did finally close, he turned to pin me in the corner. "This is new," he mused, burying his nose in my hair. His hands inched up to my neck, grazing claws over my jaw. The rumbling purr that pushed through his chest radiated through me.

I squeezed my thighs together to fight the flood of heat that had done nothing but give me away any chance it got. His body locked around me in a protective manner as he continued to take me in.

The elevator came to a stop, and when the doors opened, a sudden wave of gasps spilled in. He turned at the sound to offer a deeper, more threatening growl as he swiftly leaned over to click another button, shutting the doors on the unsuspecting group. He returned to my hair, taking in whatever scent he was clearly enjoying.

"What's new?" I sputtered out, still fighting off the flood of need that was probably filling up the small space.

"This scent. What are you doing to create it?" he groaned into me.

I honestly thought we had figured that out, but I was not going to say it knowing he'd just reject it altogether.

"Nothing. I'm literally just enjoying life." It wasn't a lie entirely; the day was still going amazingly.

He pulled away, his expressions harder to read in his form but if I had to guess by the widening of his eyes and press of his lips, he was shocked by my words. "You can feel joy?" he asked slowly.

I hadn't done a good job of tracking what emotions I could feel and what had slipped. There had been times over the last month I could say I enjoyed it. This was a bit more than that. Undivided attention wasn't my closest friend as a child and as I grew, it just felt gross to experience. But this wasn't any of that. No pressure for it to be transactional.

"Yes," I responded.

Erius pushed away from me right before the elevator came to its final stop. He took my hand in his and we stepped off.

I sat on the couch while Erius looked through the book he had the lady grab for him. He didn't want to tell me what he was looking for, but he said he hoped it would help me with shifting forms.

"You cannot wait until you feel threatened to change. With your inability to sense danger, it may not be until that danger is digging into your skin," he explained.

"Maybe I can trick my brain into thinking I'm being threatened," I suggested.

He considered it for a moment before closing the book. "What do you find threatening?"

"Being grabbed at or chased," I suggested.

"Similar to when the blond mortal grabbed you?"

I crossed my arms over my chest and leaned back. "As I said, I had it under control. I felt it coming on, you interrupted me."

"Yes. And what would you have done next, after transforming before your boss?"

The demon had a point. It was one thing to have broken his arm, but turning into a full monster would have only put us at risk.

"You need to control shifting when you need to and holding it off when you do not. Yes, it would have been nice to watch you transform and make a meal out of that mortal. But that would only cause us more problems."

I nodded. "Ok, I see what you mean. Maybe I can try and replicate the feeling."

"Go on then," he said with a wave of his hand.

I closed my eyes, focusing on the memory of yesterday's assault. The invading feeling of Andrew's hand flared over my arm as if he were next to me, lifting the hair on the back of my neck as it had the first time. The sting radiated up my arm and through my entire body. But just as excitement tuned in, the pulsating energy simmered down until the feeling was gone.

"Hm, you almost did it. Why did you stop?" he asked.

"I didn't mean to."

"Well, go again." He waved his hands at me to proceed.

I thought of the same irritating instance, letting the memory of it enrage me rather than allowing the success to snuff it out.

Again, the searing memory of Andrew's hand lit my arm, burning right down to the bone. My body ignited, vibrating through until the tingling sensation boiled to the surface. Visions flashed before me of the blond man I once knew slowly morphing into an eyeless creature. His face contorted into a twisted scream that looked to dislocate his jaw. Sounds of screams echoed through my mind, sending full body shivers to consume me.

The heat washed over my skin, leaving my body covered in spotted brown and blonde fur. My tail whipped out at my side, startling Prometheus and sending him running up the stairs. I stretched my fingers out, the claws growing instantly.

Erius's lips pulled up as he looked over me. "Very good." He inspected my form for a few moments, moving my horns around and examining my tail with a prideful smile.

"Now change back," he instructed.

My shoulders slumped as I glared at him. "Can I have a minute?" I groaned.

"You may not have even five seconds in some cases. Change back. Please." He definitely tagged on the please as an afterthought, but I'd try because he said it.

I took a deep breath and focused on something more positive. The pleasant morning spent with my demon friend and the lengths of kindness he held. My sweet bonding quickly shifted to the morning's foreplay that left me wanting. I focused on the moments leading up to him pulling away, the feeling of longing and frustration met with the euphoric release of his lips pressed against me.

Chilling pricks washed over my body, draining the form as if to be rinsed from my skin.

His smile grew with encouragement. "Wonderful, what did you think about?" His lips curled up into a sinister smile, telling me he had an idea.

"That's my business," I muttered.

He chuckled softly and waved a hand for me to continue. "Again."

A bell echoed through the flat, pausing us from the lesson. "Azal, it's me, open up," Alius' voice called from the entryway.

Erius stepped away to answer it while I tried to focus once more on the feeling. "Alius?" he greeted upon opening the door.

"Azal. I hear you and Little Bird have made quite the appearance. But I have some words."

Chapter Thirty-One

Mira

Erius and Alius spoke in the kitchen about someone showing up and how it would be wise for me to stay in the flat, which was highly irritating considering I was having a nice time learning about this whole new world that had been only a few miles from me this entire time.

"Little Bird!" Alius greeted me as they stepped out of the kitchen. Again with the nicknames. Did nobody use given names around here?

With mixed looks of concern and amusement, they gathered around the couch to examine me like some lab rat.

"How's the transforming going?" He didn't seem like someone I should distrust, and my body didn't get any sort of negative reaction from him. Yet it felt odd to share. One demon in my business was enough, I didn't need another and his mysterious sister, not to mention his niece.

You need to be careful who you change around, he said—but then went around telling all his demonic buddies.

I narrowed my eyes at their approach. "Wondrously."

Erius hid a laugh as he came to my side.

"My sister, Vex, has some questions for you. I hope you do not mind I ask," Alius said politely.

Erius said we were laying low but had his friend out here running his mouth. I folded my arms and leaned back.

"You can trust him, Mortal. Not everyone in the Circles thinks the *Nipans* are dangerous. Vex and Alius are a few of them," Erius explained. I looked back up to Alius with a soft nod.

"I am assuming by your calm nature that you are not in any pain," he began. "Is it painful when you transform?"

"No, it is more like water washing over me. Sometimes it's hot, sometimes it's cold, but it's never hurt."

"That's good." He nodded enthusiastically as his locs lightly swung in rhythm with his movements. "Do you know what that form eats yet?"

Erius shook the couch as he chuckled to himself. "Oh, we have learned what it is she eats. However, it does not benefit *Acrana*."

Alius furrowed his brows as his lips turned down, "How so?"

"I eat men," I tossed blankly.

Erius cleared his throat, hiding a laugh as he turned from us. Alius just looked at me in wide-eyed disbelief.

"I witnessed it for myself. It was a mess," Erius mused. I snapped my head around to him.

"Why did you do that?" Alius finally asked.

I returned my gaze to the interrogator and leaned forward, running my hand through Prometheus' fur. "The first smelled like steak, and I was hungry. The rest were because Erius wanted to test a theory."

His eyes widened as he turned to the demon. "And what was that?"

"All the men had a darkness about them. One had been under investigation for some murders, while the others were inmates in a medical facility," Erius informed bluntly.

Alius looked over us with no hint of concern, but he did not share the same amusement as Erius in my new dietary habits.

"Well, regardless of *Acrana*, that is the most information we have ever gotten. Anything else? I'm sure Vex will have more questions for her." He turned to address Erius as if I was not there, but my demon kept his gaze on me as he spoke.

"She is seeing apparitions that I cannot. It guides her and recently." He paused with a sharp downturn of his lips before turning back to Alius. "It has plagued her with visions."

"Visions?" Alius echoed with rounded eyes.

Erius nodded as both eyes fell on me, waiting for me to explain.

"I didn't see much, as I told Erius. I just heard noises. Like crashing, creatures growling and making a fuss."

Alius pressed his lips flat, chewing over the new information before turning back to Erius, "I think that will do for now…I shall get this information off to my sister. She will have more questions, I'm sure. Along with a few other things…" Alius began mumbling his assumptions as he climbed to his feet. Erius joined him before they both headed toward the front door.

"Are you sure your serpent will not get snatched?" Erius clarified.

"My dear friend, I do not commit acts that cost me such privileges such as my messages not being monitored." From his tone, I could tell he was making a jab at whatever it was Erius did that cost him his wings.

"Yes, well—what about Vex?" the demon poked again, ignoring the remark.

After a short pause, Alius began to explain, surprisingly in English so I could understand. "Something has sparked between *Chaonia* and *Roshus*. A'trox has challenged Ozeth, so Vex has been at his side."

Ok, maybe it didn't matter because I couldn't understand anyway.

"What does A'trox want?" Erius grumbled.

"Alaura. As you can imagine, the three worry any serpents out in their markings will be tracked. I use burrowed serpents, much smaller than my sister and her husband's. But Ozeth is not the only one challenged. A'trox claimed a challenge with Drokadan and Urran as well."

Like most things in this world, I was unfamiliar with the odd names being thrown around, but this A'trox seemed like a dick.

"Anyhow," Alius said a bit louder, "I will be seeing you, Azal. Good day, Little Bird," he called out before the door closed again.

When Erius returned, his skin was colorless and void of any stars to decorate him, but when his gaze met mine, faint nebulas returned in a slow swirling pattern. I didn't want to ask about what all that meant and who all those names were. It sounded like a history lesson on Alius and his family tree.

There was one thing I wanted to ask him now that there was apparently someone here to keep away from. It didn't sound like it was the same person he owes something to, but still, someone to be wary of for some length of time.

"How long do I have to stay here?" I asked quickly before he had a chance to change the subject.

"Just until our little friend has had his fill at the bones table."

"Does he hunt *Nipans* or something?" I pressed.

"No. He hunts humans." Erius looked over me, a smile gracing his lips. "Are you hungry?"

I scanned the empty kitchen, unsure how he planned to cook with no ingredients unless he was going to bring forth food with his mist. "I thought there was no food here."

"I can acquire food." He laughed.

I narrowed my eyes at him. I didn't even know what food there was to be had aside from barracuda stew and steak. "You won't bring me some odd food, will you?"

"I will try and find something that matches your mortal food." He chuckled again. He reached out and gently swept his clawed finger along my cheek. The heated trail sent a shiver over my skin. I looked up to him, locking eyes for a brief moment before he swiftly turned and headed out, leaving me alone with my cat in his living room.

I flipped on the TV and signed into my Netflix account. It took a minute of surfing through some things before I settled on whatever. It wasn't long into the show *The Witcher* that I remembered the books I had recently gotten. With something of more interest now on my mind, I jumped up and made my way to the kitchen where the bag had been left. I dug through it, pulling each book out one by one to set along the counter.

I grabbed *N.S Records of the Circles, Priests, and Priestesses* and headed back to the living room to learn a bit more of this world. I flipped through the pages, stopping on any random one and got comfortable on the couch.

THE DEMONS

349

MAZARINE, PHTHARTIC, AND RASASVADA

Mazarine Demons – *Due to their willingness to aid the mortals down paths of graciousness, they are well loved by their Priestess Tikara. With her doting, they had been granted the most generous of blessings to set them aside from their less favorable counterparts. And while they can be identified by their deep mazarine eyes and iridescent skin, it is wise to avoid if possible.*

Phthartica Demons – *Vile Creatures that follow the dark path. As with Mazarine Demons, Phthartica Demons have been gifted their vile nature through their priestess Chimeriea. They know nothing more than to cause ill-will and hate. They find much joy in taunting mortals with natural disasters and are the likely cause of many horrific ends in the mortal realm. With deep crimson eyes that melt into the blackness of their essence – they can guide one to do the most monstrous of offenses. AVOID BY ALL ACTS.*

Rasasvada Demons – *Tricky by nature. One must never trust a Rasasvada Demon as they take pleasure in guiding their self-interests. For trusting a Rasasvada is a positive route for misfortune and disaster. Can be identified by their icy white to frost blue eyes. AVOID BY ALL ACTS*

I looked over the last description matching Erius. It definitely wasn't too far off. It sort of explained the looks and the shopkeeper's concern. It was better than being with the Phthartica ones, I supposed. Besides, the author of this particular book didn't have much praise for demons of any sort. Even the ones with the nicest description had some form of negativity written. I mean, they weren't wrong; misfortune had followed me since meeting him. But they weren't necessarily right either.

I flipped through a few more pages in hopes of finding more about Rasasvada in particular. Unfortunately, that was all I'd learn about him from this book, but a name Erius had previously mentioned caught my attention and soon I found myself engrossed in a new topic.

The Priestesses and Their Five Serpents

Creation began with three immortal divine sisters so named the Priestesses. With their gifts, each one created a realm to rule. Earth for

Tikara, The Spirit for De'mordia, and The Five Circles for Chimeriea.

From earth, the sisters plucked five serpents. From the spirit, they bred life into the creatures, and for the Circles, five priests were born to take claim over a single domain amongst them.

Together the Priestesses created life to occupy each realm as they saw fit. Each Circle constructed the same by each priest.

The Five Circles? Erius mentioned there being six. *There must be more information about it further into the book.* I flipped through more pages, skimming as much as I could before I reached the final page. Nothing about the Sixth Circle.

Before I could move back to the front of the book to check again, Prometheus began his wild yowling for dinner.

"Oh! My apologies." I giggled, jumping up from the couch to make my way to his crate where his bowl and cans of food waited. I set it down and he got to work licking it up. When he was done, he gave me a pleased whisker flick before turning to prowl behind the couch. My gaze followed him, trailing up towards a black cabinet mini bar tucked in the corner. Red and silver trim and hardware helped it stand out, but also made it look as if it were from some sixteenth-century Dracula dungeon.

Three expensive and ancient-looking bottles sat on the top shelf with a row of shot glasses and a decanter in the shape of a diamond resting in a holder.

A mini bar! Now, let's see if it is fully stocked. I headed over and gently tugged at the elegantly shaped handle. Sadly, the inside had far too little to view, just another bottle of scotch and a fourth older expensive bottle of whatever he appeared to collect.

Other than the bar, couch, TV, and kitchen, the downstairs was pretty minimalistic which was more fitting than all of the technology. Really, the only thing I hadn't seen was the balcony upstairs. I crossed the open floor and marched up the large set of steps.

The room flooded with the orange glow of the setting sun, making everything seem that much bigger. But it was not the open space or high-rise ceiling that got my attention this time. It was the balcony pool that sat outside surrounded by potted palm trees and enormous seats.

I made my way to the overly sized double door that led out. The shimmering light of the water bounced off the window that cast the reflection across the ceiling and down the wall his bed sat against. I paused at the door to inspect the overly luxurious pool. Crystal clear water called to me, and my skin begged for the cool release from the blazing summer heat.

With a light push, the door popped open, filling the quiet space with the low sound of chirping from the crickets already starting their noise. The suffocating scent of chlorine washed in but was soon masked by the abundant number of short potted palm trees scattered around. When the mix of fragrances faded to a less aggressive cloud, I stepped out with Prometheus close behind. We circled the deck while I looked for the unseen bottom of the pool. With all the modern fancy shit he had going on, I figured he'd have a glass bottom pool. But the closer I got to the edge, the sooner I noticed that not only was the bottom not glass, but it ran deep and dark.

Finally, I found the depth plate at the end wall and my eyes nearly popped free of my head when I read thirty feet. Something that would seemingly be impossible. That would mean was about three stories deep, something that also wouldn't make any sense architecturally which should have been expected by now; nothing here makes sense.

Prometheus pranced around, prowling on the little bugs that buzzed and hopped on the floor, completely distracted from the task at hand. That left me on my own to venture. Though there wasn't much else to be seen, it was all extravagant but minimal. I couldn't imagine Erius did much else here other than shower and sleep... *and fuck Ennaza.*

Get off it, get over it. Build a bridge and move on.

I don't know why I keep letting it affect me. It wasn't affecting him. Not that I thought it would really matter, his lack of emotion seemed even more absent than mine.

Making my way around the pool to the railing, I could see out over the city to the ocean. The rhythmic motion of the waves was calming as they swayed in and out. From this distance it was mesmerizing but was nothing compared to watching on the beach itself. Maybe that was why he always sat in the front of the van and watched the waves.

Prometheus weaved between my legs, finished with his games with the creatures as I was finished with my balcony exploration. I spun on my heels, ready to march off when I slammed into Erius hard ass chest. The collision sent me stumbling back against the railing with a blinding pain shooting through my face. I rubbed my nose with a feral hiss as I shot him a look of disdain. Not that it did anything. He scanned the balcony without care before turning his focus on me.

"Did you enjoy your tour?" Erius inquired with a smile.

"If I'm going to be trapped here, I'd like to have something to do." I looked over the pool. "Can I swim?" I asked kindly as I headed back in.

"Of course." He laughed, following close behind as we crossed the room and headed downstairs. "Did you learn anything from your book?"

I looked back to him, remembering I had left the book out and there were in fact a few things I had to ask. "I do have a question about the little I did read."

"Proceed," he said with an amused smirk.

I sorted out the questions as we made our way to the couch, debating if I should start with the type of demon he was or the priestesses. I caught sight of the interesting bar, figuring he'd speak more with a bit of his own alcohol in him. He was not too open about anything involving himself, but with the right leverage, I was sure I could squeeze it from him.

"First, I have some questions about the fancy-looking rum you have over there." I pointed to the corner where the small bar sat as we took our seats.

"It is scotch," he corrected.

"Scotch? But I thought you liked whiskey?"

"Whiskey was all that was ever offered where we went." He got up and walked around to the bar and pulled two glasses out.

I waited patiently, ready to try whatever demon world alcohol he had. He pulled out an ice tray and dropped a single cube into each glass before pouring the deep red liquid from the diamond-shaped decanter.

"Do take it easy with this. Now, tell me of these questions," he said, handing me my glass.

I took a sip. The spicy tart burn of the alcohol slid down smoother than I had ever felt before. "Um—Oh, yeah. You said they are called the Six Circles, but this book says Chimeriea took rule over the *Five* Circles."

"Yes," he said, pulling his glass to his lips.

"Why are they called the Six Circles if there are only five?" I pressed further.

He took a deeper drink from his glass before setting it down on the table beside the bag of food he brought for us. "Because, for a time, long ago, there were only five. Do you recall when I told you she was imprisoned in the Sixth Circle? It was *created* for her." He began to dig through the bag, pulling a very mortal-looking take-out box out and sliding it over to me.

"It seems unwise to keep her in her own realm, does it not?" I asked as I pulled the food to me. It smelled amazing, but who knew what it was he picked since he thought I'd like barracuda enough to make it the first offer.

"She is well guarded by three ancient titans and will not be escaping. Nor will anyone ever get as far as the Dolent Peaks that surround her," he informed me casually, as if I have any clue of the names or words he brings up.

"Let's pretend for a second I don't know what you're talking about. What are Dolent Peaks?"

He laughed into his cup before finishing it off in one gulp. "The Dolent Peaks are the cliffs and—what you all would call volcanos—that encompass the entire plot she is kept on. She is also well chambered underground, surrounded by enchantments cast by her sister and three of the five priests." He explained everything so calmly, eyeing my box of food as he waited for me to open it, making me nervous, yet again, in entrusting him with food.

"Should I be worried?" I asked, pulling the box closer.

"It is a simple burger." He laughed again and pulled out another box for himself, tilting it away from me so I couldn't see. Now I was even more curious to know what he ate along with souls.

I would have continued the questioning, but I was hungrier than I thought. We ate and drank down two glasses each of scotch. He wasn't over exaggerating when he told me to be careful. Two glasses in and I was feeling pretty good.

"So, what do you do here?" I asked, leaning back on the couch.

He joined me, resting his head back with a sigh. It was easier to make out his features when I was looking at the side of his face.

He crinkled his nose with a soft sneer before answering, "I have my own business and dealings I conduct on the lower floor."

"I mean, in here." I waved my arms around the empty space.

He looked around the Livingroom and offered a soft shrug. "Not much."

I knew it.

"Can we swim?"

His eyes swept me from head to toe as he sipped his drink, only speaking once the glass left his lips. "I thought you didn't like me seeing you naked."

"I have a bra and underwear on." I shrugged.

He looked at me with a raised brow, finishing off the last of what was in his glass. Without a word, he set it down and stood with his hand out to me. "Let's go then."

I took it happily as he helped me to my feet, and we headed up. I was a bit wobblier than I anticipated but he made great support as we made our way across the room.

He opened the door, flipping a few switches on to light up the balcony before we stepped out. I placed my glass on the table beside the pool and began removing my jewelry. Erius placed his glass beside mine and began unbuttoning his shirt. I slipped my dress down when I remembered exactly what matching set I decided on for the day.

Me and my lace obsessions.

I looked up, finding Erius just free for the world. Instead of avoiding it, I dropped my gaze at the star-filled dick before me. Who knew demon dick would be so…exotic looking? I mean, how else do you describe a dick with notches on it? I never really sat and fantasized about it before, but I wasn't expecting rivets and other unique things. My mind wandered to Saturday night, and I tightened my legs at the throbbing memory.

I shot my eyes back up to him with a heated face, "You don't have something to wear? Trunks, boxers, anything?"

His smile grew wide, baring his fangs. "You wanted to swim." He entered the pool, keeping his eyes on my pants. I finished undressing, watching him as he watched me.

"You like what you see?" I snapped.

"I told you before, it is pleasant." He shrugged.

I narrowed my eyes at him, pulling my legs free and placing my pants neatly beside my shirt. The heat of his gaze pressed into my skin as I lowered myself into the equally hot water.

"It's heated?" I mused.

"Only when I am in it," he tossed.

"Are you being cocky or is that some sort of demon thing?"

"It is a demon thing." He made his way to my side, reaching for his glass to cage me against the pool wall and his chest. I struggled to keep my breathing even as my body ignited, ready for whatever unexpected thing he would try. I know he had a reason for being all up on me, but I need a little relief from it.

"Do you have anything besides scotch?" I tossed out as a hopeful distraction.

"Did you have a preference?"

"Rum," I suggested.

He chuckled to himself. "You are trying to get drunk on a weeknight?"

"It's not like I have work tomorrow," I pushed.

He cracked a smile and waved his hand, manifesting a black vapor. From it came a black bottle with a diamond skeleton hand encrusted to the bottom. The top was plugged with a diamond-embedded skull.

I watched in amazement as he poured the deep red liquid into the glasses. "This is not like the rum you are accustomed to," he warned again.

"Rum is rum in my eyes." I shrugged, snatching up my cup and taking a deep drink. The liquid burned like acid with the faint hint of cherry and spice. I scrunched my face at the flavor and Erius laughed.

"As I said, do take it easy." He chuckled again.

"I will. Can you manifest yourself some swim trunks?" I finally suggested.

He rolled his eyes with a sigh but snapped his fingers. The vapor wrapped around his waist and when it cleared it left him in black trunks with a goat head stitched into the leg. I hid my giggle behind my cup, taking a sip in the process.

"Did you do that on purpose or is it your preferred animal?" I snickered.

"It was for you since you requested I wear them."

"Well, that is kind of you," I began. "And thank you for earlier. Today was nice."

His body straightened as he looked at me. I took a deep drink of the rum again and held it out for more.

"With this one, one glass is enough. For a mortal." He pulled the glass from my hands and set it aside.

I clicked my tongue and sat back. I wouldn't say I was ready to stop, but I wasn't in the right state to argue or fight either.

"Do you plan to drown?" he asked, his tail instantly wrapping around my waist as if the threat were a real worry.

"We are at the shallow end," I pointed out.

"Yes, but you mortals are susceptible to the simplest of injuries."

My lips twisted up into a mischievous grin. "Mr. Goat, are you saying you care if I get hurt?"

He looked down at me with a half-smile. It was alright if he didn't want to say it aloud, if it would make this all too real for him, but it felt nice to know. I leaned into him, resting my head against his shoulder.

The sky above wasn't nearly as beautiful as the one that swirled beside me. The explosion of green and blue nebulas drifted down his arms and rumbled across his chest. disrupted by the low purring coming from him.

Who knew the demon who took my soul would treat me better than my own family and literally every mortal man I had come across?

His body stiffened, gripping my waist with his tail that still clung to me. "We should go in."

I lifted my head to look at him, his glowing eyes already burning into me.

"Why? Are there Watchers here, too?" I asked, looking to the shadows around us for any sign of the creatures.

"No," he laughed. "It's of the same magic that keeps the mortals from seeing all this; it keeps Watchers out." He climbed out first and kindly helped me after my first failed attempt, thanks to the effects of the drink. I leaned against the chair beside the table.

"Wait here," he ordered, ducking into his room. I drank down the little bit of rum left in my cup.

As I was looking into my empty glass, I could see the open bottle on the table just calling my name.

"Well, if you say so." I giggled, filling the cup to the top.

"Mortal," his voice came from behind me as he reached around to take the bottle.

"My apologies. I didn't realize you were such a proper demon," I teased.

He pulled his brows down as he looked over me. "You can air dry then," he said with a scoff.

My eyes shot to his swim trunks, something he had brought from nothing. Like the rum.

I wouldn't need for him to get me a towel.

"That's fine." I closed my eyes with a smile and imagined the shimmery slip maxi dress I had seen in a fashion magazine last summer.

It was black, sheer, and slit on both sides with a shimmering glow. Rhinestones, or diamonds, I was not sure, but I imagined diamonds for the sake of practice.

I ran my hands from my neck over my breasts and stomach then hip, feeling the soft flutter of fabric drape over my skin. I opened my eyes to find the dress, better than I had seen in the magazine.

"Oh, wow! It worked!" I cheered, looking up to Erius. I knew he wouldn't share the same excitement and I was expecting a look of indifference. But he looked to be more in disbelief that I managed it.

"That's fancy," he pointed out.

"It's a swim cover."

"With diamonds?"

"I added those as an attention grabber." I walked through the door into his room, his eyes on me the entire time. "I see they worked."

He grabbed the bottle of rum and followed behind. We made our way downstairs, and I took a seat on the couch once more.

"Does that play music?" I pointed to the stereo under the TV. He had speakers around the room in odd spots so I would only assume it did. But who would really know with him?

He walked over and picked up the remote from the coffee table, and with a few clicks, soft classical music began to play. His skin reacted to the tune with the sound, slowly expanding as it drifted over his arms, chest, and face.

"Symphony number five, in C Minor?" I mused after a moment. "So you like the classics."

His hands consumed my waist, pulling me up his chest so he could bury his face in my neck as he had been doing.

"Have you been enjoying smelling me whenever you like?" I asked—not that I disapproved of the new friendly contact.

"Your scent has sweetened throughout the entire day," he muffled into my skin. The heat of his vanilla-scented breath sent fire over me. A guttural groan rumbled through his body as he sat me down just as quickly as he swept me up.

"My bad," I breathed, stepping back from him. His jaw flexed, shoulders tensed, and his hands clenched at his side as he struggled to maintain control of whatever he was holding back.

"Is it that *distracting*?" I asked innocently.

He tilted his head back, closing his eyes to take in a deeper breath.

"Enticing."

Chapter Thirty-Two

Mira

I sat on the couch reading more from the history book while Erius took off to grab food or something. He wasn't too clear, but wherever he went tested the limits of our distance several times, igniting the glow and burn every time he stepped a bit too far.

As for the book, it mostly was on a group of people called NightSkins, blood sorceresses native to a place in Macaria that I couldn't pronounce even if I tried. Demric wasn't used much in the book, except for a few passages that seemed highly needed. It did not go into any deep explanation about Macaria, and all the information about NightSkins drifted between English and what may have been a new language entirely. The letters looked a bit different than what I had seen on the menu, but who knew? Because I sure the fuck didn't.

I closed the book after a few more pages of concepts and phrases

I didn't understand. It had already been well over an hour, and I was drumming my thumbs together like an idiot. Being trapped in a demon's lair was not as exciting as the world outside it. Granted, everything was a lot larger, with subtle hints of a world unknown, but mostly it was mortal and modern.

The glass wall allowed for a beautiful show of lights and beams as the sun moved across the sky. Stretching waters reflected the bright light, tossing it back to flood the white room in even more blinding light.

Nothing to do but watch the ocean and read.

And practice changing. The thought suddenly invaded my mind. Not that it was wrong, and as Erius said, it would be wise to have better control of it. Now that I had a general feeling locked away, I needed to be able to tap into it sooner and without it fading because I lost focus. Whatever imaginary battle Erius was worried about, I was sure those extra seconds wouldn't be granted.

I sat up, getting in a comfortable position to pull up an uncomfortable memory. Unlike before, the thought of an invading hand instantly brought fire to my skin. The phantom touch gripped my wrist in the same spot, sending another flare through me. Trickling ripples fluttered up my arm and traveled through me down to my toes.

The fangs pushed through with a sting, which they hadn't done before, so that was new and painful. They even protruded out a bit more than before. Probably because I fed in this form and had been changing more frequently. I was sure more random new, fun things would present themselves the more I did it. Or maybe it was proximity based. There were a bunch of strange new threats at every corner. My body was overstimulated with it all.

My tail draped over my lap, bored with no demon to wrap around. The blonde tuff of hair on the end was cute—I guess. It definitely resembled more of a lion's tail than a goat's or even the kind of tail Erius had. The curl pattern matched my hair in color and texture, which was interesting because the fur over the rest of my body had more of a fine, silky feeling to it. I had never really taken the time to inspect myself, which would also be wise.

I can run faster than normal as a mortal, and this form could go even faster. But what else could I do? I'd spent more time avoiding it than trying to accept it. Knowing there wasn't much information on my situation didn't leave too much hope for me being changed back. I might as well get to know myself all over again, something that took me twenty-three years to do as a human to fully accept and love unconditionally.

This is my life now. At least until we get caught.

The door opened with Erius's arrival and my tale reacted immediately, perking up with excitement at the very scent. I slammed it down into the couch before he stepped into the room.

"What happened?" he asked darkly, looking around the living room as if there were a threat to spot.

"Nothing. I just thought I would try to do it."

He came to my side with a bag in hand. Despite him not having very distinguishable features in this form, his look of confusion shaped his eyes the same way as his human form.

"What?" I asked.

"I brought your mortal food. But if you'd like, I'm sure I can get you out to the sea of mortals to feast upon," he teased.

"And have you comment on my eating etiquette? I don't think so," I snipped.

"I will not say anything about your mess, promise." He chuckled darkly and I knew he was lying—it would be the first thing to leave his mouth at the smallest drop of bloodshed.

A wave of ice shifted over me, washing the form clean off to present my mortal skin. The corners of his lips fell, disappointed with the rejection of human slaughter. He dropped the bag on the table with a soft grumble and sat down.

"Do you plan on drifting off again today?" I asked, pulling the BLT from the bag. Though it was well-wrapped, the smell of bacon and tomatoes was delightfully overpowering.

"Do you miss me when I leave?"

"You would like that, wouldn't you?" I teased. "No, that isn't why I'm asking. I'm just, sort of, bored."

"You are bored. You were spending your hours in a compact van, and you are bored here?" He scoffed.

"Well, I wasn't originally. But being trapped here when there is so much to see out there. Having nothing to do in the van was my life because I've seen all that shit my whole life. This world is something I could only read about or watch on TV. Now, I'm living it and instead of exploring, I'm forced to stay in this fish tank of a flat."

"What do you have in mind?" he asked.

"Well," I looked to the book that was still sitting on the table. "That said something about what kind of demon you are – I can't remember the name."

"Rasasvada," he said proudly.

"Yeah—that. It mentioned that you only do things that fall on your benefit, but that was about it." *That and the fact you should be avoided.* I took a bite of my sandwich, looking over him with a raised brow.

"Yes," he said with a slow nod.

"Well, what else do you do, or can you do besides what aids you?"

"I can show you, but I doubt it will affect you as it should."

"And how should it affect me?" I asked, still enjoying the BLT as I calmly waited.

"You should feel a sense of hopelessness and fear—worse than any fear you've ever felt."

I waited for him to proceed, taking another bite to show I was no longer talking, but listening or watching since he enjoyed demonstrating everything.

After a moment, the room shifted as shadows crept out from the floor, stretching up to consume the room. The glass wall was blanketed, cutting out the sun and any light that had flooded the flat. As the shadows reached across the ceiling to meet in the center, screams swirled around us, quietly at first but soon growing to an ear-shattering volume. Gentle, fluttering wisps of shadows ghosted over my skin.

I froze, not from fear but anticipation as I waited for what was next to come. The wisps lightly wrapped around my wrists and ankles, while more spun around my neck with a tighter grip. Several more shot out from the darkness to push me into the couch while the ones around my ankles began to creep up my leg. They tightened at my thighs, keeping me held down though I didn't plan to struggle. I hoped for it to continue, encouraging the wisps by inching apart my legs.

I'm sure it was all supposed to be quite frightening, but it had the opposite effect as my body ached for him.

A low chuckle filled the space. "See? You are unlike most, even for a soulless mortal." His voice echoed around me in a low bellow.

"You started it," I poked.

He chuckled again, releasing me from the wisps and draining the room of shadows to allow the light once again.

I looked around, stopping on Erius who still sat unmoved beside me. "What was that?"

"An expansion of my demonic presence," he said matter of fact, as if that explained it any better.

"Mmhm."

"It allows me to be all around and disorient you. But you find ways to distract yourself with other thoughts."

"Yes, and you keep touching me to initiate it but won't do anything about it."

He looked at me with his frost blue eyes, the nebulas moving across his cheeks as if he were blushing. "Did it not seem dangerous enough the first time?"

"I cannot sense danger," I hinted.

He released an exasperated sigh, flicking his claws as he examined them.

"As I had mentioned before, you are easy to harm. With your breakable bones and—" His eyes slowly traveled over me before rushing his words, "Incredibly soft skin."

There was a simple fix to that on both ends; he would just need to stay in his human form. But I didn't want to push it and seem desperate. Although it would be a lie to say I wasn't.

"Alright, *Hannibal Lecter*, relax," I teased, knowing he probably wouldn't understand the reference, but I found it fitting. The rest of the day went by with Erius showing me a few other things he could *safely* do inside. After he was bored of that and my dissatisfying reactions, he asked me who *Hannibal Lecter* was, and of course, that was an introduction best shown.

I messed with the different options in the shower. Having done the varieties of rain and storm, I decided to go with the waterfall options, of which there were several. With a few more taps I found the settings for the glass including the option to frost it, which would have been nice to know the last few nights.

Not that Erius was an intentional creep, but not having a door to close the bathroom and a whole wall made of glass left me feeling exposed and uneasy. The energy of the entity had never really left, and Erius was clear that I inform him of anything out of place for the mortal realm. Not that there was much he could do about the energy; he couldn't see it and no magic he waved at it would make it appear.

I pressed "Begin" and the heated liquid washed over me like a waterfall would have. I gasped out, my mouth filling with water from the full-on assault. I threw myself from the downpour and tapped against the pad to return to the calm rainfall.

"Are you alright?" Erius asked from outside the glass doors already up to ensure I wasn't blacking out again. The frosted glass did well, at least from my side, blurring out his figure as he stood in the center of the room.

"The waterfall settings are a bit much," I coughed out.

"For your size, yes. But it is well suited for my form." That would explain it. In fact, that would explain the size and need for so many oddly shaped shower heads.

I managed to get it back to the right setting and Erius drifted out of the room once more, giving me the needed privacy to finish the shower. With the frosted glass I was able to dry and moisturize my body in peace. One thing I did miss about house living was the sizable shower and space to move.

The thick towel sat heavy on my head until I pulled it free to work on the day's style when low muffled voices caught my ear. Clearly, Alius had more questions to pester me with. Unfortunately, they held their conversation in Demric. Whatever Alius was telling Erius was clearly not meant for my ears, which probably meant bad news from his sister.

I stepped out and headed downstairs, finding the two over by the glass wall. They both turned to me as I made my way to the couch, their expressions unmoved. Erius spoke in Demric once more before walking around the coffee table.

"I have some business to handle downstairs. Alius is going to be adjusting a few things for me in the kitchen. Feel free to do as you like, just please stay here," he explained.

I looked to Alius and back to Erius with a soft shrug. "Ok?" That had been the rule for the last two days. I didn't need to be reminded every time he left to get food or whatever else he did. He didn't bother with what he called "scent sharing," which was fine. I didn't need an audience to my frustrations.

"I'll return later." He looked to Alius with a soft nod and headed out.

Alius followed behind, turning off at the kitchen to begin whatever maintenance he needed to. We hadn't used it at all, but I would figure if there was anything wrong with it, Erius could just use his vapor to fix it. Maybe his magic had its limits.

I grabbed the remote and flipped on Netflix to search for something new to watch, skimming through all the titles in every category before settling on a collection of painting shows. The narrator's voice was relaxing enough and watching the simple magic of art being created was a peacefulness I didn't often set aside time for.

The first episode began with the sweet, curly-haired man describing what scene he planned, mixing in all his inspirational goodness into it. I settled into my spot with Prometheus at my side as the painter constructed a beautiful snowy mountain piece.

Over the course of the episode, I could see Alius drifting around the kitchen out of the corner of my eye, not really inspecting or fixing anything in particular. He stood by the oven, checking inside and along the top. It wasn't a very thorough inspection, as he moved to the opposite side to simply open and close several cabinets, not taking any time at all to really look at what was in them. Not that there was much; I had already snooped. But for someone inspecting something, it was no time at all.

My skin tensed as if an electric current had been sent through me. The realization of what was really happening finally clicked. Perhaps it was because Erius had left me alone before that had me overlook it, but Alius wasn't inspecting anything. He was watching me, ensuring that I didn't leave.

I wasn't sure which was worse: that Erius thought I needed a babysitter rather than just telling me to stay here—as he had been, or the fact neither had the decency to be truthful about it. What reason was there to lie? What could be so dangerous for me that I needed a sitter?

I was not a fucking child. In fact, technically, I was no longer even mortal. I was not as delicate as I once was, even in my regular human body. Being under threat was no longer an issue to ensure I change; I could do that.

I could protect myself, and how fucking dare he think I couldn't or that I needed to be looked after?

Alius moved again, this time to the fridge, opening and closing it without any time to truly inspect it. He turned around, locking eyes with me for a moment before rushing to appear busy.

"What are you inspecting?" I pried.

His eyes slightly rounded as he moved back to the oven.

Very subtle.

"Azal feels the kitchen should be in working order with you here. It is currently set up as a sort of storage space for him. None of this is hooked up to work," he explained.

A decent enough reason. I couldn't argue with it. Maybe I was just overthinking it all. Erius had really gone out of his way to try and make it comfortable, which was probably a lot for him.

I rested back on the couch and continued to watch as the man added the fog to his trees.

"You enjoy art?" Alius suddenly asked from beside me.

I looked over him, noticing the distance he had just cleared in less than a second.

"Is sneaking up on people all you demons do?" I asked.

Alius shook his head with a smirk. "I'm not a demon."

I raised a brow to him and waited for him to continue explaining. He was not about to leave it at that. I didn't think he was a mortal running an underground club and hotel, and he did mention something about his niece being a sorceress. Maybe I should have taken that into account before blurting out an assumption.

"I am what your kind calls a shapeshifter. Well, half. I am also from the bloodline of a prominent magic race. I hear you have acquired one of our history books." His eyes flashed to the book resting on the table. "Oh! That brief introduction?"

"It mostly talked about the Five Circles with brief explanations on the priests," I admitted.

Alius picked up the book with an amused grin. "It is meant as a novice introduction for the new spirits entering the Circles. They aren't normally sent this far. But Nic is a divinationalist. She may have sensed you'd need it. She owns the shop you two patroned on your adventure."

"A *divinationalist?*"

"One who studies and practices in all forms of divination. Nic is one of the best." He flipped the book around as he examined it before returning his attention to me. "Hm, if Erius wants you to defend yourself, it is only right you know why. I have a few books I can lend you if you want something more interesting. But you must stay here while I gather them."

He wasn't wrong; it would be something to do while I sat here and waited for our next step. But what really caught my attention was his offer to leave while I stayed. My assumption about being *babysat* was not wrong at all, and the flame of irritation lit my skin. I looked over Alius, forcing a pleasant smile as I nodded. "That would be wonderful. Thank you."

A *wonderful* few minutes to transform and sneak out because if there was one thing I could not stand, it was being told not to do something without reasonable explanation. If there was a human hunter downstairs, then I just wouldn't go down there as a human. Besides, there had to be more than this scotch to enjoy.

"Right, I'll just be a few moments then. Remember, stay here with your cat," he wavered, probably wondering if that was too much. It was, but I continued to smile up at him as if I didn't catch it. With a parting grin, he turned and headed out.

As quietly as possible, I tiptoed to the door and waited until his heavy footsteps drifted down the hall. Prometheus meowed at my feet, my little sidekick always ready encouraging me to do the worst.

"Sneaking out is for children, Prometheus. I'm *leaving* to go to the bar." The familiar tingle trickled over my skin, revealing the fine fur and tail. The transformation was getting much easier, aiding in the confidence I already had in myself.

"But now, what to wear?" I muttered to the cat. His whiskers flicked and his tail swished from side to side before he darted up the steps. I ran after him, following him to the bathroom. He hopped up on the counter and my form instantly caught my eye. I looked over myself in the mirror, making it a bit easier to imagine what would pair well with the new form of mine.

I imagined several dresses I had seen in magazines and on TV over the last few months, one I had found on a mood board that would not only look nice but would allow my tail to move more easily.

"I got it," I whispered, pulling my hands up to my chest and running them down the length of my body. The black velvet fell over me, splitting at the bottom of my ribs on either side and dropping into a double-sided slit. Belts encrusted with diamonds swept over my hips to connect the fabric, hugging the dress to me like a second skin.

Perfect. Alius never saw my demon form, and Erius had never seen this dress. I just needed to lay low and head straight to the bar. No detours, no attention.

I turned to Prometheus with a hopeful smile, getting a simple meow in return.

"Thanks, I know," I giggled to him as I sped back downstairs. I strained my ears, struggling to hear footsteps from either direction, but it was clear and quiet. With a deep breath, I opened the door and stepped into the bright, empty hall.

"Not so hard," I whisper to myself. I tossed one last look to my right before making my way down the hall to the elevator doors. My triumph was short lived. As I came up to the first turn, Alius appeared with three heavily thick books in hand, his attention on them for the time being.

With a steady breath I forced myself forward, not missing a step in fear his senses were just as strong. He glanced up at me with a half-smile but continued down the hall without notice. I quickened my step toward the corner as I watched him from over my shoulder. His steps slowed to a full stop as he turned around with a confused look.

"Little bird?" he called, turning to make his way back to me.

I jumped into a full sprint, racing around the corner toward the empty lobby.

"Little bird!" he called again.

I turned the last bend and, to my great surprise, a group of what Erius called Gnolls were stepping out of one of the lifts. I pushed past them, stumbling onto the elevator before frantically hitting the button for the lowest level and then closing the doors. The Gnolls watched with bewildered expressions as Alius finally came into view. We locked eyes just as the doors began to close and he lunged himself forward just a little too late.

I smiled at him with a soft wave as the doors sealed closed and the elevator made its way down to the bar floor.

CHAPTER THIRTY-THREE

Erius

The lift doors opened with a maddening buzzing noise, spilling a ghostly black gas onto the floor. I followed the burbling gases up to the misshapen head. His glowing white eyes peered at me from the black mist creation. A permanent smile spread his lipless face, making it hard to distinguish his true emotions, though I suspect he was always grimly satisfied with his place working alongside his creator, Dazron.

"Jafeki," I greeted as I stepped off the lift to move around him, keeping a decent distance between us. Despite my attempt to mask Mina's scent, I could still smell her on my clothes.

I suppose I should find myself lucky Dazron did not know what the mortal looked like. I doubted he would catch her by scent. But I did not need him questioning me about what mortal I was with. The less he knew, the more I could find out from this surprise meeting.

The shifter attempted speech with a wet gargle as he struggled to catch up. All three of Dazron's shifters weren't too well off with speech of any kind, and the damned Sentient Elm hadn't felt need to teach them. I suspected it had to do with all these souls he had me collecting.

We headed from the lift lobby to the Firebar where Jafeki proceeded to lead me to the back to a more secluded section. It wasn't long before I spotted the twisted, smoldering branches of Dazron's head. His red eyes locked on me instantly, spreading a spiked tooth smile my way. His branch-like fingers reached out, pointing to the spot across from him, as if I would not have guessed.

The shifter at my side snorted once again before taking his place beside his created siblings. They likened him in the misty fog that surrounded the glowing eyes and lipless smile, but even with the strong resemblance, they had their slight differences. Mostly in how they held themselves together and moved about.

"Eriusazal," Dazron greeted with false joy. His gritted smile instantly fell as he looked over me. I sat between Marble and Muffa, the two other Shadow Shifters owned by the Sentient Elm.

"Dazron," I responded.

His eyes moved over me once more, and the hole in his face where a nose would be flexed disgustingly as he inhaled. He closed his eyes as a sickening smile curved his lips again.

My hands fisted under the table, locking me down from reaching across and snapping his neck. It was depleting enough that others found her sent appealing, but Dazron enjoying it set rocks in my stomach.

"I will admit, Azal, I did not expect you to be back to your searches so soon. But I see you are not too invested in that, now are you?"

"It is a minor distraction," I admitted.

"I would hope so. Word spreads fast, Azal, as you know. I did not think you to be easily captivated, fawning over some mortal woman when you have yet to locate the soul I am in need of. Should you be allowing yourself so close to them?"

"I thought it would look well on my part if it appeared as though I have come to enjoy them," I offered.

If only he were clever enough to make the connection, but that was exactly why I requested Alius keep Mina in the flat. For centuries Dazron had me hunt down and capture particular souls for some ritual he had yet to inform me or anyone else of. There were only a few of us he entrusted with this task, and for so long I had done as asked without question. Until now.

"The mortal I have with me has information on the one you seek. I am simply trying to extract it from her," I offered calmly, words he clearly did not accept as he tilted his head to the side with down-turned lips.

"If you wish to release your own fantasies upon these creatures, do so on your own time. You owe me a soul; it would be wise to collect it."

I took a deep breath, not wanting to outright say I claimed it for myself, nor that I had her just a few floors up from us. His intentions were vague to begin with but now, I was curious as to what her part in it all would have been.

"You have asked me to collect six souls of six very specific mortals, all on the word of a ritual that will do what again?" I pressed.

Muffa rolled his head back, gargling the clearest word I had ever heard any of them utter, "Release—"

"Shh, you gaseous blocks!" Dazon hissed, snapping his thick branch-like fingers at Muffa. He turned back to me, his red beady eyes narrowed and dark. "I will assume by your diversions that you do not have the soul, nor its location."

"I have a general idea," I said.

The rough bark-like skin above his eyes pulled down as he leaned over the table. The shifters began their ominous cackling as embers rose around Dazron in his irritation.

"Then I suggest you finish up with your mortal and find the soul in question. Or do you wish to continue your imprisonments here? Given the scent you carry about yourself, I would say you have lost interest in that all together. Is that it? You have found yourself a docile little mortal and you no longer wish to return to the Circles?" He cackled condescendingly.

My claws bit deep into my palm as I forced the words through my teeth. "She will give me the information you seek. I simply thought I would—have a bit of fun with her before I dispose of her."

His lips curled up again, delighted and interested as he leaned over the table. "Ah, do tell how you plan to dismember this one?"

I forced a smile, maintaining the ruse for as long as needed. I opened my mouth to speak when a strong fragrance of the sweet sunflower encompassed me. My muscles locked and my body fell rigid. I forced myself to maintain eye contact with Dazron despite the nagging pull to search for her.

It was one task. Keep her in the flat. How hard is that?

A waiter soon came by with a tray of glasses filled with an overpowering scotch that masked the scent. But only for a moment as he set them at the center and darted off.

Dazron clicked his teeth together and pushed the tray my way. "Help yourself, Azal." His lips curled up into a sinister grin, but he didn't seem to notice the scent or my reaction.

I grabbed the glass and took a slow sip before breaking contact to scan the floor, not wanting to raise Dazron's suspicions. I could hardly see over much through the crowd, and the lights flashing did little to assist.

"Do tell me what it is you know about this soul. Where is it?" Dazron asked stiffly, pulling my attention back to him. I did not believe I mentioned knowing the location. But he was not a hard one to read. It was clear he was low on patience and ready to cut me out entirely to search on his own. The thing was, Sentients weren't too welcome in the mortal realm. Not only were they quite unfriendly, but they also had no real magic to disguise themselves. He wouldn't last a day searching for a single mortal in a world full of them, especially with no sense of what he was truly searching for.

He didn't even give me much, simply that those with the marked essence would not only see but find interest in the blasted book. And even that he had to learn from someone else. Without Elpos, Ennaza, and myself, he would be lost, scrambling for even a shred of a clue.

"I am working to ensure it is the true soul you seek," I pushed through clenched teeth. My body and muscles reacted to the scent that was beginning to fill my mind. "I should get back to—"

"That mortal you have, you said she can lead you to the one I seek? Should I speak with her instead?" Dazron interjected.

The threat set fire over my skin, thrashing the colors around to give away my irritation.

"Calm yourself, Azal. I will not bring harm to your creature, yet." He drummed his fingers against the tables as another smile curved his lips. "I suppose you do have a right to enjoy yourself how you see fit after all you have done." He paused, distracted by a passing thought that brought him joy. "Very well, if taunting the mortal woman is your fancy, carry on. But do not keep me waiting. I expect to have the soul soon. It is imperative for what I have planned." He stood from the booth, motioning for his shifters to exit with him.

"You have until the next full moon," he said dismissively as they turned to leave. I waited until they disappeared and I was sure they were gone before jumping from the booth to search for my insolent mortal. a task that took seconds before I spotted two bronze ram horns nestled in thick blonde curls. To her left stood Alius, seemingly attempting to pull her from the bar.

My tail flicked up with heated agitation. It was one thing to have the mortal disregard my word; she seemed to have issues with authority for some time now. But for Alius, this was unacceptable. Fire burned my skin, spinning the deepest burgundy over my hands and arms, marred under the scarred impression from the tether. I fought to stamp down the irritation before approaching her. The less attention I drew to us, the better.

I pushed through the crowd to reach the bar, knocking a few drinks and patrons over in the process. The complaints went unheard as I raced to the bright red counter. Nobody appeared aware of the slight human scent that drifted around, which was a decent sign. Still, it did not bring me comfort. That hunter may catch it if he was anywhere near. Then again, Barren wasn't the best at what he did.

I turned around the last table near the few steps up to the bar when the person to Mina's right finally came into view. Broad shoulders covered in a deep shaggy fur shook over the counter with a roaring laugh. My body reacted, ready to jump between her and the very hunter I wanted to avoid.

Alius turned to me as I neared, wide-eyed and defeated.

"How did she get past you?" I growled.

His brows pulled down as he spoke through clenched teeth. "You said she still had a human sent to her. She doesn't," he snapped back in a hushed tone to keep Barren from hearing.

Her human scent was faint but there. Maybe I had spent too much time with her in her human form, or perhaps I was more in tune with the variety of fragrances she made.

I looked up to Mina, who appeared well off, laughing along with the shapeshifter without care, but it was clear her tail did not find the same joy as it whipped around erratically behind her, calming only when I stepped to her side so it could wrap around my wrist as it usually did. Once she learned to control it, I would miss the subconscious comfort it sought.

The sudden contact caused her to swirl around with a set grimace until she realized it was me. Her eyes brightened, dazzled by the diamonds that surrounded us. The words burned my tongue, but her captivating attire caught my eye, silencing me instantly, a skin-tight dress with flimsy diamond straps tugging it together at the hips. Every slight twist of her body presented more of her, drawing my attention further away from the situation at hand, a distraction like everything else she brought around me.

"Erius!" she slurred happily as she flung her arms around my neck. Her greeting caught Barren's attention instantly as he turned to face me as well.

I leaned into her to keep the shapeshifter from overhearing, but the noise around us did not allow for much quiet conversation.

"You were supposed to stay in the flat," I reminded her. Her body heated under me, blooming out the tantalizing scent that was becoming more of a struggle to ignore. "Do you remember why?"

She pulled a large, dark bottle toward her and poured some into the glass in her hand. She took a sip, scrunching her face at the taste. "The flat was boring. Besides—" She paused and leaned closer. "I'm not a mortal so there is nothing for the mortal hunter to find."

"There is much you do not understand. Grab your drink, we are going back upstairs," I ordered.

"Hey now, Azal, that is no way to speak to such a creature," Barren belted from beside us. "If you want someone to order around, go find your own." He reached out, ready to grab her arm when I pulled her from the chair into me.

"Right, well, you see, this one here is mine. Perhaps it is you who needs to find your own," I bit back.

Before I could shuffle her away, Barren gripped my shoulder, yanking it back with a hard jerk. "Not everything is deemed yours, Azal. Dazron's favor on you goes so far and from what I hear—"

I gripped Mina to my chest and swung back with my free arm, tearing my claws across the shapeshifter's face before he could finish. I flicked my wrist, sending his blood across the counter before wiping the remainder off on his torn shirt.

A bellowing howl erupted from the shapeshifter as his hands shot up to the three new gashes across his face. While he thundered and roared in pain at the bar, I tugged Mina to the elevator lobby. She was silent as I pressed the button, but the smell of her arousal only grew.

Is it danger? Is danger what gives her this feeling? Or the sense of dying?

When the lift door opened and we stepped on, I turned to her, the bottle of liquor still in her hands.

"You did all this for alcohol?" I hissed. "Do you understand who you were sitting with? Do you have a taste for death? You hear that there is a mortal hunter about and you think taunting him at the bar is wise?"

She shrugged and took a slow sip from the bottle. "I didn't know. It's not like you give much information. Besides, he sat there after I had already been drinking. I didn't invite anyone. Secondly, I am not mortal, so there is nothing to hunt," she slurred.

"You have no idea the dangers you gamble with." The lift stopped with a ding as the doors opened. I turned to ensure it was the proper floor and not just a stop along the way. The soft press of her hand slid around my waist before she was gone, running full speed down the hall.

The pull in my chest tightened as it had when I asked her to run. The instinct to chase after her was much higher, pulling me from the lift and down the hall. She tossed a look over her shoulder and held up her hand, presenting the door key to my flat that she must have snuck from me.

She picked up speed as she turned the corner, somehow managing well on her drunk feet, only stumbling once she reached the flat. With the bottle in one hand, she unlocked the door and pushed through before I had a chance to reach her. I slammed into the hard metal as I followed her in, chasing her into the kitchen where I finally managed to catch up with her.

I reached out, changing to human form as I gripped her arm to yank her back. She slammed into the fridge and did not fight as I pinned her in place, locking her arms to her side and bracing her between my legs. She shivered under me, the form melting away to present her mortal self. A small flash of what looked to be fear lit her eyes before falling to something more haunting.

"He doesn't know what I smell like as a mortal, and besides, isn't that the whole point of the scent sharing and invasion of space?" She rolled her hips against me as she spoke, drawing my attention to the dress that hugged her. Her every movement tore at the perfectly constructed resolve I set for myself, shredding it before me with a simple smile pulling at her full lips.

"I told you that only goes so far," I warned, struggling to ignore the sensation building in my groin.

She pulled the bottle to her lips, her eyes still on me. "Maybe we should try the other way you suggested that will make it stronger." She took a drink without care of her offer.

Her eyes darkened with a desire and need that called for me, a need I had been denying us both of for far too long. A sensual curve touched her lips as she brought the bottle up for another sip, rolling her body against me as she did. Her free hand smoothed over the front of my slacks, gripping my dick until if found purchase at my belt buckle.

Heat raced through me, creating an uncomfortable pain. The very thought of being inside her again loosened the thin shred of control left.

I snatched the bottle from her and tossed it to the side without care of where it landed. Her eyes widened and breathing spiked as another wave of the fragrant scent lifted from her, breaking me.

"On your knees then," I ordered.

A smile curved her lips once again as she slid down, nestling herself between my legs as requested. Her hands fumbled with my belt until it was loose enough for her to work on the button. After what felt like an agonizing few seconds, the heat of her hand slipped around me. I sucked in air through my teeth, dropping my head back as she stroked me.

She paused for a moment before the heat of her mouth covered me. I trembled and looked down to enjoy the view I had only ever fantasized, her full lips taking me in until tears began to collect at the corners of her eyes. I pulled back but she took me in again, taking me down to the hilt. The heat of her tongue swirled around as she slowly pulled back. My body shivered with anticipation and I fought to keep still, carving my fingers into the edge of the counter to keep from pounding into her.

She took me in again, pulling back just as slowly, swirling and flicking her tongue as she came to the tip. I groaned out, unable to control the jerking of my hips to be deeper. More tears collected and spilled over, and her mouth grew warm and wet.

"You take me so well." I pulled back a bit, not trying to hurt her but fuck, was it a sight I wanted to see again. She blinked a few tears free and wiped them away without dropping me. She gave a soft nod and dipped her head down as far as she could go. The fire that had been building felt as though it was ready to explode, sending chills over my body as it numbed my mind.

But I wasn't ready to finish here. I pulled out and tugged her up onto the counter. My hands worked at her dress, moving the front flap from my way, finding nothing underneath. Her hands ran through my hair while I ran my fingers over her dripping cunt, taking the offered shiver it brought. A faint moan escaped her, urging me forward as I thrust into her tightness. She cried out but pulled me in deeper, gripping me with every pump.

The bittersweet pain flooded my mind. A war between wanting every sensation heightened and wanting to grab her without hurting her began to rage.

"You feel so good," I groaned, marveling in the flood it caused.

My skin lit up with the prickling strain, ready to shift—but I wasn't ready to be through even as my fangs began to swell and burn, begging to dig into her skin. I kept going, drinking in each sound. Savoring every look that fluttered across her face.

The growing pressure flooded down from my head to my cock, begging for release in any way. I paused, holding her in place while I held on to the shred of control I had. A low growl rumbled from my chest in irritation, something she seemed to enjoy as another bloom of her scent clouded the space.

She looked up to me with searching eyes. The heat of her palm pressed against my cheek while her thumb smoothed over the bulge my fangs created.

"It's ok," she encouraged breathlessly before pressing the softness of her lips to mine, the invading blaze consumed me. She had no idea how wrong she was, but there was no time to explain. The hold I had on myself slipped as my mind wandered too far to rein back. Every nerve ending felt as if they were exploding, releasing any sort of control I thought I had in a washing wave.

I pulled away from her, shifting to my form with a thunderous roar. My tail slammed down between us, stealing away more of the small space available. The room rattled with a booming growl that tore through me, none of which seemed to phase Mina as she watched in amazement.

"I am not opposed to this, but I do not know how we would make it work." She giggled as she ran her tiny hands through the strands of my hair that fell over her. After a moment she began tracing along whatever pattern fell upon my face. "Your skin is mesmerizing," she hummed.

I inhaled deeply, trailing my lips over the softness of her legs. "As is yours," I panted, snaking my tongue out to slide it along her inner thigh. She shook against me with pleased moans. Her arm knocked against something on the counter, sending it crashing down to the floor.

"I can replace that," she gasped as she tried to see what it was, but I gently cradled her into my hand. This all would be much better enjoyed where there was more space. I climbed the stairs to my room where I was sure she'd find more comfort than a hard countertop.

I knew she wouldn't have the sense to fear this form, but I never expected this. She remained quiet as I set her on the bed and rocked back to give her space.

"So, how would this work?" she asked with a confused tilt of her head.

"We wait until I can return to a safer form for you."

"There are other things we can do while we wait," she offered. *No sense of danger.* I stifled a chuckle, knowing she was correct, but someone had to be concerned for her safety if she didn't know to be. I looked over the dress that still clung to her. "Are you partial to that dress?"

She looked down, running her hands over the fabric to the odd diamond straps at her waist. "I am."

"Then it would be wise to remove it."

Without hesitation, she reached around her back for the zipper she struggled to grasp. I pulled her into me, gently hooking the tip of my claw through the loop and slid it down until it stopped. She pulled her arms free to remove the dress before turning to me with darkened eyes.

I leaned over her, pushing her to lay back so I could admire her body without the obstruction of lace and sheer fabric. I trailed a claw from her collarbone down to her navel, marveling at the shudder it sent through her. The drawing scent pulled me down to her warm skin where it flooded my mind.

A scent so strong, I could taste it begging for me. I parted her instantly with my tongue, melting into her with a deep groan. She arched her back, releasing a soft squeak of a moan that drove me over the edge of self-control. My hands clamped down on the mattress with a harsh rip.

Pain radiated from my teeth to my dick with the need to sink into her, not feasible in the current form for either. I lifted, taking my exploration up her stomach as I shrunk down to a more fitting size. Her hands found their way to my hair, gripping my horns for support. I shoved her thigh down as I lined myself up, dipping into her one notch at a time until I filled her completely. A purring moan rumbled through her, a beautiful sound I wanted more of.

"Let me hear you," I groaned.

Her hands gripped me, her body tensed, and she throbbed around me. A scream mixed with a moan burst from her lungs as her face melted into blissful pleasure. I moved my lips over her neck, welcoming the sting that flooded my mouth and pulled at my fangs once again.

She tilted her head to the side as she did the first night, presenting the supple smooth skin of her neck to me. It was as if she was well aware of the torment it caused.

Pressure began to build in more places than one as she continued to wiggle under me. I gripped her neck in one hand, keeping the smooth patch of skin open to me as I pumped into her. Would it be a selfish act if she so blindly encouraged it? All the complications of claiming her seared into my mind, but all the pleasing outcomes reined over that, stamping them out to irrelevant consequences that could easily be mended. Her place in my realm may not have been set, but her place in my world had been carved deep.

I need to keep her.

I must *keep her.*

Without a second thought, I closed my mouth around the delicate curve of her neck and bit down. She froze against me, stunned at the sensation but not at all displeased with the unknown marking.

I pulled away, licking the wounds as I did to admire the eight nearly healed holes.

Now everyone will know you are mine.

I rocked back on my heels to take in the sight of the beautiful creature before me. The soft noises that had escaped her grew silent, paining me with the absence of their soft song. My tail ensnared her waist as I reached to lift her. In one swift move, I pulled her into me as I turned to lay back on the bed. She moved effortlessly with the sudden switch in positions. She looked down over me with hooded eyes as she slowly lowered herself onto me, pausing at each notch that popped in.

When I was fully buried in her soaking cunt, she paused, adjusting to the size and new position. She kept her eyes on me as she began to move, rolling her hips before pulling up a few notches and inching back down. I forced myself to remain still, grounding into her each time she came down. Her bottom lip began to tremble and her legs began to shake, but the sounds I had longed for were silent. Her cunt gripped me as I bucked into her a few times in hopes to pull those lovely moans from her again.

My claws dug into the soft flesh at her hips as I held her steady, driving into her with the only shred of sanity I could manage to not squeeze her too tightly. She leaned down, gripping me for better support as I relentlessly bucked into her. Her silent screams were cut short, replaced with the musical sounds of her finish. A heated gush spilled over me again as her cunt continued to contract around me. My notches flared in my own release, locking me to her for a moment to ensure a proper seal, though I doubted anything would come of it with her being mortal born.

Mina snuggled against me, unaware of the lock between us both physically and metaphorically. I brushed my lips against the mark on her neck. I had never claimed anyone for myself before, and the whole idea of it was never a concern to me. With a mortal, it may not take properly, but my claim to her would not be challenged again. A few more properly placed marks wouldn't hurt.

CHAPTER THIRTY-FOUR

Mira

A sharp pain shot from my neck down to my thighs, disturbing my peaceful sleep. My eyes weren't even open yet, but my muscles screamed as I rolled over to a blinding glow already clawing at my lids. I rubbed my eyes before peeling them open to the clear morning. The nagging pull returned, jerking me up straight in the bed, and an unforgiving soreness pulled at my back and shoulders. The silk sheets slipped free from my bare chest, exposing the discolored, hand-shaped bruises and shallow cuts from Erius's claws.

Heat raced over my cheeks as I looked around the empty bed, the memory of the night slowly surfacing. Heavy footsteps ascended the stairs, louder than needed to announce his soon appearance. I lifted the blanket to cover myself—not that it mattered—and caught sight of a reddened, irritated mark on my inner left thigh. Eight puncture wounds lined up with the indentation of more teeth.

Erius cleared his throat to alert me of his presence as he stood at the entrance.

"You bit me, you beast!" I snapped instantly.

"Well, good morning to you, too." He shrugged with a bright smile. It was too early for him to be this chipper, especially about mauling me. He ignored me as he walked over with his attention on my left wrist. Before I could look down to see what it was, he took it in his hand and pulled it closer to examine. He gently traced his finger over a purpling bruise. "Does this hurt?"

It didn't but I snatched my arm from his heated grip with a hiss. "Yes, so does the bite you left on my thigh!"

His lips turned up as his eyes raked over me. "There are worse things to be done."

"Like what?" I pressed further. Not that I was mad, I just didn't see why it needed to look like I was under attack. The biting was fine, I agreed to that, but this was a full-on mauling.

He sighed with a drop of his shoulders and a slight flicker to his eyes. "Do get dressed. We are going out for food."

"I thought I was trapped here," I shot, confused.

"Alius has informed me our human hunter has been banned from the property. And we will be going to the mortal restaurants in the actual hotel today." He looked over me with a sinful smile. "I thought you might be hungry after last night," he added in a teasing tone.

The ghosted sensation of his heated body against mine lit my skin. My hands gripped the blanket at my chest as I tried to recall the whole event.

"Can you move your legs?" he asked with another slick grin.

"I'm sure I can walk just fine. Thank you." I kept my gaze locked with his as I pushed the blankets from my naked body and stood.

His eyes dropped to my neck. The odd flush of his demon skin fluttered across his cheeks and nose. With rising shoulders, his eyes slowly crawled up to my face. "Are you upset by it?" he asked with genuine concern.

I shook my head with an honest answer. "Will it get infected?" I asked. He responded with the same smile spread his lips.

"Get dressed, Mortal," he said with a chuckle as he exited the loft and headed downstairs.

I sat there for a moment, trying to decide if him ignoring me would be better than him using me as a literal snack or whatever it was he decided to do. When I said it was ok, I meant a little playful bite, not a wound.

A painful sting scratched at my neck, and I reached up to find several more marks, another bite I should have accounted for given he couldn't take his eyes off it.

"What the hell?" I whispered mindlessly, running to the bathroom to investigate what I already knew was there. The natural light spilled in from the window, providing enough for me to see the extent of the second bite. To my dismay, it was far worse in terms of looks than the one on my thigh. I was honestly surprised I didn't feel it first.

"Erius," I growled under my breath, more irritated than mad. He did tell me I was "fragile," and I did sort of edge him on. I couldn't really expect a demon to fully grasp the concept of gentleness.

I traced a finger over the discolored mark as I inspected it in the mirror. Prometheus joined me at my feet with a few good meows in protest of his empty bowl.

"I know, I know," I chanted as I continued to look over the bite. "First I'm a prisoner, now he wants to parade me around with this. How does he expect me to go out?" I rambled off to the cat.

"With it on full display," Erius's voice came from the entrance warm and heavy with wandering eyes as he walked toward me.

I spun around, pressing my ass against the counter as he locked me in. A single claw slid down my cheek to hook under my chin. "I can get you a scarf once we reach the mortal lobby. But through *this* lobby, I want all to see." His finger skimmed over the marks before grasping my neck.

"Why?" I breathed.

"What did I tell you when we arrived here?" He tightened his hold around me.

My body froze against him, melting into the hardness of his chest. The heat of his skin ignited in his transition, filling the space around us in the black swirling vapor that smelled of warm vanilla.

"To lay low?" I panted.

The rough heat of his tail slipped up around my leg. "I said that while we are here, you are mine. This ensures nobody questions it again." He traced the mark on my neck while his tail inched further up my thigh. I didn't bother fighting the flood that warmed me, or the throbbing need he was causing. I trembled under him, watching as the reaction brought a hungered curve to his lips.

"What does that even mean?" I knew what it meant when we arrived, a means of cover and protection. But now, I no longer felt that was his same reasoning or meaning of it.

"Well, I have your soul, and now you have my marks." None of which seemed as though it actually benefited me.

"All of that sounds like I am property," I hissed.

"Not at all like property." His body shook as he chuckled out his response. His tail pulled at my leg while he lifted me onto the counter, holding my gaze as he worked at his pants.

"What's it like then?" I breathed. The tip of his dick slid up the slit of my pussy, melting my mind from the connection. I arched my back with a sharp breath.

"I am a selfish creature, Mina." He pushed forward, filling me with a deep growl. I gripped his arms with a ragged gasp. My free leg hooked around his waist while my other still sat captive in his tail. "Sharing is not in my nature. I claim what I want for my own."

"And what is it you want?" I asked.

His thumb traced over my bottom lip as he purred. "Right now, I want to see those pretty lips quiver."

My breath caught in my chest as he began pounding into me. He held my face in his hands, hovering his lips with a need he wasn't allowing himself. As much as he clearly wanted to, he seemed to be holding himself back, fighting the desire to melt into something so harmless. The gentle warmth of his bottom lip swept across mine as the tip of his tongue traced along.

I tilted my head, closing the small distance he left. He locked up but didn't pull away to break the kiss. I gave him a second if he wanted to but when he didn't, I took the lead, deepening the kiss until his body relaxed into mine. His hands moved to my hair as he fell into the same rhythm to take control.

His lips were surprisingly soft and he was alarmingly gentle, tasting of whiskey and spice, intoxicating in every sense. It clouded my mind and numbed every nerve in my body.

He didn't seem so much a stranger to it as I had thought, growing hungrier in his passion as he buried himself as deep as he could, slowly fucking me until the building pressure became unbearable. I broke the kiss to catch my breath, moaning out as he ground into me. My body flushed, becoming overly sensitive to each notch that popped in. Once he was at the hilt, he pulled out quickly before slowing his thrust to split me a second time. The mind-numbing sensation had me crying out, rolling my hips against him for more.

A deep growl ripped through him as he paused his movements,

his hands gripping my hair and neck. His dick pulsated, stretching me further.

"Please do not do that. It is hard enough to maintain control," he groaned. His lips collided into mine, taking advantage of the wait and the new freedom he felt. I remained still, moving only to kiss him back as I clung to him. When the fullness subsided, he began grinding into me, inhaling every breath I panted out until they grew into gasps and moans.

Raging fire ignited at the pit of my stomach, zapping every nerve ending into high gear. Pressure filled my head and chest as he maintained the same blissful tempo. The notches felt as though they were flaring out, slowly growing until his movements were shortened and he was hitting every spot that mattered. A heated gush flooded from me as the thin strand of sanity broke.

I buried my head in his chest, whimpering out against each body trembling wave. His hand gripped the hair at the nape of my neck and tugged back so I was looking up to him. His darkened expression and hungered eyes looked over me with a satisfied curve to his lips.

"That's my good girl," he groaned, dropping his head to the crook of my neck. At first, I thought he was going to bite me a third time, but instead, it was the wet heat of his tongue trailing over my skin. When his hands finally left my hair, they locked onto my waist, holding me down while he buried into me. His claws dug into my skin, pulling a slight sting but I only gripped him tighter, wanting more.

The tremors started in my legs, rattling my body until it shattered under him. The small space filled with the sound of my weak and breathless moans falling faint under the growing sound of smacking skin and the demonic noises that rose from him, feral and unrelenting as he ground deeper into me, pinning me to the counter as he worked up until his own finish.

His hands slipped up my body and over my chest, finding purchase around my face as he held me still. His lips crashed into mine once more, hungry and passionate as his thrust became more erratic. His tongue slipped in, parting my lips to explore me in a way he hadn't before. I did the same, drinking in the vanilla scotch taste he offered.

He broke the connection to gaze down at me, trailing his thumb over my lower lip with a quivering breath. "My sweetest sunflower," he panted out. His tail constricted my leg, opening me up to him even further. Warmth flooded me with one last jerking thrust before Erius relaxed, holding his weight up against the counter as he inspected me.

He tilted my head from side to side to look over my neck and shoulders. The swelling of his dick slowly subsided, allowing him to more easily slip out.

"You don't think the bite is enough?" I sighed, still catching my breath.

He did his little eye trick as the corner of his mouth kicked up, sizing up my body as he spoke. "Get dressed. You are going to be hungry soon." He pushed off the counter and adjusted his pants with his eyes locked on me the whole time—well, on the bite. "Preferably something that will display your neck."

"You mean your mark," I corrected. Not that I would have really had a choice. All my clothes flaunted my neck and shoulders in the summer months.

"Precisely."

I narrowed my eyes at him and hopped from the counter with the perfect dress in mind. I had a strong feeling it would fit his little request. I ran my hands down my body just as I did the night before, calling upon a black off the shoulder maxi with a slit on the side that allowed enough thigh to show, allowing both marks to be perfectly presented to his liking.

"Does this work for you?" I asked as I turned to the mirror to fluff out my hair. I watched him nod from the reflection as he looked over the dress. The frost blue of his eyes flickered as they focused on my neck.

"We should go," he said in a near exasperated voice. When I got to his side, his tail slipped around my waist as his arm fell around my shoulder to guide me out.

We stepped into the bedroom as my phone began to buzz across the glass top nightstand. The annoyingly loud clatter it caused felt as if it were shattering my eardrums. I broke away from Erius to race over and snatch it up.

We have your stuff.
What floor is the van
parked on?

        -Jasmine

We?

You all came?

*We wanted to make
sure you were safe!*
-Amber

I couldn't blame them for wanting to be sure after Erius broke someone's arm. It was a bit of an unstable action for one to commit. I sent them the location of the van and told them I would be up in a few minutes to meet them.

Please leave the demon!
-Jasmine

*I can't make any
promises on what
he does.*

Erius looked from my phone to me as I made my way back to him, but he didn't ask what it was about. After last night, I doubted leaving his sight would be on his top to allow again.

"The girls have all my stuff from work. They are going to meet me by the van in a few," I informed him, assuming he would invite himself, but he was quiet as we made our way downstairs.

Before we could even make it to the bottom, the door was attacked by thunderous pounding.

"Azal, it's me! Open up!" Alius called from the other side. His banging continued until we arrived at the door and Erius opened it.

"What is it, Alius?" he grunted, tucking me behind him as if to shield me from some invisible threat.

Alius froze for a moment, his eyes locked on my neck as he tried to gather his thoughts before us.

"Um—well, if you still care, I have gotten in connection with my niece," he began.

Erius straightened up as he looked to me, grabbing my hand to guide me off toward the elevator lobby. Alius followed behind without question, but clear concern etched his face as he eyed the mark. Erius pressed down and a lift opened instantly. He guided me in and hit the lower mortal lobby level before stepping off again.

"Go meet with your friends I will be by for you after. Please go

387

straight to them once you reach the lobby and wait in your van," he ordered before the doors closed.

I stepped out of the elevator lobby door into the bright open parking lot. The summer sun baked down on the black asphalt and sent the blazing heat back up into the air like a fiery oven, the early morning dewy fog long gone as the sun climbed the sky.

Blinded by the light, I scanned the empty lot until I spotted Amber's red convertible beside my van. The three of them stood outside leaning on her trunk with the overflowing boxes in each of their hands. The closer I got, the wider their eyes grew as they caught sight of the mark on my neck.

"Oh, Meems. No." Jaz sighed with slumped shoulders as she searched my body for more.

"I thought he was a demon, not a blood-sucking vampire," Amber tossed in.

Mickey remained quiet, her rounded eyes glued to my neck with a hung jaw.

"He's not. I mean—it's nothing." I waved the topic off as I made a beeline for my van, not wanting to hear whatever lecture they would soon give. I unlocked the door and pushed it open.

"Mina, enough is enough. When are ya'll breaking the tether? He is hurting you!" Jaz shot as they all stepped in and placed the boxes on my bed.

"He's not hurting me," I corrected, but it clearly did not faze them as they each rose a brow at me and pressed their lips.

"Then why did he bite you?" Mickey interrogated in a soft voice.

"I asked him to. We were…" I looked over their faces, knowing they knew exactly what I was going to say. The looks of anticipation varied but none seemed too thrilled. "I asked him to, and he did. There," I snapped as we stepped out for the last few boxes.

They shared glances with each other before turning back to me with concerned eyes.

"Did it hurt? Did *he* hurt you?" Amber asked after a while.

I shook my head. From what I could remember, I hadn't even felt anything, and had I not seen them, I would have never known they were there.

"No, I—"

A loud bang followed by the rain of shattering glass suddenly cut through the silent air as the lobby door smacked hard against the yellow stopper. I turned to find Erius and Alius sprinting toward us with stark and grim expressions.

"Start the van!" Erius roared as they drew near. Before any of us could move, they were at our side, shoving us into the van and slamming the door shut.

Erius raced to the driver's side, snatching the keys from my hands as he did. Before I knew it, he was pulling the van into drive and speeding out of the lot, leaving Amber's convertible behind.

"What's going on?" Jaz shot out.

I stumbled to the passenger seat, my eyes on the door of the elevator lobby as it flew across the lot. Erius sped off, swerving around the door to cut left, narrowly missing the crumbled metal. As we passed the hole seeping of smoke and fire, a creature that likened that of a tree emerged. His deep red eyes pierced the van as he lifted his pointed, branch-like fingers toward us.

"Erius?" I called as I fell into the chair. "What's going on? What was that?"

"We have to go," he pushed through clenched teeth. His hands fisted around the wheel so tight that his knuckles grew white, and the tendons were poking out. He jerked the wheel and pulled a maneuver I never thought my van capable of as it drifted around the turn and down the ramp.

"Go where?" Jaz gasped as the van bounced and jerked with every turn Erius whipped around.

"Prometheus!" I shot frantically.

Erius waved his hand over my lap, pulling my poor cat from the mist in what was clearly a journey for him. I pulled him into my chest as the conversation continued.

"Somewhere safer," Alius supplied.

"Safer?" the girls gasped together.

I looked to Erius, his eyes on the road as he turned onto the main streets without looking for any oncoming cars.

"You said the hotel was safe!" I snapped.

"That was before your little show last night."

I thought over the creatures I had seen on my way down to the bar and while drinking, and that monster was not amongst those. I would definitely remember something that looked like that. "I never saw that creature last night! What does it have to do with me?"

Erius kept his eyes on the road, weaving between cars and cutting through traffic. "He is the one I owe something to, and he is not the most agreeable or understanding sort."

"Could you not just give it to him?" I suggested.

"No," he shot angrily. "Even if I had it in my possession, I do not know what he plans to do with it."

"*Chǔs ǔzh tǎk zhǔhu zhu?*" Alius hissed. Erius shook his head stiffly.

I looked between the two, feeling the tension that began to build. It wasn't until I turned to face the road that I realized we were getting on the freeway.

"Where are you taking us?" Amber questioned as she realized the same.

"Sorry for your involvement, ladies. I've been told you three were a part of the ritual," Alius said smoothly, a weak attempt at trying to distract them, but knowing them, nothing was going to divert their attention from what just happened. They haven't been around it near as long as I have, and even I haven't been mixed into Erius's world for too long.

"Where are we going?" Amber repeated after a long death glare to Alius.

"The Mahogany Resort," Erius said stiffly.

"That is a place, not an actual location," Jaz snapped.

"It is in Salem," Erius finally informed us.

My heart sank at the sound. Of all the places for us to go, it had to be Salem?

I pulled out my phone and looked over the message app icon. The red bubble with the big number of 52 stared at me with a heated vengeance. I pulled open the app as a reminder to why.

Parasite #2

32

Parasite #1

10

Parasite #4

5

Parasite #3
7

My thumb hovered over #2, my sister, as I contemplated opening it. The last time I had spoken with any of them, they informed me that our mother's health was declining and asked me to come home and help them all transition and finalize everything. I hadn't been in contact with them for ten years and all of a sudden, I was needed once again.

"Is there any other place?" I asked blankly.

"It is the entrance to the Circles. Paris would be next, but Alaura is not trying to meet us in Paris. She will be in Salem in three days, it will take us two to get there," Alius informed us from the back.

"Less if we can find a better vehicle," Erius added.

"I can't just dump my van!" I shot.

"I think I may be able to help, Meems," Mickey said. Everyone's heads turned to her. It was the first time she had spoken the entire escape as she strangely sat ever so calmly at Alius's side.

"I—uh—can shrink things," she said with a shrug.

Alius perked up in his spot, his gaze brightening with curiosity as he looked over her.

Erius considered it with a stiff nod. "Problem solved."

"Problem not solved. My family lives in Salem and I've been working to avoid them," I informed him.

"Then do that. We are not there for a social visit. No one even needs to know you are there."

I don't know how he expected to do that in a small town when we had to wait, at most, a day and a half for Alius's niece.

"Do we have a say in this adventure or are we now captives?" Amber shot from her place on the bed.

"It is best you come with us," Alius answered flatly. Jaz and Amber turned to him with furrowed brows, but Mickey gazed at him with equal admiration as he was her.

"Why?" Amber snapped.

"Would you rather we left you to deal with what tore that door off its hinges?" he countered just as quickly.

His words sent a noticeable chill over her body as she shook her head.

"Having taken powers from Erius, you are linked to him in a way that could be traced. You would have been a distraction for only a moment," Alius said darkly.

"You mean he's tracking us?" Mickey squeaked.

"Do not fear, little dove. He has no clue where we are headed, and by the time he learns of it, their tether will be broken and Erius can lead him away from you," Alius said in a smooth, comforting voice.

My chest tightened at the words, a returning feeling that sunk my heart and twisted my stomach. It was time I stopped refusing to see it for what the feeling was: a nervousness or maybe anxiety in not wanting to be apart. Whatever it may have been, I just knew I didn't want to break the tether even if that means I couldn't go a mile from him. I didn't ever want to.

I could get over the possibility of seeing my siblings; they were in fact easily avoidable. But what was not avoidable was Alius's niece breaking the tether.

What was I even going to do in a world full of mortals when I was no longer one? Work a desk job? Eat men on the weekends and file papers on the weekday, thoughts that only sunk my heart further.

"Mortal?" Erius whispered "It will all work out."

Chapter Thirty-Five

Mira

We made it as far as Vegas before Erius was fed up with the speed of the van and demanded we collect a better car. Alius assured us that the creature they called Dazron only had a handful of locations he could step foot on and no way of travel, allowing us to breathe easy on our journey to meet his niece.

The brightly lit city seemed less interesting when you took the back streets down the less pleasant parts of town, something Erius seemed to know well enough to navigate around. He pulled into a dimly lit dirt parking lot with a suspicious-looking portable building that had several closed storage garages lined in the back.

"Ah, still in contact with Fletch?" Alius broke away from Mickey for a moment as he came over to look out the windshield.

I couldn't help but notice Alius had fawned over Mickey as he sat beside her, talking her up about her life and what she did. It was actually pretty sweet. How he and Erius were friends was beyond me because Erius seemed so much less friendly upon introduction.

"Only for transportation," Erius said as he pulled us to a park. He looked around the van, stopping at me. "Stay here… Please." He stood and beckoned Alius to join him as they left us in the van.

"Mina, what is going on?" Jaz asked as she came to sit beside me.

"Alius has this niece that is supposed to be some powerful witch that can help break our tether. As for the Dazron situation, I have no clue."

"No, Meems. I mean between you and Erius," she whispered. I looked to her with furrowed brows. She could already see it so I didn't know why she was asking. It's not like it was a big deal.

"We had sex," I droned slowly.

She dropped her head to the side. "I think we could all see that. It's all around you." She watched something I couldn't see floating around my head with interest.

"Is it that loud?" I looked around, searching the empty space for something I already knew I couldn't see.

She watched whatever it was she saw with great intent as she spoke. "It was a show for the first few weeks. They were clashing but not mixing. Now, I hate to say it, but it's the most beautiful color mix I have ever seen."

"Why didn't you say anything before when they were clashing? What does that even mean?"

She looked back to Amber and Mickey who were gushing about Alius before turning back to me with a shrug. "It looked like something you two needed to figure out yourselves. And I was waiting to see what would happen when they mixed."

"You didn't seem too concerned," I poked.

Her eyes glistened as she looked over the invisible fog around me. "Hey, if you want to fuck a demon, who am I to tell you not to? I don't think it's wise and I didn't think you'd let him feed off you like that. I didn't even know demons drank blood."

"I don't think he did much more than bite me." Though I didn't really ask at the time, but now that she brought it up, it wouldn't hurt to know for sure.

"Yeah, did you even clean it? It looks infected," she said as she looked over the wound.

"Erius didn't give me too much information about it." Not that I had asked many questions after the whole *"I'm a selfish creature"* statement he had made.

"I think it just makes me smell like him more," I thought aloud.

"What?"

"It's hard to explain. He needed everyone in the hotel under the impression we were together so they wouldn't try anything."

"Like what?" Jaz pressed with a disgusted sneer.

I shrugged. "Eating me, I guess."

Amber and Mickey's conversation cut short as they all turned to look at me with wide eyes. "Mina, what Hell have you been living in the last week?" Amber cut in.

"I wouldn't call it Hell. It was all fascinating and interesting. I even got a little book with some history of his world." The mention of the book suddenly reminded me that I had left it in the flat with all my other things. But that wasn't a bad thing, not anymore.

"Watch this!" I focused my intent. If I could manifest two dresses I had never owned, I was sure I could conjure my belongings back, even from this distance. I circled my hand around until the green flame appeared, keeping my focus on the things I had left behind and creating a green fog as Erius did. When the fog drifted away, my luggage appeared around the van, including the book which landed in my lap.

The van filled with a wave of *ohs* and *wows* and hushed gasps.

"How'd you learn that?" Jaz asked.

"Erius showed me. You should try it. I'm sure you'll need a change of clothes soon."

"How are you so sure we can do it, too?" Amber quizzed.

I shrugged, not sure if it would work for them or not. But it wouldn't hurt them to try. Truthfully, I had been so consumed in my own power that I hadn't even checked on the extent of theirs.

They did as I did, holding their hands out before them. Each one of them closed their eyes with various looks of concentration on their call. Within seconds, their hands lit up with flames and mist in varies shades of purple, pink, and orange. They maintained focus without notice of their new flames, pushing the energy through their palms until tightly stuffed shoulder bags appeared in their laps.

"Shit! I didn't know we could do this," Jaz cheered.

The door slid open with a whoosh, and the men stepped in.

"Gather what things you need. Tie down what you do not," Erius ordered.

Alius walked by Mickey with a soft smile. "You mentioned something about mass manipulation?" He asked her.

Jaz turned from them to me with a soft smile and waved a hand around her head as if to present the aura around them. Probably a silly sight from the outside, but it was clear she saw what was evident to everyone else.

"Yes. Well, I had been practicing with fox skulls and grasshopper heads," she admitted.

"Dear, those are a bit small. Are you sure you can—" Amber began.

"I am sure she will do lovely. Come, let us put your things in the car," Alius encouraged as he took Mickey by the hand and led her out.

"Will we all even fit in this new car?" I asked Erius.

"It's a Lexus RX. Fletch said it was the fastest he had for all of us."

"I wouldn't know, as you know," I reminded jokingly.

His lips twitched at a smile. "Yes, your lack of knowledge in motor vehicles." He grabbed the bag and helped me pack things. He even handed me my bonnet from the hook and my Kindle from my pillowcase. Not sure how he knew that was where I kept it, but that was a topic for another day. Once everything was packed away, I scooped up my sweet boy and headed out to join everyone else.

Amber and Jaz stood by the silver Lexus, admiring the interior as they placed everything in it. Alius stood near Mickey as she explained her practice of shrinking fox skulls and enlarging grasshopper heads. The fox skull I wouldn't mind watching, but I could do without a monster-sized hopper head.

"Alius and I will alternate driving," Erius informed us, squeezing everything into the open spots before leaning over me with his weighing energy. His eyes scanned over my dress with a growing smile. "Sit with me in the back. Alius wishes to sit with Meklit. He fancies her."

"Yeah, I gathered that," I giggled.

He gently trailed his finger down my cheek and hooked under my chin. "Are you hungry?" he asked softly.

"Oop!" Jaz gasped.

"Let's go watch the van shrink," Amber whispered next as they walked off.

"Hm, I am surprised they did not accuse me of harming you," he mused.

"Oh, they did. Amongst other things," I said, shutting the trunk to the car. "I told them you did something I asked for, so I don't think they will be bothering you about it."

We rejoined our small new group as Meklit held her hands out in front of her. She spoke in Kanuri, which I knew to be her grandmother's native language, and she had mentioned a lot of her journals were written in it.

She waved her hands out in front of her, creating the same orange flame as before. The wisps shot out of her fingers, wrapping around my van like tight gripping tendrils. The chanting continued as the flames constricted my home, shrinking it down with a horrendous crumpling sound as it morphed to the size of a toy RC car. Once the vibrating stopped, I picked it up with two hands, being extremely careful not to tilt it or shake it up too much as I gently set it in my bag.

"Get that packed away, and we will head off. I am sure you all don't mind if we grab food on the way out of town," Alius said smoothly.

"Oh, finally! I actually haven't eaten since this morning," Amber admitted.

I hadn't really thought about it over the last few hours, but Erius and I never even made it out to breakfast before all this.

"I'm sure there is something to get before we get back on the freeway," I suggested, pulling my phone from my pocket to look for the closest place. Around the corner from our current location and right before the freeway entrance we would need to get onto anyway sat a fast food stop.

It would have to do.

"There is a Sonic not even a mile away. Let's get that and go."

"Ugh, my ass hurts," Jaz complained to Amber as she tried to find comfort with the limited space she had. Alius and Erius switched sometime after we entered Utah, and in doing so, I switched spots with Mickey as she took rest in the far back with Alius.

Jasmine, Amber, and Prometheus took up the middle row, struggling to get their work schedules and affairs in order for this sudden out of state trip.

I waited until they were all asleep and night darkened the sky before asking Erius for the explanation I thought I was well owed.

"What's going to happen after the tether is broken?"

"It all depends on what we can do about you being a *Nipans*. As I see it, whether we break the tether or not, it looks like in some way or another, we are still connected."

I looked back to Alius whose eyes were now open and staring out the window.

"What about his sister?"

"You would need to go to the Circles for more—" Alius began.

"No," Erius growled instantly.

"And that is why I had not brought it up just yet."

I looked between the two, reacting to unspoken words that they both seemed to understand.

"I would like to go if I can help find out more about what I am," I said.

"It is dangerous enough for you here. But in the Circles, where everyone is going to want to kill you, capture you or study you, it is not as if they will sit you down and ask you how you are feeling. There are tests they will force you to perform."

"Nobody would force her to do anything. Do not be so overly sensitive about it. *Mich mŭpfutsham rŭb bup moi bekkoù pàt tŭn, biech,*" Alius said with curved lips.

Erius shot another discerning look over his shoulder. The blue glow of the car's dash shined off the light glow of his eyes.

Both were probably right, but at the end of the day, it was really my choice to go—if needed. As they put it, there was nothing known about what I was, and if I could help those who sought answers to find them, I would.

"I recall you agreeing to start your drive once the sun broke. Maybe you should rest," Erius told Alius. After a low chuckle, the cramped space fell silent once more.

"You should sleep as well," he suggested.

One of the few times I wasn't going to argue. After the day we'd had, sleep was a wanted escape for once.

By the time we made it to Denver, everyone was begging for a moment to stretch outside of the car. We stopped to grab food before pulling into a dirt lot. The patchy dry grass covered the field with two netless soccer goals on either end, a park that had long since seen better days. Trees enclosed us all around, making for a perfect spot to stay out of view.

In the distance sat a horribly rusty metal slide with three broken steps on the ladder. The swings were just crusty chains hanging from the large bar, and the sandbox had weeds growing out of it. All and all it was safe to say no one visited the ghostly park.

We sat at a table riddled in Sharpie and graffiti of various tags and slurs. Perhaps not the best place to rest for most, but we sought seclusion.

We pulled out our food, and the smell should have been enough to tell me that the taste was going to be trash, but I was not one to notice red flags right out the gate.

I took a bite of the dry burger, scrunching my face at the instant regret. Without drawing notice from the others, I spat the half-chewed slop into a napkin and set it all aside. Not that I would have been able to enjoy it in peace had it been edible. The crawling itch began creeping along my skin and up my throat until my mouth grew sticky and dry.

I itched at my arm aggressively until I was paused by a rough, warm hand. "Are you alright?"

"My mouth burns," I choked out.

Erius stopped to look over me. "Are you *hungry?*" he quizzed with a teasing grin. He didn't mean hungry for mortal food, it had been a few days since my last hunt in my demon form and I was sure I needed to alternate my diet and feed that form a bit more often.

"Yeah," I drone slowly.

A large smile split his face as he checked over his shoulder to the group. Before I could turn to look as well, he tugged me off behind the patch of trees.

"Go on then, change," he ordered once we were out of sight.

"Why did we come over here?"

He looked around the trees out to the center field where everyone else sat laughing and joking for the time. "Did you want your friends to know what your form eats—or how it eats?" Even if I didn't care about what I was now eating, Mickey was extremely squeamish, Jaz would make jokes about it, and Amber would just find it disgusting. Regardless, I would have to mention it at some point to them.

"Maybe some other time." I changed over, delighted at how easy it seemed with each conscious shift. Erius changed next, pushing us into the darkest parts of the shadows, cover for only him since I had fur. We hadn't hunted in the middle of the day when people could clearly see, and it wasn't like we wandered into an extremely secluded place.

"Stay low, there are hunters out and about," he warned.

"I'm not sure it is the right season for goat hunting," I commented.

He turned to me with a stark expression, clear confusion on my knowledge of Denver hunting laws, an unfortunate outcome of my father's yearly hunting trips. At least that was what he told my mom.

"Well, be that as it may, not all mortals follow the law as you well know and you look like a rare creature from afar," he warned.

Yes, a human goat hybrid with the fluidity of a feline—very rare. I crouched down, creeping along the brush as I listened to our surroundings. Erius lurked behind me, enjoying his little show as always.

Beside the soft conversation from the field we left was a low crunching of leaves in the far distance. We turned to face the noise, moving in sync as we stalked through the thinning cluster of trees.

"Shh! Do you hear that?" a man said.

"Dad!" a young girl whined next, "can we please go home?"

The scent surrounding them didn't exactly scream meal for me. I lowered myself to the ground and ducked under a bush while Erius morphed into the shadows to allow them to pass on. From my position I could see the florescent orange hunting hat over the tops of the leaves as they left the path, taking their overly floral scent along with them.

"I take it neither of them matched your taste," he teased as he crept out from behind a tree.

"No," I said flatly. Pine and lavender smelled more like a chemical fragrance than an edible one, and they both were drenched in the sickening scents, "He seemed like a present father. We should go somewhere where there are more fucked up men."

His lips curved up as he reached for me. "I know just the place. We must run." He took my hand, and we sped off through the trees. It wasn't a long run. It felt as if just as my speed got picked up, we were at a sudden stop by a fence line. The mouth-watering scent hit me instantly, filling my head with a mindless fog. I took a step forward only to be pulled back once more.

"Where are we?" I hissed.

"Denver Department of Corrections."

"A prison?" My voice cracked from my dry throat.

"Yes. Even most of the guards have a black mark to them. A pen full of prey, just for us," he explained.

"How do we get in?"

"Do not worry on that." He held out his hand for me, ready to lead me into a literal human buffet. "Change back for a moment." His horns receded into his skull and his skin melted away to present his mortal form. I did the same, adjusting my clothes from the run. When I was situated and didn't look like I had just ran through the woods, we made our way across the street.

We arrived at the copper red entrance with the words "Denver Department of Corrections" plastered in an ugly, mustard yellow hung beside the main entrance. Erius tightened his grip on my hand as we stepped in and walked up to the front desk.

"Visitation is on Thursdays," the guard grunted without looking up from his computer.

"Is that so?" Erius quizzed with a deepening voice. The lights above us flashed as the outside world darkened around the building. Between the flashes I could feel my body begging to shift back as the drawing scent grew more tantalizing and my mouth flooded with saliva.

The man finally looked up, fear quickly marking his face. Erius reached over the counter and placed his finger on the guard's forehead. Without another word, the man mindlessly lifted a ring of keys to Erius. The temperature around us dropped as my demon returned to his hunting form, snatching the keys with a distorted cackle.

I released my own hold as it clawed to break free. He pulled me along through the first door, using the shadows and flickering lights to our advantage as we trucked through the empty halls.

"Where are all the guards?" I asked.

"Tending to the cell blocks. A lot can happen when the power fails in a prison. Now, lead the way." He released my hand and allowed me to seek out the cell block worth our attention.

I knew nothing about the layout of prisons, let alone this particular one, yet the smell of roasted meat carried me, moving my feet in whatever direction it called. We crept down the flickering hall toward a thick red door that looked to be made of strong metal. But the barrier didn't halt the strong scent that seeped from it.

"Through there," I said.

Erius stepped to the door without hesitation and gripped the handle. With a loud crack, the metal broke in his grasp and the door slowly opened.

Blaring sirens began to sound at the vandalization, but it didn't seem to bother Erius as he remained perfectly calm. We moved between the darkest parts of the shadows as I led us to the bottom cell block where the scent flooded the floor like a pool—a bowl full of evil intent.

The rambunctious whooping quickly died to hushed whimpers as Erius and I stepped to the middle of the block. Several cells surrounded us with nothing more than a four-inch window to view the horrified captives inside. Each passing second that they gaped at us flooded the room with a more concentrated mix of smells. The engrossing scent of summer BBQ tugged at all my senses, setting my nerve endings on fire with the anticipation of what was to come. My tail whipped violently from one side to the other as I tried to pinpoint the most delicious prize.

Faces of the captured men pressed against the small windows of their doors. Contorted features twisted into horrific, eyeless creatures. I slowly spun around, eyeing each fear-filled inmate until I spotted one who looked less fearful, if at all.

I lunged forward toward the door, eyeing the man with growing hunger. He shrunk back a step or two but maintained eye contact with me. The sweet scent of fear rolled off him, yet he remained detached from it all as he watched me, filling his room with mouthwatering goodness. I inhaled deeply as I inched for the handle.

"This one," I breathed.

Erius shot his hand out to grip the lock and tore it free with ease as he had with the last. The tantalizing smell pulled me in before the man had a moment to realize what was happening. I was at his back with his head tightly gripped between my clawed hands. His body shook rapidly but he said nothing. Not even a whimper escaped his tightly sealed lips while Erius slunk up to him.

"Again with the neck snapping?" he chuckled grimly.

"It's the quickest way," I groaned.

The man's shaking intensified, yet he still did not scream.

"Yes, but do you not ever wish to enjoy the kill?"

"Not really." I shrugged stiffly with a tightening grip. Finally, the man let out a groaning gasp.

Erius shook his head as he looked at him, "You, what was your crime?"

"What?" the man pushed between gasps.

"Your crime. What was it?" Erius asked again.

"Do answer him!" I snapped. My stomach ached and my mouth

burned. I could feel my hands tightening around the man's skull with each second that ticked by.

"Tell me," Erius ordered in a deep growl.

Despite his racing heart and heaving chest, the man remained silent.

"Hm, a silent one," Erius mused with a slight nod.

Through with the games, I flicked my wrists, whipping the man's head to the side with a sharp snap. Erius sighed heavily as he watched the limp body crumple to the floor.

"You play too much!" I snipped, straightening out the body.

"I am only interested in seeing what it is you crave from him." He chuckled as he bent down to pull the soul free.

"The fact they all had a record of violence isn't enough?" I questioned, ripping open the jumpsuit to free the man's extending belly.

Erius consumed the soul as he did the others, absorbing it into his skin so that it joined the other cluster of soul stars. I used my claws to slice into him and rushed to grab what I could before the other inmates could figure out whose cell was busted and the guards could come down. With no time to enjoy any of it, I devoured what I could and we exited through an emergency door that led from the cell block to a shaded alleyway that took us out to the main street.

"That is convenient yet dangerous," I said, licking the blood from my hands as my form shifted back.

"Alius should be here," Erius whispered.

"What?" I shot as I turned to him.

He looked down at me with a pleased grin before smearing his thumb over my chin to wipe away the last of the blood. I figured he'd taste it like he did the last time, but he just smeared it on my already stained shirt. He pulled his hand back for a quick inspection before throwing his arm over my shoulder with a low chuckle.

"I informed Alius where we were going and told him to meet us on the most deserted road. Dumb luck that the block you chose led right out to it." His devilish smile twisted at his lips.

Before I could wipe myself clean, he grabbed my face between his hands and bent his head until his lips were on mine, licking up the remaining blood from my skin while maintaining the deepening kiss. The sirens continued behind us as guards began racing around on the court and fields in search of the unseen threat. By now we looked no different than two civilians walking the sidewalk.

Erius pulled away from me with reddened lips. "You were much cleaner this time."

"Well, thanks for that," I groaned.

We watched as the cops continued to scurry about, screaming orders and code numbers, frantically looking everywhere but where we stood. Finally, the Lexus pulled up with a screeching halt and the back door swung open.

Alius looked at us from the back seat with a disapproving glare. Amber and Jaz sat in the front with wide eyes as they looked over my slightly stained clothes. Mickey was, thankfully, napping.

Erius and I climbed into the back row with the three sets of eyes still locked on us.

"Is that your doing?" Amber asked as she nodded toward the scrambling guards in the field.

"In a way," I admitted. Erius and I quickly used our mists to change from the soiled clothes into something cleaner and less riddled with death. Once we were buckled into place, Jaz pulled off from the curb following the navigation at hand.

"So much for us switching off," Erius scoffed to Alius.

"So much for you two maintaining a low profile. What is that?" Alius waved his hand over to the frantic guards now making their way inside.

"This facility held the worst of the worst. I am trying to find out what it is she desires," Erius explained.

"Did you learn anything?" Amber asked curiously.

"No. She snapped his neck before I could find anything out." Erius sighed disapprovingly.

"Mina!" Jaz and Amber shot as they spun around to face me.

"I can't help what I do in that form. Lions need to eat lambs," I countered.

"So, is this what you do now?" Jaz asked. I could see how it would be discomforting to them. They weren't a hybrid, illegal creature. I doubted it would be able to be reversed seeing as how I was also an unknown on top of it all.

"This is my life now." I shrug. "I can't help it. It's like an uncontrollable need once the smell hits me."

"But you're eating people, Meems," Amber whined.

"Just men—and it's not like they are even innocent men. One was a registered sex offender, two of them killed their wives, another was—"

"Another?" Jaz interjected with widening eyes. "There's more?"

"There is an endless supply of mortals with an essence as dark as the night sky. Look at it as if she is cleansing the earth," Erius explained.

Chapter Thirty-Six

Mira

After another two days of driving and stopping to rest, eat, and hunt, we finally arrived in Salem. It had been years since I had last stepped foot in my hometown, dreading the day I'd ever come back. Nothing had changed over the years. Even the smell remained the same heavy scent of bitter magnolia and musky earth pine.

Alius drove to an antique-looking building that sat beside the town cemetery. During my childhood, the building had been rumored to be haunted and most certainly vacant, a fact that soon fell clear in Jaz's mind as she turned to look at me with concern. At this point, it wouldn't surprise me if it was another hidden demon hotel of some sort.

We pulled into an empty lot and parked near the front boarded-up entrance. "Keep Out. Haunted" was sloppily written in red spray paint along the plywood that covered the doors.

"Are we walking from here?" Amber guessed as she looked around.

"No. This is the Mahogany Resort entrance," Alius informed her with a cheery grin.

"But this place is boarded up. Mina, what is this? Are you sure it's safe?" Amber turned to me, ready to ignore any protest from the men. Mickey and Jaz turned with the same questioning expression which is understandable. They got tugged along with two men they didn't know, miles away from home and now they were being told a busted down building was where we would be staying. I'd have concerns, too, if I hadn't already seen what their magic was capable of with my own eyes.

The men smirked at each other before exiting the car to wait.

"Look, I know it all seems weird as fuck. But I'm positive the inside isn't nearly as bad. I promise," I said with a convincing smile. All I had to go off of was the appearance and layout of the last demon hotel I was captive in. And that one was attached to a fully occupied building.

They chewed over the idea, with no hint of fear—mostly agitation and mistrust which were completely valid for them. I fucked up and they were dealing with it just as much as I was.

When they felt sure enough, we all climbed out to grab our bags before meeting with Erius and Alius again.

"I am sure Erius has already had this discussion with little bird, so she should be familiar with what will be beyond these doors. You three lovelies, I must warn. Once we cross this threshold, you enter a realm that dances the line between your world and the Circles. Try to maintain composure. Mortals are not welcome beyond this point, as it is the main entrance. Lucky for us all, you four are no longer '*mortal.*' At least, not in the sense the resort will care to see. From here on, the four of you are sorceresses by birth. Never been mortal a day in your existence. Understand?" Alius explained kindly.

We nodded and watched as he ran his hand down the panel nailed to the door. Before our eyes, the plywood and red writing faded to present a thick dark wood entrance with a heavy gloss finish and stained-glass windows along the side.

He opened the door to present a brightly lit lobby that smelled heavily of mahogany. Natural light poured in onto the dark tile that reflected the several oval-shaped chandeliers that hung above. We walked down a long entryway lined with tropical potted plants on either side of us. A long, black reception desk sat at the far end of the lobby.

Behind it hung a lovely set of ivy vines that rained down over a large opening in the wall that led to a separate office. With a swift flick, Alius rang the small bell on the countertop.

The echoing ring bounced off the tiles and walls, fading slowly to nothing. Once the reverberations cleared, a tall woman with snow-white hair and violet-colored eyes slipped through the parting plants to greet us.

"Hello," she greeted with a thick accent.

Alius greeted her in return before pausing. "How many rooms will we need?" he asked as he turned to the group.

Erius's hand quickly found purchase at my waist as he tugged me closer. "I need to ensure you don't sneak out and go on a hunting spree," he whispered into my ear.

I suppressed a groan and pushed down the desperate need that began to grow between my legs before he could sense it. But by the grip of his hand around me, I could tell I was too late.

"We will take our own room," Mickey informed sweetly, gesturing to Amber and Jaz.

Alius nodded with a faint smile before turning back to the receptionist. "Three rooms please."

"Would you like those joined or separate?" she asked as she began typing on the computer.

Alius shot a glance back to Erius. "Separate will do. Thank you."

She typed away some more before announcing the fee to us. Alius pulled out a small sack and spilled its noisy contents into his palm. He picked out three golden crescent-shaped coins and dropped them into her hands. With a nod, she looked over the pieces before carefully placing them in a drawer at the desk and stepped to the back room for a few moments before returning with three old-styled keys.

"Alright. Rooms 731, 727, and 724," she announced as she placed each key down with the corresponding room. Erius plucked up the one for 727 and returned to my side. Alius scooped up the remaining two and handed one to Mickey before leading us up to floor seven.

The halls of the hotel were far from outdated or untended as it looked from the outside. It was a building that was very much in operation and well-kept with dust-free chandeliers and glossy tabletops that lined the hall. Greek-styled vases filled with flowers sat spread out between the black tables along the side, and paintings depicting times throughout the ages decorated the walls.

We stopped at the room marked 724, which happened to be the

girls' suite. Jaz unlocked the door and pushed it open to present a luxury flat with three beds and a turn-off that led deeper in. From what I could see, it was spacious enough for several more people to sleep in. With wide eyes and no goodbye, see you later or anything, Amber and Jaz wandered into the room while Mickey and Alius parted with a lengthy goodnight.

Before they could finish, Erius was tugging me into our own room. Though our suite was just as big as the first looked, we had one bed to share. I plopped on the mattress, snapping my fingers to call Prometheus and his carrier into the room. With a quick glance around, it was easy to see this was some sort of honeymoon-like suite. Aside from the single bed and questionably placed mirror above it, a whirlpool tub sat in the corner by the window overlooking the center court garden.

I shot a narrowed glance Erius's way as he busied himself with what was in the mini fridge. I wondered if he had picked this room knowing it looked like this. But he looked at some of the amenities with confusion.

"Am I yours here as well?" I sighed after a moment.

A rumbling laugh filled the room as he pulled a bottle of wine from the fridge. "You make it sound as if you are property."

"Well, when you go around calling me yours, pulling me around, and not allowing people to touch me without some sort of physical assault coming their way, it makes a woman think."

"It ensures your safety. Anyone may find you to be their next meal or play toy or any number of things. I need them to see a claim placed on you in some form."

"So, I am yours while we are here?" I pushed a second time.

He paused pouring the drinks to look over me. His brows pinched at the center and his lips pressed flat, flashing his gaze to the mark on my neck and back. "You are simply *mine* anywhere we go. That is all anyone should be aware of."

"But, I mean, when this is done? When the tether is broken, what are we doing?"

He handed me the glass without a word and took a long sip of his own.

"You don't have to answer. I just feel if you are going to go around, snapping arms of people who touch me, and biting me to show claim, that makes me something more to you."

"Do you like when people touch your things?" he asked defensively.

"Ah, so I'm a thing! That's better than being—I don't know—a pet. Mortals don't usually fornicate with their pets and those that do are frowned upon, Erius. Will you be frowned upon?"

"You are not my pet, and you are no longer a full mortal," he reminded me. "Now, would you like to eat?"

The question brought an immediate rumble to my stomach that curved his lips up. "I thought you would. Get ready, we will be leaving the hotel to eat."

"Why do we need to leave?" I didn't mean for my voice to crack the way it did, but I didn't want to chance running into any of my siblings.

"Because I do not want to risk anyone seeing me and recognizing this form," he said but something about his reason sounded incomplete. I considered the likeliness my four siblings would be out in the exact spot I was. They hardly tore themselves from our mother's side for anything more than shopping and work, which was all on the other end of town, a decent distance from us. With years between our last visual encounter, I would hope they had forgotten most of my features since they didn't liken their own to begin with.

They all had dark brown to black hair, whereas I was born with the blondest curls. My skin was a few shades darker than theirs, which matched both our mother's and father's. Since our last visit, my style has drastically changed, and I stopped dyeing my hair black to fit under my mother's standards. Not that she didn't like my blonde hair. At least she never said it aloud. But she made consistent statements about how I didn't match the rest of them in more ways than one. That was the only thing she ever got right about me, that I was different from them, and I was so glad I continued to be.

After the short convincing, I nodded to Erius and we both changed into something we hadn't been sitting in for the last few days.

We hadn't really had time to talk about the night he bit me or really even a moment to talk about breaking the tether since that was what we were here for, after all.

My stomach ached at the thought. Not that I didn't want to be free; I just wasn't sure what that meant for him and I. If he would just return home, leaving me to teach myself and curb my own hunger. He said he'd stay to ensure his safety, but what did that mean for me?

I attempted to stamp down the feeling that nagged at my stomach as I pulled on my black lace skirt. I buttoned up the sheer bell sleeve top and fluffed out my hair before heading out.

Erius waited at the foot of the bed, adjusting his sleeves to their usual place below his elbow. When he caught sight of me at the doorway he paused, sweeping his eyes over me with a slack jaw. He put his hands in his pockets with a deep inhale. "Well, are you ready?"

I made my way over to his side with a soft nod. The frost blue changed to the mortal shade he sported and held up a hand. I was ready for him to tug me from the room and lead the way out. Instead, he brought my hand to his face and placed a gentle kiss over my knuckles.

"I know you must think this is all for show. But I have…grown fond of you," he admitted.

As much as his words sent chills through my body and sent my heart pounding into my chest, I couldn't shake the feeling he only felt that way because of this tether. Either way, I was literally a dot in his life, and with what little I did know of him, I was more than likely some weird phase he was going through.

"Ok, let's go then." I tried to pull my hand down, but his grip didn't offer a moment of retreat. His eyes flickered with a devilish smirk that sent the heated fluttering through my chest in a violent attack. I sucked in a deep breath in an attempt to steady the feeling, but Erius was already chuckling in amusement. He placed another unreasonably soft kiss on the top of my hand before turning to lead me out.

Dinner was no different than it had been back in L.A. with all the people staring as if we were some unlikely pair, stammering over their words and whatnot, just embarrassing themselves. Not that it took away from what was very much a date—and who knew a demon could be more romantic than any male mortal?

After we paid the check for dinner, we walked along the path heading in the opposite direction of my childhood home. It wasn't until we were passing by that I realized the very occult shop that had gotten me into my practice was still up and running. It had the same old flickering fluorescent sign in the window. Once we hit the curb, I grabbed Erius by the hand and we made our way over.

We stepped in and I was surprised to see that little had changed since my last visit over ten years ago—newly painted walls and shelves but the coffin-shaped bookcase and display tables remained true and strong.

"Welcome in," a young girl called from the back. I thanked her and continued to look over the crystal collection.

"I can't believe this place is still here," I muttered to myself.

"Did you come here often?" Erius asked curiously as he followed me around the table. He did look over the crystals and books when I drew near them but mostly he kept close.

"Sort of. My mom and dad didn't really let me get out of the house much. I was always on babysitter duty for my younger siblings. But my uncle had brought me here whenever he and my cousin were visiting. Danni is younger than me, so she didn't really understand. To her it was fantasy magic. But it resonated with me in a way I couldn't find anywhere else. And when he died, it was his spirit that led me to necromancy and aiding others in speaking with their past loved ones." It was more personal information than I had ever given him, but it felt right to share something after so long.

He didn't ask anything else after that as he followed behind me, holding whatever I handed him. I ended up grabbing a few bags of herbs, some crystal shards, and a new cauldron to test some of the spells I had highlighted in the Death Magic book during the trip over. I paid with the last of the mortal cash I had left, not that it mattered, and we headed back to the street.

Perhaps the trip here wouldn't be so bad. The mixed scent of sage and myrrh was surprisingly calming. I guessed they had no rosemary lit to attack my senses, thankfully.

All in all, the evening was proving to be less stressful than I had expected. With no sight of my family and a visit to the only happy place I had here, I was able to find my center again. It was crazy to think all this time I had been fearless and anxious about nothing, but my family troubles were probably more powerful than demon magic. Only the wickedest of families could master such a feat.

We crossed at the light and headed back to the resort, discussing some of the spells I hoped to try once we returned.

"Mina!" a deep voice called from behind us.

I turned around instinctively at the sound, immediately regretting my decision as my eyes landed on thick curly brown hair bouncing our way. Under the curls were a set of heated eyes stabbing into me.

Fucking fantastic. Miles.

Chapter Thirty-Seven

Mira

My youngest brother looked between Erius and me with a heated gaze, staring even harder at the matching scars along our arms.

"Have you finally gotten our messages?" he asked.

I had never been scared of any of my siblings—I was their second mom—but the small bit of guilt I used to feel over the resentment I had for them was gone, leaving nothing but the hollow feeling of indignation.

"No," I said honestly. Which he clearly didn't appreciate, but I was not sure if it was the honesty or bluntness of the response. Either way, his face turned a deep bronze as anger flooded him. He was always the short-tempered one.

"Mom needs you," he pushed through clenched teeth.

With that, I turned on my heels and marched off. I told them all when I left I didn't want to speak with them again. They had been blocked for the longest but when my mom became sick and I found out months later I unblocked them, and not for the reasons they think, I only did it so I would know when she was finally gone. When the messages started piling up, I had assumed she was.

Until I received an invitation last year to celebrate her year milestone of "defying the odds." The only odds she'd ever beat were the ones of how often she and my father could pass out high on a park bench while I watched their litter of children when I was only a child myself, cleaning themselves up only after I started high school and doting on the four children they didn't "ruin."

I didn't know how she expected me to forget all that now that she was slowly dying.

Miles called after me, meeting my pace with ease. He kept his eyes locked on me and away from the demon at my side. Every short glance stolen ended with a deep flush and returning eyes.

"Mina," he barked.

I stopped to look at him, keeping my face composed and my voice calm to not draw attention from the few people on the sidewalk. The heat of Erius's hand circled my wrists, not gripping me, but it felt as though he was waiting.

"I spent ten years helping her. She has the four of you now and I have a life." I turned again, deciding to take the long way around with my brother still on our trail.

"You aren't going to at least see her?" Miles pressed.

"For what? So she can tell me what a disappointment I am? Tell me how, despite the fact I literally gave up my childhood to raise you all, that you four somehow turned out better and I'm the fuckup? Or was she going to finally give me a reason why she didn't show up to my graduation but managed to hold off on the needle long enough to go to each and every one of your guy's plays and games? I'm sure she can pass on without having to make herself feel better before she meets her God. I'm not her Forgiveness Free Plan. It's not my job to make her feel less guilty about the way she treated me!" By the time I was finished, I was gasping for air with heaving shoulders.

Erius continued to watch wide-eyed while Miles's face deepened by three shades. His mouth hung open with nothing to say because he didn't have shit to respond with. He knew I was right, and he knew I wasn't budging on my stance.

"Then why the fuck are you here?" he blurted.

Erius stepped forward, and I paused him before anything drastic could happen. But his near chivalrous action gave me an idea.

"I wanted to show my fiancé the horrors I had to live through. I was hoping to avoid all of you. That's why I'm on this end of town. Shouldn't you be—I don't know—getting *your* mother's prescriptions?"

His eyes widened as he looked at Erius, who froze at my side.

"Take that back to Mom and let her know I didn't end up the occult whore she said I'd be." I grabbed Erius's hand and marched off down the empty sidewalk, taking the path that would lead us around the back of the seemingly abandoned building.

This time, Miles left us, taking off back toward the direction he had come from. When he was out of sight, I dropped Erius's hand and turned around to head to the front entrance.

"Why did you tell him that?" Erius asked.

"Because it would piss them all off knowing I am living a full life and don't give a fuck about them. That my decision to leave and never speak to them is why they now suffer here taking care of her. All they want is for me to go there so they can push it off on me. I guarantee you, had I gone to visit my mom, they would have given me a sob story about how she can't be left alone and they need a break. They'd all leave town and leave me with her."

"So this estrangement is because your mother was a bad one?" he asked curiously.

"I wouldn't say she was a bad mom. She was just a shitty one to me. For my brothers and sisters, she was a star parent but was an addict for most of my childhood and left me to watch them all by myself. When I turned sixteen, they decided to get clean and actually be present parents. Just not to me."

"What of your father?" he pushed next.

I looked at him from the side of my eye. I've already shared so much with him, might as well share it all now.

"He left when my uncle died and we haven't really heard from him since." I shrugged as we headed up the steps to the front entrance.

Erius grabbed the door for me as I explained the not-so-bright parts of my childhood, listening intently as we headed to the elevators and allowing me to spill everything that I had only ever told Jaz before. I was not sure if he truly cared, but he appeared to. And honestly, having someone else to tell felt like a weight had been lifted, one that I hadn't even realized was pushing me down until it was gone. The fog cleared my mind, and I could breathe deeper than I ever had.

He clicked the button to head up and while we waited for the doors to open, his phone began going off. He answered it with a short greeting before falling silent for a few minutes.

"I'll meet you there," he grunted before ending the call. He shoved the phone in his pocket and looked back at me. "Head up to the room. I'll return in a moment."

"What?" I blurted. The doors to the elevator opened as he handed off the key and walked off.

So much for our heart-to-heart, I guess.

I arrived on the seventh floor, going straight to the girls' room for a little venting. I gave the thick wood a good knock to be sure they heard and waited less than a minute before Jaz answered.

"Hey!" she said in a cheery tone, but just as soon as her smile came, it fell once she got a decent look at my face.

"One of the *pups*?" she asked. 'Pups' was the term we used to call my siblings since they were back-to-back pregnancies and each was an Irish twin with the one before and after them, like a litter.

I nodded and stepped into their flat, "Miles saw Erius and me leaving the Seeing Crystal and aggressed me about our mom. As I knew they would. Trying to get me over there and all," I complained.

Mickey and Amber sauntered into the main room from the bathroom, midway through putting on makeup.

"Where are y'all going?" I asked curiously, taking notice of Jaz's outfit and done-up locs.

"We've never been to Salem, and Jaz was going to take us to some shops. We were going to ask if you were up to it once we were all ready," Amber explained.

"Dinner sounded nice, too. Something...*mortal* to do during all of this," Mickey added.

"I don't think I'll be joining you. I already ran into my brother, so I'm just going to turn in for the night." I was tired and worn out from the irritations he caused. Risking going out and running into the rest of my siblings didn't seem like a grand outing for me.

I said goodbye and wished them a fun night as they wished for me to have a better one on our way out. The door swung open to present Alius and Erius. The heavyweight sunk to the pit of my stomach as I looked at them, knowing that we were that much closer to being tether free.

"My niece has arrived," Alius informed with a glowing smile.

The men led us through several long halls decorated with skulls of many kinds, all of which caused my skin to crawl and itch. I shoved my hands into my sides to fight the need to scratch myself. The energy that seeped off the walls and skulls ranged in feelings from being light to heavy. Some spots were thick and felt as if I were treading water while other spots were airy and free. By the time we reached a spiral stairwell, I had dug my nails so deep into my palms that all I could focus on was the stinging pain it caused.

"Remember, remain calm, and try not to speak too much. There will be few we can trust and even fewer to trust with Mina's—condition," Erius reminded.

"Condition?" I repeated.

"We do not want to even utter such words aloud until we are more than positive it is safe to do so."

We entered a room nearly identical to the front lobby, only everything was on the opposite side. The empty and silent space didn't seem to raise concern for our guides as they crossed the floor, ignoring the reception desk altogether. Opposite the desk sat a high climbing window that looked out onto a beautifully lush courtyard full of colorful flowers I had not seen in my world before. Some had enormous cruciform petals that glowed bright orange while other small flowers that resembled gray umbrellas lined the paths.

"This way," Alius said as he ducked through a door that led out to the garden court. He waited until we were all out before continuing. "We are meeting Alaura at Ion's Inn."

I wasn't sure of the history between him and his niece. It didn't seem my place to ask but I was growing exponentially interested each time he brought her up. It was clear she was hiding from something, or someone like we were. If she was as powerful as Alius claimed, someone being after her certainly checked out.

We walked around the court, staying in the shade as much as possible without being too inconspicuous as Alius led us all to this mysterious inn.

Once through the court, we entered a room with a glass dome ceiling and rounded bar at the center. A man with forest green skin and bottom protruding fangs stood behind the counter with a growing smile. The sides of his head were shaved, with long enough hair left on top to braid it down and rest over his shoulder.

"Alius, Azal! It has been some time," his deep voice bellowed from his position. Erius hushed him instantly before looking around the empty space.

Jaz grabbed my arm and whispered, "Mina, what is that?"

Amber and Mickey hung back with gaping eyes, taking in what was as shocking to them as it was to me at first.

"And who is Azal?" Amber questions softly.

"That's what they call Erius. And he said we were leaving the world we knew. You are going to see things that are…different," I reminded them flatly.

"This isn't what I imagined," Amber grumbled.

"Nothing will be," I pointed out softly before focusing back on the newcomer.

Alius and Erius stepped up to the counter and spoke with the man they called Ion, an orc by the looks of it. After a few shared words, the orc-man looked back to us with a beaming grin before nodding to Erius. They waved us over as Ion opened a hatch that allowed us behind the bar. I stepped off first, already slightly accustomed to this world as I held Jaz by the hand and guided her as she tugged along Amber and Mickey with hesitant steps.

"Ladies, nice to meet you. The name's Ion," he greeted the second we crossed in, holding out his hand to Amber with a warm smile. She shook it reluctantly and he moved down the line to each of us.

"Now, if you will follow me," he said as he led us around to the other side of the bar. He moved a few crates and boxes from the wall to present a hidden hatch against the large center pillar.

"Mind your head," he warned as he opened the small door. Alius stepped up first, holding his hand out to Mickey to assist her in, then Jaz and Amber before he entered and Erius took his place to guide me in.

"It is a wide step down," he warned. With my hand gripped in his, I ducked under the low entrance, stretching my foot down into the darkness until the tip of my shoe grazed the loose rocks.

As I lowered down onto the floor, I caught sight of an odd carving tucked up on the high left corner of the hatch. Out of sight from the frame that covered it, but with it held up and open the way it was, gave sight to a crest of some sort with what looked to be a dragon's head, but I couldn't be sure. By the time I released Erius's hand, he was jumping through, followed by Ion who shut the hatch and sealed out any light. My vision at night was better but not completely clear in my human body, leaving me partially reliant on Erius to guide me. As if to read my mind, the heat of his hand found mine to gently aid me along the narrow hall.

"Alaura arrived a few minutes before you all and has requested I close the bar down for the evening," Ion informed us as he continued to guide us through the darkness. His abrupt stop caused Amber and Jaz to pile up behind him with startled shrieks.

The girls groaned and apologized as Ion brushed it off with a smooth laugh. "We are here," he said as the small space filled with the clicks of the changing lock. The door opened to a small but bright room, illuminated only by the torches and odd number of candles scattered around. The walls and ancient-looking stone pillars flanked the room with a sizable granite carved table in the center that housed more candles clustered about the top.

Beyond the flames, with her arms resting upon the table, sat a young girl with deep brown skin. Her dark curls were pulled from her face with a golden wrap while some free strands fell over her shoulders. Her eyes remained closed, unaware of our presence as she took slow, steady breaths, stuck in her own meditative trance that didn't seem much different than how us mortals did it.

"Alaura!" Alius exclaimed as he rushed to her side. Her eyes shot open and instantly locked with his.

"*Bif!*" she cried out with a shaky voice as she jumped from her seat. They threw their arms around each other with tear-filled eyes. Clearly this was a long-awaited reunion all on account of a silly little tether.

"Your mother is worried about you!" Alius whispered to her.

"Yes, I knew she would be," she said, pulling away to turn to the rest of us. "But your serpent mentioned something about the '*sacred dragon head?*'" She looked at me, the corner of her lips turning up. "Is this her?"

"Yes. Well, it is more of the tether that connects them. Once you release it, then you may ask her your questions," Alius informed.

Alaura turned to her uncle with an instant downturn of her lips. "Yes, of course. Please sit, everyone."

We all took our seats around the table, Erius and I together as she inspected the scars over both our arms. She traced her fingers delicately over the swirls on each of our wrists with a deep pinch at the center of her brows.

"Hm?" she hummed to herself. It didn't seem too convincing. "You say she was intoxicated and misspoke the scripture?" Alaura asked, her eyes locked on the scars.

"That is the only thing that makes sense. I haven't a scripture in the book for such a tether," Erius informed.

"Hmmm," she hummed again as she finished tracing our scars, examining her fingers as if there were residue left. She rubbed the invisible substance between them as she thought. "Do you have the book with you?"

"The last time I saw the book was on the floor of the van the morning I woke up to find Erius. Since then, he has had it." I pointed to him, already twirling his black vapor above his palm. When the smog cleared, it left behind the dusty old book in his hand.

"*Vŭkbik*. Perfect," Alaura said with a thick accent as she took it from him. She inspected the cover with a fading grin. "Hm, how did you come by this?" She opened it, turning each page with caution.

"It showed up at my job a few weeks ago. It was extremely— um—drawing in a sense, like it wanted me to use it. It's what we used to bring him," I explained.

Alaura looked over the pages with a twisting expression. "What was your purpose in summoning him?" she inquired.

"Well, we were a bit drunk when we had the idea originally, and it sort of escalated from there."

"Mina is the one who set the deal, we were passed out," Amber added as she gestured to Jaz, Mickey, and herself.

Alaura continued to look over the pages, not seeming to find what she was looking for. "Do you happen to remember which page?" she asked me.

"I think it was the one covered in charcoal."

Alaura turned a few more pages before landing on the one in question. She searched the seemingly blank page in confusion which didn't make me feel any more confident.

"Are you sure this is the page?" She flipped the page to search both sides, finding nothing but the black residue smeared over the old parchment.

"Yup, that's the one. The words weren't there one minute and then, when we looked for a ritual, they appeared," I explained.

She placed her hand flat on the page, and within moments the book illuminated, engulfing the pages in a white light. Alaura's eyes lit in the same fashion. Her lips began moving as if she were speaking but no sounds were heard. When the glowing died down and the theatrics were over, Alaura's brows pinched at the center.

"Hm. Interesting," she murmured, still analyzing the page as if something were going to appear. Yet it remained blank with nothing but black charcoal dust.

"Since it wasn't in the scripture, there's nothing about how to reverse it through this. But I know a ritual that might work." She didn't sound as confident as Alius made her seem.

"And if that does not work?" Erius probed.

Alaura was silent for a minute, her faint smile twitching to a frown for the briefest moment.

"It is for common bindings, not tethers. We will start with that." She turned to Alius. "Can you send a serpent to my mother for me? It is too risky I send one in my name. If A'trox got word I was this near the entrance, he would send his disgusting *dwau* for me."

"What is it he wants with you?" Alius asked, but Alaura began shooing him into another room.

"Never you mind. Now listen closely…" Her voice trailed off behind the door as she slammed it shut.

"What does *'send a serpent'* mean?" Mickey asked innocently, breaking the short-term silence.

"It is how the residents send messages to each other. You lot had a similar system not too long ago with carrier pigeons," Erius explained. The room went silent again while we waited for the two to return.

Eventually, the door opened with Alaura entering first. "For now, we wait for the serpent and the next full moon."

"Why the next full moon?" I inquired.

"That is when I can perform the ritual. Lucky for us, it is only three days away. The serpent will take about a day and a half to reach my mother, so we should have her response around the same time," she explained.

"Where will you stay?" Alius asked with thick concern.

"Ion has a room down here he said I can stay in. I will be safe. And I have some resting and gathering to do before then," she assured.

Erius stood and walked over to grab the book before returning to my side. He was neither pissed nor excited about the news, his already blank expressions hard to read. After Alius said his goodbyes to his niece, we headed back to the main lobby where the girls parted from us to have their night out.

Erius and I headed back to the room in silence, but it wasn't the usual quiet, and that made it all the more concerning. Alaura didn't seem too confident in her own ability to break the tether which probably was more relieving than stressful on my end. But given the circumstances, I'd say he was right. We had bigger things to be concerned about.

CHAPTER THIRTY-EIGHT

Mira

    I sat across the street staring at the front yard of my childhood home. Four cars sat crowding the driveway and parked on the street. The once green grass was now brittle and brown with large patches of bare dirt. With not much to see or hear from my position, I sent my raven and fox spirits in to see what I could not.

    "Are you sure you want to do this?" Erius asked. He sat patiently on the seat beside me, dressed up in disguise just as I asked. It wasn't more than a hat, sunglasses, and clothes that were much more casual than his usual attire. Alaura was kind enough to teach the girls and me a useful glam spell to disguise ourselves, and I felt this was the best time to practice.

I altered my hair to a fine, straight texture in a deep orange and red shade with dark brown eyes. I squared out my jaw and shifted my nose so that it was slightly crooked and off-center.

"Why are we here again?" Erius asked with a bored sigh. He leaned back, folding his arms over his chest as if he wasn't enjoying himself.

"Don't act like you aren't enjoying everyone avoiding us at all costs," I said in my altered voice.

"I am. But that does not answer my question."

We could add that to the grand list of questions that had gone unanswered. Like him, I had my own reasons.

"Shh. I'm trying to focus." I held up a finger to keep him quiet while I tapped into the raven as it landed on a windowsill looking right into my mother's room. The same burgundy paint clung to the wall, fading over time and covered with layers of dust, as was most everything else. The side tables, the lamps, and the chest at the end of the bed all covered in a thick layer of grime while my decrepit mother lay in the bed at the center of it all.

Her once deep brown hair was grayed and patchy in some spots. Her dull eyes were even more lifeless than I remembered. She looked over a delicate piece of paper with teary eyes, sniffling and mumbling to herself her sorrows and woes.

The back screen door opened with a loud squeak as the old wood rubbed against the loose floor—just as I remembered it. It slammed shut with a bit of force from whoever closed it, breaking my focus from the room.

"Go back and try again," I heard my sister Tia snip.

"Look, I don't know what she has going on, but she's with some guy that looks like he knows a hitman or two, if he's not one himself." I giggled at his assumption and continued to listen in, guiding the raven to land closer. "I'm not going back. You can go since you think it's so easy."

"Why wouldn't you have just said it flat out? I doubt she wants any of it, I'm not sure why mom left it to her in the first place," Tia said.

The raven hopped closer, keeping to the shadows but giving me better sight of my four siblings as they stood in a circle discussing what clearly was something about me.

"It's the fact you think Mina will come back to watch her for us just because of the will. Mina doesn't give a fuck about anyone but herself and always has. I told you messaging her was pointless. She isn't even here to see our mother. She's here to parade her boyfriend around," my youngest sister, Asia, tossed in. I knew they just wanted to dump our mother on me, and they planned to bribe me to do it. My hands fisted in my lap as I continued to listen to them.

"Fiancé," Miles corrected with a scoff.

"Yeah, sure. She probably sold her soul to the devil to find a man willing to put up with her."

Before I could stop the sweet raven, he shuffled into the air, flapping and tangling his claws in her hair upon the attack. Warm hands wrapped around my wrist, tugging me down onto the bench once again.

"Did you plan on slaughtering your entire family?" he whispered. "Call them back. We should return for the ritual. It is getting dark."

"Oh, fine. Let me just see what the fox has seen." I waved off his hand, shifting my vision to my sly creature as he slipped up the stairs of the house.

Sneaky little thing. I hadn't even realized he had gone inside.

The top step came into view as the fox slipped around to the corner and made a straight shot for my mother's room. Her door was left ajar with a thin light shining a line across the dusty wooden floor.

My siblings may have been watching over her health, but they were not caring for her or the house—and that was what they wanted to push off onto me.

The fox slunk in without notice and trailed around the bed to the side where my mother had set the paper. Along the floor sat a small folder of scattered pages. I couldn't make out the words on the paper, but the folder had my name, so I figured all of it was my personal information, like the birth certificate and Social Security card I had asked her to send me for months until I ordered copies of them myself.

I beckoned the fox to collect the folder and all the paperwork before requesting its return.

With a few blinks, the house became clear. I focused on my raven as he shot up into the sky above the roof and flew back to me while I could still hear Asia's screaming. My precious creature, on the other hand, looked full of joy and spirit as he flew effortlessly through the sky. His flight pattern looked more like a dance as he made his way to us. He circled above us for a moment before swooping down into the necklace, leaving only the skull.

My fox was next to pop free of the side bushes with the manila folder in his mouth. I opened my arms as he bounded toward me and

425

jumped right into my lap. His cool fur brushed over my thighs as he took a seat, dropping the file at my side before shifting down to the skull.

"Ok, I'm ready." I rolled the folder up as best I could and tucked it into my bag before standing to head off to the nearest alley to drop the glamor. I decided to leave the new hair but return my blonde strands. I hadn't straightened it since high school, and this was a perfect way to avoid heat damage.

Erius trailed behind, doing the same to shed the clothes he had and shift them to his usual. He kept his eyes locked hard on me as we moved out onto the main sidewalk.

"Remember what I said about taking pictures?" I joked, but his features hardened as deep creases folded between his brows.

"Those are the ones you say you took care of?" he finally asked.

"Unfortunately. We don't get along very well, if you haven't noticed." I took the route that trailed the lake, taking in what parts of town I did enjoy before it was time for me to return to L.A. After this trip, I won't be returning, that was for sure. But there were still parts that I loved and had good memories of. Those were the places I wanted to remember.

I took in the sky above, a beautiful mix of blue and white as it shifted to the sunset. A perfectly round moon sat just above the treetops as if to be held up by their branches, its beams of light touched down across the water's surface. Lilacs crowded my nose as we passed a patch of them. It was a delightful evening and the raven scaring my sister was just a cherry on top. I didn't understand why he would want to ruin it with questions regarding them.

"Do you plan to take it?" Erius suddenly asked.

"Take what?"

"What your siblings were trying to use to bribe you." His gaze was soft, and his features relaxed aside from the small pinch between his brows.

"I don't even know what she would leave me. I may see what it is out of curiosity, but I don't think I could ever accept anything from any of them, least of all as payment to take their place in caring for her."

He didn't ask anything more regarding them after that, and I was thankful he at least knew when to not pry. With the little bit of time we had left, we took streets rarely walked as I pointed out the few places I did enjoy. By the time the sun was half submerged and the moon was nearing a high point, we were crossing the lot of the resort to meet Alaura in the cemetery across the street. The dark patch of land had a single flickering light illuminating a path as she set up for the ritual.

The thick and overgrown vines that took over the unkempt cemetery made it difficult for us to push through, but Erius was able to locate the small, cleared patch where Alaura and the girls waited. The cemetery was eerily quiet with not even the whistle of a slight breeze to hear. No chirping of crickets or the hooting of owls, not even the sound of the twigs snapping beneath us could be heard.

A large salt circle was created with five black candles placed around it. She had herbs and flowers piled beside one candle while snake skins and dead beetles were piled by another. Bones had been placed by the third, meticulously arranged to form a pentagram. Lastly, a dusty bottle of a clear liquid and another of a darker liquid sat along the final two candles.

Jaz and the others sat on a bench near a large tombstone with various objects in each hand. Not that I could make out any of it, as they gripped the objects with dear life. They held their heads down and eyes closed, but their mouths moved in sync with one another as they silently chanted something. I assumed Alaura gave them a task in the ritual and they were dead set on breaking this tether more than anyone, I think.

They didn't even stop to say hi or anything.

"Welcome. Take a seat at the center of the circle. You must face each other and grasp the inflicted arm of the other," Alaura instructed as soon as she spotted us. She flipped through a few pages of a book with heavy concentration. The golden marks on her forehead began to glow as she returned her focus to the pages. Her setup was much more efficient than the one we had crafted almost a full month ago, so hopefully that counted for something.

Erius and I sat as requested, taking each other's right arm as we had the first night. The contact sent a chill up my arm that spread through my chest. Erius's body stiffened and his gaze locked on our joined hands, feeling the same reaction to the touch.

Alaura moved around us, sprinkling a crushed herb along the chalk border as she chanted in Demric. The heavy scent of burning wood and charcoal filled the air as her voice grew louder with each verse repeated. Screams filled the cemetery from all around us, raising the hair on my arms in a way I hadn't felt in weeks.

A dry, cold burn gripped my arm where the scar rested, glowing brightly as golden embers appeared to fall from it. The brighter it grew, the more the searing pain dug into me. I screamed out as I had the first time I suffered such pain, yanking back from the demon to break free.

But just like before, we were locked together.

Erius's face twisted with pain, but he only clenched his jaw. No other sound came from him other than a low growl rumbling from his chest. His eyes flashed, pulsating with the mounting pain that continued to carve away at us.

Alaura watched our arms closely, her chanting growing more aggressive. The illuminated marks on her forehead pulsated the louder she got. Her voice brought a storm of dark clouds that thundered and crashed over us. But the incoming storm did little to drown out the symphony of screams that swirled around the cemetery.

I sucked in a sharp breath as I continued to fight off the fire that engulfed my hand and wrist, clawing its way up to my elbow. Just as everything peaked and the pain grew to its most unbearable, it all began to fade. It slowly trickled from the tips of my fingers as the glowing in my arm subsided to the scar that now climbed up to my shoulder.

The darkened smog cleared from the sky to present the bright, full moon and cluster of stars. Sounds of the crickets returned to fill the air, and the heat of the summer night warmed my chilled skin.

Erius released me to examine the new scar that swirled wildly up his arm.

"Was that it?" Jaz questioned from the side.

"Erius," Alaura began, "head out of the gates." She turned back to me, taking my arm in her hand to investigate as she began tracing the scar once again. Erius's weighing energy never subsided as he leaned over to look at it as well. Alaura snapped her head toward him with a heated gaze. "Go! Now!"

Without hesitation, he jumped to his feet and stormed toward the entrance. It was odd to see since I usually had to fight with him a bit to get anything done.

"How'd you do that?" I asked mindlessly, my eyes still on the gap Erius exited from.

"It comes with the family name. Here, come this way." From what I read in the small book, their world did seem to have a sort of class system and with everything else I'd heard, it sounded to me that she was some sort of royalty or of some sort of high-standing bloodline like Alius mentioned.

Alaura guided me to the furthest corner from the cemetery gates. Before we made it to the final tomb, my arm lit up and yanked back as Erius and I reached the maximum distance. And unless Erius was running, I didn't think we had the same distance anymore.

I turned to Alaura with wide eyes as my hand dropped back to my side. Within a few minutes, Erius returned with Alius on his side. Both held equally grim expressions as their darkened eyes looked over us.

I rubbed at my arm, the pain still searing into my shoulder. Alius took to Alaura while Erius came to examine my new scar. He looked over it, following it up past my elbow and then my shoulder.

"It shortened the distance," he said softly. My heart shot into my throat, and breathing soon became a struggle, at least for a moment. I didn't want to break the tether, not really anyway. But I also didn't want us to have less of a distance in it all.

Alaura marched over, looking over me intently with a crumpled piece of thick paper in her grasp. She handed it to Erius, her eyes still on me and the new length of my scar. He quickly unfolded it, reading the words with a growing anger that pinched his face.

"Out of the question," he snapped as he shoved the paper back into Alaura's hands. She looked at him as if she were planning murder right then, but her composure relaxed with a soft clearing of her throat.

"This is an ancient magic, dark and out of my power. There is only one who can undo it," Alaura explained as gently as she could.

"How do you know they can?" I asked skeptically. We were already told she could possibly help, and it had quickly proven no help at all.

"Because it is *her* magic. My father knows far more of it, and he is certain it is the power of Chimeriea, and only her power can break it."

"Do you have any idea how dangerous that is?" Erius snapped.

"Yea, Alaura. Even for the residents it is risky. Traveling that far is certain death for the mortal. Not to mention forbidden," Alius tossed in.

"Yes, but as you two have said. Neither she, nor her friends, are fully mortal. And from my understanding, she is the least mortal of them all," Alaura mused with excitement.

"And say we entertained this ludicrous idea of yours. Do you know how to get there? Safely," Alius asked his niece.

She thought for a moment, her smile growing wider. "I don't, but I know a few who will."

Alius's eyes narrowed as he looked to her, ready to ask the question I think we were all wanting to ask, but he was cut short by a deep rumbling that echoed through the trees. It almost sounded like a laugh, but I had never heard one so dark and creepy before. I looked around in search of the source while my skin began to react, ready to shift at any sign of danger I could not see. But there was nothing for my mortal eyes to focus on.

Erius grabbed my hand and tugged me back to the entrance before I had a chance to locate the laughter. With everything happening so fast and the darkness blurred by the sudden speed, I couldn't make out where we were headed. All I could feel was the cold air rushing past.

A strong gust of wind whipped around us, tossing my hair about until I was blinded by it and stumbling around. Air pushed from my lungs and my stomach dropped seventy feet below the earth's crust. My feet lifted from the ground for a few seconds before reconnecting with a softer earth. Thrown off balance, I stumbled forward into dirt and rocks, struggling to push my hair out of my face as Erius's hand remained locked around my arm.

"Ow! What the fuck was that?" I barked out. The screams and cries of the girls stumbling through came next, followed by a wave of gasps and inquiries about our location.

I flipped my hair back out of the way to find us in a narrow corridor that led down a long flight of steps.

"Alaura!" Erius snapped.

"It's the only way! Besides, Ion isn't the only one with a special inn. His sister has one, too. She will help us," Alaura assured confidently.

"How are we so sure we can trust so many people? Where does this even lead?" Jaz snapped from the back.

"For once, I agree with her," Erius growled.

"Look, you wanted my help. Here it is. You read my mother's words—do you have any other plans?" Alaura snapped as she pushed toward the front.

"I know what you are trying to do, Alaura. I will not have her tested on," Erius growled.

"She is the key we have all been looking for," Alaura began bluntly. At this point, there really were only two options—for me, anyway. I still didn't know everything about my new form, and there wasn't anyone to help—or anyone willing to, except for this select few. It was all I have to learn more about my new self.

I could either embrace it or live the rest of my existence in fear of something completely unknown.

"I don't mind being tested on," I blurted out. "If I'm going to be like this, I'd like to know everything I can. Besides, being the first of something is kind of cool."

"Yea, Meems, this is all so *cool*!" Amber snipped sarcastically. Her irritation was well warranted. They really got sucked into all of this for just agreeing to set up a fun little ritual. Granted, none of us saw this outcome, but I had been the one to lead us from one bad decision to another.

"You guys don't have to come," I offered.

"I want to!" Mickey pipped from beside Alius, who was ready to protest when his niece interjected with a shaking head.

"It would be best. You all will not only carry a bit of Erius's essence, but Mina's scent is all over the three of you. It is best you all come along. We will figure it all out once we get to Merlot's," Alaura explained.

"What even was that thing?" Mickey asked. I looked back to Erius who was busy staring blazing daggers into Alaura. Whatever it was, it didn't sound like a Watcher, and with that tree thing after us, I could only assume it was someone or something sent by him.

With them reluctantly agreeing to this adventure, there was only Erius left to object to the entire idea.

He tugged me closer to him and leaned over with softer word. "Your form presents itself at any sign of trouble and you believe it wise to set yourself in the line of it…again?"

"I've gotten better at controlling it. I can hold it back if I need to. Besides, where else are we to go?" I waited for a response, but I think he knew that we had little to no options at this point. His jaw flexed but he nodded forward. The weight of his energy fell over me, wrapping me in a protective embrace as we descended.

The darkness faded to a deep red glow the further down we went. Not that there was any other direction for us to go. When we finally did hit flat, solid ground, it was nothing more than a small room with a single black door leading out.

Alius turned to us, ensuring we were all ready before pushing the door open with a deep, echoing groan. The energy around me tightened as we stepped into a red station that looked like a subway platform. But there were no benches, no tracks for the train. No people stood waiting and no sounds to be heard. Just one tunnel that led to blackness.

Alaura took the lead, climbing from the platform and waiting for the rest of us. Everyone stepped down one by one, and when it came my turn to go, Erius pulled me back.

"Mina," he began, "you haven't the fear to understand the dangers we are all about to face. You cannot change or come close to it. From here, you four must be sorceresses by birth. Nonmortal. There are things in my world that you lot are not meant to see in these forms. When I say run, you run. When I say hide, you hide. When I say act frightened, please for the love of everything, act frightened. Do you understand?"

I looked over him, already knowing the answer as I had known for weeks now. Well, at least from the first week after my first change. My world of reality and mortal things ended the night I shook a demon's hand and offered my soul. Every day since had been as if the universe has been screaming at me to leave this realm. I was more than ready to leave it, and I think I always had been.

I nodded slowly. "I understand."

He helped me down from the platform and we joined the group, entering the tunnel that would take us to the Six Circles.

BONUS

Back at the shop Andrew stood aimlessly in what was once the reading room. The faint scent of Mina's Honey and Milk shampoo still clung to the air along with the overpowering scent of sage. His arm hung in sling a size too small, left over from the time Lily had broken her arm skating down a hill. The cast was set and heavy with poles and screws sticking out and was adorned in nothing more than his mother and sister's signatures and a lie to go along with the cause. Tripped carrying a delivery up the stairs, is what he had told them. Knowing the truth would have garnered him questioning looks. He had been going on about Mina's mysterious intern the last month and they had already begged him to leave it alone.

But he knew deep in his soul something was not right with the man. From his odd voice to his inhuman eyes. The ones that burned into

Andrew's memory while his arm was being shattered under the crunching grip. There was something not right about the guy, Andrew knew, and despite how impossible it all seemed, he knew something was not human about Mina's new friend or their matching tattoos.

The bell rang with the entrance of a new customer and with Mina being fired and the rest of the girls quitting on the spot, he was left short staffed and in need of not only new hires, but a new reader. He had already notified all Mina's clients that she was gone.

"I'll be right down," he huffed as he turned to leave the room. By the time he reached the downstairs lobby, he found a dirty looking fellow with greasy red hair, ripped jeans and a matching jean vest with the sleeves ripped off. Not generally his customer base, but who is he to judge, the last person he judged shattered his forearm.

"Can I help you?" Andrew asked the man on his way down the stairs. The grease ball of a man turned with a distant expression and a crumpled paper clutched between his hands. The lost look in the man's eye sank Andrew's heart to the pit of his stomach. It was the same lost look he had stared at in the mirror for the last month after the whole incident.

"I'm looking for someone named Mina. I've been told she does readings here," the man said.

"Not anymore. We have been looking for a new reader for the last month – until then, no readings," Andrew answered flatly. The man didn't say anything as he looked over Andrew, his gaze stopping at the cast. His eyes grew wide as they seemed to drift off to something in the distance.

"You've seen it too," the man eventually whispered. The words sent a frigid chill over Andrew's skin, freezing him as visions of an auto shop and a deadly fire filled his mind. The frightening glowing eyes gripped his heart as new terrors filled his soul. Once it all cleared Andrew and the man held each other's frightened gaze for several long moments before Andrew sucked in a ragged breath.

"I don't know what you're talking abo –"

"The demons. Her and the monster that hangs around her. They did this to me." The man turned and lifted his shirt on his right side to expose part of his lower back. Webbed scars stretched over his skin, pink and raw from the recent inflicted attack he had to endure. But Andrew was far more distracted by the man's words. If he hadn't witnessed the haunting eyes, he wouldn't believe it to be true, at least for the man. But Mina? Andrew had known her the better part of the last three years and though she dabbled in dark occult shit, he never noticed anything demonic up until *he* showed up.

"Demons?" Andrew echoed blankly.

"Yes, her, that man, their friends – they have all fucked up my life here. I was told she worked here," the man hissed.

Andrew lifted a brow, the familiar ache to protect Mina swelled in his chest, but for what? She was more than clear and he had kept pushing. And now he lost the only connection with her he had. Not because of her or her friends, but because of Erius.

"What were you planning to do if she was here?" Andrew pressed, "Who are you?"

The man's lips twisted up into a grizzly wicked grin, "The name's Billy, and I've found someone who is searching for the both of them. Someone who may be able to help you as well. He sensed her essence here… as he calls it." As the last of the words left his lips, the entrance bell sounded off again as a dark haired man walked in. His skin was too pale for the LA sun and eyes a blood red with the same dark sclera as Erius. He cocked his chin towards Andrew with a slow climbing look.

It sunk Andrew's heart and cleared the air from his lungs, the temperature around him fell drastically, leaving the tiny bumps to rise across his skin. He sucked in a breath, too horrified to say a thing as another demon stared him down. One that held a grin that looked as if he'd sooner make a meal of Andrew than help him.

"Hello," he greeted in a thick Scottish accent, "I'm Elpos and I hear you've had a run in with a long lost companion of mine."

Thanks for Reading

Thank you so much for joining Mina and Erius on their journey in this reality meets fantasy tale. I hope that you do stick around to see what they have coming for them in the Six Circles, who they come to meet and trust – while also discovering who is not to be trusted along their journey.

There will be ups and downs, fights and losses, battles and well deserved triumphs – along with a discovery long since buried that is now at risk of coming to the surface.

About the Author

Ambrosia R. Harris, author of The Taking of Persephone Series, is delighted to present this novel as an introduction to her fantasy/dark fantasy line. She is a full time author working from her overly heated home in Las Vegas, NV. She studies herbalism and practices in the craft and has incorporated her knowledge of such topics throughout her works.

She lives with her high school sweetheart and their three children along with their dog, Cerberus, their cat, Prometheus, and their ball python, Juju.

Ambrosia currently has her book release schedule up for the years 2024-2028 on her site. For more information or to receive updates, you can sign up for her newsletter or follow her social medias.

Acknowledgments

I would first like to thank my long time beta reader, Jaeden Beauchef. If it wasn't for their help in each and every release, I'm not sure where I would be. From detailed edits to heartfelt feedback, I do not think I can thank them enough for the time and work they have put in to help me. This was a bit different from most of my projects since I did have the lovely work of Megan Harris to do edits, I do hope that gave Jae a bit of a break from the heavy work.

I would also like to thank Megan for her work with the edits, they were informative and all in all it was an amazing and easy process.

Lastly I would like to thank my cover designer, Alexandre Levasseur for his lovely work not only with the front and back covers but also with the character art he continuously surprises and amazes me with.

If it was not for this glorious team, Sunflower in the Shadows wouldn't be who she is today!

Printed in Great Britain
by Amazon